Praise for the novels of Heather Cullman

Scandal

"Wonderfully poignant romance that offers readers superb character development and subtle wit."
—*Booklist*

"A warm, charming tale." —Kat Martin

"Delightful . . . lusty passions and tender love."
—*Rendezvous* (Rosebud of the Month)

"Positively shimmers . . . delicious." —Heartstrings

"Delicious, sensual, and compelling . . . will entertain and enthrall readers with its love story and breathtaking love scenes!"
—The Romance Reader's Connection

Bewitched

"Readers will be *Bewitched* by Heather Cullman's tender late Regency romance. . . . Delightful."
—BookBrowser

"Touching, entertaining, and oh-so-romantic."
—All About Romance

A *Perfect Scoundrel*

"A delightful, lighthearted Regency romp from a talented writer. Enjoy!" —Kat Martin

continued . . .

For All Eternity

"Moves like a whirlwind . . . humor in just the right places . . . wonderful characters." —*Rendezvous*

Stronger Than Magic

"A delightfully romantic tale." —*The Literary Times*

"Ms. Cullman weaves a magic spell with every word."
—*Rendezvous*

Tomorrow's Dreams

"Intriguing . . . steamy sexuality and well-drawn characters." —*Romantic Times*

Yesterday's Roses

"Witty, lusty, and thoroughly delightful."
—*Affaire de Coeur*

"Exciting . . . combines dynamic characterizations, romance, and mystery." —*Paperback Forum*

HEATHER CULLMAN

SECRETS

A SIGNET BOOK

SIGNET
Published by New American Library, a division of
Penguin Group (USA) Inc., 375 Hudson Street,
New York, New York 10014, U.S.A.
Penguin Books Ltd, 80 Strand,
London WC2R 0RL, England
Penguin Books Australia Ltd, 250 Camberwell Road,
Camberwell, Victoria 3124, Australia
Penguin Books Canada Ltd, 10 Alcorn Avenue,
Toronto, Ontario, Canada M4V 3B2
Penguin Books (N.Z.) Ltd, Cnr Rosedale and Airborne Roads,
Albany, Auckland 1310, New Zealand

Penguin Books Ltd, Registered Offices:
80 Strand, London WC2R 0RL, England

First published by Signet, an imprint of New American Library,
a division of Penguin Group (USA) Inc.

First Printing, January 2004
10 9 8 7 6 5 4 3 2 1

Printed in the United States of America

PUBLISHER'S NOTE
This is a work of fiction. Names, characters, places, and incidents either are the product of the author's imagination or are used fictitiously, and any resemblance to actual persons, living or dead, business establishments, events, or locales is entirely coincidental.

To my Le Salon de Bleuette
friends, for your kindness,
generosity, and the hours of joy
you have given me.

And as always to my wonderful
husband, Chip. I might not write a
dedication to you in every book,
but every book is written with you
in my heart. I love you.

Chapter 1

For the third time in as many days, the Turkish soldiers came for him at dawn. As they had done the previous two mornings, they led him up to the stone-flagged courtyard where they stripped him of the filthy rags his captors had tossed at him to replace the fine clothing they had stolen from him upon his arrival at the *bagnio,* as slave prisons were called in Algiers. When he stood naked, save for a pair of short, queerly draped white pantaloons that hung almost indecently low on his lean hips, they marched him through a squat archway and out a brass-studded oak door, the sole exit from the octagonal fortress.

Today he was to be sold at the slave market. Today he would become an object, a mere thing to be prodded and inspected, used and perhaps abused, kept or sold, little better than a dog at the mercy of his new owner's whims.

Today his humanity would be flayed from his soul.

Or so his guards had informed him in the odd slave language of Lingua Franca, a dialect he had immediately recognized as an amalgam of bastardized Italian, French, Greek, Arabic, and Spanish. Exactly why he so readily understood it, as well as several other languages that were spoken among his fellow captives, he did not know. Then again, he could remember nothing that had happened in the time before he had awakened from a terrible brain fever a month earlier, including his name and how he had come to be in his current straits.

In short, he was a man without a past. As for his future, well, he didn't dare contemplate it for fear that he would break from his horror at what his guards said awaited him there. For as he knew from the chilling examples that had been made of those prisoners who had succumbed to their panic, his captors had little patience and no sympathy whatsoever for unmanly displays of weakness.

Just thinking about his captors' brutality filled his mouth with the metallic taste of fear. Their favored punishment was the bastinado, a hellish torture wherein the victim's feet were thrust through loops of rough rope attached to a stout pole, which was then twisted to tighten the loops until they cut into the victim's ankle flesh. When the pole had been hoisted up on the shoulders of two strong men and the victim dangled helplessly upside-down, he was beaten with thick sticks, half the blows directed to the soles of his feet while the other half landed on his bare buttocks. For minor infractions the sentence could be as few as a dozen blows, with more serious crimes commanding five hundred, a lethal number that few survived.

Having suffered the savage punishment himself several times before his captors were satisfied that he had indeed lost his memory and was not merely pretending so as to avoid paying the enormous ransom demanded from wealthy captives, which by his appearance he was suspected of being, he had taken pains to be a model prisoner to prevent further encounters with the bastinado. Thus when one of the six Turkish soldiers escorting him viciously elbowed him in the kidney to propel him toward an alley that twisted between the high whitewashed walls to his left, almost bringing him to his knees from the pain, he stoically swallowed the cry that sprang to his lips and docilely did as directed.

Though it was just after dawn the raw heat from the newly risen sun had already seared the air into an irradiated haze that now undulated in the early morning glare, distorting the surroundings like the view through the rippled glass of an ancient window. As with so much of what he thought, he was struck with curiosity at why he would conceive such an analogy. Could it be that he was an architect and would take such notice of windows? Or was he perhaps a solicitor in the business of property management, who made a practice of assigning dates and values to buildings by assessing telltale details such as their window glass?

He gave a mental shrug, resigned to the fact that he could not even begin to answer such questions, or the ones that arose from simply contemplating them. Whatever he was—or more correctly, had been—the only thing he knew for certain was that his life had been one of relative ease. For as his captors had so astutely pointed out, his hands were soft and free from the calluses that would have marked him as a member of the laboring class; a gentleman's hands, they called them. He only prayed that whatever he had been in his former life had left him endowed with a skill that would prove valuable to his new owner, thus saving him from being relegated to a life of backbreaking menial drudgery.

It was blessedly cooler in the alley they now traversed. Only the faintest wisps of sunlight escaped down into the shadowy passage, the bright beams having been shredded by the sharply protruding upper floors of the windowless houses on either side. Now and again they passed an open door where dark-robed figures paused from their work to peer outside, their gloom-shrouded eyes drawn by the clatter of the soldiers' iron-tipped shoes as they punished the pavement beneath them. The entire passage held the putrid stench of rotting refuse mingled with the nauseating reek from the dung-fouled drains below.

While most slaves were herded through the streets in groups in order to be seen by prospective buyers, those determined to be particularly valuable were paraded singly, guarded on all sides by muscular Turkish soldiers dressed in showy red-and-gold vests over white silk shirts and pantaloons, their hands poised on the gilded hilts of the deadly scimitars that were tucked into their twined red sashes. Exactly why he was considered to be more valuable than most of the other captives, he did not know, especially since many of the other men were much stronger than he was in his current illness-wasted state.

Hmmm. Perhaps it was for the reason another prized captive, a handsome golden-haired Italian youth named Matteo, had suggested: it was because of his pretty looks. Not having access to a mirror and unable to remember what he looked like, he could not say for certain that such was the case. All he knew for sure was that there was something about his person his captors had deemed remarkable.

Up and down the winding streets and alleyways they continued to troop, each passage presenting an exotic new world of sights, sounds, and smells. There was a tiny bazaar with crude wooden stalls where Arabs swathed in white burnouses rubbed elbows with black-robed Jews and hooded desert nomads, and an alley of cavelike workshops where skilled Moorish artisans in wide-legged pantaloons wrought their colorful wares. At one corner they passed a gathering of wealthy Turks sporting ornate silk turbans, several of whom paused in their conversation to stare at him with dark, assessing eyes, as if seriously considering his purchase. Soon thereafter they stopped in a small, shady square where he was displayed before a fountain, around which men in white cloaks sat crossed-legged on woven rugs, serenely smoking clay pipes.

There were even several occasions when servants chased after them and bade them to enter a grand house along their route, in which the owner, usually accompanied by an attendant or two, inspected him in the entry hall. After the inspection was completed and the commanding soldier had conversed with the potential buyer, the soldier barked either "Christian!" or "English!" thus signaling the conclusion of the interview and that they were to take their leave.

Christian. English. During his imprisonment he had been addressed by those names so often by both his captors and fellow prisoners that he now automatically responded to them. As a result and for the lack of a real name to call his own, he had begun to think of himself as Christian English.

By now they were mounting a seemingly endless flight of stone steps that led from a cool, dank alleyway back up into the sun-parched world above. When the steps at last terminated, Christian found himself at the edge of a wide road that was currently being used as a marketplace. The stark fear that had been curdling in his belly for the past month exploded into panic at the sight of it, almost shattering his fragile control.

Was this the place, then? Was this where he would be sold? It was said that a man lost a part of his soul the day he entered into slavery. Were these his last moments of being whole?

Wanting nothing more than to bolt, to somehow escape what awaited him, but knowing that there was no escape for him, Christian allowed the soldiers to promenade him through the marketplace, bleakly resigned to his fate. With each step his panic grew, rising from his chest in great, wrenching sobs that threatened to escape with every breath he took. Desperate to tamp them down, to maintain what little dignity and composure he had left, he tried to force his thoughts away from what awaited him by studying the sights around him.

Produce and goods of every description were laid out for sale on the cobblestones. Peddlers bearing baskets filled with trinkets and treats wove through the milling throng, loudly hawking their wares. At one end of the makeshift marketplace stood a number of tethered donkeys, camels, and horses; at the other a crowd had assembled to watch fancifully garbed acrobats perform gravity-defying balancing acts. Rather than divert his mind, as he had hoped, the chaotic noise and pungent foreign smells served only to deepen his chilling sense of foreboding.

Apparently, the slave auction was not being held at that particular market, for after displaying him atop a stone block and calling out what Christian assumed were his selling points, they jostled him off down a street leading toward the sea, not halting again until they reached a small piazza near the docks. One glance at the ragged men squatting on the hot pavement of the open courtyard, their naked flesh slick with sweat and turning red beneath the broiling sun, instantly told him that they had at last reached the *Bedestan,* as the slave markets were called. Today there appeared to be close to a hundred slaves for sale, with every color, age, and nationality represented among their ranks.

Rather than being ordered to join the group, as he fully expected to happen, Christian was instead escorted to where a half-dozen men squatted near the domed mosque bordering the far side of the piazza. When he spied Matteo's curly golden head, and that of a muscular, copper-haired Dutch giant named Gregor, he easily deduced that the prized slaves had been segregated from the less valuable ones, most probably to better exhibit them. Now assuming the required squatting position next to Matteo, as indicated by his guards, he watched the buyers congregate from beneath his lowered lashes, gritting his teeth against the pain in his feet as they were seared by the scorching pavement.

The buyers were predominately Turks and Moors, with an occasional Jew or Arab apparent here and there, all of them decked out in opulent trappings that marked them as important men. As the buyers wandered among the slaves to engage in a last-minute inspection, the servants accompanying them rushed to spread their masters' rugs and cushions beneath the shaded arcade built along three of the four piazza walls. That task completed, they retreated a respectful distance away to brew coffee over portable oil stoves.

Of all the offerings there today, Christian and Matteo seemed to excite the most interest, and they spent the better part of the next hour being poked and examined. Sometimes they were made to run and jump, after which the prospective buyer pressed his ear against their chests to assess the soundness of their hearts. At other times the customer would jam his hands into their mouths, prodding and peering at their teeth in an attempt to judge their age and health. There were even several occasions when palmists were brought forth to read the lines of their palms, so as to tell whether they would give their masters a long lifetime of service and bring them good fortune.

Or so the guard overseeing the exhibition of the prized captives had told him. The guard, a fierce, hawk-faced man with dark, leathery skin and hard, obsidian eyes set deep under the prominent ridges of his bushy black eyebrows, seemed to take sadistic pleasure in whispering to Christian each potential buyer's most perverse proclivities in the aftermath of every inspection. Christian had just returned to his place for what seemed like the hundredth time, his knee joints screaming in agonized protest to his constant rising and squatting, when the group was approached by two bejeweled men in the company of a Turk whom Christian had identified as the slave dealer.

After the party had strolled past the prized offerings, pausing briefly before each man to appraise his qualities and converse among themselves, the dealer barked something in his native language, pointing first at Christian, then to Matteo. Promptly Christian was seized and dragged forward by the guard at his side, while one of the guards accompanying the slave dealer did the same with Matteo. When one of the buyers, an Arab by his appearance, indicated an American youth whom Christian had heard the other captives refer to as Samuel, he too was brought forward.

Now standing several feet from their companions, each captive was shadowed by a guard, and the dealer and his customers moved in for a closer inspection. They began with Matteo. After examining his teeth and seeming to find them to their liking, the Arab murmured to his fellow buyer, who grinned and stepped back. Now whispering to the slave before him, saying something that made the handsome Italian blanch beneath his tan, the buyer began brushing his fingertips across Matteo's broad chest, touching and stroking the sculpted planes, pausing at each flat nipple to tweak it until it pebbled.

Matteo stiffened beneath the Arab's foul caresses, his jaw clenching and lips crimping tight, as if struggling to stifle his protest.

Smiling at his response the Arab moved downward,

lightly tracing the tapering lines of his torso. Over his ribs he drifted, petting here, teasing there, pausing on his belly to thoroughly explore the muscular grid. After doing something to his navel, something that made the Italian flinch and gasp, the buyer dipped lower yet, following the tawny line of hair leading from Matteo's navel down into his filthy white pantaloons. Now watching Matteo's face, hungrily gauging his reaction, the Arab gave the garment a jerk that sent it sliding to the ground, leaving Matteo fully exposed.

To Matteo's credit he remained stock-still, his blue eyes fixed and staring straight ahead as both buyers leaned in to inspect his male parts. As Christian watched the Arab began to fondle Matteo, deftly stroking and teasing, coaxing an erection. It was all Christian could do not to vomit from the bile rising in his throat, aware that he, too, would most probably be subjected to the same humiliating treatment.

Apparently, he looked as sick as he felt, because the guard at his side chuckled and whispered, "It is your unlucky day, English. Ghassan bin Hanif seeks a new *garzóne*." At Christian's frown, he grinned in a way that exposed several rotten teeth and explained, "A *garzóne* is a male concubine. Not a bad life for a slave, unless his master has a taste for the dark pleasures, which Ghassan bin Hanif is rumored to have. It is said that any slave unlucky enough to be chosen as his *garzóne* is doomed. Those who do not kill themselves out of misery die from his perversions. Sometimes one does survive, but by the time Ghassan bin Hanif is tired of him he has been reduced to something less than a man, and his life is hardly worth living."

By now the Arab had finished with Matteo and was repeating his obscene performance with Samuel. Samuel, who could not have been a day over fourteen, was a comely youth with straight dark hair, clear green eyes, and the smooth, gangling body of a boy struggling to grow into manhood. Unlike Matteo, who had borne his demeaning ordeal with stoicism, Samuel wept and tried to shrink from the Arab's touch, only to be immobilized and forced into submission by the guard at his side.

Unable to watch, Christian looked away.

Again his guard chuckled. "Take heart, English. Perhaps the other man, the mulatto slave breeder, will buy you. Every year he buys a handsome white male slave to serve as a stud for the black females he keeps on his farm outside the city. Sadly"—he heaved an exaggerated sigh, his lips twisting into a cruel smile—"once the slave has planted his seed in the women, he is sold to labor in the stone quarry. Shall I tell you about life in the quarry?"

Christian closed his eyes, his heart now drumming in his ears too loudly to hear what the guard said next. *A stud or a whore. Dear God!* He was doomed either way. The bubbling panic he had held at bay since entering the piazza burst at the ghastly prospect, rioting through his veins to erupt in his brain in a delirious flash of frenzied rebellion.

No. No! He would not do it! He would never yield to such degradation. His integrity was all he had left, and he would rather die than surrender it. Indeed, should either man purchase him, he would fight their sordid purpose with a ferocity that would leave them with no choice but to kill him.

At that moment he caught a whiff of spicy, musk-laced perfume and felt the presence of another body moving close to his. In the next instant soft fingers began probing his lips, coaxing them to open. The feel of those hands invading his mouth, knowing where they had been and where they were about to go, further fueled his resolve. Unwilling to suffer the Arab's slightest touch, he roughly seized the wrist of the offending hand, flinging it away with a force that made his tormenter stumble backward. No doubt he would have fallen had he not been caught and steadied by the slave dealer.

"You shall not touch me, you depraved bastard! You will have to kill me first," Christian snarled, his now raised hands knotting into fists, ready to fight to the death to defend the tattered remains of his dignity.

The words were barely out of his mouth before three guards lunged at him, slamming him to the ground in a punishing tackle. After gut-punching the fight out of him, they dragged him back to his feet, tethering him in their immobilizing grasps.

The slave dealer was speaking with the Arab in his native tongue, his speech rapid and gestures placating. Judging from the wrathful looks he kept darting at Christian, it was apparent that he was offering to punish the recalcitrant slave. The Arab, however, shook his head, raising his open hands in a motion that made the slave dealer fall silent.

The guard pinioning Christian's arms at his back laughed quietly in his ear. "Ghassan bin Hanif admires your spirit, English. Perhaps he will buy you for the pleasure of breaking it."

The Arab had turned and was staring at Christian, his pale blue eyes gleaming with a peculiar light and his lips parted into what on other lips would have been an amiable smile. After a moment of savoring the sight of his victim struggling impotently against his restrainers, he closed the short distance between them, crooning in heavily accented English, "There, there now, pretty one. Ghassan seeks only to worship your beauty." Trapping Christian's hostile gaze with his strange unblinking one, he slowly reached up and traced the shape of Christian's lips.

Christian bared his teeth in a feral growl and tried

to jerk away, but his head was held firmly in place by the guards.

The Arab laughed. "Good. Your teeth are as fine as the rest of you." His hand was now gliding over Christian's rigid jawline, his fingertips making love to the flesh beneath them as they slowly skimmed down his tense neck and across his collarbone. "So pretty, so pretty. Pretty, pretty man," he murmured over and over again in a low, throaty chant.

Again Christian tried to evade his touch, and again the guards prevented him from doing so.

Again the Arab laughed, his touch growing teasing as he outlined the boldly defined contours of Christian's chest. "Such a wild one. Ghassan would take great pleasure in taming you," he purred, his fingers circling inward to fondle Christian's nipple.

Christian sucked in a sharp, hissing breath, hating the resulting sensations yet unable to stop his body from responding to them. For several torturous moments the Arab continued to woo his nipple, his unnerving smile broadening as it hardened and peaked beneath his fingers. He then moved to the other one and repeated his vile manipulations on it. Once more Christian's body betrayed him. Despising it for its mortifying weakness and himself for not having better control over it, Christian gritted his teeth hard, trying desperately to ignore the hands that now caressed his belly.

Damn it to hell! What was the matter with him? The last thing in the world he was feeling at that moment was sexually stimulated. Revolted? Yes. Resentful, hostile, humiliated, enraged, degraded, and bitter? Oh, yes! In fact, he hated the Arab with such vehemence that were the devil to appear and offer him the chance to kill him in exchange for his soul, he would accept the bargain without hesitation.

Ghassan bin Hanif's fingers were on Christian's

waistband now, toying with the fabric. "Are you so magnificent everywhere, my pretty one?" he inquired. His voice had grown husky and breathless, betraying his mounting excitement. Trailing his fingertips along the fabric, tickling the flesh edging it in a manner that made Christian's groin lurch and tighten, he added, "You do not mind if I satisfy my curiosity, do you?"

Like hell he didn't! Christian gave a savage jerk, freeing himself enough from the guards' holds to shake off the Arab's hands. Fighting with all his strength, unmindful of everything but his desperation to escape the Arab's depraved defilement, he hissed, "I will kill you if you touch me there, I swear to God I will!"

But, of course, his resistance was in vain. The guards merely tightened their hold, with one almost wrenching his arms from their sockets while another grasped his neck in a stranglehold and the third ripped off his pantaloons, after which he forced Christian's legs apart.

Ghassan bin Hanif couldn't have looked more pleased by his outburst. Raking Christian's naked length with his gaze, pausing at his manhood to openly leer, he murmured, "Just as I suspected. You are big, like a stallion. Pretty and virile—the perfect *garzóne.*" He lifted his eyes then, his gaze hot and desirous as it met Christian's. "You *shall* be my *garzóne*, pretty one, if you rise to my touch."

Christian closed his eyes and bit the inside of his cheek until he tasted blood, determined to lose himself in the pain. As he dug his teeth deeper into the lacerated flesh, wincing at the lancing pain, he felt the Arab begin to fondle him, with one hand expertly stroking his length while the other manipulated his masculine sac.

He bit his cheek so hard that tears sprang to his

eyes. He would not rise, damn it! He could not. Indeed, how could he possibly get an erection when the very feel of the Arab's hands made him shrink inside with disgust? Then he felt the Arab's hand leave his sac and slowly snake between his buttocks. Before he knew what was happening, the bastard's fingers slipped inside him, violating his most private place. Christian froze, a strangled scream ripping from his throat in his shock.

The Arab laughed. "Ah. You like that my pretty *garzóne*."

"No!" Christian spat.

"But you do," the Arab retorted with another laugh. He nodded at the guard, who forced Christian's head down so that he was staring at himself.

He was fully erect.

"No, damn it! No!" Christian screamed. This wasn't happening, it couldn't be happening . . .

Like a crazed feral thing caught in a trap, he began to thrash and fight, striking furiously at his guards in an attempt to free himself.

Thud! His flailing elbow rammed into one guard's groin, connecting with bone-jarring force.

Oww! The guard crumbled to the ground howling, his hands convulsively clasping his abused flesh.

Whack! Christian's leg slammed backward into that of the guard restraining him from behind, hooking around it to yank it from beneath him.

Splat! Aargh! That guard, too, hit the pavement.

Spurred by the success of his attack, Christian redoubled his struggles against the remaining guard, violently arching and straining, his fists flying as he lunged this way and that, battling to beat off the iron grip on his waist and throat. Now he bucked, now he kicked, now he pummeled and punched. Now—

Crack! His head smashed into something hard. In the next instant his brain exploded into a swirling vortex of red-hot pain and the scene around him dissolved into nothingness.

Terrified by what he knew would befall his body if his mind succumbed to unconsciousness, he fought to open his eyes, frantically willing himself back to his senses. After several fruitless attempts, he managed to lift his eyelids.

Or did he? He remained surrounded by blackness. Not certain what to think but unwilling to surrender the fight to his confusion, he prepared to launch a blind attack on the foes he feared lurked in the gloom. As he tensed to spring, his eyes began to adjust to the darkness, and he was able to make out several murky forms. For a moment or two he stared at them, his eyes straining and his mind grappling to identify them. Then the clouds shrouding the moon parted, and thin silver light spilled in through a window that only seconds earlier had been lost in the darkness, further unveiling his surroundings.

He was in a small but cozy chamber, tangled in the covers of a simple tester bed.

His chamber?

Yes. It was his chamber, his bed.

In England.

He was in the comfortable dowager cottage that sat on the edge of the Critchley Manor estate, which belonged to his best friend, Gideon Harwood.

Too limp with relief to move, Christian remained as he was, caught in a snare of twisted sheets and blankets, his flesh still fevered from his panic and his breath tearing from his lungs in harsh, ragged sobs.

A dream; it was just a dream.

No. Not a dream. If only it were just a dream. But of course it wasn't. It was a memory, one that had escaped its prison at the back of his mind to haunt him through a nightmare, as the painful memories of his enslavement were often wont to do.

Suddenly unbearably hot, feeling like he was suffocating from the lingering heat of his fear, Christian ripped the covers from around him and stalked naked across the room to the window.

Though the cottage had two much larger and grander bedchambers than the one he currently occupied, Christian found the homey simplicity of this one comforting, and had thus chosen it for his own. Decorated in muted shades of yellow, green, and red, it boasted plain, whitewashed walls, the north one occupied by a tiled fireplace, a rustic beamed ceiling, and a wide planked oak floor scattered with several gay rugs. Aside from the Spartan bed, which dominated the humble space, the only other furnishings were a clothespress, a dressing table, and a rushseated chair, all as austere in design as the bed.

By now the coal that had been burning in the fireplace brazier had been reduced to ash, and though the winter's chill had encroached upon the room's prior warmth, his skin remained uncooled as he walked the short distance to the window. Reaching it, he gazed out into the still Christmas Eve night beyond.

Virgin snow lay in wind-swirled drifts upon the sleeping earth, glowing dimly in the shadows like sleeping ghosts, while that reposing in the moonlight glittered as if dusted with diamonds. The stand of trees separating the cottage from the sweeping manor park had long ago shed its autumn finery and now stretched black and barren against the deep night sky, the skeletal limbs pocked by snow and scabbed with ice. In the distance crouched the massive shape of Critchley Manor, its featureless darkness studded here and there by a candlelit window.

Comforted by the sight of it, Christian rested his hot cheek against the cold, frosted glass, his warm breath forming misty halos upon the pane as he pictured the occupants within. They were both friend and family to him, his saviors and his salvation, and he didn't know how he would have survived without them. He owed everything to them, especially Gideon and his sister, Bethany.

To Gideon Harwood he owed his life, for it was Gideon who had liberated him from slavery and offered him not only his friendship, but also a life to replace the one he could not remember. To Bethany he owed his soul. As always happened when he thought of gentle, beautiful Bethany Harwood, Christian was filled with a bittersweet yearning.

With Bethany he felt whole, as if he were everything he was meant to be, like he had found his place in life. She was his love, his finest hope, and there was nothing he would not do for her. . . . except for the one thing he must do before he could speak his heart and make her his wife: find out who he was. For without knowing his past, they could have no future together. After all, it was possible that he was already wed; that he had a wife and perhaps even children somewhere to whom he would be forced to return should he rediscover his former life. And the thought of having to abandon his love for Bethany was more than he could bear. He might also find that he was a criminal or a rogue or some other despicable creature unworthy of loving her. So like the coward he was, he continued to avoid seeking his identity, terrified of what he might find.

Ignorance afforded him hope, and while he knew that he must someday seek knowledge of his past, he was not yet ready to gamble his hope on the chance that he might find himself free and worthy of Bethany. Yet until he did gamble it . . .

Soul-sick and weary, Christian turned from the window, sighing his despair. But where was the good in agonizing over the matter? He had done so a thousand times before and was still no closer to finding his courage or a solution. It was Christmastide, a time of celebration and joy. Tomorrow he would attend the Christmas Day festivities at Critchley Manor.

Tomorrow he would see Bethany, they would dance and laugh, and he would bask in the warmth of her company. For now, that was enough. It had to be enough.

Chapter 2

"Bethany? Whatever are you doing in that alcove?"
Bethany Harwood started at the sound of her sister-in-law's voice, almost dropping the beribboned parcel she held in her discomfiture at being caught in her stealthy venture.

Not that she was doing anything to be discomfited about.

Not in the least.

To be sure, there was nothing the tiniest bit condemnable about stashing her Christmas token for Christian, a small watercolor portrait she had painted of him and her sister, Bliss, behind the cushions of the secluded window seat alcove, where she could present it to him in a modicum of privacy during the festivities to be held that afternoon. Unfortunately, were her sister-in-law, Julia, to learn of her plan, she might be inclined to use it as yet another opportunity to promote her campaign to match Bethany and Christian.

And there lay the reason for her discomfiture. Though Bethany had repeatedly rejected the notion of such a union, sometimes by pointing out the impossibility of it and at others by denying her love for Christian, Julia remained undeterred from her purpose.

Despite her exasperation at the situation, Bethany could not help smiling at the thought of Julia and her romantic tinkering. Stubborn, meddling . . . dearest Julia. For all the times that Bethany repeatedly claimed to view Christian as a brother and nothing more, something she took great pains to illustrate through her actions toward him, Julia had somehow managed to discern the truth: that she loved and desired him in a way that was far from sisterly. To further justify her belief that Bethany and Christian belonged together, Julia also professed to having seen evidence that Christian shared Bethany's tender feelings.

Bethany sighed. She supposed she could understand her sister-in-law's determination in the matter. As a happily wed woman, Julia naturally wished the same sort of bliss she had found in her marriage to Bethany's older brother, Gideon, for Christian and Bethany.

Oh! If only she would see that it was impossible for them to find such bliss in each other's arms. If only she knew how much it hurt when she spoke of a marriage between Bethany and Christian, painting vivid word pictures of the union that depicted a heaven on earth that Bethany would have given anything to possess, but knew she never could.

Julia, tenderhearted creature that she was, would of course put an end to such talk were Bethany to tell her that it pained her. However, she would also be stricken to learn that she had wounded Bethany, and Bethany would do anything, endure anything, to save the woman she regarded as both her sister and best friend from grief. Besides, confessing her hurt would be akin to admitting her love for Christian, and that was bound to provoke conversations that would prove far more painful than Julia's simple weaving of impossible dreams.

Now plagued by the all-too-familiar ache that came

from thinking about those dreams, and determined to avoid saying or doing anything that might prompt Julia to build on them, Bethany hastily shoved the painting into place, then poked her head around the elaborately swagged and tasseled yellow drapes that partially separated the window seat from the ballroom. Smiling brightly at Julia, who stood just inside the room with her head at a quizzical angle and her face set in lines of polite query, she fibbed, "I was just searching for the third volume of Mr. Richardson's *Clarissa.* I was reading it here yesterday morning, and have been unable to find it since."

Coming forward to relieve her sister-in-law of one of the two workbaskets draped over her arms, she hastily changed the subject by peering at the scissors and ribbon in the basket she had taken and asking, "What is all this?"

To Bethany's relief, Julia readily accepted both her explanation and her diversion. Nodding at the basket on her own arm, which contained small packets of either silver, gold, or iridescent white paper, all tied with pale blue satin ribbon, she replied, "These are Christmas tokens for our party guests. I have fans for the ladies"—she indicated a gold package—"toys and sweets for the children"—those were wrapped in white—"and there are watch fobs for the gentlemen"—the silver packages. "I am going to hang them from the kissing bough with the ribbon in your basket. I thought to make a game of cutting them down."

"How so?" Bethany quizzed, eagerly seizing upon the innocuous topic of their Christmas festivities.

Julia slanted her a mischievous look, an impish smile tugging at her lips. "I shall invite each guest to climb the ladder the footmen have decorated for the occasion and claim their prize. As they cut it down the assembly will select either a lady or a gentleman, depending on the person doing the cutting, to join the person under the bough for a kiss." She clapped her hands in her glee. "Oh! Just imagine how very diverting it shall be to see who our guests select to kiss one another!"

For one brief, delicious moment Bethany did imagine, her pulse quickening as she envisioned Christian beneath the bough with her, sweeping her into his arms and claiming her lips with his.

Then the vision abruptly shattered, crushed by her ever vigilant prudence, which always sprang forth to dash her hopeless dreams, especially those that dared to picture her and Christian as more than just friends. Ignoring the way her heart grieved their loss, she forced herself to return to the conversation at hand, resuming it by frowning at Julia's swollen belly and chiding, "Please do not tell me that you intend to climb up and hang those tokens yourself. A woman in your condition—"

Julia cut her off with a laugh. "I am fine, dear. Why, the doctor says that he cannot recall the last time he saw a mother-to-be in such prime twig. Besides, I am not so very great with child yet that I cannot do simple tasks."

"But Gideon says—" Bethany tried again, only to be foiled by another peal of amused laughter.

"Gideon worries about me far too much. I daresay that he would lock me away in a trunk full of featherbeds if he thought that doing so would keep me from harm."

"It is just that he adores you so, as do we all, and he wants only what he thinks is best for you," Bethany replied, reaching out to take the second basket from Julia.

Julia relinquished it, but not before sighing and rolling her eyes to show exactly how silly she found the household's constant coddling. "You should all know by now that I love you far too much to allow anything untoward to happen to either myself or the baby. However, since you are determined to take Gideon's part in this and insist on treating me like an invalid, I shall allow you to tie the tokens to the bough for me. In truth, you make much more elegant bows than I do, so it is just as well that you assume the task."

Bethany nodded, pleased by her sister-in-law's easy capitulation. "I promise that I shall tie them in my best fashion. You have only to tell me how you want the ribbons arranged and I—" The remainder of her vow was cut off by the arrival of two footmen in green-and-gold livery bearing a ladder gaily festooned with garlands, ribbon, and holly.

After they had set it into position beneath the kissing bough and Julia had directed them to pull forth two chairs and a small table, the men took their leave.

Looking to Julia for instruction, Bethany asked, "What should I do first?"

Julia considered for a moment, then said, "It will be easiest if we tie the ribbons to the packages and then hang them from the bough. So I suppose that we must start by deciding how long the ribbons should be and cut them to the proper length."

Ordering Julia to sit, Bethany lifted her lavender muslin skirts and climbed the ladder. When she had measured and cut the initial piece of ribbon to Julia's specifications, she settled in the chair next to her at the table. As they sized the remainder of the ribbon, using the measured piece as a guide, Bethany conversationally inquired, "Where are the children? I have not seen them since early this morning."

The children consisted of Bethany's younger sister, Bliss, who had turned twelve two days earlier, and Julia's three siblings: twelve year-old Maria, eight year-old Jemima, and little Bertie, who was almost two. Since Julia could not bear to be parted from her siblings, and her parents, the socially prominent Marquess and Marchioness of Stanwell, had no time for them, Gideon had suggested that they take up residence at Critchley Manor. It was an arrangement that all involved found most agreeable.

As always happened at the mention of the children, Julia smiled. "They are outside with Jagtar and Mr. Hubert, sharing Christmas plenty with the animals." Jagtar was Gideon's manservant, a Sikh who had accompanied his employer from India, which is where Gideon had amassed his impressive fortune. Mr. Hubert was the jolly head gardener and the younger set's preferred guide among the creatures inhabiting the estate grounds. Now gazing at Bethany, Julia broadened her smile and added, "By the bye, dear, Leonie did a splendid job arranging your hair. You look quite lovely with your curls draped over your shoulder like that. I daresay that you shall be the most elegant lady at the gathering today."

Bethany smiled her thanks, though she knew that that last would be impossible since Julia would be in attendance. Julia—Lady Julia, by birth—was the epitome of well-bred elegance; everything one expected a noblewoman to be. She was aristocratic yet gracious, utterly refined in both bearing and manner. Everything she did she did with grand style. She was also sophisticated and cultured, charming and witty, always knowing exactly the right thing to say and do in every situation, no matter how difficult. As for the way she looked . . .

Bethany stole a glance at her companion from beneath her lowered lashes. If ever a woman looked highborn, it was her sister-in-law. Everything about her appearance was so graceful, so polished and perfect. Indeed, with her gleaming golden-red hair, pale, flawless complexion, almond-shaped amber eyes, and fine features, she was blessed with a classic beauty that paid homage to her genteel heritage. This morning she wore a becoming gown in a luscious shade of coral, with her hair done up in a modish coiffure of coils and curls. Though she was five months with child and beginning to show her condition, she still somehow managed to look fashionably slender.

As Bethany reached into the basket to retrieve a fresh bolt of ribbon, the color of which matched to perfection that of the ones binding the packages, Julia murmured, "It is a shame that Christian did not join us for our Christmas Eve feast last night. We all missed him dreadfully, especially the children. You know how they adore him." Bethany glanced up in time to see Julia shoot her a sly sidelong glance as she finished, "Considering the way he dotes on them, I daresay that he will make an exemplary father someday."

It was all Bethany could do not to groan aloud. Here Julia went with her blasted matchmaking again. Thus cued to don the polite but dispassionate air she always adopted in such instances, Bethany shrugged one shoulder and said, "You know how uncomfortable Christian is around strangers. No doubt he calculated the hours he would be trapped at the dinner table and decided that the occasion would afford our guests far too much time to pump him about his person. I must confess that I myself found their questioning disconcerting to the extreme."

Julia patted her arm. "You were magnificent, dear. Everyone said so. Why, they thought you so lovely and charming that they are clamoring for me to bring you to town for the season."

Bethany's stomach gave a sickening lurch at the thought of London society. "You know that I cannot possibly go," she demurred, carefully measuring a length of ribbon to hide her alarm.

"Bethany—" Julia began.

But Bethany had heard her arguments on the subject dozens of times before. In no mood to hear them again now, she cut her off, saying firmly and with finality, "Enough, Julia. I do not wish to discuss the matter."

Julia fell silent, and for a moment or two Bethany thought that she had heeded her wishes. Then she softly retorted, "You cannot hide from your past forever, Bethany. Like it or not, Gideon and I are a part of the *ton,* which makes you a part too. Given the *ton*'s fondness for gossip and prying into each other's affairs, the truth about you is bound to be uncovered sooner or later. Would it not be better to face what happened before they do so and find a resolution on your own terms? You know that Gideon and I will do everything in our power to help you. All you need to do is ask us."

Julia was right, of course, and Bethany knew it. She must address her past someday, and she would. But not today. She simply did not have the strength to do it yet. Feeling suddenly fragile, as she always did at the prospect of reopening the terrible wound to her soul, Bethany pleaded, "It is Christmas, Julia. Can we not enjoy the day and speak only of agreeable things?"

Julia gave her arm another pat. "I am sorry, Bethany. I did not mean to distress you. Truly. It is just that I am so proud of you and wish to show you off. However, you are correct in that it is Christmas and that we should speak only of agreeable things. And what could be more agreeable than the fact that Christian has accepted our invitation to our gathering this afternoon?" She laughed softly, a warm, bubbling ripple of sound. "Then again, how could he have possibly refused when you begged him so prettily to come?"

"I hardly begged him," Bethany demurred, though she had to admit to herself that she had been required to coax him at length.

Julia slanted her the knowing look that Bethany had come to recognize all too well. "No, of course not, dear. How very foolish of me. We all know that you have only to smile at Christian for him to do anything you ask."

"You know that isn't so," Bethany protested. "While it is true that Christian has been gracious in accommodating my requests, he has been equally indulgent in obliging those of the rest of the family. He has been an exceedingly good friend to us all."

"From the way he looks at you, I daresay that he wishes to be more than just a friend." Julia's words were charged with unmistakable meaning.

Seeing where the conversation was leading and determined to curb its direction, Bethany chided, "Julia, please. You promised that we would speak only of agreeable things today."

"Are you saying that you do not find the subject of Christian English agreeable?" Julia glanced up from the ribbon she was cutting to meet Bethany's gaze, her eyebrows raised in barbed query.

"No, I—"

"And can you honestly say that you find the thought of Christian as more than a friend disagreeable?"

"No, of course not," Bethany blurted out before she could stop herself. Hoping to rectify her slip, she carefully added, "Any woman would be honored to be courted by a man like Christian. Not only is he kind, considerate, and gentle, he possesses a fine sense of honor and a keen intellect."

"Mmm, yes," Julia murmured, her words accompanied by the soft snip of scissors slicing through satin. "And we must not forget to add his sinfully handsome face and spectacular body to his list of credits."

Since no one with eyes in their head could possibly argue with that, Bethany reluctantly acknowledged, "Yes. He is a fine-looking man." In truth, his looks were more than just fine. With his silky sable curls, thickly lashed dark eyes, and stunning features, Christian English was the most beautiful man she had ever seen. Why, just picturing him never failed to give her a funny little quiver in the pit of her stomach.

"Well, then? If everything about him is so agreeable, how can you possibly object to me speaking about him?" Julia inquired archly.

"Because I know where this conversation is leading, just as you know that anything more than friendship between Christian and me is impossible," Bethany countered, now at the end of her patience with their game.

Ignoring her less-than-subtle cue to cease play, Julia doggedly pressed on. "I agree that it is impossible until he finds out who he is, but afterward—" She broke off, leaving the rest of the sentence to float tantalizingly in the air.

Bethany sighed her frustration. "He could already be married, you know," she reminded Julia for what must have been the hundredth time.

And for the hundredth time Julia sniffed at the notion. "Considering his youth and the length of his enslavement, both Gideon and I agree that the possibility of him being already wed is highly unlikely."

"But we do not know his true age," Bethany argued. "He could be much older than he looks."

"Or he could be younger." Julia shrugged. "Whatever the instance, if he does have a wife somewhere you would think that she would have reported him missing. Indeed, I cannot imagine a woman not moving heaven and earth to reclaim a man like Christian, and you know as well as I that Gideon was unable to find any record of a man fitting Christian's description being reported lost in that part of the world."

Bethany had to admit that Julia had a point. Were

she Christian's wife, she would have appealed to every available authority for help, pursued all avenues, and overturned every stone on earth in her determination to find him. And she would not have ceased her search until he was back safe in her arms. Not about to share that particular sentiment with her companion, she simply said, "I guess that we shall just have to wait and see."

"I guess so," Julia murmured.

For a short time thereafter the women worked in silence, with Bethany tying the ribbon to the packets while Julia finished cutting the remaining lengths. Just when Bethany had begun to relax, certain that the topic of Christian had been put to rest, Julia said, "What will you do if he discovers for certain that he is unwed and asks you to marry him?"

Bethany forced herself to laugh as if such a thing were the most absurd notion in the world, though the last emotion she felt at that moment was amusement. "Such stuff and nonsense, Julia! Christian has said nothing whatsoever that might lead me to believe that he thinks of me as anything more than a friend."

"He has said nothing because he is a gentleman, and he does not wish to see you hurt should it turn out that he cannot wed you," Julia returned. "Nonetheless, we have all seen the way he looks at you, and you at him. You both could not wear your hearts on your sleeves more plainly were you to pin them there for the world to see."

Bethany made a show of adjusting the bow she was tying to hide her chagrin at Julia's observation. "Even if what you say were true, and Christian was free and wished to marry me, you know very well that I could never accept him. He deserves someone far better than me for a wife."

Julia sniffed. "There is no one better than you, Bethany, and Christian knows it."

"How can you say such a thing when you know what I have done . . . what I have been?" Bethany exclaimed, spoiling her formerly flawless bow in her mounting agitation. Oh, why did Julia have to be so very blind where she and Christian were concerned?

"You did what you had to do to save Bliss. Christian understands and accepts that fact," Julia replied in a reasonable voice.

In an attempt to right the bow, Bethany gave it a furious tug, one that perfectly reflected the turbulence of her emotions. "Well, I cannot accept it!" she snapped. "I was a whore! Worse yet, I bore a baby out of wedlock, and I could not even do that right. It was born dead." She gave her head a jerk to the negative. "No, Julia. No matter what happens, I shall not marry Christian. I can never be worthy of him."

"You were a nobleman's mistress, and you have been with only one man. That hardly qualifies you as a whore, especially in view of the fact that you sacrificed your virtue to save Bliss from a ruinous life in the rookery. Why, anyone with half a grain of sense would agree that you had no choice in the matter, what with you and Bliss being left destitute by the death of your mother and uncle, and Gideon seemingly lost in the wilds of India," Julia pointed out, in what Bethany was beginning to view as her annoyingly pragmatic manner. "If it makes you feel any better, I can truthfully attest to the fact that there are women in the *ton* who indulged in liaisons with several men before they were wed, and no one thinks any less of them."

"Perhaps, but they never bore the shameful title of mistress, nor were they abandoned like a cheap trollop for conceiving a child." By now Bethany had given up on her attempts at tying the ribbon.

"It is the man who abandoned you that should feel shame, not you, Bethany." Julia stamped her foot beneath the table. "O-o-o! It infuriates me to no end every time I think of what that bastard did. One expects so much better from a nobleman. I do wish that you would tell me his name so I can serve him up his just deserts."

Trying to persuade Bethany to reveal the name of the man who had ruined and then abandoned her was another of Julia's favorite pastimes, second only to matchmaking. Shaking her head, as she always did when Julia broached the subject, Bethany replied with a weary sigh, "You know I cannot do that."

And as with her matchmaking, Julia did not easily surrender this particular game. "I do not know why. Gideon has promised to limit his vengeance against the scoundrel to a well-deserved thrashing, so you no longer have to worry about your brother being hung for murder."

Bethany sighed again. "It is because I wish to forget the man and that part of my life." As if such a thing would ever be possible. Nonetheless, she was determined to try. Indeed, for all she knew she could never forget her shame, but she hoped to someday succeed in reducing its sharp, haunting pain to a dull, intermittent ache.

Apparently, Julia was satisfied with her response, because she let the subject drop. Gradually, Bethany's hands became steady again and she resumed her tying. She was working on the last package when Julia suddenly said, "If you will not marry, what do you intend to do with your life? I cannot imagine an intelligent and spirited woman like you being satisfied with burying herself in the country and passing her days painting watercolors."

Bethany took her time knotting the last bow while she debated whether or not to confide her dream to Julia. When she could procrastinate in her response no longer, she set the finished package aside and met

Julia's gaze. One glance at those amber eyes, so loving and filled with such gentle concern, settled the question for her. Now staring at her hands for fear that that concern would turn to disapproval when she voiced her ambition, she said, "I have thought a great deal about that question, and have decided that I would like to dedicate my life to helping females in the position Bliss and I were in when I was forced to sell myself."

There was a long pause, then Julia quietly replied, "I think that is a very worthy goal, Bethany. How do you propose to help them?"

Bethany shot Julia a grateful look, thankful for her understanding. "I wish to create a place where destitute women can find not only food and shelter, but also aid in gaining honest employment. I daresay that I shall be required to offer schooling, since most of the women will be without skills and education."

Julia looked thoughtful. "What you are proposing, then, is a charity school of sorts?"

"Of sorts, yes, but it will be for girls and women of all ages and stations, so that all destitute females will have a chance at a better life. Of course, in order for my plan to succeed, I will need to build my haven in one of London's impoverished areas." Julia's eyes did register disapproval at that. However, before she could voice it, Bethany hastily explained, "Those are the areas where the women I wish to save are most likely to be, and I know from my own experiences from living in a rookery that poor women are reluctant to stray beyond their own social boundaries. Besides, how are the women to learn of my project unless it is somewhere they can see it and hear about it?"

Julia seemed to consider her argument, then slowly nodded. "Hmmm. I do see your point, though I suspect that Gideon will be less than thrilled with the notion of you spending your days in such a place. And you will need his financial assistance to take on such a project."

"But of course you are right," Bethany murmured, her heart sinking at the prospect of trying to sway her overprotective brother to her scheme. She sighed. "Oh, dear. Whatever shall I do?"

Julia reached over and gave her arm a reassuring squeeze. "You leave your brother to me. If you are truly in earnest about all this, I am certain that I can convince him to help you. However, before I speak to him, you must consider the fact that Gideon will insist on you living at his Grosvenor Square townhouse, which means that the *ton* cannot help but to see you as you go about your business. When they do, they will insist on taking you into their fold."

Bethany shrugged, having already contemplated that hazard. "I shall evade their company by politely but firmly informing them that I am still in mourning for my husband and baby, and am not yet ready to attend social functions outside those hosted by our family."

When Gideon had returned from India to find Bethany pregnant, he had promptly put about the rumor that she was the widow of an American sea captain named Nathan Matland, who had recently perished at sea. Thus she was addressed by those outside the family as Mrs. Matland, and took care to dress in mourning whenever they had visitors or she went into Low Brindle, Critchley Manor's small village. Since her fictional husband had supposedly been dead for close to a year now, she was in half mourning, which allowed her to discard her black gowns in favor of ones made up in drab shades of gray, brown, white, and lavender.

Julia laughed at her reasoning. "What a slyboots you are, Bethany! Not only will you be able to avoid society, but you will also appear to be a model of decorum for adhering so strictly to the rules of mourning."

"Then you think that my strategy will work?"

"I think that it shall most definitely work in allowing

you to avoid parties and such. However, you still run the risk that the man who ruined you might see you and cause complications."

Bethany shrugged again. "I know for a fact that he does not live on Grosvenor Square or any of the adjoining streets, so I should be safe enough. After all, I shall be spending most of my time in an area of town that is seldom patronized by aristocratic gentlemen."

Julia sniffed. "I assume that you are plying the term *gentleman* loosely in describing that beastly creature."

Not wishing to reopen the subject of her former keeper, Bethany let the comment pass without response, instead saying, "So you see? You can speak to Gideon with the certainty that I have thought the matter through."

"So it would seem," Julia murmured. After a moment, she nodded. "Very well, then. I shall speak with him right after the Twelfth Night, when our houseguests have all departed."

Bethany threw her arms around Julia and gave her a mighty hug. The sooner she left Critchley Manor, the sooner she could escape Christian and the disturbing effect he had on her heart.

CHAPTER 3

"Mr. Christian English," Fitzroy, the staid Critchley Manor majordomo, announced to the crowd in the ballroom, though it was doubtful if anyone could hear him above their mirthful raucousness. To be sure, no one so much as glanced in Christian's direction as he stepped over the threshold.

And for that Christian was grateful. Nothing unnerved him more than strangers, for they never failed to ask him the polite but personal questions one always asked a new acquaintance, which inevitably forced him to confess his lack of memory. Making matters all the more uncomfortable was the manner in which they treated him in the aftermath of his confession.

God! How he hated the way they spoke to him in that hushed, funereal tone people always used when trying to project sympathy. How they carefully measured each word and uttered it slowly, as if they assumed that his condition had robbed him of his wits as well as his memory. Equally vexing was how they looked at him, their eyes wide with shock and filled with pity, gazing at him from faces that seemed frozen into somber masks.

Unfortunately, their pity was never such that they felt obligated to stifle their curiosity about his ordeal. Quite the opposite. When they learned that he had lost his memory during his capture by corsairs, their horrified fascination simply refused to allow them not to probe for details. And of all the things he despised about strangers, he despised their probing most. In truth, there were times that he could not help despising the people themselves for not having the decency to realize how painful it was for him to relive his enslavement. Thus, he had made it a rule to avoid any situation that might require him to hobnob with strangers. He most certainly would have shunned this gathering had Bethany not been so set on him attending.

For the first time since his arrival, Christian smiled. Sweet, darling Bethany. How could he deny her anything when she begged him so prettily? Eager to see her now, to have his jangled nerves soothed as they always were by her comforting presence, he skirted the well-dressed assembly, taking care to stay far enough away to avoid being drawn into conversation. Retreating near the musicians to an alcove, one that housed an imposing statue of Icarus, the spread wings of which further hid him from view, he gazed about the room, searching for her.

Though the heavy draperies had been drawn to stave off the winter chill, the newly renovated ballroom glowed like the inside of a rainbow, the gloom lifted by the prismatic illumination from the hundreds of colored globe lamps that had been strung on gay garlands of holly, ivy, pinecones, and evergreen, and draped throughout the room. Joining the globes in their battle against the shadows were scores of expensive beeswax candles, many of which twinkled among the diamondlike pendants of the four cut glass chandeliers overhead, while others flickered in girandoles or sparkled in mirrored wall sconces.

Looking to his right, Christian saw that the row of double doors leading to the grand dining hall had been thrown open to reveal several long tables and side-boards heaped with fantastical confectionary creations and foods of every description, all arranged on highly polished silver platters that reflected the kaleidoscopic light. The doors to the crimson salon at the far end of the ballroom stood open as well, and though he could not see the interior he knew from his conversation with Gideon the day before that it had been out-fitted with gaming tables and all the accoutrements required to indulge their guests' love of gambling. Everywhere he looked there were people and more people, among whom moved footmen bearing trays of orgeat, wine, capillaire, cakes, and both red and white negus.

As Christian continued to scan the room, the sickening knot in his belly began to ease. Aside from a score or so of people, who judging from their dress and manner were the aristocratic guests Gideon had wryly warned him had accompanied Julia's parents from London, he recognized almost all the merrymakers as being neighboring gentry. Despite his intention to avoid the noble strangers, he could not resist pausing in his search for Bethany to study them, viewing them with the wary curiosity one usually reserved for exotic creatures with dangerously sharp teeth and claws.

Julia's father, Lord Stanwell, was easy enough to identify, what with his distinctive copper hair and amber eyes, which were reminiscent of his daughter's autumnal coloring. And he deduced from the way she clung to his arm that the pretty, if rather fatuous-looking, blond woman by his side was Lady Stanwell. As for the rest of his lordship's circle . . .

One by one Christian examined them, experiencing a disquieting sense of familiarity as his gaze touched several of their faces. Like most of his queer vagaries, he dismissed the sensation, not considering it worth his contemplation. If there was one thing he knew for certain, it was that he was not an aristocrat. Gideon had made thorough inquiries in both India and London about missing noblemen, having been convinced by Christian's speech and bearing that he was from the aristocracy, and none matching his description had been reported missing. And everyone in the *ton* knew that nothing untoward could happen to an English aristocrat without hue and cry being raised.

Everyone in the ton knew? Christian frowned at his latest conceit, wondering how *he* knew such a thing with the unwavering certainty he felt. As he had done with his sense of familiarity, he shrugged off the thought as yet another of his unexplainable whimsies. Ah, well. Whatever the instance, he knew from Gideon's cynical remarks that the aristocratic entourage had come only to curry Julia's parents' favor. Apparently, one was nothing in the *ton* unless they held the enviable but tenuous position as one of the Marquess and Marchioness of Stanwell's select group.

Now shifting his attention from the Stanwells and their toadies, who clustered together at one end of the room, as if coming in contact with the local gentry might contaminate them with the stench of their commonness, he resumed his search for Bethany. As he again glanced toward the dining hall, he spied Bethany's sister, Bliss, and Julia's sisters, Maria and Jemima, darting through one of the doors with their faces wreathed in grins and their hands full of what appeared to be Cook's famous gingerbread cakes.

Christian grinned at the sight of them. Jemima, a winsome little moppet with golden curls, and her pretty, copper-haired older sister Maria were both appropriately attired for the occasion in frilled white muslin gowns tied with wide blue silk sashes. Bliss, on the other hand, the willful leader of the group, wore the peacock-and-gold sari she had begged Gideon to buy her for a Christmas gift. Ever since Gideon had returned from India and had regaled the children with tales from that exotic, far-off land, Bliss had become enamored with all things Indian.

Christian's grin broadened in amusement at the child's unorthodox attire, which was currently raising eyebrows and drawing disapproving looks from the nobles. While Bliss was not as pretty as her companions, and most probably never would be, her thin, sharp-featured face possessed a sparkling vivacity and her steel gray eyes a keen intelligence that made her looks arresting in a way that would someday pale those of more traditionally pretty women. As Christian fondly marked the girls' scampering progress through the room, a group of elderly gentlemen near the dance floor stepped aside to allow them passage, and he finally saw her.

Bethany. His heart seemed to still in his chest. Though she was always beautiful, she looked even more so today with her hair swept up in a formal but artless coiffure of waves, curls, and ringlets, and her cheeks flushed pink from the heat of the room. In keeping with her pretend mourning for her fictional husband and her true mourning for her baby, she wore a demure gray silk gown topped by a black net overdress, both of which were trimmed in black velvet points and flattered her splendid figure to perfection. At the moment she was speaking to Julia and three young women who clearly ranked among the aristocracy. Unlike their peers, however, who continued to segregate themselves at the opposite end of the room, the three women appeared agreeably disposed toward everyone there, for they smiled and nodded at all who passed by, be they servant or guest.

After sparing the women enough of a passing glance to note that two of them were blondes, one pretty and the other plain, while the third was an elegant brunette, he focused all his attention on Bethany.

For a long while he stood there watching her, savoring her every expression, her every gesture and smile. Dear God, but she was exquisite. There wasn't a woman present who could hold a candle to her beauty. Everything about her was enchanting. Flawless. Her smooth, glowing complexion . . . her graceful figure . . . her bewitching face, with its slightly slanted sapphire eyes and lusciously full lips. And then there was her glorious hair, so thick and glossy and gleaming like polished mahogany in the candlelight.

Yet for all her dazzling appearance on the outside, he knew her to be even more so on the inside. To be sure, she had the most marvelous heart in the world, big and tender and filled close to bursting with kindness and generosity. In his mind it was her greatest beauty. And no matter how life and age might alter her face and figure, in his eyes the loveliness of her heart would always make her appear as radiant as she was today. For hearts such as hers did not wither and fade with the passage of years like flesh did; they simply grew more magnificent, their timeless beauty strengthened and enhanced by the wisdom, goodness, and faith that came from living a loving life.

Though Christian ached to spirit Bethany away to a quiet place and kiss her until they were both breathless, he knew that he had no right to do such a thing since he could not claim her for his own. Besides, if he were to approach her now he would be forced to meet Julia's friends, and at the moment he was unprepared to do so.

"Hiding from your legion of female admirers, Christian?"

Christian almost jumped out of his skin, startled to hear Gideon Harwood's amused voice so close at hand. His startlement promptly turning to chagrin at being caught spying, he shot his friend a sheepish smile and lamely echoed, "Female admirers?" all the while praying that Gideon hadn't discerned the exact target of his covert gaping.

Gideon's dark eyebrows shot up in an expression of genuine disbelief. "Good heavens, man. Do not tell me that you haven't noticed the way the local chits moon over you? Why, they practically trip all over themselves trying to draw your attention every time they see you. Mr. Elbourn told me that his poor daughter, Florinda, was so absorbed by the sight of you riding through Low Brindle last week that she failed to watch where she was going and almost broke her nose from running into Mrs. Smith's garden wall."

Though Christian secretly thought that the featherbrained Miss Elbourn's large hooked nose might actually be improved by a break, he was too much of a gentleman to ever voice such an ungallant opinion, so he instead shrugged and replied, "I cannot say that I have noticed Miss Elbourn or any other lady paying me particular attention."

Gideon's eyebrows arched a fraction higher. "Surely you jest? One cannot ride Little Critchley Road without passing a gaggle or two of giggling girls either coming from or going to your cottage. They have all but worn out the pavement in carrying baskets of delicacies to your door."

Again Christian shrugged, forcibly resisting his almost overwhelming urge to steal another glance at Bethany. "Since everyone in the village knows about my condition, I assumed that they felt sorry for me and were being kind out of pity, rather in the manner of Julia and Bethany when they take baskets to your invalid tenants."

Gideon gave an out-and-out laugh at his reasoning, drawing smiles from several passersby. "I can assure you that their charity has nothing whatsoever to do with pity. Indeed, when Owen Henson lost his leg in that wagon collision last month, not a single unwed female under the age of thirty bothered to take him a basket more than once. Ditto for Peter Dawkins, who is only now recovering from three broken ribs." He laughed again and shook his head. "No, my friend. It isn't pity that has those women beating a path to your door; it is that pretty face of yours."

Christian cringed at Gideon's description of his face as pretty, remembering all too vividly the previous night and the painful memory his dream had dragged forth. For as much as he could recall, which was admittedly very little, his looks had been more of a burden than a blessing. A curse, almost. Nonetheless, he knew that his friend had intended his teasing comment to be a compliment, so he smiled and bantered back, "If what you claim is true, then I feel obligated to plead in my own defense by saying that I have never said or done a single thing to give those women the slightest encouragement."

"Of course you haven't. Then again, encouragement is unnecessary in these situations," Gideon countered, taking a sip from the glass he held. "Women, and men, for that matter, know no reason when in the throes of a crush, and they have the most confounding tendency to interpret even the most innocent glance or comment from the object of their infatuation as a requital of their tender feelings. Everyone knows that it is so."

Christian made a wry face. "I hope you are correct. The last thing I need is to further complicate my life by gaining the reputation of being a scoundrel."

Another laugh from Gideon. "There is hardly any danger of that. I happen to know for a fact that there is a rumor flying about the village that says you took a vow to live like a monk until you discover your true identity. . . . not that it seems to have done much to dissuade your admirers."

It was Christian's turn to laugh. "Shall I venture a guess as to who is responsible for starting the rumor?"

Gideon shrugged one shoulder. "Never let it be said that I do not aid my friends in their time of need."

"Never," Christian agreed with a smile. And it was most certainly true. Since they had become friends, Gideon had always been there when Christian had needed him, and he suspected that he always would be. He only hoped that he would someday have the opportunity to return all the favors Gideon had granted him.

Gideon fell silent then, his laughing gray eyes growing shuttered and a mask of inscrutable austerity falling over his smiling face as he turned to survey the crowd. This was the hard, formidable Gideon Harwood that Christian had first glimpsed when Gideon had lifted him, bleeding and on the verge of death, from a battlefield in India. The Gideon Harwood that Gideon wished the world to see: cool and enigmatic, intimidating in both his superior strength and keen intelligence, a man with the confidence to take on the world and win. Gideon Harwood, the proud, conquering warrior.

Christian's smile broadened at his thoughts. If anyone looked like a warrior, it was Gideon, with his imposing stature, muscular build, and a face so starkly sculpted that it appeared to be hewn from stone. Yet for all his fierce, almost piratical looks, there wasn't a more honorable man or a better friend to be found in England. Judging from the tender way his wife gazed at him, it was apparent that he was a stellar husband as well.

At length, Gideon slanted him a sidelong glance and murmured, "Well, then, if you are not hiding, what the devil are you doing skulking in this alcove?"

"I didn't say that I am not hiding. I freely admit that I am. From them." Christian jerked his head in the direction of the nobles.

"Ah, yes. Them." Gideon chuckled dryly. "You are a very wise man indeed to stay clear of that lot. Were I not the host, I would be tempted to follow suit. However, since I am the host, I must not only be hospitable to them, but I must also make certain that all appropriate introductions are made. And I fear that there are several individuals among their number that I must insist you meet."

Christian grimaced. "I cannot imagine why. I doubt if any of those individuals harbor the slightest desire to make my acquaintance." The knots in his stomach again tightened at the thought of being presented to Julia's aristocratic guests. After listening to Julia's accounts of life in the *ton,* he suspected that the villagers' probing would seem like a pleasant little tête-à-tête compared to the imperious grilling he was bound to suffer from the aristocrats.

Gideon gave his shoulder a reassuring squeeze, as if discerning his alarm. "I can assure you that they will be delighted, the Marquess of Shepley in particular. He happens to own the bank in which we deposited the bulk of our fortunes, and by his own admission we rank among his largest depositors."

Christian experienced one of his odd pangs of recognition at the name. "Shepley," he echoed, testing the feel of the word on his tongue. Like the name, it too seemed familiar.

Apparently, his expression mirrored his thoughts, because Gideon eyed him quizzically. "Do you think you might know the man?"

Christian snorted, dismissing the sensation. "How would I possibly know a marquess, unless, of course, I was once his valet?"

Gideon continued to stare at him, his gaze searching and his steely eyes narrowing as if in conjecture. He looked about to voice his thoughts, then seemed to change his mind. Glancing away to again observe his guests, he said, "I do not see Lord Shepley at the moment, but his daughter, Lady Amy, is the pretty blond minx dressed in green talking to Bethany and Julia. She very much favors her father in looks."

Having thus been given permission to look openly at Bethany's group, Christian followed Gideon's gaze, saying, "I noticed earlier that Julia seems rather well acquainted with Lady Amy and her companions. Bethany appears to be getting on with them as well."

Gideon nodded. "Bethany met Lady Mina, the other blond lady, several months ago when she stopped at Critchley for the night while on a journey home to London. They became fast friends. You were in Liverpool at the time, which was a stroke of luck on your part, since she was accompanied by the odious Duchess of Hunsderry and her equally detestable daughter, Helene. The brunette is Lady Caroline, the Earl of Hollamby's girl. While I cannot claim to know her as well as I do Ladies Amy and Mina, Julia counts her as a bosom-bow, so I am certain that she and Bethany will becomes friends, as well." He glanced at Christian, a smile tugging at his lips. "Would you like me to introduce you to them? I am sure that they would be pleased to make your acquaintance—perhaps too pleased in regards to Lady Amy." He emitted a snorting laugh. "The chit is famous for developing a crush on every handsome man she sees, so it should not take more than a single glance for her to become utterly and completely infatuated with you."

Christian made a face. "As tempting as that offer is, I do believe that I would prefer to postpone the honor until later."

"In that instance, perhaps you would like to accompany me to the dining hall and sample the wassail I concocted." Before Christian, wishing to remain where he could see Bethany, could open his mouth to decline that offer as well, Gideon gently reminded him, "You cannot hide in the alcove all day, you know."

Of course, Gideon was right. Not only would it be cowardly to do so, but also Bethany would be terribly disappointed in him if he didn't at least try to partake in the festivities. And the last thing in the world he wished to do was disappoint Bethany. Stealing a final glance at Bethany, who had taken Lady Amy's arm and was now escorting her through the crowd, Christian sighed and nodded. "All right, then. Wassail it is. I trust you made it strong?"

"Naturally." Gideon's sudden grin was almost boyish in its deviltry. "It is my belief that the tradition dictating that the master of the house must make the wassail springs from our manly ancestors' need for strong spirits on Christmas Day in order to survive the exhausting influx of gaiety and goodwill."

Christian laughed. "My father thought much the same thing. I remember that he used to say—" he broke off abruptly in his shock when he became aware of what he was saying, instantly losing the remainder of whatever his unconscious mind had prompted him to reveal.

"Remember what, Christian?" Gideon gently probed.

Christian's mind raced to recapture the nebulous thought, but to no avail. It had vanished without a trace. At length he shook his head. "I—I do not know. Whatever the memory was, it is gone now."

"But you did remember your father?"

Christian shook his head again. "No. I cannot say that I precisely remembered him. I did not picture anything in connection with my words. They simply sprang from my mouth without any thought behind them." He had, however, remembered the taste of the wassail in question, with its aromatic blend of ginger and nutmeg steeped in sugared ale and fine rum.

Gideon gave his back a thump, a man's way of expressing sympathy to another man when he did not want the man receiving his sympathy to feel like he was being pitied. "Well, it is something, Christian, a start, and a very good one, to my way of thinking."

Christian smiled faintly in response, suddenly overwhelmed by an odd, almost wrenching sense of yearning, though for what he did not know. Could it be that he was homesick for a home he could no longer remember, his longing stirred by hidden memories of happy Christmastides past?

Before he could fully contemplate the notion, Gideon began to lead him toward the dining hall, cutting a wide swath around the crowd, no doubt out of consideration for Christian's diffidence to strangers.

Now in the dining hall, standing before the table where an enormous gold wassail bowl sat surrounded by several perfectly aligned rows of punch rummers, as the large-bowled, footed glasses were called, Gideon waved away the footman who had stepped forward to assist them, preferring to serve them himself. As he ladled the beverage into two glasses, three aristocratic ladies entered the room, one of whom snapped her fingers at a nearby footman, indicating that he was to serve them. Christian watched as the servant was joined by two of his colleagues, marveling at the precise choreography with which the three men armed themselves with plates and then discreetly shadowed the ladies.

All of late-middle years, all slender and garbed in highly embellished gowns with flowers and plumes in their upswept hair, the women leisurely perused the delectable offerings, conversing in low voices as they went about the business of making their selections. Each had only to point her closed fan at whatever dish she wished to sample for the footman carrying her plate to instantly move forward and add a serving.

"The attractive brunette in blue is Lady Fairhope, a countess," Gideon said, handing Christian a glass of wassail. "Lady Stinson, whose husband is a mere viscount, is in yellow. And the bilious-looking redhead with a neck like a turkey is the Duchess of Poltimore, the latest in Julia's mother's ever changing entourage of bosom-bows. It shall be entertaining to see if they acknowledge my lowly presence, which I would venture to guess is highly unlikely given the fact that there is no one around of any consequence to gossip about their breach in propriety should they elect to do so." Grinning wryly, he raised his glass to Christian. "Ah, well. Here is to us, and friendship among commoners. Happy Christmas, my friend."

Christian echoed the toast, touched his glass to Gideon's, and took a quaff. As Gideon had promised, the wassail was indeed strong.

"When they reach the roasted peacock, they will either pretend to suddenly see us and greet me, or feign distraction and turn away without acknowledging our presence," Gideon murmured. He took a deep swallow from his glass and added with a chuckle, "Five pounds says that they turn away."

"Five pounds," Christian agreed, praying that he would lose the wager. If the women acknowledged Gideon, Gideon would be forced to introduce them to him. And from the look of the trio, they were masters in the art of grilling—merciless ones.

It appeared that God might favor him with his wish, because after rejecting the peacock the women made a show of becoming interested in something across the room. As they pivoted on their heels, Lady Stinson stole what was no doubt meant to be a surreptitious glance at the men, abruptly abandoning stealth in the next instant to regard Christian with open interest. After out-and-out staring for several seconds, her brown eyes slowly narrowing as she did so, she snapped her fan open and whispered to the Duchess of Poltimore from behind it. Her grace in turn nudged Lady Fairhope and hissed something to her. After a brief conference behind their fans, during which their gazes remained pinned on Christian, the duchess nodded and approached the men.

Now smiling in a way that formed cracklike creases in her heavily rouged cheeks, she said, "I wish to compliment you on your excellent table, Mr. Harwood. Judging from the array of continental-style delicacies, I daresay that your cook is French."

Gideon smiled back, the very picture of urbane charm. "Alas no, your grace. Our cook hails from Liverpool. However, she is wed to a Frenchman, which could account for her mode in cooking."

"No doubt," her grace murmured, shifting her attention to Christian, thus signaling her desire for an introduction.

Gideon decorously did the honors. "Your grace, please allow me to present Mr. Christian English."

"Mister . . . English, you say?" A frown knit her forehead, and she was staring so hard at his face that Christian could almost feel her sharp blue eyes slicing into his flesh.

"Mr. English, yes," Gideon confirmed with a nod. "Mr. English, the Duchess of Poltimore."

Christian bowed, praying that the woman would lose interest and leave him in peace now that they had been introduced. "A pleasure, your grace," he said, though, of course, it was nothing of the sort.

By now the other two ladies had joined the duchess, so Gideon introduced them as well.

"And where are you from, Mr. English?" Lady Stinson quizzed in a conversational tone, joining the duchess in her unnerving scrutiny. While her ladyship could not by any stretch of the imagination be judged as pretty, what with her lank mouse-brown hair and buckteeth, she more than made up in elegance what she lacked in looks.

Christian cringed inside. Here they went with the grilling. Forcing himself to smile in what he hoped was a cordial manner, he pretended to misunderstand the question, deftly dodging it by replying, "I reside at the Critchley Manor dowager cottage, my lady, at the edge of this estate."

"I believe that Lady Stinson wishes to know your birthplace, sir," Lady Fairhope chimed in. Like the other two women, she made no effort to conceal her curiosity.

So much for being evasive, Christian miserably thought. Before he could decide on a new, hopefully more effective tactic for putting off the women's questions, Gideon came to his rescue by saying, "Mr. English is an Englishman, like me, lately from India."

All three pairs of eyebrows rose in unison at his response.

"How very interesting," the duchess intoned, exchanging a meaningful look with the other two ladies. "Tell me, Mr. English, were you in India long?"

"Several years," Christian replied, wondering if he should just spit out his tale and be done with it. At the rate the women were prying, they would have it out of him soon, anyway.

"Indeed? And what was your business in India?" quizzed Lady Stinson.

Again Gideon rescued him, this time interposing, "He was there in my company, my lady. He assisted me in training Indian troops."

"Oh." This was from the Duchess of Poltimore, who uttered the word in a short, brusque syllable. Looking away, as if suddenly bored by their conversation, she murmured to her companions, "I do believe that I see apple puffs on the sideboard across the room. As I recall, they are Lady Stanwell's favorite." With that she turned away from the men, dismissing them without another glance.

"I do believe that you are correct," concurred Lady Fairhope, turning away as well.

"In that instance, we must take her a plate." Lady Stinson followed her companions' lead, but not before stealing a final glance at Christian. Unlike her friends, she appeared unsatisfied by what she had learned.

Gideon shook his head as the women walked away. "They rather make one question the validity of the *ton*'s claim on the term *polite society,* do they not?"

Christian grimaced and took a long pull from his glass. By now another trio of aristocrats had entered the room, this one comprising two women, one a sour-faced matron and the other a pretty blond who couldn't have been a day over fifteen, both clinging to either arm of an ancient gentleman.

"The Earl and Countess of Markland," Gideon murmured, indicating the new group with a faint nod in their direction. "The woman accompanying them is Lady Gristock, his lordship's daughter by his first marriage."

Christian frowned, taken aback by that last piece of information. "Lady Gristock strikes me as being rather young to be wed," he observed. At the moment the chit was giggling in a high-pitched, childish squeal, her incongruously full breasts threatening to pop out of her low neckline as she playfully tugged at his lordship's ears. Judging from his lordship's gleeful cackling, he was enjoying her silly game immensely. Lady Markland, however, did not seem to approve of their antics, because she scowled and loudly reminded the man of his gout.

Gideon laughed. "The girl is the wife. The older woman is the daughter."

Christian shot his friend a cynical look, certain that he jested. But Gideon shook his head. "It is true. Julia said that the girl was only fourteen when his lordship wed her. Then again, he had no choice but to meet her at the altar since she claimed to have been compromised by him. Not that he was complaining about doing so, mind you." He laughed again and shook his head. "The chit's claim turned out to be a source of pride for his lordship. Indeed, according to Julia, he went about London all puffed up and boasting of his conquest to anyone who would listen. It supposedly created a most delicious scandal."

Christian drained his glass. "I daresay that I would not be wrong if I ventured to guess that his lordship is wealthy?"

"No, you would not. You would also be correct if you were to surmise that the girl's father owed his lordship a rather large sum of money."

"And of course it is only right that a son-in-law forgive his father-in-law's debt," Christian sardonically concluded.

"Of course."

Christian continued to study the unorthodox group, not missing the enjoyment the old man seemed to be deriving from his child bride and her youthful tomfoolery. Judging from the way the girl smiled at him, now and again patting his withered, age-spotted cheek, there appeared to be a measure of genuine fondness between the couple. Turning back to Gideon, he commented, "I would say from watching the pair that his lordship does not regret his bargain."

"Not in the least, which is why his daughter looks so peevish," Gideon replied, replenishing both their glasses. "It seems that the woman and her husband had designs on the old man's town house, thinking to retire him to the country to rusticate in his dotage. Unfortunately for them, he loves nothing more than to show off his young wife to society, and she adores buying out the London shops, both of which naturally require that they reside in town. That being the case—"

"Northwick, my dearest boy! Where the devil have you been keeping yourself?" a jovial voice boomed, followed by a hearty slap on Christian's back. "I have missed seeing you gadding about town. Been a bloody dull place without you to liven things up."

It was Lord Markland, who had descended upon them with a speed that was astonishing for a man of his advanced years. More astonishing yet, he was grinning at Christian in a most familiar manner, his liver-colored lips stretching broadly over his yellowed and stained teeth to reveal a wide expanse of surprisingly healthy-looking gum. A short, slightly built man with spindly extremities, an age-hunched back, and a rather oversized head topped by an enormous powdered wig, he could not have looked more delighted as he gave Christian's back another thump. Lady Markland, who still clung to her husband's arm and looked even younger up close, emitted another high-pitched titter.

Christian merely stared at the pair, uncertain how to respond.

"Papa, please! Do come away this instant," the daughter hissed, ignoring Christian as she reattached herself to her father's arm and tried to lead him away. "This man is not the Marquess of Northwick."

Lord Markland impatiently shook off her tugging hands. "What the hell has gotten into you, Sybil? Of course he is Lord Northwick, though where he has been keeping himself these past years, I would like to know."

Lady Gristock had the good grace to toss Christian an apologetic look as she countered, "Think, Papa! Think! Remember? Lord Northwick was killed by Barbary pirates on his journey home from India. The ship's captain saw him die. How could you have possibly forgotten something that was all the talk for close to a year?"

"Nonsense, girl!" his lordship barked. "How can he be dead when he's standing before me, as wicked and handsome as ever? Just look at him. Does he look like a ghost to you?"

For the first time since beginning their discourse, her ladyship seemed to actually see Christian. After studying him at length, she murmured, "I admit that his resemblance to Northwick is striking, but he cannot possibly be him. If his lordship had been discovered alive after all these years, we would have been among the first to hear the news." Now glancing at Christian, she pleaded, "Please tell him that you are not Lord Northwick, sir."

Christian shrugged and obliged her. "I am not Lord Northwick."

"Are you certain?" Gideon interjected. All four pairs of eyes promptly turned to him. He nodded. "It is possible that you could be this Lord Northwick, Christian. In truth, it would make perfect sense. That you were born into the aristocracy would account for your education and breeding, and the presumption that you are dead would explain why no one reported you missing. Then there is the part about pirates. You were initially captured by corsairs, during which you were grievously wounded. It could be that the captain simply assumed that you were dead from your wounds, and left you as such."

Christian considered the theory, concluding that Gideon could be right. The pieces of Lord Northwick's story did indeed fit the puzzle that was Christian English's life. So could it be true? Was it true? Was he indeed the lost Marquess of Northwick?

Lord Markland was clearly convinced that it was so. "Of course he is Northwick," he snapped in an indignant voice. "I know the lad when I see him. . . . known him since he was in swaddling, though I can't for the life of me imagine why he is denying who he is." A sudden look dawned on his face then, and he chuckled. "Ah. Perhaps I can imagine the reason after all.

You always were a bit of a scapegrace." Another chuckle. "So what is it this time? A chit, a duel, or a debt?" He shook his head and clapped Christian's back again. "Well, never you mind. Whatever your trouble, your father and I will straighten it out quick enough. No need to continue hiding like this."

"Is it true? Have you been hiding?" This was from Lady Markland, who was gazing at him with something akin to awe.

Christian shook his head. "No. I can assure you that I have not been hiding, my lady. The truth of the matter is that I have lost my memory and do not know who I am."

"What!" The utterance was chorused by eight voices instead of three, for the Duchess of Poltimore and her cronies had joined their group, along with two gentlemen whom Christian had yet to meet.

Casting an uncertain look at Gideon, who nodded, Christian proceeded to explain his situation. Rather than dredge up painful memories, as doing so in the past had always done, disclosing his plight in this instance served to quicken the sense of excitement humming through his veins. After all, he might not only be of the aristocracy, a station that would most certainly make him worthy to offer Bethany his heart, but by the tone of the conversation it appeared that he was also unwed. Wishing to verify that last, he asked, "Is, ur, was Lord Northwick married at the time of his presumed death?"

Lord Markland guffawed. "Hell no, much to the frustration of every unwed chit in the *ton*. For all that you were a notorious rakehell, your wealth, title, and dashing looks made you the most coveted marriage prize in England."

It was all Christian could do to stifle his whoop of joy at the news.

For a short while thereafter the group remained silent, each reflecting upon what they had learned. At length Lady Fairhope said, "I believe that Mr. Harwood and Lord Markland could be correct in that Mr. English is the Marquess of Northwick. My friends and I marked the astonishing resemblance the instant we laid eyes on him. It quite piqued our interest in him."

Both Lady Stinson and the Duchess of Poltimore nodded, with her grace adding, "Yes. And the more I look at him, the more convinced I am that he is indeed his lordship."

"Then there is the fact that he was found in India," contributed Lady Stinson. "The parallels between Mr. English's and Lord Northwick's situations are far too great to be shrugged off as a mere coincidence."

The two men mumbled their agreement.

"Well, there is one way to know for certain," Lord Markland declared. When everyone stared at him in query, he nodded and continued. "It so happens that my third son, Brice, and Lord Northwick were quite good friends—thick as glue since their nursery days. One of their favorite pastimes used to be swimming naked in the reflecting pool in our town house garden. Couldn't walk past there on a warm day without seeing them splashing about in it." He cackled and shook his head. "I remember the last time I saw them there. It was right before Northwick's father shipped him off to India. The boys were deep in their cups at the time, as were the actresses with them. You should have seen the tits on those dolly-mops, they—"

"Father, please!" his daughter gasped, casting the group an embarrassed look. "I really do not see what such things have to do with the matter at hand. You said that you know of a way to tell for certain that Mr. English is Lord Northwick."

He snorted. "I was just getting to that, damn it."

"Then please do so without any more unnecessary embellishments," she retorted primly.

His lordship snorted again. "I daresay that the gentlemen didn't find my embellishments the least bit unnecessary."

"Papa!" Lady Gristock more wailed than uttered the word.

Lady Markland tittered and patted her husband's cheek. "You really should not tease Sybil so, Bumpy. You know that she lacks the humor to bear it gracefully."

By the look the woman shot her ridiculous stepmother, it was apparent that she had a great deal of trouble bearing her with grace as well.

Unlike with his daughter, Lord Markland actually heeded his wife's reprimands. "But of course you are correct, dearest," he cooed, chucking her under her pert chin. "I was being naughty. My apologies, Sybil."

His daughter sniffed. "Do you or do you not know a way to determine if Mr. English is Lord Northwick?"

Lord Markland tore his gaze away from his prettily simpering wife to frown at his daughter. "I said I did, didn't I?"

"Well, then?" This was from the Duchess of Poltimore, who was clearly as weary of his lordship's nonsense as his daughter was.

"Lord Northwick has a birthmark, a bright red one, shaped like a starburst high on his left buttock," Lord Markland disclosed. "It is most distinctive. I mentioned seeing him swimming naked to explain my knowledge of it."

Christian's soaring hope promptly sank. He had no such mark. At least he had never seen one while drawing on his breeches. He sighed, crushed and suddenly weary. So that was that, it seemed. "Well, that settles the matter then," he murmured. "I have no such mark, so I cannot possibly—"

"Yes, you do," Gideon cut in. "I saw such a mark while nursing you in India. I am not surprised that you have not noticed it. It is far too high on your buttock for you to see without the aid of a mirror. I did not mention it because I thought it might be a brand of your slavery, given its shape."

Christian could only stare dumbfounded at Gideon, his hope renewed.

Gideon smiled and nodded. "It is true, Christian."

"If he is Lord Northwick, his name is Alexander Moncreiffe, and he is heir to the Duchy of Amberley," Lady Stinson pointed out.

Christian felt his jaw drop. Good heavens! A future duke?

"Well, the only way to know for certain is for Lord Markland to examine the mark and verify that it is indeed the same one," one of the nameless gentlemen commented.

"Be glad to," Markland replied. "Can't tell you how happy I'll be to have Northwick back in society. Brice will be delighted, too, as will all the unwed chits." He chuckled and shook his head. "There will be no peace for you, boy, once it is known that the Marquess of Northwick is back on the market."

Chapter 4

"He is so handsome," Lady Amy sighed.

"Like a storybook prince come to life," whispered the ever romantic Lady Mina, her pale blue eyes dreamy as she stole a glance at the object of their admiration, who currently stood at the opposite end of the room surrounded by their aristocratic elders.

Lady Caroline nodded her agreement. "He is certainly the most exciting thing to happen to the *ton* in ages. I daresay that the competition for him in the marriage market will be nothing short of vicious, poor man." She cast their subject a pitying look. "He shan't stand a chance against the *ton*'s matchmaking mothers."

He, of course, was Christian English, or more precisely, Alexander Moncreiffe, Marquess of Northwick. And he had been all the talk for the past hour, ever since it had been discovered that he was the long lost heir to the Duchy of Amberley.

Lady Amy giggled, something she did whenever she was about to say something outrageous or naughty. "Poor man, indeed! They will run him to the ground like frenzied hounds after a prize fox, with Famous Helene and her horrid mother leading the pack." She shook her head, emitting a heavy sigh. "For all that his lordship has lost his memory, I do hope that he has retained enough of his wits to see Famous Helene for the termagant she is and not become trapped in her web of counterfeit charm."

Lady Caroline sniffed. "In view of the fact that her mere smile has reduced scores of sensible men to sonnet-spouting dolts, it seems rather too much to hope that his lordship will escape should she decide to add him to her collection of suitors, which she undoubtedly shall. How could she not want a man who more than matches her in beauty, rank, and fortune? Indeed, he is exactly the sort of match she and her mother have been waiting for."

Famous Helene, as the women referred to Lady Helene Dunville, daughter of the politically powerful Duke and Duchess of Hunsderry, was considered to be the most beautiful woman in England and was so widely praised in poetry and song for her exquisite looks that she had become somewhat of a celebrity in London. Hence the title of "Famous" Helene. Unfortunately, she was also the most disagreeable chit in town, a spoiled, slyly malicious creature with such an overblown sense of self-importance that she was an agony to be around. Of course, she was only odious to those she considered beneath her and to other young women, particularly those she considered to be potential rivals. To any man she deemed worthy of her attention she was all that was gracious and pleasing, easily turning him into her fawning slave.

Or so Bethany had heard. Having only experienced the Famous One at her most petulant, when Helene, her harridan of a mother, and Lady Mina had stopped for the night at Critchley Manor several months earlier, Bethany could hardly judge her effect on men for herself. What she did know for certain, however, was that Lady Helene's looks merited every bit of praise they garnered. And the very thought of such a beautiful woman setting her sights on Christian made a hard knot form in her throat.

Caroline was right: Christian hadn't a prayer of resisting Helene's wiles if, or more correctly, *when* she chose to exercise them on him. . . . even less of one since he had no memory. After all, if he could not remember something as simple as his own name, he most certainly would not recall the artifice and tender traps marriage-minded women employed to snare a husband. She could only pray that someone in society would take pity on him and advise him of the perils before he fell victim to them.

"So what do you think of all this, Bethany?" Caroline inquired, cocking her head to view her companion from an inquisitive angle.

"Of course, I am happy for Christian," Bethany somehow managed to squeeze past the lump in her throat.

Amy snorted. "Then you are a far more charitable person than I. If I were you, Bethany, and had had that glorious man all to myself these past months, I would be beyond chagrined that he had been found."

A true innocent and thus always slow to pick up on the subtleties of conversation, Mina frowned and asked, "Why ever would you be chagrined, Amy?"

"Because now that he is found, dear, he will leave Critchley Manor for London, which is where his family presently resides, and he is unlikely to return here anytime soon, if ever. That means that poor Bethany will be bereft of his dazzling company," Amy explained in an indulgent voice.

As if poor Bethany needed to be reminded of that fact! Her eyes now burning with tears at the heartbreaking prospect of being parted from Christian, Bethany willed herself to smile and say as brightly as she could manage, "Christian has been a wonderful friend to our entire family, Amy, so I can hardly claim to have had him all to myself. However, you are correct in that I will miss him dreadfully when he goes. We all will."

Apparently, her performance wasn't as convincing as she hoped, because Mina reached over and gave her arm a gentle squeeze, her pasty, spot-marred face the picture of sympathy. "You know that you are always welcome to visit me in London, Bethany, and I shall be more than happy to take you about in the *ton* so you can renew your acquaintance with him."

"You are welcome in all our homes," Caroline declared stoutly. "Indeed, I would love nothing more than to introduce you to society. With your beauty and fine nature, you are certain to topple Famous Helene from her pedestal as toast of the *ton*."

Amy clapped her hands gleefully. "Oh! Do say that you will come, Bethany! I will have Papa throw you a grand ball to introduce you to society, and we shall all accompany you to Madame Manette's shop to help you select the perfect gown." Another fit of clapping, this one accompanied by a sharp, tittering giggle. "What fun we shall have putting Famous Helene's celebrated nose out of joint!"

Bethany nudged her feigned smile a fraction wider, lowering her eyelashes to hide the tears that threatened to escape as she demurred, "You are all far too kind."

"Then you will come?" This was from Mina, and judging from her voice she was genuinely delighted by the notion of Bethany's visit.

"I shall most certainly take your generous invitations under consideration." But of course Bethany would do no such thing. She could not even consider appearing in society. Now desperate to escape the other women's company, certain that she would burst into tears at any moment and not wishing to do so publicly, she added, "I promised Julia earlier that I would check the refreshment tables for her. If you will please excuse me?"

Lingering only long enough to be excused by her companions, she took her leave. After going into the dining hall to cast a cursory glance at the tables, just in case the other women were marking her actions, she retreated to the alcove where earlier she had hidden her gift to Christian, and took refuge behind the drawn drapery.

It was cold in the alcove, where a frigid December draft had become trapped between the ice-glazed window and the heavy drapery, and none of the warmth from the overheated room had managed to seep through the tightly woven velvet barrier. But Bethany didn't care. She barely felt the chill in her distress, though her skin prickled beneath it. She was alone, and at the moment that was the only thing that mattered. Alone to weep for the love that should never have been born, alone to grieve for the loss of the man she desired above everything else in the world, though, in truth, he had never really been hers to lose.

And he never would be.

By now her tears flowed freely, and harsh, ragged sobs tore from her chest. How could she survive without him when she practically lived for his company? His presence sustained her, charging her every moment with a life-affirming exhilaration that came from the anticipation of seeing him. . . . of hearing his beloved voice, always so warm and gentle, his every speech thoughtful and touched by tender humor. Then there was his endearingly rakish smile . . . the sight of it never failed to make her pulse race. And when he casually took her hand in his, as he so often did when they sat together, she experienced the most marvelous thrill that raced through her body and made her feel more alive than she had ever felt before.

Oh, how she loved him! She had from the moment she first met him. And since that time she had been unable to think of anything but him. She daydreamed about him when she was awake, proper maidenly fantasies that turned highly improper when she slept, disturbing her slumbers with titillating images of Christian naked and in her bed, his sleek muscles bunching and knotting, and his smooth skin glistening in the candlelight as he took her over and over again. So vivid were those dreams at times that she could almost taste the sweetness of his mouth and feel his hot breath fanning over her flesh as he electrified her with his kisses. The way he looked, with his long sable curls tousled from their passion and his beautiful dark eyes hot and desirous as they gazed at her from beneath eyelashes like lush black lace . . .

But she didn't want to think of him like that, not now, not ever again. Of course, she could not control her dreams, so they would no doubt continue to plague her, breaking her heart over and over again. But when she was awake, well, then she could at least try to keep her thoughts from constantly straying to her wanton desire for Christian.

Striving to do so now, she rested her cheek against the window glass and looked out at the misty winter scene beyond, gazing into the distance toward the quaint dowager cottage, the snow-covered roof of which was barely visible from her vantage point. How many nights had she sat at her bedchamber window, staring at the cottage, wondering what Christian was doing and wishing that she were doing it with him? Truth be known, she had selected her chamber not for its grand plasterwork ceiling, like she had told Gideon, but because it provided a clear view of the cottage.

As always happened when she admitted that fact to herself, Bethany berated herself for her foolishness.

She really should have taken greater pains to guard herself against such romantic indulgence, for it had served only to encourage feelings that should have been discouraged. She could see that now. . . . now that it was too late and she had completely lost her heart to Christian.

The tears that had eased during her dreamy reverie resumed with a fury as she ruthlessly reflected upon the hopelessness of her love. While it had been impossible before, it was doubly so now. Christian was a marquess, heir to a duchy, and by all reports a member of a particularly wealthy and noble family. As such he would naturally be expected to make an advantageous marriage, to wed a woman whose lineage and virtue were beyond reproach.

A woman like Famous Helene. The very thought of Christian married to another woman made her feel as if she would shatter to pieces.

Fool! Silly, pathetic little fool! she harshly chided herself, trying desperately to harden her mind and heart to the inevitable. *Marquess or no, he could never have been yours. He is much too good for the likes of you. No decent man deserves to be shackled to a woman like you, a harlot who sold herself to the highest bidder. You have known that all along, and yet you have stupidly allowed yourself to hold out hope in the back of your mind.*

It was true. She had held out hope that someday, somehow, she would be able to share her love with Christian. In her wildest dreams she had even imagined them married and living happily ever after. Perhaps, just perhaps, if he had turned out to be a scandal-ridden scoundrel, or even a minor criminal . . .

But no. He was an aristocrat. One who would soon return to his family in London, where he would resume his rightful place as heir and reclaim the glittering life that was his heritage. Once there he was bound to forget all about her. And who could blame him with nobly born temptresses like Famous Helene to turn his head?

Heartbroken, more desolate and wretched than she had ever been in her life, yet determined to move beyond her pain and somehow get on with her life, Bethany swiped her hand across her eyes, fiercely rubbing away her tears. Matters were as they were, and there was nothing she could do to change them. Weeping over them and pining for Christian would serve only to make them worse. Besides, the last thing she wanted to do was show her grief to Christian. To do so would only cause him pain. It might also destroy his future, for though she would deny the knowledge to her dying breath Bethany knew that his feelings for her had grown beyond anything that could be described as brotherly. And were she to in any way betray her love for him, he might offer her marriage.

Heaven help her, but she might not have the strength to turn him down, and wedding him could only lead to disaster. After all, if she were to marry a marquess she would have no choice but to take her place at his side in the *ton,* which would no doubt lead to society's discovery of her past and bring disgrace to Christian. There was also the distinct possibility that Christian would regain his memory and regret that he had not made a more suitable match. Then he would hate her.

Bethany hugged herself, the thought filling her with a terrible hollowness. Better to suffer a broken heart now than to spend her life loving a man who hated her.

"You have certainly set our assembly on its ear, Lord Northwick," Julia said, waylaying Christian as he wended through the crush of revelers in search of Bethany. He had yet to so much as catch a glimpse of her since Lord Markland had examined his mark and confirmed that he was indeed the Marquess of Northwick, and he was eager to share all he had learned about himself with her.

Now smiling fondly at his best friend's beautiful wife, who in her pregnancy grew more radiant with every passing day, Christian replied, "So it seems. I have been so besieged by people wishing to make my acquaintance that this is the first opportunity I have had to catch my breath."

"Well, I think it is perfectly marvelous news, and we are all so very thrilled for you. A marquess—just imagine. Not that I am surprised," she amended, looping her arm through his. "I always suspected that you were from the nobility, and I am seldom wrong about such things." By now they had begun to stroll through the crowd, with Julia nodding now and again to her guests as she escorted him across the room.

Christian grinned at her clever ploy. Given the way she was hugging his arm and leaning into him, they gave every appearance of being engaged in a serious conversation. Aware that her performance was calculated to give him respite from the other guests' questions, since most of those in attendance were far too polite to interrupt them when they were so clearly engrossed in each other's company, he hugged her arm back in gratitude and responded, "You said that you are all thrilled by my news. I take it, then, that Bethany has heard it as well?"

Julia slanted him an amused look, a knowing smile playing on her lips. "Everybody here has heard. They cannot avoid doing so, unless they are stone-deaf. But to answer your question, I saw Bethany discussing the matter with Ladies Mina, Caroline, and Amy a half hour earlier. She was smiling, so it was evident that she is quite pleased by your good fortune."

"I am glad she is pleased. There is nothing in the world I want more than to please Bethany—to please you all," Christian rushed to revise, barely catching himself before he revealed too much. Though Lord Markland was certain that he was Lord Northwick, Christian thought it best to wait until he had been to London and verified his status with the Moncreiffe family before declaring his feelings for Bethany. After all, it was always possible that they might for some reason refuse to recognize him. Thus, wishing to further rectify his slip, he added, "You are my family, at least the only one I know, and I could never be happy if you were not."

But of course Julia wasn't fooled. And as always happened whenever he inadvertently dropped a hint that he cared for Bethany beyond friendship, she seized upon his careless words to drop a few hints of her own in a transparent attempt to promote a romance between them. Hugging his arm yet tighter to her side, she did exactly that. "How could she not be happy for you? Not only are you from a fine family, but you are also heir to a grand fortune and a duchy. Why, by all reports you have everything in life a young man could desire. Surely you know that Bethany, darling creature that she is, has always wished only the best of everything for you?"

Christian nodded, taking care to keep both his tone and words neutral as he replied, "How could I not know? Bethany has such a generous nature that she could never wish for anything less than the best for anyone."

"Yes. Our dear Bethany has the best nature in the world." Glancing away long enough to greet the newlywed vicar and his rosy-cheeked bride, she slyly commented, "Such a happy couple, the vicar and his wife, a true love match. I must say that it is most fortunate that you are not wed. Why, just imagine the awkwardness of returning to a wife you do not remember."

Christian, too, greeted the couple before returning,

"Yes, I can imagine, and I must admit to being relieved at not having to face that particular situation."

"In view of the fact that your doctors believe that you may never fully recover your memory, given the length of time it has been lost, I daresay that you have every reason for relief. To be sure, that you are now free to follow your heart and marry a woman you love rather than having to struggle to rediscover your feelings for a stranger shall make it all that much easier for you to resume your old life."

Indeed it would. And if all went as he hoped, he had every intention of following his heart back to Critchley Manor and offering it to Bethany.

"I was saying something to that effect to Bethany just last week," Julia continued with a smile and a nod to Sir Whiting, an ancient knight whose small estate lay just west of Low Brindle. The normally cantankerous man actually smiled back and gaily lifted his glass in salute. Raising her eyebrows in surprise, Julia added, "When I mentioned that I hoped you were not wed so you would not have to suffer the discomfort of not knowing your own wife, the poor dear turned quite pale. Caring for you as she does, she naturally finds the notion of you enduring such a trial distressing to the extreme."

"Then I have reason to be doubly glad that I am not wed, since I do not wish to cause Bethany distress." Judging his remark as an appropriate opening to inquire after Bethany's whereabouts, Christian said, "Speaking of wishes, I wish to bid Bethany a happy Christmas, but she seems to have disappeared. Do you, by chance, know where she has gone?"

Julia came to a stop in front of the musicians, who were presently being served glasses of wassail by two footmen, and jerked her chin to indicate a place to their right. "I saw her slip into the second alcove a quarter of an hour earlier. Since you have been unable to find her, I would venture to guess that she is still there."

It was all Christian could do to bridle his grin at the prospect of being alone with Bethany. Without the prying eyes of the other guests to mark their conduct, they would be able to act naturally toward each other, to speak openly, completely free from the danger that their most innocent actions might be misinterpreted and judged as improper.

Apparently, his glee showed despite his efforts to hide it, because Julia laughed and gave him a playful shove toward the alcove. "Go on with you, now. I am certain that the two of you have a great deal to discuss."

They did at that. Pausing long enough to smile his thanks, Christian stepped behind the drawn draperies.

Bethany was indeed there, snuggled in the window seat with her feet drawn up beneath her and her forehead resting against the frosty window glass. She appeared to be deep in thought. Keeping his voice soft so as not to startle her, Christian called, "Bethany?"

Despite his precaution she jumped, jerking from her relaxed attitude to sit as stiff and straight as a primly posed statue, staring at him as if stunned by his presence.

As Christian returned her gaze, baffled by her odd response, he could not help noticing that her normally rosy cheeks looked ashen and that her beautiful eyes were red, making him wonder if she had been weeping. When a faint sniffle escaped her he was certain it was so. Instantly alarmed, he rushed to her side, sinking down on the seat cushion beside her. Taking both her hands in his, he urgently inquired, "What has happened, Bethany? Is something amiss?" To his consternation, her hands were like ice. Then again, it was close to freezing in the alcove.

Bethany continued to stare at him for several more beats, her eyes wide and face inanimate, almost as if she were in a trance. Then she smiled with an abruptness that made him promptly suspect that the expression was feigned. "Why, whatever makes you think that something is amiss?" she exclaimed in a bright voice—a shade too bright to ring genuine, at least to Christian's ears.

He frowned. "Because you are as pale as a ghost, and judging from your red eyes and sniffle you appear to have been weeping."

"Weeping? Me?" She emitted a short laugh that was no doubt meant to project amusement, but instead came out sounding as false as her smile and voice. "Silly man! Why ever would I be weeping when there is so much to be happy about? Such wonderful news, you being a marquess and all! Are you not thrilled?"

But Christian wasn't about to be put off by her change of subject. Ignoring her question, he leaned nearer, studying her face through narrowed eyes as he demanded to know, "If you were not weeping, then why, pray tell, do you look as though you were?"

"Oh, that." Another of her overly gay little laughs. "I have a slight cold. The sneezing and sniffling always make my eyes red." She released a dainty sneeze, as if to substantiate her claim.

Not at all convinced yet unwilling to spoil the day by pressing her to confide something she was clearly reluctant to share, Christian pretended to accept her explanation, logically pointing out, "If you have a cold, you should not be sitting in this icy draft. Here," he braced his hand under her elbow to help her rise, "let me escort you back into the ballroom where it is warm. It would never do for us to allow your cold to worsen into something more serious."

She pulled her arm away, shaking her head. "Perhaps in a moment or two, after I have finished cooling myself. I must admit that I find the ballroom rather overheated today."

"The ballroom cannot by any stretch of the imagination be considered overheated, Bethany," Christian retorted, his alarm renewed by her words. "My guess is that you are feverish." Not waiting for her to respond he felt first her forehead and then her cheeks, letting his hand linger longer than necessary against her skin, savoring the feel of its softness beneath his palm. To his eternal relief, her temperature felt normal.

When he said as much, Bethany laughed. This time it was her true laugh, the light, lilting trill that never failed to enchant him. "I told you I was fine and I truly am, so please do stop fussing over me. You are behaving like a hen with one chick." The way she was grinning at him now, so broadly and with such beguiling sauciness, made Christian ache to pull her into his arms and sample the sweetness of those teasing lips.

Forcibly checking the urge, he smiled back and replied, "I am fussing because I care about you. Surely you cannot fault me for that?"

"No, of course not." Her fetching grin faded then and her face again grew serious. "I care about you too, Christian—or should I call you Lord Northwick now?"

"We are friends, Bethany, and I like to think that we are close ones. And close friends do not stand on ceremony. Besides, I prefer being called Christian. It is the name to which I am accustomed to answering. Since it is also my true one—"

"What?" She held up her hand to halt his speech, shaking her head. "But I thought your name was Alexander?"

"It is. However, according to several of Julia's parents' friends, who claim to know me and my family well, my full name is Alexander Edward Christian Moncreiffe, so I truly do have a right to the name Christian."

Bethany's smooth forehead furrowed as she digested that tidbit of information. At length she mused,

"Hmmm. Perhaps the reason you have elected to go by Christian all this time is because a part of you recognized the name as being your real one."

"Perhaps," he concurred with a shrug. "Whatever the instance, I wish for you to continue calling me Christian."

"Since you will always be Christian to me, I shall be more than happy to oblige you." Not that she would have many more opportunities to do so. Once he rejoined his family, which would no doubt be soon, he would no longer be at Critchley Manor for her to address at all. The tears that had begun to dry in Bethany's eyes again welled up at the devastating reminder that she was losing him, and before she quite knew what was happening a gasping sob slipped out.

Christian dipped his head in response to the sound, frowning at her in query.

She forced herself to laugh and lightly exclaim, "Oh, dear! Please do pardon me, Christian. I was trying to stifle a sneeze and failed."

Rather than lift his frown, her explanation merely deepened it. "If you ask me, it is a wonder that you are not sneezing more. This terrible chill cannot help but to be aggravating your cold."

"Oh, but I was sneezing far worse in the ballroom," she fibbed. Since her story about stifling a sneeze appeared to be working to disguise her tears here, she might as well ensure its use in the ballroom, just in case she should again succumb to her heartbreak while in his presence there.

Christian's expression grew positively black. "It sounds to me like you should be in bed."

"But then I would miss the festivities, and I could not bear to do so. Julia has ever so many cunning games and amusements planned," she countered. "Besides, I wish to hear all about Lord Northwick, everything you have learned about yourself thus far. Do tell. Please?" As an afterthought, she smiled. Broadly. If she were truly as thrilled about his splendid new station in life as she claimed to be, she would most certainly smile at the mention of it. Wouldn't she?

Christian eyed her with such displeasure that for a moment she thought he might deny her plea. Then he nodded once and replied, "Fine. I will share what I know, but only on the condition that you return to the ballroom where it is warm."

"I shall do so the instant you finish telling me," she vowed, deliberately misunderstanding his intimation that she return that very minute.

"Bethany," he began.

But she cut him off. "You know as well as I that we shall never be able to have a proper conversation in the ballroom, not with the other guests sniffing about you and clamoring for your attention."

He opened his mouth to argue, only to close it again as if reconsidering whatever he was about to say. When he finally spoke, he said, "All right, Bethany, you win. However, I shall expect you on your feet and ready to be escorted into the ballroom the second I finish telling you."

"But of course. Your wish is my command, my lord," she teased, though the last thing in the world she felt at that moment was a sense of humor.

Christian smiled at her pert response in a way that made her heart turn over. Oh, but he was magnificent! Mina had not been wrong when she said that he was like a fairy tale prince come to life. With his tall, athletic build, thick tumble of glossy sable curls, and a face so handsome that it would have been pretty had it not been on such a masculine man, Christian was indeed blessed with spectacular looks. Now gazing at her from beneath the fringe of his impossibly lush eyelashes, he inquired, "So? What exactly do you wish to know?"

Certain that he could hear her pounding heart, she reminded him, "I believe that we agreed on you telling me everything."

He laughed, something that further quickened her pulse, if such a thing were possible since it was already racing. Again taking her hands in his, this time to casually twine his fingers through hers, as he so often did when they sat together, he said, "Then I suppose that the logical place to start would be at the beginning."

"Very logical, indeed," she agreed with a nod.

"The beginning would be my birth. I was born on my parents' estate in Surrey on October 9, 1768, which makes me thirty years old now. I was the fifth of six children, but the first son."

"Then you have four older sisters?"

"Four, yes." Another fascinating smile curved his beautiful lips. "Caroletta, Justina, Viola, and Lucilla, all wed, I am told, and a younger brother named Godwin. While I have learned that my brother is twenty-six and that we were quite thick in our youth, I have yet to glean any specifics about my sisters."

"Well, judging from your winning way with the females at Critchley and Low Brindle, I would venture to guess that you got along as splendidly with them as you did with your brother," Bethany commented.

Christian made a face. "From what I hear, I have a reputation for getting on rather too splendidly with every female I meet." At Bethany's sharp glance, he sighed. "I was a rake, Bethany, a notorious one. My exploits with women are quite famous in London, even to this day. I also appear to have had an excessive fondness for gambling and drink."

"But you never engage in serious gambling, and I have yet to see you drunk!" Bethany exclaimed, unable to believe what she was hearing. "Furthermore, you have never been anything but a perfect gentleman to any of the women in your acquaintance here." She shook her head. "Perhaps you are not Lord Northwick after all, because you cannot by any measure be considered the least bit of a rake."

"Well, they do say that experience changes a man," he returned, "and I have had more than my share of sobering experiences these past few years. Enough, certainly, to subdue the most dissolute rake."

Though Bethany could only imagine the nature of those experiences, since he had never volunteered to share them with her and she'd never had the heart to pry, she'd deduced from the bits and pieces she had learned from Gideon that he'd suffered unspeakable atrocities during his enslavement. Not wishing to say anything now that might conjure painful memories of those terrible times, she let the reference pass without comment, responding, "Be that as it may, Christian, I still cannot believe that you were ever all that wicked."

"Believe it," he retorted grimly. "While much of what I have learned about my past is unfit for feminine ears, I can tell you that it was my wickedness that led me to be shipped off to India. It seems that my father has rather vast holdings in the East India Company, and he arranged for me to be employed in the company in hopes that the responsibility would improve my character. According to Lord Markland, my parents feared that I would get myself killed in a duel or during some other reckless escapade were I to remain in England."

"That certainly explains how you came to be in India," she mused.

He nodded. "From what I have been able to ascertain from the various accounts I have received thus far, it appears that I was captured and enslaved while returning home from there."

"Indeed," she murmured, for lack of a better response. What else could she say? For all that her tongue practically ached to quiz him on his capture, she was determined to hold fast to her resolution to never trespass upon his privacy.

Christian nodded again. "Apparently, my father fell gravely ill while I was in India, and my mother sent an urgent message bidding me to return home post-haste. Since the only available ship sailing for London at that time was an American one, I booked passage on it. What I failed to take into consideration, or perhaps did not know, was that America had yet to pay the dey of Algiers his annual tributary for safe passage through his waters, which left American ships vulnerable to corsair attacks."

"That is what happened, then? You were attacked by corsairs and taken prisoner?" Since he was volunteering the information, the question could not be considered prying. Could it?

"Something like that, yes. It was said that I was badly wounded during the attack and left for dead. When the corsairs discovered me alive, I was taken prisoner and enslaved."

"Oh, Christian, no! How could anyone have been so heartless as to desert you in such a manner!" Bethany cried, stricken by the thought of the man she loved wounded and abandoned.

He shrugged, but in its stiffness the gesture was far from nonchalant. "Judging from the ship's captain's report, I cannot really fault him for leaving me behind. He had good reason to believe me dead."

"The only good reason to believe a person dead is to check for a pulse and not find one, something the man clearly did not bother to do with you," Bethany interposed indignantly.

"True. Then again, I was said to have fallen overboard when I was wounded. By the time the captain and his crew managed to free their ship from the corsairs' tethers and make their escape, I had disappeared, so they naturally assumed I had drowned." He shrugged again, sighing. "My guess is that I was fished from the water by the corsairs when they were rescuing their own men."

More horrified by his harrowing experience than she had ever been by anything in her life, Bethany choked out, "Good heavens, Christian! It is a miracle you are alive."

He chuckled, a harsh, bitter grating sound unlike any laugh she had ever heard pass through his lips before. "Please believe me when I say that there were many days that I viewed my survival more a curse than a miracle."

"My poor, poor darling," Bethany cried, the endearment slipping out in her distress. "Your ordeal must have been very dreadful indeed for you to view life as a curse."

"It was." He glanced away then, but not before she saw the shadowy pain in his eyes.

At a loss as to what to say or do to chase it away, Bethany tightened her hold on his hands, mutely giving what little comfort she could.

He gently squeezed her hands back, as if acknowledging and accepting her attempt at solace. When at last he returned his gaze to hers the shadows had lifted from his eyes and a feeble smile tugged at his lips. "For all that I once wished myself dead, I must admit to being very grateful to be alive now, and that gratitude can be credited directly to you and your family."

"I am glad you are pleased to be alive," Bethany murmured, her heart swelling with tenderness, as it always did whenever she caught a glimpse of his scarred soul.

"I am very pleased indeed. And I want you to know that no matter what happens in the future, I shall never forget all that you have done for me. You, more than anyone, have done much to heal my wounds from my ordeal in India. You have treated me with such kindness and given me so much joy these past months that I could not help but to again feel the pleasure of being alive."

"You have helped me too, Christian," she said. By now the tenderness in her heart had swollen so large that her chest felt close to bursting.

Christian tipped his head to view her from a quizzical angle, his weak smile strengthening at her words. "I have?"

She nodded. "Yes. You have accepted me in spite of my sins and been a good friend at a time when I desperately needed one. After my baby died and I felt like my world was crumbling—"

"I was simply returning the favor of caring for you the way you have cared for me since the day Gideon introduced us," he interjected softly, "and I have loved doing it. Indeed, one of the things I shall miss most about Critchley Manor is the pleasure that fussing over you brings me." His smile broadened into a roguish grin. "I shall miss it almost as much as I will miss being fussed over by you."

Though doing so made her feel as if her heart were being ripped from her chest, Bethany forced herself to ask in as even a voice as she could manage, "When will you be leaving for London?"

"In two days. I shall be returning with Lord Markland and his party. His lordship has offered to write the necessary letter of explanation to the Moncreiffe family and send it ahead, so that they will be expecting us when we arrive."

"So soon?" Bethany exclaimed. "But—"

Before she could fully voice her dismay, her younger sister, Bliss, unceremoniously burst through the draperies, announcing, "Bethany, Julia says that you're to return to the ballroom this instant and show everyone how to cut the Christmas tokens from the kissing bough. She said that you're supposed to come, too, Christian." As usual, her long, dark hair was in a tangle and her clothing was rumpled, the result, no doubt, of a rough-and-tumble romp with the neighboring boys, whom she delighted in besting at all their athletic feats.

Christian's eyebrows rose at her message. "What is this about a kissing bough, Bliss?"

"Oh, just one of Julia's silly games." Bliss rolled her gray eyes in an exaggerated fashion, drolly conveying her exasperation at her sister-in-law's games. "I offered to climb the ladder and do the demonstration myself, but she insists that Bethany must do it. I can't imagine why." She emitted a soft snort. "I can climb a ladder ever so much faster and better than Bethany can."

"Perhaps it is because she fears that the gentlemen will all fight for the honor of kissing you if they see you beneath the bough, and she does not want there to be a brawl," Christian bantered.

Bliss grimaced. "Jest let the friggin' buggers try! I'll knock their bleedin' blocks off."

"Bliss!" Bethany cried in reprimand, while Christian laughed. Despite her and Julia's attempts to tame Bliss's wayward tongue, whenever the child's emotions ran high she had a disconcerting tendency to revert to the street cant she had learned from a gang of pickpockets. The cant was, unfortunately, only one of several regrettable habits she had adopted during the time she and Bethany had been forced to live in a wretched Westminster rookery.

Now recovered from his fit of hilarity, Christian teased, "Thank you for the warning, Bliss. I must confess to having had every intention of claiming a kiss from you if I caught you under the kissing bough. Since I wish to keep my block firmly in place, however, I shall take pains to check the impulse should I see you there."

"Oh, but you're not a bugger. You're handsome and I love you, so you can have a kiss any time you wish," Bliss cheekily retorted. "Here." She darted forward and pressed a childish peck to his grinning lips. "There. Satisfied?"

At that moment Bethany could not have envied her sister more. Oh, to have such freedom to kiss Christian!

Christian chuckled. "Very satisfied indeed. You may be certain that I shall cherish your kiss forever."

Never one to have her head turned by pretty speeches, Bliss merely shrugged. Now latching on to Bethany's arm with one hand and Christian's with her other, she gave them each an impatient tug, urging, "Come on. If you don't come this instant Julia will think that I dawdled in fetching you and have my head."

"Well, now, we most certainly would not want Julia to have your head, would we, Bethany?" Christian said, slanting Bethany an amused glance.

Bethany smiled at him, loving him all the more for his kindness to her impossible little sister. "Absolutely not."

"Shall we, then?" Rising, Christian gallantly offered each lady an arm and escorted them back into the ballroom.

By now Julia had assembled the guests in a circle around the kissing bough and was explaining the rules of her game. When she saw their trio approaching, she exclaimed, "Ah. Here is Mrs. Matland to demonstrate."

Naturally, everyone turned to stare, with several pairs of aristocratic eyebrows raising when their owners saw Bethany on Christian's arm. Self-conscious at being the center of so much scrutiny, Bethany hesitated at the edge of the gathering, suddenly overwhelmed by the urge to flee.

But of course Julia wouldn't let her. Moving to where Bethany stood frozen in her tracks, she gently disengaged her arm from Christian's and led her to where the festively festooned ladder stood beneath the kissing bough. Nodding to the green-and-gold liveried first footman, who stood by the ladder, she said, "Albert will steady the ladder while you climb, Bethany, dear. Once you are in position, he will hand up the shears."

Seeing no choice but to cooperate, Bethany lifted her skirts as high as modesty would permit and did as Julia instructed. By the time she reached the top, her nerves had begun to settle. After all, there was nothing so very embarrassing about simply claiming a Christmas token, was there? Shears now in hand, she reached up and cut the ribbon suspending one of the gold-wrapped packages from the bough. Shaped out of greenery to resemble a huge crown and decorated with lit beeswax candles, plump red apples, mistletoe, and glittery gold tinsel, the kissing bough was a most impressive creation. Token now in hand, Bethany returned the shears to the waiting footman and began her descent back to earth.

She was almost there when she heard Julia gaily exclaim, "Now, then, who shall we elect to kiss our lovely Mrs. Matland?"

Bethany almost missed a rung in her chagrin. *Oh, blast!* She had been so busy wallowing in her misery over losing Christian that she had completely forgotten about the kissing part of Julia's game, though how such a thing could possibly slip her mind, she could not imagine. The bough *was* called a *kissing* bough.

A number of gentlemen in the crowd eagerly volunteered for the task, among them several nobles, while the ladies called out suggestions. Julia made a show of studying the assembly, then announced, "Lord Northwick may have the honor, I think."

Bethany was tempted to strangle and hug Julia at the same time. In the hundreds of fantasies she'd had in which she'd kissed Christian, she had never once envisioned doing so before an audience. Kissing the person one loved, especially for the first time, was something that should be done in private, someplace dark and intimate where the parties involved would be free to explore their passion. The very notion of kissing Christian here, before what at the moment seemed like the entire world . . . why, it was unthinkable. Impossible.

On the other hand, this might very well be the last and only chance she would ever have to kiss him.

"What do you say, Lord Northwick?" Julia asked, deferring to Christian.

Christian stepped forward to join Bethany under the bough. "It will be a pleasure, my lady," he replied. His roguish grin had returned and he was gazing at Bethany from beneath those extravagant lashes, his dark eyes irresistibly magnetic as they captured hers. Her heart seemed to melt in her chest and for the life of her she could not move, so transfixed was she by the absolute power of his attraction. Before she could resume thought, much less rouse herself from his captivating spell, he swept her into his arms and claimed her lips with his.

The moment their lips touched, her passion ignited and her senses were swept away on a spiraling sense of excitement. Oh, but his kiss was wonderful, even sweeter than she had imagined. His lips were firm yet soft, eager yet tender, as they moved over hers, stirring the most unimaginable feelings inside her. Those feelings . . . o-o-o . . . what they did to her! They pulsated through her veins, quickening her desire and filling her with such a joyous rush of abandon that she mindlessly melted against him, parting her lips in uninhibited response, her mouth shamelessly begging him to deepen their kiss.

The instant her mouth opened he pulled away and stepped back, but not before Bethany saw his face. He could not have looked more flabbergasted. And was it really any wonder? Bethany's cheeks burned in her humiliation. She had responded to his kiss with a hunger that was as brazen as it was shameful. She had behaved like a wanton, and Christian had obviously been shocked by her lewd display. How could he not be? Were someone to have asked Bethany to name her greatest burden at that moment, she would have said without hesitation that it was her overly passionate nature.

By now Christian was sketching a playful bow to their cheering audience, grinning as if nothing untoward had happened. Hoping to salvage a morsel of her dignity, Bethany followed his example, forcing herself to smile as she dipped into a curtsy. Judging from the faces beaming back at her, it was apparent that no one had noticed her impropriety.

No one except Christian, that is, she grimly reminded herself.

Moving toward Julia, who beckoned to her from the sidelines, Bethany miserably told herself that it was for the best that Christian was leaving. Indeed, after her performance today he was certain to view her with disgust, and she could not bear the thought of seeing repugnance in his eyes every time he looked at her. Yes, it was for the best.

If only she could convince her heart that it was so.

CHAPTER 5

He had hoped to feel a sense of familiarity here, to see or hear or perhaps even smell something that would stir his memory. At the very least he had expected to experience one of his odd twinges of recognition, especially during those moments when he was reunited with his family.

But no, everything and everyone here at the Moncreiffe family's imposing town palace seemed utterly foreign to him. So foreign, in fact, that he would have been inclined to believe that Lord Markland was mistaken about his identity had the Duke and Duchess of Amberley not confirmed it with such certainty. To say that their heartfelt response to his appearance had stunned him would have been a sweeping understatement!

Indeed, never in his most wishful dreams had he imagined that his mother would burst into tears at the sight of him as she had done and promptly pull him into her embrace, sobbing her love for him over and over again. Nor had he expected his father to accept him without hesitation, as had been the case. Why, Christian had no sooner set foot inside the house than his father began referring to him as Lord Northwick, his heir, emphasizing the title to the servants as he directed them to see to Christian's comfort. Though neither parent had asked to view Christian's birthmark, so sure were they that he was their son, Christian had insisted that they do so, needing further confirmation of his identity for his own peace of mind. When the viewing had led to another round of misty-eyed hugs, this time with his father joining in, Christian was finally able to relax and accept his good fortune.

Wondering anew why he had not felt even the slightest stab of recognition for his parents when they had embraced him, Christian nodded to his father's valet, Frederick Collins, who had been sent to assist him in dressing, approving the red-and-black patterned silk waistcoat the man held up for his inspection. Absently extending his arms to allow the servant to slip it on him, he meditated upon his disheartening lack of cognitive response to his estranged family.

Hmmm. It could be that he had simply been too tired upon arrival for his mind to fully assimilate everything it was experiencing. After all, it had been late when he'd arrived, nearly two in the morning, and he had been practically dead on his feet from exhaustion. Christian nodded to himself. Yes. That had to be it. His brain had been numb with weariness and was thus not functioning properly. No doubt things would be different now that he was rested.

Christian lifted his freshly shaven chin to allow the valet to adjust his neck cloth, smiling faintly at that last thought. He could not remember the last time he'd been so well rested. He'd just slept more than twelve hours, not rising until almost three this afternoon, a rarity for him, who seldom slept more than five hours a night and never rose past six in the morning. Then again, he couldn't recall ever having fallen asleep with such ease, not even after his most grueling days in India. Nor could he remember ever passing a full night without being awakened by a nightmare at least once. But last night, well, last night he had fallen into a deep, dreamless slumber the instant his head touched his pillow, and he had awakened more refreshed than he could ever recall feeling before.

Could it be that his brain had unconsciously identified this elegantly appointed wine-and-gold chamber as his own, as a place where he had felt safe and happy in the past, and had thus found the peace it needed to allow him an untroubled sleep? The more he considered the theory, the more sense it made.

"My lord?" Collins's voice intruded.

Christian glanced in query at the thin, balding man. He now displayed Christian's newest coat, a charcoal gray double-breasted affair that boasted what Christian privately considered rather overly wide lapels, despite the fact that his Liverpool tailor had assured him that wide lapels were all the rage. At his nod, the servant assisted him in donning it, as well.

As Collins fussed over his attire, aligning the seams of his pearl gray breeches, puffing his cambric shirt frills, smoothing a wrinkle here and plucking at invisible lint there, Christian felt his first surge of familiarity since arriving at the house. For all that he could not remember ever being attended by a valet before, doing so now felt like the most natural thing in the world. So natural that he had been going through the motions without thought, automatically presenting the required limbs, lifting this, lowering that, stepping and turning, all without prompting, as if he had been dressed by someone else every day of his life, which had no doubt been the case in the days before his enslavement.

A wave of relief rolled over him as he savored the welcome sensation. To his way of thinking, sensing his memories was a promising step toward remembering them.

By now Collins had finished primping his clothes to

perfection and had stepped back to survey his handiwork, a frown creasing his narrow forehead as he eyed Christian's mane of unruly black curls. Clearing his throat twice, he said, "Are you quite certain that you do not wish me to arrange your hair for you, my lord? If I were to set your curls in ringlets over your forehead and tie the back—"

"No, thank you, Collins. It is fine the way it is," Christian interjected, curbing his impulse to grimace at the thought of sporting one of the stiff, contrived coiffures favored by the men in the *ton*.

Collins couldn't have looked more dismayed. Nonetheless, his tone was even and his manner composed as he responded, "As you wish, my lord." Moving to the remnants of the meal a footman had served Christian the instant he'd stepped from his bed, he inquired, "Would you care for another cup of coffee, my lord? Or perhaps you are of a mood to sample the chocolate? Cook informs me that chocolate with sugar, cinnamon, and vanilla was always your favorite morning drink."

Personally, Christian had always considered the sickeningly sweet chocolate concoction favored by the English to be repulsive to the extreme. *Well, not always, it would seem,* he amended wryly. Wondering if perhaps there was something in this particular preparation that might spark a memory, Christian nodded. "Yes. I do believe that I will try some chocolate."

As the servant poured the steaming brew into a cup and added a grating of fresh cinnamon, Christian wandered over to one of the four full-length windows at the far end of the room and drew aside the light-filtering subcurtain. Hoping that something in the landscape beyond would strike him as familiar, he gazed outside.

Alas, no. He felt nothing but a hearty admiration for the perspective the window provided of the nearby park. With its sprawling lawns and gracious tree-lined avenues swathed in a pristine mantle of newly fallen snow and its frozen canal gleaming like polished silver in the feeble winter sunlight, there was nothing quite like St. James Park at this time of year. Especially when brightly clad skating parties took to the ice and—

St. James Park? Christian's breath caught in his throat as sudden awareness of his thoughts slammed through his mind. No one had told him the name of the park. That could only mean . . . His arrested breath escaped in a jubilant rush. It could only mean that he remembered more than he realized about his home, provided, of course, that the park was truly called St. James. Without turning from the window, he softly inquired, "Collins, what is the name of the park across the way?"

"Why, St. James, my lord."

Christian gave an out-and-out grin, his flagging hope of ever remembering his past now revived by his success. Eager to see if he could recognize more, he carefully scanned the rest of the scene. As his gaze touched what appeared to be a palace in the distance, the name Buckingham House popped into his mind. Again he asked Collins for confirmation and again he received it. His hope now soaring, he glanced down at the Moncreiffe house's geometrically landscaped courtyard below, only to have his grin fade when he saw a queue of carriages lining the long, curved drive.

Though he almost hated to ask, fearing that he already knew the answer, he said, "There appears to be a rather large number of carriages in the courtyard. Are my parents having a party?" God, he hoped not. The last thing he was in the mood to do was suffer the grilling he knew awaited him when he was reintroduced into his old circle.

Collins came to his side to present him with his

requested cup of chocolate, chuckling dryly as he, too, observed the conveyance-cluttered drive. "I daresay that it would appear so to the casual observer, my lord. However, the preponderance of the carriages belong to your family. Your sisters and brother arrived around noon, and your aunts, uncles, and cousins followed suit shortly thereafter. They all presently await your appearance in the Gothick drawing room. Counting your sisters' husbands and children, I would venture to guess that there are close to fifty people in attendance. Naturally, everyone is eager to see you for themselves and verify that you have indeed returned from the grave."

Christian choked on the chocolate he had just swallowed, as much in his shock at the size of his audience as in response to the nauseating sweetness of the drink. Ever the perfect valet, Collins solicitously pounded his back. As soon as Christian could speak, he gasped out, "Why in heavens name was I not awakened when my siblings arrived?"

"Everyone agreed that you needed your rest and must thus be allowed to sleep as long as you wished," Collins returned, frowning as he plucked an errant piece of lint from Christian's sleeve. "But please do not fret about the assembly downstairs. When I last passed the drawing room the atmosphere was decidedly gay. The occupants there were engaged in what appeared to be a rather lively game of crambo."

Having gained nothing from sampling the chocolate, save for a reminder of why he detested the drink, Christian set his cup on the nearby writing desk, shaking his head. "Nonetheless, it was rude of me to have kept them waiting so long."

Another dry cackle from Collins. "As I recall, my lord, you once made a habit of making company wait, sometimes not deigning to appear at all."

Christian cringed at the man's reference to his less-than-sterling past character. Determined to begin mending his reputation now, he replied, "Those days are in the past, Collins. I am no longer the man I was before my time in India."

"Indeed you are not," the servant retorted with one of what Christian had noticed were his rare smiles. "If you will pardon me for saying so, my lord, before your departure to India you had developed a reputation among London's valets for being an exceedingly—ahem!—difficult master. So difficult, in fact, that were it not for the generous wages you offered, none of the better valets would have suffered your employment."

"Was I truly so very beastly as all that?" Christian asked, though again he hated to ask for fear of the answer.

Collins's smile broadened a fraction. "Let us just say that your disposition has improved vastly over the years, and I am pleased to report that, judging from your demeanor this morning, you have become a singularly agreeable gentleman. That being the case, you may be certain that I will put about word of your improvement, which will allow you to have your pick from London's finest valets. Your father mentioned to me this morning that you will need to hire one posthaste."

"Mmm," Christian murmured, at a loss for a better response. Though a manservant had clearly tended him in the past, he now found the personal nature of the services rendered by a valet far too intimate for his comfort. On the other hand, he knew nothing whatsoever about what society expected from a man in his position, so he supposed that he should swallow his distaste and employ a valet to advise him, like Gideon Harwood had done when he was required to enter the *ton* to court his aristocratic wife. Christian sighed. Ah, well. The matter was hardly his most pressing concern at the moment. Deciding it high time to address his top priority in the concern department, namely facing his audience downstairs, he said, "I believe I am ready to greet my guests, Collins."

Collins paused in folding Christian's discarded nightshirt to glance up and nod. "Very good, my lord. There is a footman just outside your door, waiting to escort you to the drawing room."

It seemed that the footman had been called away, because he was gone by the time Christian stepped into the hallway. Rather than return to his chamber and ask Collins to direct him to—had the valet said the Gothick drawing room?—Christian decided to test his instincts about the house by trying to find the way himself. Besides, he needed time alone to compose himself before facing his forgotten family and the questions that would inevitably arise during their reunion.

After glancing up and down the hall in an attempt to determine the direction he had come the night before, Christian elected to go to his right . . . not because it was the way he remembered coming, but because there was an intriguing arched opening at the end of it that something inside him urged him to explore.

Down the hall at a brisk clip Christian proceeded, carefully noting his surroundings as he went. That the Moncreiffe family was indeed as wealthy as he had heard was apparent from the abundance of decorative moldings and intricate plasterwork relief adorning the vivid pea green walls—a true extravagance when one considered that the costly embellishments would be seen only by the family, servants, and perhaps an occasional houseguest. Then again, everything from the beautifully loomed carpet that spanned the entire length of the hallway, to the gilded wall sconces with their costly white beeswax candles, all the way up to the elaborate stuccowork ceiling overhead, demonstrated that no expense had been spared in turning what in most homes would be viewed as a strictly utilitarian space into an oasis of breathtaking beauty.

As much as Christian appreciated the grandeur around him, he could not help being disappointed that he did not find any of it the least bit familiar. Of course, the paint and plasterwork did look quite new, unmarred by time and carelessness. Could it be that the hall had been recently renovated? With a shrug, he added the question to his long list of mysteries about his life. Now noting with a measure of amusement that even the handles on the gold-and-white paneled doors were like works of art, Christian stepped through the graceful arch at the end of the hall to find himself in a long gallery.

Impressive in both size and structure, the gallery was set at a transverse angle to the hallway he had just left, and it ran the entire length of the north wing's third floor. At one end there was an arcade of circular recesses, some display cabinets filled with what appeared from a distance to be ancient artifacts, while the others exhibited classical statues and spectacular tapestries. At the opposite end spanned a row of magnificent Venetian windows, each one flanked by black marble half-columns crowned with gold scrolls and acanthus leaves. On the deep red walls in between hung scores of paintings in gilt frames, mostly portraits.

Family portraits, perhaps? Christian advanced toward the near wall for a closer look, the flat, square heels of his japanned leather shoes scraping against the marble inlaid floor as he went. The soft noise echoed off the barrel-vaulted ceiling and whispered in the emptiness around him.

As he studied the portraits, he noted that many of them were very old indeed. There was a sour-faced woman wearing a jeweled gable headdress from the time of Henry VIII, and a group of laughing young men sitting around a table littered with the remains of a feast, all clothed in the extravagant style of Charles II's court. One particularly large painting appeared to depict a fifteenth-century wedding feast, while a simple but skillfully rendered sketch portrayed three young sisters in pleated lace ruffs from Elizabeth's time.

Past warriors on horses, mothers with babes, idyllic family gatherings, blushing maidens, and rakishly posed youths Christian strolled, searching each face for traces of his own. Now and again he thought he saw his dark eyes returning his gaze from this face or that, and he spied an occasional head of Gypsy-wild black curls peeking out from a staid headdress here and coiling from beneath the sweeping brim of a hat there. *Hmmm.* And was that his mouth on the lady in the yellow brocade gown with lavishly flounced lace sleeves and broad panniers?

Christian leaned in for a closer inspection, then smiled. It could very well be his mouth, for if he did not miss his guess, the subject of the portrait was his mother in her youth. Though his mother was now long past her prime, what with her two eldest daughters firmly entrenched in middle age and their children near an age to bear children of their own, the Duchess of Amberley still retained much of the beauty pictured here at least four decades earlier.

For several long moments Christian gazed at the painting, hoping that the sight of his mother's clear green eyes and pretty heart-shaped face would evoke a childhood memory. The only thought to cross his mind was the observation that, aside from his mouth, he in no way bore the slightest resemblance to his mother. Thinking back, he couldn't say that he much resembled his father either, except, of course, for his dark eyes. He was about to move to the other side of the room and view the pictures there when a portrait of a lady dressed in ice blue satin and holding a small golden spaniel abruptly arrested his attention.

She was beautiful. Then again, how could she not be? With her lustrous cascade of chocolate brown ringlets, her angelic features, and sapphire eyes, she bore a striking resemblance to Bethany.

Mesmerized, Christian reached out and reverently traced the line of the woman's blushing cheek with his fingertip. Now that he really looked at her, perhaps the resemblance wasn't so very remarkable after all. Nonetheless, it was enough to draw forth memories of Bethany and the kiss they had shared beneath the kissing bough on Christmas Day. As always happened when he remembered those moments, Christian was moved by a deep, powerful longing.

Bethany's lips had been so sweet and responsive, her body soft and pliant as it melded to his. The feel of her luscious form, slender yet feminine and rounded in all the right places, had dangerously kindled his long-smoldering desire for her, sparking an urgency that had threatened to prove quite embarrassing for his body's inflamed response. God! How he'd wanted her! It had taken every last ounce of his self-control not to scoop her up then and there and carry her off to his bed for an afternoon of lovemaking.

A smothered groan escaped him at the mere memory. After all the times he had dreamed of loving Bethany . . . tender but sensual fantasies in which he kissed her into submission and where she lay spread before him in voluptuous surrender, her satiny skin blushed with passion and breathy little moans of ecstasy escaping her kiss-swollen mouth as he pleasured her . . . was it really any wonder why the feel of her lips parting beneath his in unmistakable invitation had almost undone him?

Christian smiled. Well, now that he knew for certain

that he was Lord Northwick and had a future to offer her, he fully intended to return to Critchley Manor and take her up on her invitation. Of course he could not—he would not!—do that last until he'd made her his wife, for to take Bethany without the benefit of marriage would make him every bit of a scoundrel as the bastard who had used her like a whore and then abandoned her, and he cared far too deeply for her to ever treat her with anything less than the perfect love and respect she deserved. Besides, he simply could not imagine living his life without her by his side.

To him there could be no sweeter paradise than falling asleep in Bethany's arms every night, no greater delight than waking to the sight of her smile every morning. In truth, she had become such an important part of his life that he knew he could never feel truly whole without her love. And she did love him. He knew it just as surely as she understood his love for her, though, of course, neither could voice their feelings.

Until now, Christian reminded himself, his heart swelling with joy at the thought that he could at last declare himself to the woman who meant everything to him. And were it not for his nagging need to gather the remnants of his past and piece them together so that he truly had a life to offer her, he would have gone to Critchley that very moment and offered her his heart. He would—

"You always did adore her," a soft voice intruded.

Christian jumped, startled, his head whipping around to stare in the direction from which the voice had come.

A woman dressed in a simple white muslin gown with a warm kashmir shawl tucked over her shoulders and arms was slowly approaching him from the arched entryway. Tall, with light brown hair, brown eyes, and a creamy complexion, which as she drew near he could see was marred by a sprinkling of freckles across her nose, the woman possessed a quiet sort of beauty that could have been easily overlooked by those granting her only a passing glance. Coming to a stop by his side, she nodded to the painting before them, smiling as she explained, "You have been attracted to the 'bootiful' lady in blue, as you used to call the woman in that portrait, since you were, oh, about this tall." She indicated a small child with the flat of her hand. "So much so that you regularly voiced your intention to marry her. Of course, you were only three or four at the time and so adorable in your infatuation that no one had the heart to inform you that your 'bootiful' bride-to-be had been dead for well over a century." She finished with a laugh; a warm, throaty ripple of sound that instantly embraced Christian in a comforting sense of familiarity.

Relishing the sensation, Christian answered her smile with one of his own and glanced back at the portrait in question. To his consternation, he saw that he was still touching the subject's cheek, almost as if attempting to cradle it in his palm as he had done with Bethany when he tested her for fever on Christmas Day. Sheepishly dropping his hand to his side, he quipped, "If what you say is true, it would appear that I have always had a discerning eye for beautiful women."

"Indeed you have, and they for you," she countered with another of her evocative laughs. "You were a born charmer, dear brother, and I can see that that has not changed during your absence. You still have the handsomest face, most winning manner, and that delightfully devilish smile in all of England. What a flutter you shall cause among the ladies this season!"

Brother? That most certainly explained his ease in

her presence. He was awkwardly trying to think of a discreet way to determine which sister she was when she presented her hand and said, "I am Lucilla, your youngest sister. Lucilla Elliott, Countess of Craythorne, by marriage. But, of course, you always called me Lucy. Goosey Lucy, to be exact."

Christian accepted her proffered hand with a grin, nestling it between his palms in a manner that felt wonderfully natural. "I did?"

She nodded. "You started calling me that when I refused one of your more hazardous dares. I believe that I was around eight at the time, which would have made you six."

"What was the dare?" he asked, eager to learn all he could about his past.

"You dared me to climb a ladder that workmen replacing the roof tiles on our Essex country house had left propped against the eaves, saying that I must crawl across the roof and spit down all the chimneys in order to prove that I wasn't a goose like the other girls in your acquaintance. As I recall, we had been arguing my goosehood status all afternoon." She shook her head, as if she could not believe the silliness of their youthful debate. "At any rate, when I refused your challenge, and most prudently I must add, you dubbed me Goosey Lucy and did the deed yourself, chanting my new nickname the entire time. That is, until you fell off the ladder and broke your arm and collarbone." She chuckled, again shaking her head. "I daresay our screams were heard all the way to Scotland, yours from your pain and mine from the certainty that you were killed."

Christian grimaced. "It sounds like I was a horrid child."

"Not in the least. Most people found your boyish pranks quite charming. You always laughed and smiled in such an engaging manner when you were naughty, especially when you were teasing like you did that day, that no one ever thought to view your actions as bad or mete out punishment."

"From what I have heard about my character thus far, it sounds like I would have benefited immensely from a switching," Christian wryly observed.

She shrugged. "That is what Carrie always said, but then our Carrie has never been known for her sense of humor."

"Carrie?" Christian echoed with a quizzical look.

"Caroletta, our eldest sister." She shook her head, her face apologetic. "I am sorry, Xander—or I believe that mother said you go by the name Christian now?" It was her turn to cast him a quizzical look, to which he nodded. Nodding back, she continued, "It feels so much like old times reminiscing about our childhood that I momentarily forgot about you being unable to remember your past. Pray, do forgive me. I am certain that your unfortunate plight is beyond difficult to bear, and I cannot be helping matters by chattering on about things you cannot recall."

Christian gave the hand he still held a warm squeeze. "Quite the contrary, sister. I am enjoying your chatter immensely. It is refreshing to have a conversation without being forced to suffer the prying, probing, and patronizing pity that most people feel obligated to engage in when they learn that I have no memory."

"Well, I can promise you that nobody is going to pry, probe, or patronize you today, not even Vi, though I am certain that it shall pain her to no end to have to bridle her curiosity."

Running over the list of his sisters' names in his head, Christian murmured, "I take it that you are referring to Viola?"

"Viola, yes. And to refresh your memory, she is the sister who always seemed to know the culprit of every transgression in the household and duly tattled the infractions to the appropriate authority. It is why you and I called her Vi the Spy. We always suspected her of spying. How else could she have been privy to everything everyone said and did?"

Charmed by his rediscovered sister's artless prattle, Christian laughed and teased, "Are you warning me to be wary of Viola?"

Lucy grinned. "I daresay that a warning would have been necessary a few years ago, but I am pleased to report that she is much reformed, thanks to her husband and his intolerance for gossip. Of course, that is not to say that she refrains completely from sticking her nose where it does not belong. It is just that she has learned discretion and thus limits the sharing of—"

"Xander? Is it truly you?" a choked voice interjected.

Christian and Lucy turned in unison in the direction from which it had come. A woman was advancing toward them from the archway, moving so fast that Christian was unable to catch more than a fleeting impression of her looks before she hurled herself at him, hugging him tight as she sobbed, "My darling, dearest Xander! It is you. It really is! I am beside myself with joy that you have returned to us."

As she grasped him yet tighter, clinging like she would never let him go, Christian instinctively returned her hug, glancing over her shoulder at Lucy in question.

Justina, Lucy mouthed.

Justina. If what he had heard from the aristocrats at the Harwood's Christmas gathering was correct, and he had no reason to believe that it was not, Justina was his third-born sister and was now married to one of the most financially powerful men in England. Before he could draw forth the remainder of what he had been told, she pulled back, holding him at arm's length, exclaiming, "Here now, brother, let me look at you."

As she did so, touching first his face and then his hair, as if she still could not quite believe that he was real, Christian studied her in return. Unlike the other family members he had met thus far, his resemblance to Justina was quite strong. True, she did have their mother's green eyes, but they were the same rather slanted almond shape as his, rimmed with the same ridiculously thick fringe of black eyelashes that Bethany had always admired. Her hair, too, was reminiscent of his, with its deep waves and fat curls, though its hue was much lighter—chestnut where his was sable.

Shaking her head over and over again in a way that made those curls jiggle and bob, she again pulled him into her embrace, murmuring, "Welcome home, Xander. We have all missed you dreadfully."

"Christian, Tina," Lucy corrected her sister. When Justina pulled back to eye Lucy in query, Lucy reminded her, "Mother informed us that he goes by the name Christian now, remember?"

After a moment of grave-faced contemplation, during which she resumed scrutinizing his face, Justina nodded. "Christian. Yes, of course. My apologies. I fear that I forgot that detail in my excitement of seeing our darling brother again." Before Christian quite knew what was happening, he again found himself in her arms, being treated to another hug, this one particularly fierce. "Oh, dear! I do not think that I shall ever be able to let you go now that I have you back, Xan-sorry, Christian."

Lucy laughed. "Tina has always been inordinately possessive of you, little brother," she explained, grinning as she glanced between brother and sister. "She claimed you for her very own baby the day you were born, though she was only seven at the time, and as you can see she has yet to relinquish that claim."

"That is because he was such a dear baby and has grown into an even dearer man," Justina retorted. Releasing Christian with visible reluctance, she added, "I suppose it makes me a wretched mother to admit to such a thing, but I do believe that he was even prettier than my own three babies, and they were impossibly beautiful when they were born."

"Speaking of children, Tina, has anyone found Amanda and Jeremy yet?" Lucy interposed. Glancing at Christian, she explained, "Amanda is Tina's daughter and Jeremy is my son, and a worse pair of brats you will never find, especially when they are together. To be sure, I cannot recall a family gathering during which they did not get into some sort of a scrape together, can you, Tina?" Justina shook her head, to which Lucy sighed and said, "Unfortunately, it appears that today's gathering shall prove no exception to that rule. The imps slipped from the drawing room when no one was looking, undoubtedly bent on naughtiness. Tina and I and an army of Papa's servants have been searching for them since in hopes of catching them before they succeed in their mischief. It is what brought me, and I daresay Tina, to the gallery."

Justina laughed. "I must say that the pair takes after their Uncle Xan—ur, *Christian*—in their fondness for madcap romps, but to answer your question, Lucy, yes. They have been found. They returned to the drawing room of their own accord, though heaven only knows what they have been about. Both are quite filthy, and Jeremy is sporting several nasty bruises and a scraped knee."

Lucy shrugged, visibly unperturbed by her son's injured state. Then again, boys would be boys, so bruises and scraped knees were hardly a rarity when one had a son. "I suppose we shall find out soon enough," she replied with an air of resignation.

Tina nodded, her mien equally resigned. "Yes, I also suppose that we should return to the drawing room ourselves. For all that I would love nothing more than to keep Xander—sorry, *Christian*—all to myself, we really must share him with the rest of the family."

"See what I mean about Tina being possessive?" Lucy quipped.

Christian smiled first at Lucy, then at Justina. "I am delighted that she cares enough for me to feel possessive, but please, Tina, do not apologize for calling me Xander. It is the name by which you know me, and if you wish to continue calling me it, you may do so with my blessing. The only thing I ask in return is that you tell me how I came by such an odd nickname."

"Oh, that," Justina replied with a short laugh. "We call you Xander because Papa has always been referred to as Alex and we found it beyond confusing to have more than one Alex in the family. Since we also agreed that Alexander was too formal a name to suit a cub like you, we decided to call you by the last half of the name, hence Xander."

Lucy nodded. "Alexander is a family name that has been given to every first-born son in the Amberley line of Moncreiffes since the fifteenth century. You will naturally be expected to carry on the tradition and name your first-born son Alexander, as well."

"I see," Christian murmured, his heart warmed by his sisters' explanations. The fact that his family was close enough to take his nickname under such serious consideration boded well for his hope for a harmonious family life. His earlier trepidation about his upcoming reunion now gone, replaced by an eagerness to rediscover his forgotten kin, he presented each woman with an arm, saying, "Shall we proceed to the drawing room?"

Chapter 6

Bantering and laughing as they went, the three siblings made their way to the drawing room, traversing what to Christian was a bewildering maze of corridors and descending a completely different staircase from the one he had climbed the night before, this one a gravity-defying horseshoe stunningly wrought of polished oak inlaid with marble. Now and again one of his sisters would pause to point out a particular feature of the house and explain how it figured into his past experiences, some of which represented milestones in his life, while others served as mere footnotes, but all providing him with valuable insight.

Though their stories did not stir his memory, their telling did much to promote Christian's burgeoning sense of kinship with the women. So much so that by the time they reached their destination he was so comfortable in their presence that he felt like he had known them all his life, which, of course, he had. His sense of ease, however, was short-lived, abandoning him completely when they reached the open drawing room door.

The crowd was even more overwhelming than he had imagined.

His trepidation returning in a nerve-shattering rush, Christian came to an abrupt halt, and for the life of him he could not coax his feet to step over the threshold. As if sensing his apprehension his sisters stopped, as well, with Justina squeezing his arm in an endearing but ineffective attempt at tender reassurance, while Lucy signaled to the wine-and-gold-liveried footman stationed at the door, to which the servant nodded and refrained from announcing their presence.

Though Christian could not claim to find anything about the Gothick drawing room the least bit familiar, he somehow knew the intricacies of how it had gotten its name.

Gothick, as opposed to Gothic, design was a popular compilation of Gothic and Chinese styles interpreted in fancifully curved and sometimes asymmetric forms and embellished with elaborate ornamentation. It was a style characterized here by windows with pointed arches and trefoil tracery, an enormous chimneypiece decorated with quatrefoils, crockets, and the inevitable arches, looking for all the world like a medieval tomb, and a heraldic ceiling, as ceilings plastered and painted to illustrate a family's heraldic glory were called.

And as if all that weren't quite enough to lend the chamber the desired, if somewhat spurious, air of antiquity, there were several pierced tracery room dividers that resembled a cross between Chinese fretwork and an ancient church choir screen, furnishings fashioned in the medieval style with florid carving, some pieces of which were upholstered in rich purple-and-gold velvet, and, of course, the requisite display of fretwork on the walls, in this instance in a gold oriental design wrought over dark red lacquered walls.

God, it was hideous! Christian had always hated the Gothick style with its oppressive gaudiness and gloomy—

Always hated it? Christian's heart seemed to still in his chest at the sudden realization that he was having one of his strange flashes of memory. To be sure, it was clear from his recognition and easy identification of the architectural details that he was intimately familiar with the room, or at the very least schooled in architecture, either of which were pieces of knowledge that could only have been culled from his memory.

"They do not bite, Xander, I promise," Justina murmured, giving his arm another squeeze.

"Well, except for Lilliane, Vi's youngest daughter," inserted Lucy. She grinned with an infectiousness that made Christian smile back, albeit weakly. "Little Lilly is teething and chews on anything she deems appropriate to put in her mouth, which is just about everything she encounters."

"As I recall, Christian did exactly the same thing," a feminine voice from behind them commented.

Christian and his sisters parted to turn to the owner of the voice. One glance and Christian suspected that she was another of his sisters. How could she not be? With her dark hair, which he could not help but notice was threaded with silver, her sparkling green eyes, and heart-shaped face, she bore an uncanny resemblance to his mother.

Lucy laughed at her remark. "So he did, Vi, and there are teeth marks on his baby chair to prove it."

Viola briefly joined Lucy in her laughter, her gaze riveted to Christian's face, as if memorizing every detail. Then her smiling face grew serious and she stepped forward to embrace him. Pressing a gentle kiss to his cheek, she murmured, "Welcome home, dear brother."

Christian hugged and kissed her back. As with Lucy and Justina, he found her presence comfortingly familiar. "Thank you, Viola. It is wonderful to be here," he replied, and to his surprise he discovered that he meant it. As intimidating as he found his return to his former life, it truly was wonderful to be home. *Home.* How he loved the sound of that word!

Now stepping from his embrace, Viola looped her arm through his and pulled him into the drawing room before he could stop her, exclaiming, "Hear! Hear, ladies and gentleman! Our darling brother has come downstairs at last!"

The buzzing chatter abruptly ceased at her announcement and all eyes turned to Christian. After a moment or two of strained silence, during which Christian was certain he would shatter from his tension, his audience burst into wild applause, with cheers going up here and there. In the next moment the crowd surged forward en masse to greet him.

The hour that followed passed in a mind-boggling blur of names and smiling faces, some of which seemed vaguely familiar, though in most instances Christian felt as if he was meeting each person for the very first time. As Lucy had promised, no one probed, pried, or patronized him, and he soon found himself relaxing. For all that his family was the epitome of breeding and almost terrifying in their elegance, they were an amiable and delightfully witty bunch. Well, except for Carrie and her husband, who were decidedly dour.

Why, even his brother, Godwin, whom Christian had feared would be less than pleased by his return from the grave, given the fact that he had been enjoying life as heir to the duchy of Amberley in Christian's absence, seemed every bit as eager as the rest of the family to welcome him back into the fold. Rather more eager, when one considered his jovial declaration of relief to be free from the duties and obligations that went with inheriting the family titles. And as with Lucy, Justina, and Viola, Christian felt an almost immediate kinship with his good-natured younger brother.

Now sitting on a settee between his mother and

Lucy, with his comically dotty great-aunt Josephine, his other three sisters, and Godwin—or Winnie, as the family called him—occupying the facing chairs, Christian accepted a fourth piece of seed cake from his bashful thirteen-year-old niece, Rosabel. Ever since he had mentioned to Tabitha, Justina's pretty fifteen-year-old daughter, that he fancied seed cake, his nieces had taken turns plying him with the treat.

Pausing in his conversation with his companions long enough to thank the girl and to compliment her on her lovely manners, something that made her blush and hide her face in her mother Viola's lap, Christian returned his attention to his own mother, who was saying, "Winnie, you must take your brother to your tailor first thing tomorrow so he can have some proper clothing made."

Christian looked down at his attire, which up until that moment he had thought to be quite fashionable. It still appeared so to him. Frowning his consternation, he glanced back at his mother and asked, "What is wrong with what I am wearing? My tailor in Liverpool assured me that the cut of this coat is quite the thing in London."

His mother eyed the coat in question, her skillfully rouged lips pursing and her nostrils flaring, as if she had just caught a whiff of something unpleasant. "Oh, I suppose that the cut is well enough for Liverpool and the country, as is the fabric. But as a member of the *ton* you will naturally be expected to be clothed in the best London has to offer."

"Naturally," Christian muttered, shifting his attention to Godwin's attire, comparing it to his own. To his apparently less-than-discerning eyes, his brother's dark blue coat and buff breeches did not look any finer than what he wore.

"Then it is settled," his mother declared with a nod. "You shall see to refurbishing his wardrobe first thing tomorrow, Winnie."

Godwin, who resembled Lucy with his light brown hair, intelligent brown eyes, and unassuming good looks, winked at Christian in a humorously conspiratorial manner. "But of course, mother. If you do not think that being seen in such barbarically clad company will ruin my reputation beyond repair, I shall gladly introduce him to London's most fashionable clothiers."

His mother smiled faintly at his bantering response and countered in like coin. "In view of the fact that your reputation is already in ruin, my dear boy, I daresay that it shall only be improved by your being seen with your poor brother on an obvious mission of mercy." Her gaze had now returned to Christian, her eyes narrowing as she took further stock of his apparently disreputable appearance. "While you are about your charitable works, please see to his hair, as well. I shall trust you to decide upon its cut and mode of dress—"

"Thank you, Mother, but no. I prefer to keep my hair as it is," Christian interrupted, his firm voice brooking no argument. Though he was willing to be biddable in the matter of his attire, the same could not be said for his hair. Bethany had often admired it in the past, teasing him that it would be a crime to cut such lovely curls. And since he had every intention of making her his bride, it was only right that he preserve those curls for her. Besides, he couldn't imagine anything more wonderful than feeling her fingers stroking and teasing them.

"Truth be known, I prefer it the way it is, too," Lucy chimed in with a decisive nod.

"As do I," Justina said, nodding as well.

Vi laughed. "I must admit that I am in accord with Lucy and Tina. Those long, tousled curls suit to perfection his romantic image of a heroic adventurer. No doubt the ladies of the *ton* shall agree when they see him."

"As if they need any more romantic rubbish stuffed into their silly heads," scoffed Carrie, the scorn on her face matching that in her voice. "I agree with mother. Christian should cut his hair. Now that he has returned to civilization, he must take pains to look civilized. It is especially true since he is of the nobility and thus required to serve as an example to his inferiors."

Great-aunt Josephine, who up until that moment had appeared to be dozing, abruptly pounded the floor with her jeweled-head cane and boomed, "To the devil with his hair! I say we summon a surgeon. The boy could have worms, you know. Worms! He needs to be bled and purged posthaste."

"Worms?" Christian sputtered, caught off guard not only by her outburst, but also by the unseemliness of her subject.

Aunt Josephine inclined her head to the affirmative, a true tribute to the strength of her scrawny neck given the probable weight of her towering hair, a preposterously arranged mountain of white powdered rolls and false curls topped by enormous blue plumes and festooned with strings of pink and white pearls. "Worms," she confirmed, her voice rising in her horror. "One hears such dreadful tales about people returning from barbarous places plagued by worms. They breed in a person's gut and feed off his bowels, which causes a ghastly, bloody flux—an uncontrollable one, I shudder to add." Her beady blue eyes seemed to bore into Christian. "How are your bowels, boy?"

"Ur, sound enough," he somehow managed to choke past the laughter building in his throat. Judging from Lucy and Viola's red faces and the tears welling in their eyes and Godwin's muffled snort, it was apparent that they too were fighting hilarity.

"Well, the symptoms usually do not appear until after a person has returned to England, and by then he has unwittingly given worms to every person he meets," his aunt retorted, nodding with a decisiveness that made her monolithic coiffure sway perilously from side to side. "I, for one, shall not rest easy in your presence until you are thoroughly bled and purged."

"He has been in England for some time now, Aunt Josephine. I am certain that if he had worms, he would have noticed by now and been treated for them. Is that not correct, Xander?" This was from Justina, who, unlike her siblings, looked more troubled than amused by their aunt's suggestion.

Christian's merriment dissipated in the face of his sister's obvious alarm. Touched by her concern and wishing to reassure her, he smiled and replied in a gentle voice, "I was thoroughly examined by doctors several times while in India and again here in England, all of whom verified that, aside from my memory, I am in prime twig."

Visibly unconvinced, Aunt Josephine shook her head hard enough to send a puff of white hair powder swirling through the air. However, before she could resume her worm tirade, Godwin exclaimed, "Ah, I see that Fielding has arrived at last, and he has brought Illingsworth, Chafford, and Avondale with him." At Christian's quizzical look, he explained, "Brice Fielding is Lord Markland's third son and your best friend since childhood. But surely Markland mentioned the fact on your journey to London?"

"Yes, he did," Christian said as he stole a glance at the approaching quartet, wondering which man was Fielding.

One man was tall, sporting an immaculately dressed head of dark brown hair that framed a roughly hewn yet undeniably handsome face. Two were blond, one of whom almost matched the dark-haired gentleman in both height and the studied perfection of his coiffure. However, where the dark gentleman was elegantly trim, the blond had a thin, gangling frame that gave him a decidedly gawky appearance. Add the thick spectacles perched on his long, blade-sharp nose and a set of teeth that seemed too big for his narrow-lipped mouth, and he cut what could only be hailed as a queer figure.

By contrast, the other blond man, though wanting in height, had an admirable build and the sort of broad, good-natured face that more than made up in character what it lacked in archetypal beauty. As for the fourth member of their party, well, the word that came to mind when viewing him was *unremarkable*. Of medium height and build, with sandy brown hair and a face composed of regular but nondescript features, he was the sort of person one could meet on several occasions and still be hard-pressed to pick out from a crowd. And yet for all that the other men's looks were by contrast quite distinct, only he struck a chord of recognition in Christian.

"Fielding is the short blond fellow," Godwin supplied as if reading his brother's mind. "The taller blond man is Clive Chafford, Viscount Chafford, or Chaffy, as your circle has referred to him since your Eton days."

"Then I was educated at Eton," Christian murmured. It was uttered not as a question, but as a point of wondering discovery.

"Yes, and at Cambridge, as well, though all you seemed to learn at either establishment was debauchery and wickedness." This was from Carrie, who punctuated her response with a disapproving sniff.

"That is unfair, Carrie," Justina protested, shooting her tart-tongued older sister a reproachful look. "You know as well as I that our Xander quite excelled in his study of architecture at Cambridge. Indeed, several of the dons there said that he possesses the talent to earn a tidy living as an architect, should he ever find himself in need of employment."

Christian smiled faintly at that last piece of information, pleased to have the mystery of his interest in architecture finally solved.

Godwin, who was clearly used to his sisters' bickering and had no intention of letting this particular spat ruin the day, cut off whatever retort Carrie had opened her mouth to deliver and continued his exposition on the new arrivals as if the women hadn't spoken. Nodding in the direction of the four men, who had now stopped to greet their host, he said, "Neville Cavendish, the newly anointed Marquess of Illingsworth, is the rather fierce-looking dark-haired fellow. The gentleman to his right is Charles Sinclair, Earl of Avondale."

Viola, who had whispered something to Rosabel that had prompted the girl to lift her face from her lap and join her cousins in their game of charades, inserted, "Lord Avondale has only recently returned to London after a lengthy absence from society. He has been rusticating in Scotland, I believe."

"Of course it was Scotland. Avondale is a *Scottish* title," said Carrie, and from the disdain in her voice as she uttered the word *Scottish* it seemed that she was critical of Scottish titles. Then again, she seemed critical of everything and everyone.

Their mother shook her head, frowning at her eldest daughter. "No, Carrie, that is incorrect. While it is true that the origin of the Avondale title is Scottish, his lordship's father was granted a patent of peerage many years ago, so both the family and title are now regarded as English."

"And a very estimable title it is, regardless of its origin. It has been ever since the present Lord Avondale's grandfather took his place in parliament, way back in the days when the title was still Scottish," Aunt Josephine contributed. She waited until all her companions' eyes were trained on her before continuing. "Yes, I remember Lord Avondale's grandfather well. A great man, very great indeed. That he was one of only sixteen Scottish lords elected by his peers to represent Scotland in the House of Lords says much about his character."

"Hmmm, yes. As I recall, the man was quite famous for his wit and talent for oration," Christian's mother interjected, her face growing thoughtful.

Aunt Josephine nodded. "Indeed he was. So famous that he was arguably the most quoted man of his day. When his eldest son showed signs of being equally gifted, the boy was granted an English patent of peerage, which, I might add, was a very clever thing to do. After all, the best way to ensure that a Scotsman keeps England's interests above Scotland's is to make him an Englishman."

"Ah, but a man like Avondale has no choice but to protect Scotland's interests, since most of his estates are there and his wealth is tied to the land," Godwin pointed out. "From what his lordship was saying at White's last Tuesday, it is the vastness of his holdings there that kept him in Scotland these past years."

"That is what I heard from Lady Boswick, as well, who got it from her husband. And you know how close his lordship was to Avondale's father before he died," said Voila, always privy to the latest gossip. "I also heard that he wishes to take a proper English bride now that he has matters in Scotland well in hand. If what is said about the extent of his wealth is true, he shall have his pick of the season's finest marriage-market offerings—after our darling Christian, of course." She smiled and nodded at Christian.

He smiled back and asked, "Were Avondale and I friends before, well, you know?" He finished the sentence with a shrug. By now the quartet of men had finished exchanging pleasantries with his father and had resumed their trek to where he sat.

"You were quite thick, all five of you," Lucy replied. "Of course, Avondale's father died shortly after your Cambridge days, and your friend had to return to Scotland to tend to matters there. However, before that time you all shared quarters that you referred to as the Bachelor Barrack." She laughed and shook her head. "None of us dared to contemplate what went on there."

"Illingsworth, Fielding, and Avondale mentioned something about establishing a new Bachelor Barrack for the season now that Christian has returned to London," Godwin said.

"Indeed?" Lucy quizzed with a grin.

"It is indeed true, my dear Lady Craythorne," Fielding confirmed, continuing toward Christian while his companions halted near where the family group sat. Without ceremony he seized Christian, who now stood, locking him in a fierce embrace as he added, "Who knows? Reliving his past might prove just the thing to restore the dear boy's memory."

CHAPTER 7

Julia peeked through the opening of Gideon's ajar study door, trying to gauge whether or not this would be a favorable time to broach the subject of Bethany and the charitable institution she wished to found for London's destitute females.

Not, of course, that that was Julia's only reason for wanting to bundle Bethany off to London, though she truly did find Bethany's benevolent dream admirable and had every intention of helping her fulfill it. No, her most pressing reason at the moment was her desire to reunite Bethany with Christian—it was *imperative* that she do so, for Bethany's sake. The poor dear had been positively melancholy ever since Christian had left a month earlier, barely eating and seldom smiling, and spending far too much time alone, pining for Christian, Julia suspected. Indeed, she had grown so thin and pale of late that Julia was beginning to fear for her health.

Nodding to reinforce her determination to help her sister-in-law, Julia soundlessly opened the door several inches wider to allow an unobstructed view of her husband.

He sat reading in front of the fire, like he did at

the end of every day, lounging in his favorite leather wing chair with his feet propped up on the matching ottoman and a glass of fine port on the side table near his elbow. As was his custom during cozy family evenings at home, he had doffed his coat, boots, and neck cloth shortly after supper and now wore one of the richly patterned silk dressing gowns he had brought from India with a pair of comfortably worn leather mules on his feet.

Julia smiled faintly, her heart overflowing with love at the sight of him. He looked so handsome sitting there, bathed in the glow of the firelight. The illumination irradiated his dark hair like the summer sun, revealing a wealth of highlights in gleaming shades of chestnut and russet, and a sheen so lustrous that her fingers ached to rake through it, knowing that it would feel as glorious as it looked. Though his face was presently cast in shadow, obscuring its details, its contours were silhouetted against the flaring brightness of the firelight, presenting her with a view of his bold profile.

Julia hugged herself, imagining all the times she had cradled that square jaw in her hands as she kissed across that noble brow and down the line of that strong nose, until at last she reached that firm mouth and claimed it with her own. How she loved Gideon's mouth! The way it felt when they kissed, his lips gentle yet masterful as they moved over hers, his tongue teasing yet seductive as it explored her mouth.

Lost in her voluptuous thoughts, Julia instinctively dropped her gaze to his body, a shiver of wanting rippling through her at the thought of what lay beneath the draped folds of his dressing gown. That body . . .

Oh, it was spectacular! Not only was it a joy to behold with its long, lean lines and powerfully sculpted muscles, but it was also a wonder to touch; a contradiction of hard, manly brawn overlaid with skin as soft and fine as a baby's. Such marvelous and amazing skin . . . how she adored it! She was remembering the way they had made love that morning and how miraculous it felt when Gideon laughed at something he read.

As always happened when she heard him laugh, Julia was embraced by a delicious sense of well-being. Her dreamy smile broadened. Like everything else about her husband, she cherished the sound of his laughter.

Chuckling and shaking his head in his amusement, Gideon glanced up to retrieve his port. She must have moved or made a noise, because he abruptly paused in his action, shooting a sharp glance in her direction. When he saw her standing there his lips slowly curled into a smile, parting to display his straight, white teeth in all their pearly splendor. In a voice as rich and warm as his laughter, he softly called out, "Julia, love? Is there something you want?"

Answering his smile with one of her own, she replied, "I am sorry to disturb you, Gideon, but I need to speak with you on a matter of the utmost importance." Judging from his warm response to her presence, this indeed seemed a propitious time for her mission.

"You could never disturb me," he countered, laying aside his book to give her his full attention. "Well, at least not in a manner that I could ever find unpleasant." His dark eyebrows arched in rakish innuendo.

Julia laughed. "Never?"

"Never, though I must confess to hoping that whatever is of the utmost importance has nothing to do with Bliss and Davy Taggert," he returned, extending his arms to invite her into his embrace. "I had a devil of a time pacifying Lady Taggert last week when she came around accusing Bliss of attempting to murder her little angel."

Julia readily accepted his invitation, laughing at his remark as she went to him. Davy Taggert was the spoiled son of a neighboring baronet, a despicable, pig-faced bully who delighted in tormenting those younger or smaller than he, which, given his generous girth, included most of the local children. When Bliss, who had appointed herself champion to those very same children, had caught him terrorizing the wheelwright's three daughters last week, she had taught him a much needed lesson in manners. That such a fragile-looking girl could have so soundly thrashed a boy three times her size was nothing short of astounding, especially when one considered that Bliss had come away with only a bruised elbow and torn gown.

Slipping into Gideon's lap and twining her arms around his neck, Julia said, "I am happy to report, sir, that Bliss's behavior has been beyond reproach this entire week."

"And some people claim that there is no such thing as miracles," he quipped. That said, he crushed her against him and covered her lips with his.

Now ensconced in Gideon's lap with her head resting on his shoulder, breathless from his welcoming kiss, Julia cuddled yet deeper into his embrace, enjoying the cozy moment.

It was a cold, blustery night outside. The darkness was alive with the screams of the wind as it raged across the park and pummeled the house, hurling shards of brittle sleet that shattered with a sound like splintering crystal against the windows. Gideon's study, however, couldn't have been snugger. The servants had drawn the drapery and lit the fire several hours earlier in anticipation of Gideon's nightly reading, thus heating the room to a toasty warmth that quite banished Julia's earlier chill from traversing the drafty halls.

True, some might view the way the candles and

firelight failed to chase the shadows from the corners and ceiling as gloomy, but Julia thought that the effect merely added to the feeling of coziness. To her the surrounding darkness was like a black velvet cocoon, warm and safe and private, creating a soothing sense of intimacy that made her feel like they were the only two people on earth.

Apparently Gideon felt the same way, because he dipped his head to kiss the curve of her breasts. "God! I love what being with child does to your breasts," he groaned.

Julia arched against his mouth, sighing her pleasure. "And I love that you love it, though I must admit that I am beginning to feel as big as a house."

"Big as a house, you say? Hmmm." He lifted his head to consider her breasts with wicked fascination, a wolfish grin curving his lips. After a beat he chuckled, a husky, provocative sound that made the fire only he could light ignite in her most intimate place. "I say hurrah to that, my love, the bigger your breasts the better. Indeed, I cannot imagine anything more wonderful than having more of them to love."

Julia sniffed at his amorous tomfoolery, willing herself to resist his seductive advances until after she had presented her plan. "In case you have not noticed, my belly is increasing at an even greater rate than my breasts."

"Oh, I have noticed," he grunted, shifting her in his lap as though he were being crushed by her weight.

Julia shot him a quick look, not quite certain by his tone whether or not he teased her. After all, she had not been jesting in regards to her size; she truly was increasing at a dismaying rate.

But of course he was teasing. It was obvious from the mischievous light dancing in his eyes and the grin tugging at his lips. Relieved, for she wished always to appear beautiful to him, she cuffed him playfully on the ear. "A good husband would tell me that I look radiant and reassure me that I am not fat, but ripening like a sweet peach," she chided, trying to look offended but failing completely. "Furthermore, must I remind you that I did not get in this condition by myself?"

Gideon slanted her a look that made her fire down below burn yet hotter. "If I say yes, will I get a demonstration to refresh my memory?" he purred.

As tempted as Julia was by the thought of a quick romp by the fire, she was determined to speak to Gideon about Bethany and she intended to do so now. With that purpose in mind, she replied, "If you listen to what I have to say and behave yourself while I do so, I promise to give you a thorough demonstration later."

Gideon seemed to consider her bargain, then heaved an exaggerated sigh. "I shall try to behave, but it will be devilishly difficult with your breasts so temptingly displayed."

Julia glanced down at her breasts, which were indeed swelling immodestly from her once modest neckline. Struck with an idea of how to broach the subject of Bethany, she feigned a fruitless attempt at adjusting what was rapidly becoming her too tight yellow velvet bodice, grimacing at her failure as she replied, "What I wish to discuss with you has to do with my display."

That piqued his interest. "Indeed?"

She nodded. "As you have pointed out my gowns are becoming far too tight, and I really must have new ones made up."

"This is about . . . gowns?" He couldn't have sounded or looked more disappointed. "You know that you do not need my permission to buy new gowns or anything else you desire."

"Yes, and I cannot say how fortunate I am to have such a generous husband," she countered, treating him to her most beguiling smile.

His eyes narrowed at her response, his expression growing wary. "But?"

Julia sighed. They had been wed less than a year and he was already wise to her wiles. Making a mental note to rectify the situation, she shrugged in a manner that she hoped conveyed nonchalance and said, "It is just that I would like to go to London to have them made. They will drape ever so much more elegantly if they are fitted to my body. Caroline wrote me just last week saying that there is a new dressmaker in town named Madame Feuillette who has become all the rage among the mothers-to-be in the *ton*. The woman is said to be a wonder at making gowns that flatter a pregnant woman's condition right up to her confinement. Unfortunately, in order for her to work her magic she must see how a woman is carrying her child so she can ascertain which cut and style will best suit her."

Never a man to deny his wife anything, Gideon smiled like the indulgent husband he was and kissed her forehead. "Then we shall go to London at the end of next month and you shall have a whole new wardrobe, the most lavish one money can buy, by the miraculous Madame Feuillette."

"But I will have burst out of all my clothes in a month's time, and it would be a scandal to arrive in London with nothing decent to wear," Julia protested, though truth be known, he had tendered the exact response she had expected. She shook her head, frowning. "No, I need to leave as soon as possible—the end of the week would be best." Gideon opened his mouth, no doubt to argue, but Julia cut him off before he could speak, quickly adding, "Besides that, at the rate I am increasing I shall most certainly be too large to travel such a distance in a month's time, at least with any degree of comfort, and we both agreed that our baby must be born in London, where we will have the best doctors at our disposal."

It was Gideon's turn to frown and shake his head. "I cannot possibly leave before the end of next month. As you might recall, there is a cotton auction in Liverpool in a fortnight that I promised our tenants I would attend on their behalf." Unlike the estate tenants in most other parts of England, whose livelihood was farming, the Critchley tenants were weavers, and under Gideon's guidance had united to form a cloth guild that was quickly gaining a reputation for producing the finest cloth in England.

Julia pretended to search her memory for mention of the auction, though she remembered it well enough. She waited a moment for effect, then slowly nodded, like she was just now recollecting the matter. "Mmm, yes. Now that you mention it, I do recall you saying something about promising the guild to attend an auction offering some particularly fine lots of West Indian cotton."

"Then you might also recall that I am having two Arkwright water-frame spinning machines installed at the guild factory next month, which I must supervise, and that there is a meeting with our new cloth finishers scheduled for the week after that." He shook his head again. "I am sorry, Julia, but I simply cannot get away any earlier than the end of next month."

Well aware of Gideon's many commitments and viewing his detainment in the country as the perfect opportunity to do some covert matchmaking between Bethany and Christian, she said, "I know how very important your work is, love, and of course I would not dream of taking you away from it, but I truly am in dire need of clothes. Oh, dear. What to do, what to do." She frowned and pretended to contemplate the problem. Speaking slowly, as if thinking out loud, she murmured, "Hmmm. I suppose that Bethany and my siblings could accompany me in your stead. My parents did mention at Christmas that they wished to have Maria, Jemima, and Bertie home for a visit before the season starts. Naturally, Bliss would be welcome to come, as well, though I doubt she will want to be parted from you. Perhaps you could bring her with you when you join us at the end of next month."

Gideon's strong jaw took on the mulish set that Julia knew all too well. "Out of the question! I cannot and will not allow my pregnant wife and family to go traipsing off to London without my protection, especially in this weather." Like his expression, his voice indicated that he would brook no argument in the matter.

Julia, who knew that a little cajoling went a long way in winning her husband over to her point of view, wrapped her arms around his neck and drew his face down to hers. Snuggling her cheek against his, she murmured, "Of course I would rather have you with me, darling. To be sure, I shall be ever so lonely without you. But you know as well as I that I shall be perfectly safe on the road. Our outriders and footmen are more than capable of protecting us, and our coachman will refuse to travel any road or in any condition that he deems unsafe." She turned her head to kiss his ear, whispering, "Please?"

Gideon groaned, a sure sign that he was weakening. "Is it really so important that you go now?"

"Very," she murmured, this time kissing his cheek. "And not just for my sake. I think it equally important that Bethany go to London, and soon."

Gideon pulled his cheek away, the wariness back on his face. "Julia," he growled, drawing her name out on an ominous note. "I do hope that this desperately needed trip is not another of your ploys to match Christian and Bethany."

Julia sniffed, as if the mere suggestion of such a thing was the ultimate in absurdity. "Of course not, though I shan't deny that we would both be thrilled to see Christian again, a feeling that I am certain is mutual, considering how often he writes to us. But no." She shook her head to emphasize her denial. "While you are correct in that I have an ulterior motive for wishing to take Bethany to London, it has nothing to do with Christian." So what if it was a lie? God was certain to forgive her since it was uttered for the sake of love.

Gideon's jaw visibly tightened at her response. "Indeed? And what, pray tell, is your ulterior motive?"

Julia reached up to toy with his hair to avoid meeting his gaze, focusing on it like it was the most fascinating thing in the world. "Surely it has not escaped your notice how dispirited Bethany has been of late?"

"And?"

She made him wait while she coiled a thick lock around her finger before replying, "And I have a plan to raise her spirits, one that necessitates going to London."

"Yes?"

Though Julia's gaze was still glued to the hair curled around her finger, she could tell from his tone that he was growing impatient. Judging it time to show her hand—well, at least as much of it as she willing to show for the time being—she replied, "Bethany has confided in me her desire to establish a place in London where females who find themselves in the straits she and Bliss once found themselves in can go for help. What she is proposing is a charity school of sorts that is open to all ages and stations of destitute females, one that will not only provide them with the skills to gain honest employment, but also help them in finding a proper post. My plan is to take her to town and encourage that ambition. It is my belief that having a sense of purpose will lift her from her doldrums. And the sooner we do so, the better for Bethany and her health." She ventured a glance at Gideon's face to see how her revelation had struck him.

He appeared to be considering her words. "I have

indeed noticed that Bethany has been plagued by the dismals these past weeks, and I confess that I have been worried about her," he slowly replied, his gaze thoughtful as it met hers. "You could be right in that having something worthy to occupy her time will cure what ails her. Perhaps . . ." His voice trailed off then as he seemed to struggle with his decision.

"Of course I am right. I usually am about these matters," Julia crooned in an attempt to weight that decision in her favor. "Besides, not only will my plan do Bethany a world of good, but leaving at the end of the week will also ensure that my siblings have a proper visit with our parents, *and* it will allow me time to have a wardrobe made up before the *ton* returns to London to prepare for the season." Having thus reiterated her case, Julia breathlessly awaited his verdict. She would save the part about Bethany wishing to build her school in a rookery for another time. A single battle was quite enough to wage for one day.

After several agonizingly long moments, Gideon sighed and nodded. "All right, Julia. You win. You may leave at the end of the week. But—"

But Julia cut him off with a fierce hug, exclaiming between kisses, "You wonderful, darling man! Thank you. Oh, thank you! I must go tell Bethany this very instant. She will be so thrilled." Planting one last kiss on his lips, she scrambled from his lap and rushed off to share her news. If the rest of her plan went as smoothly as this part just had, Bethany was certain to be a June bride.

Chapter 8

"If you cut it this way, Maria, you will avoid the stains and worn places completely. See?" Bethany said, indicating her arrangement of pattern pieces on the scraps of bottle green broadcloth the girl had salvaged from an old footman's livery coat.

Maria looked up from the sewing project before them, her brown eyes shining and her previously puzzlement-pursed lips flexing into a delighted smile. "I do see, yes! Oh, Bethany, you are so very clever. I never would have thought to arrange them like that," she exclaimed, her voice breathless in her worshipful admiration. "I do hope that I shall be as clever and beautiful and utterly wonderful as you when I grow up."

Bethany, who sat at a small worktable in her bedchamber with Maria by her side, was touched by her artless idolatry and affectionately smoothed an unruly copper curl from the girl's pretty face. "But you are already all those things, dear, as are Jemima and Bliss. And I do not doubt for an instant that you will all grow up to be the most fascinating women in England."

Maria blushed and dipped her head in maidenly modesty, visibly thrilled by Bethany's praise.

Equally thrilled to have so pleased the child, Bethany picked up the pencil and sketchbook she'd abandoned to help Maria and resumed her work on the portrait she had begun of the girl several days earlier.

Like her younger sister, Jemima, Maria had spent most of her childhood in the care of her Aunt Aurelia, a woman who had ruined herself in her youth by eloping with a scoundrel her parents had forbade her to wed. When the scoundrel had died several years later, leaving her penniless and in debt, she'd had no choice but to throw herself on the mercy of her brother, Julia's father, who had banished her to the nursery to serve as governess to her nieces in punishment for her sins.

Bitter over her wretched lot in life and determined to create company for her misery, Aurelia had cruelly withheld all approval and affection from her young charges, so depriving them of even the simplest pleasures that they had become desperate for human warmth and were thus pathetically grateful to anyone who tossed them the tiniest morsel of kindness.

Loving her siblings as she did, Julia had naturally been distressed by their situation and had begged her parents to release them from their odious aunt's care. But her pleas had fallen on ears made deaf by uncaring hearts. No doubt matters would have remained unaltered had Julia not confided her worry to Gideon. As a man to whom home and family meant everything, Gideon had promptly devised a way to liberate the girls from their aunt, after which he had convinced the Duke and Duchess of Stanwell that the air at Critchley Manor would be far more healthful for their young daughters and infant son than the miasma that passed for air in London. Since that time everyone at Critchley had made it their mission to ensure that Julia's siblings had all the affection they could ever need and want.

Not that providing it was a chore. Bethany looked up from her drawing to glance first at Maria, then at golden-haired Jemima, who sat crossed-legged on the floor in front of the fire with Bliss by her side, both girls carefully picking the gold trim from yet more remnants of the discarded livery. How anyone could not adore the girls was a mystery Bethany could not begin to fathom. They were a delight—utter darlings! Both were pretty, well-mannered, and sweet-tempered, with just enough youthful mischief in them to give them a charming ebullience. Bethany had loved them from the very beginning. Though it had taken Bliss, who was wary by nature, longer to accept them, the three girls were now the best of friends and there was nothing one would not do for the others.

"Kesin will look ever so cunning in his new coat," Jemima commented, turning over the cloth in her hands to tug at the stitching that attached the trim to it.

Kesin was a slow loris, a queer, tailless little primate with woolly brown fur and round, owl-like eyes, that belonged to Jagtar, Gideon's Sikh manservant. Though everyone in the household fawned over the beast, with the three girls often resorting to drawing straws to settle their arguments over who got to carry him on their frequent outings, Maria had been the first to claim him for her baby and so it had fallen to her to provide him with a wardrobe suitable to his new station. When the other two girls had seen how funny he looked in the infant bonnet Maria had first made him, they had insisted on aiding her in the undertaking, with Bliss, who normally loathed anything to do with stitchery, eagerly joining her friends in their nightly sewing sessions in Bethany's bedchamber.

As for Kesin, who at the moment napped in a flannel-lined basket at Maria's feet, his fuzzy form garbed in a wrapper made from the colorful Indian silk that Gideon had donated to the girl's project, well, the greedy little animal tolerated their fussing docilely enough as long as he was regularly plied with fresh fruit.

Nodding in agreement to Jemima's comment, her voice accompanied by the soft snip of her shears cutting through fabric, Maria responded, "The lace you are picking from the old coat should be wide enough to work into an elegant waistcoat, and Julia has promised me one of Gideon's old frilled neck cloths which I will cut down to make a little one for Kesin. I thought I might add whatever frills are leftover around the edge of the coat cuffs so that it will appear that he is wearing a shirt." She paused in her cutting to heave a heavy sigh. "If only Kesin would wear breeches. Just imagine how perfect he would look."

Jemima giggled. "Especially since he refuses to wear breeches. Do you remember the time Maria tried to put them on him? He was so mad! I thought that Jagtar would never get him out of the drawing room drapery."

"Of course we remember," Maria countered, joining her sister in her giggling. "How could we forget? I doubt I shall ever see anything quite so funny as Kesin scrambling from valance to valance while Jagtar chased him." She succumbed to another fit of giggles, helplessly shaking her head.

By now Bliss's hearty guffaws mingled with her companions' girlish twitters. "Good thing Bethany mended the fringe he tore before Gideon and Julia returned from the village, or there would've been hell to pay," she gasped out, choking on her words in her mirth.

"Bliss! I have told you over and over again not to curse, and hell most definitely qualifies as a curse word," Bethany chided, though she couldn't help smiling herself at the memory. The episode *had* been comical.

Bliss shrugged one shoulder, unrepentant, as usual. "Well, there would've been hell to pay. What's wrong with saying so when it's the truth?"

"I think Bethany wants you to say something like, 'Imagine what a pickle we would have been in had Julia and Gideon seen the damage.' Is that correct, Bethany?" This was from Jemima, who looked up at Bethany with wide blue eyes that begged for her approval.

Bethany smiled and gave it. "That is exactly right, dear."

Jemima smiled back. "I am glad. I do so want to be an elegant lady, just like you and Julia."

"In that instance, you must get a good night's sleep every night," interjected Julia's voice from the open doorway. "For in order to be considered elegant, a woman must possess bright eyes and an agreeable nature, both of which require plenty of sleep."

The three girls groaned in unison at the mention of sleep, knowing that it signaled their bedtime, with Bliss voicing her usual protest: "But it is too early to go to bed!"

"It is half past nine," Julia returned, stepping into the room. "By the time you change into your nightclothes and say your prayers, it shall be close to ten. And let us not forget the fact that you always stay awake whispering and giggling for at least an hour after you are in bed." Though the house was more than large enough for each girl to have her own bedchamber, the trio insisted on sharing one. Now clapping her hands three times to urge them to action, she briskly ordered, "Now off with you. I shall be in to tuck you in after I speak with your Aunt Bethany."

Grumbling their disgruntlement, as they did every evening when bedtime was announced, the girls obediently packed their projects into their sewing hampers, knowing that further argument would be fruitless. That done, Bliss picked up both her hamper and Maria's, while Maria carefully retrieved Kesin's basket from the floor, trying not to wake the sleeping animal.

Shweet!—Shweet!—Tat! Tat! Tat! Kesin's wooly, nub-eared head instantly popped up and he emitted a sharp, scolding twitter in complaint for being disturbed.

"Poor baby. Mama is sorry," Maria crooned, gently massaging his back in an attempt to pacify him.

Kesin grunted and emitted a low, buzzing hiss, unappeased.

"Here. Give him to me, dear," Bethany said, holding her arms out to take the basket from Maria. "I will return him to Jagtar for you."

Unfazed by the beast's rather ferocious display of displeasure, aware, as were the rest of them, that he would never harm her or her companions, Maria wrapped her arms protectively around the basket, shaking her head. "Jagtar said he could sleep with us tonight, and Gideon gave his permission, too, saying it was all right with him if you do not mind, Julia."

Three pairs of hopeful eyes were now trained on Julia. "Do say yes, Julia," Jemima begged.

Julia made a show of looking from one eager face to the other, tapping her chin with her index finger, pretending to debate the request. Then she smiled and nodded. "Yes. It is fine with me, too. Now bid Bethany a good night and go tuck the grumpy little beast into his bed before he grows any more cross." Kesin's bed was an elaborately carved cradle that Christian had purchased for the girls when they had told him about their plans to make the animal into a baby. Like all new forms of luxury, Kesin had immediately taken to the idea of sleeping there.

Now grinning from ear to ear, the girls each kissed and hugged Bethany, who treated them in kind, then went to where Julia still stood near the door and did the same to her. When they had exited and the sound of their chattering voices had faded with their progress down the hall, Julia advanced toward Bethany, exclaiming, "I have the most wonderful news, Bethany! I have spoken to Gideon about the charity school you wish to found and he has given his approval. We leave for London at week's end."

Bethany stared blankly at her sister-in-law for several beats, having completely forgotten, in her misery over Christian, their Christmas Day discussion. When she did remember it, she felt the blood drain from her face. At the time of their conversation, she had viewed London as a haven to which she could flee from Christian's all-too-tempting presence, with the establishment of a charity school serving as a diversion from her hopeless love for him. But now—now!

But now Christian lived in London, and their love was more hopeless than ever. In view of that fact, she would be a fool to go there now, knowing as she did that she was certain to see him. It would be impossible for her to avoid doing so. After all, Julia would naturally invite him to call. Yes, and there wasn't a doubt in her mind that Julia would also resume her well-intentioned but misguided matchmaking attempts. And the mere thought of being thrust into Christian's path at every turn was—was—well, it was beyond unbearable.

Indeed, as if the prospect of having her heart broken every time she saw him wasn't devastating enough, there was the humiliation of facing him burdened with the shameful memory of her unbridled response to his kiss and how he had pulled away in disgust. And he had been disgusted. How else was she to explain why he had avoided meeting her gaze for the remainder of the Christmas gathering, why he had not bid her a private farewell when he had taken his leave from Critchley, or included a personal missive to her in the frequent letters he wrote to the entire family?

No. There was no doubt in her mind that her passionate display had made him see what kind of woman she truly was, and that he now viewed her as a wanton. How could he possibly believe otherwise? Decent women, the kind that a fine man like Christian could love and should take for a bride, did not crave the fleshly pleasures like she did whenever she was near him. A decent woman most certainly did not lose her head to those cravings, as she had done during Christian's admittedly chaste kiss.

Oh, that was not to say that Christian would treat her with anything less than perfect courtesy when they next met, despite his revised view of her character. Christian English, or, more correctly, the Marquess of Northwick, was a gentleman and her brother's dearest friend, and he respected Gideon far too much to ever do or say anything that might be perceived as a slight to any member of the Harwood family. And while it was doubtful that anyone else would discern a difference in his demeanor toward her, she would see it. It would be there in his face, his dear, beautiful face . . . in his smile . . . and in his eyes . . . that terrible, impassive cordiality that would inform her more brutally than words that he no longer cared to recognize her as anything more than an acquaintance he must acknowledge out of duty.

And it was that prospect that she found most unbearable of all.

Oh, true. She should be glad that there was no longer a danger that they would do something foolish, like declare their love or elope in a moment of passion-filled madness. She should also hope that his tender feelings for her had continued to wane in his absence. But to her shame, she simply wasn't that strong or that unselfish. For though she knew that he could never be hers, she could not bear the thought of him belonging to another woman. And as long as he had harbored feelings for her, he had never so much as glanced at another woman, which had allowed her to at least pretend that he was hers.

But that was in the past. No doubt he was casting plenty of glances at other women now—beautiful, desirable, *unmarried* ones, *ton* members all, any one of whom would be a proper match for him. Why, it was entirely possible that one had already caught his eye! The pain of that realization hit her heart like a physical blow. Dear God, it would kill her to have to see them together!

"Bethany, dear? Are you quite all right?" Julia inquired, cupping Bethany's cheek in her cool palm to scrutinize her face.

Bethany blinked, surprised to see Julia now sitting in the chair Maria had vacated, frowning at her in concern. Though Bethany was, in truth, far from all right, she could not bring herself to confide her lovelorn despair to Julia, so she forced herself to smile and reply in as light a tone as she could manage, "Of course I am all right. Why do you ask?"

Julia's gaze didn't waver from her face, her amber eyes unnerving in their probing intensity. "It is just that you looked so queer when I told you my news, like you had just had an exceedingly nasty shock," she replied.

Bethany shrugged and emitted what she intended to be a carefree little laugh but instead came out sounding more like a desperate titter. "Did I?" She shrugged again. "Perhaps it is because your news took me by surprise. I must confess that the last thing in the world I expected you to announce is that we are to make a hasty departure for London." That much, at least, was true.

Apparently, Julia found her excuse acceptable, because she released Bethany's face. Moving her hand to the small of her back to massage it, she retorted with a miffed little snort, "I do not know why you should be surprised. I did promise to approach Gideon about the matter, and you should know by now that I always honor my promises."

"I know you do, Julia," Bethany rushed to reassure her, "and I am grateful. Truly. The only reason I was surprised is because I was thinking about other things and our conversation was the farthest thing from my mind." Another truth.

Julia, who was now flexing her spine, her hand still braced against her lower back, nodded at Bethany's apologetic little speech. "Well, now that I have reminded you, is it not the most wonderful news you have heard in a long while? Gideon thinks your ambition is quite admirable and has offered his full support. It is because he is so amenable that he has given us permission to leave on Friday. Just imagine! By the middle of next week we shall be in London."

Bethany did not want to imagine it any more than she wished to experience the proposed journey. She could not go—she would not! Well, at least not this week. While she truly did desire to help London's destitute women, doing so would have to wait until her heart had healed enough to endure the sight of Christian without breaking all over again. And only distance and estrangement would allow it to do that.

Now searching for a way to postpone the trip, though the search was sluggish given her bruised state of mind, she tossed out the first excuse she touched on. "But surely it would be better if we waited until after your baby is born? It cannot be safe or comfortable for you to travel in your condition."

Julia rolled her eyes, sighing her exasperation. "I am pregnant, Bethany, not an invalid at death's door. And now is the perfect time to go. Gideon and I have agreed that our child must be born in London, and at the rate I am increasing I shall most definitely find the journey a misery if we put it off much longer."

"Still, I cannot imagine what Gideon could have

been thinking to give his blessing for you to travel in this weather," Bethany argued. "The roads are certain to be rutted and muddy, not to mention icy. And then there is the snow. Why, it would be a hazardous journey for anyone, much less a pregnant woman."

"Gideon had a special post from his London solicitor this morning, and the man who delivered it reported that the roads are in a remarkably good state for this time of year." Julia shook her head, clearly not about to be dissuaded. "You are a dear to worry so about me, but we shall be perfectly safe."

"But what about the children? You cannot think to leave them for so long," Bethany countered with growing desperation. "Besides, they will be desolate to miss the birth of the baby."

Julia shot Bethany an odd look, a faint frown creasing between her brows. "They shan't miss a thing, because I intend for them to be in London for the birth. I thought we would take my siblings with us on Friday, so they can have a visit with my parents, and of course Bliss is welcome to come, as well, though I doubt she will want to abandon Gideon. If she does not, he can bring her when he joins us at the end of next month."

"What! Gideon is not coming with us? Oh, but we simply cannot travel so far without him," Bethany protested. She was grasping at straws now, admittedly flimsy ones, but they were the only ones left.

"And why not, pray tell?" Julia returned, the crease between her elegant eyebrows deepening. "We shall have more than enough men with us for protection, and I have not grown so dependent on my husband that I cannot do without him for a month."

"But—but," Bethany stammered, frantically grappling for yet another reason to cancel the trip.

"But what, Bethany? More objections, more excuses not to go?" Julia cut in.

"Well—" Bethany intoned, still at a loss.

Julia shook her head, pushing aside her lame attempt at a response. "So many excuses, Bethany. One would think that you have had a change of heart about your school."

"No—oh, no! Never!" Bethany cried, vigorously shaking her head. "The ambition is as dear to my heart as ever, and I cannot imagine anything more satisfying than saving those poor creatures. It is just that—"

"Is it society, then?" Julia interrupted, visibly impatient to cut to the heart of the matter. "Are you afraid that the *ton* will see you and pry into your past?"

Bethany shook her head again. "Of course not. I already explained my plan to avoid the *ton,* and I have every faith in its success."

"Ah." Julia's brow suddenly cleared and she nodded, as if in confirmation to a new thought. "Then it has to be Christian. There is no other logical reason left as to why you would wish to avoid going to London."

Bethany opened her mouth to deny Julia's conclusion, but to her horror only a sob came out, followed in quick succession by another and yet another. Before she quite knew what was happening, all the pain and grief she had kept bottled up inside her the past month broke free, and the tears she had struggled to contain began to stream down her cheeks.

"Ah. So I am correct. This does have something to do with Christian." Julia fumbled about in her side slit pocket and withdrew a neatly folded handkerchief. Pressing it into Bethany's hand, she added gently, "I rather wondered if there was some sort of trouble between you."

Bethany wiped her eyes with the handkerchief. "You"—*sniffle!*—"did?"

Julia nodded, both her face and voice soft with compassion as she replied, "It has struck me as rather odd that you have not written to him in his absence, or him to you. After all, you were so very close. And yet I feel that whatever happened between you cannot be all that terrible, because I have noticed that you have his likeness displayed in a rather prominent place." She indicated the framed painting hanging by Bethany's bed.

It was the picture of Christian and Bliss that Bethany had intended to give Christian on Christmas day, but had instead kept, having been not only too embarrassed to present it after their kiss but also deeming it too shabby a gift for a future duke. Gazing at it now, like she so often did, Bethany blew her nose and brokenly replied, "I fear that what happened is worse than terrible. What I did—I—I—well, he cannot help but to despise me now."

"I cannot imagine you doing anything so awful as to make him despise you," Julia replied, giving Bethany's arm a sympathetic squeeze.

"But I did!" Bethany sobbed. "Oh, Julia. Whatever am I to do? I—I—"

"You love him," Julia finished for her.

It was on the tip of Bethany's tongue to refute the charge, as she always did. Yet how could she do so when her tears had made the truth so very obvious? Though she hated to admit the fact, even to herself, she knew that her and Christian's feelings for each other had most likely been obvious for months to everyone who was close to them. That being the case, why bother to continue denying her love for him, especially when nothing could possibly come from her confession now? Besides that, it would be a relief to share her heartbreak with someone who loved her as much as Julia did.

Still unable to speak for the sorrow constricting her throat, Bethany miserably nodded.

Julia nodded back. "Well, I am glad that you are

finally willing to own up to the fact that you love him. Perhaps now you will also acknowledge that Christian loves you in return, and realize that he cares for you far too much to set his feelings aside over a lover's quarrel."

"If only it were just a lover's quarrel, but it was more than that," Bethany managed to croak. "Much, *much* more."

Julia sighed. "All right, then. Perhaps you should tell me what happened so I can judge for myself." When Bethany hesitated, embarrassed to confess her wanton behavior, Julia squeezed her arm again and softly prompted, "I shall no doubt see the matter with much clearer eyes than you, and my guess is that whatever happened is not so very dire as you believe. Who knows? Perhaps I will be able to help you think of a way to mend the problem. After all, I am an old married lady now with much experience in dealing with difficult men." She made a droll face as she uttered that last.

Bethany smiled weakly at Julia's joke, grateful for her attempt to rally her spirits. "Perhaps you can at that, but what would be the point? Christian is a future duke, and even you have to admit that a match between us would be highly unsuitable. That being the case, do you not think that it would be prudent to simply let the matter be?"

"I will admit to no such thing because it is not true," Julia retorted with a sniff. Bethany opened her mouth to argue, but Julia cut her off, saying, "Oh, and do not hand me that silliness about you being unworthy of Christian in your soiled state. If Christian thinks you are worthy then you are, and his is the only opinion that matters in determining your suitability for him."

"That is his opinion now, but what if he regains his memory in the future and regrets his choice? I can think of no greater misery than spending my life with a man who resents me and is bitter that he did not make a match more suited to his station," Bethany replied. There! She had finally voiced her greatest fear.

Julia snorted. "Such stuff and nonsense! Love is ruled by the heart and memory by the head. If Christian's love for you is true, and I would wager the baby in my belly that it is, whatever memory he recovers in the future will in no way diminish his love for you. If anything it will strengthen it, because he will remember the chits in the *ton* and thank God for being wed to you instead."

Though Julia's reasoning made sense, Bethany still could not bring herself to believe that there was hope for her and Christian. Desperately wanting to believe it, yet too fraught with concerns to do so, she skeptically pointed out, "Even if you are right about the steadfastness of his love, there is still the matter of society and Christian's family. As you, yourself, pointed out, society loves nothing more than to gossip, and they are bound to pry deeply enough into my past to discover the truth should they become curious about me. And you know as well as I that they would be curious to the extreme were I to become romantically linked with Christian." She shook her head. "I could not bear to bring such disgrace to Christian, and I shudder to think of what his family would do when they discovered that their heir wished to wed a discarded mistress."

"There might be a scandal, true, but do not forget that there will be no real proof to support whatever talk is bandied about," Julia replied. "Even if the father of your child were to step forward and confess his vile behavior, which I doubt the bastard would have the courage to do, it would still be your word against his. Also do not forget that your word carries the weight and support of my family and the Barham name wields a great deal of power in the *ton*. Certainly enough that most of society would not dare to cross my parents by questioning the character of a Barham family member, which you are through my marriage to Gideon."

When Bethany continued to look unconvinced, Julia sighed and added, "You probably do not know this, but when Gideon first arrived in London it was gossiped that he was a pirate or worse. He most certainly was not viewed as a person suitable to associate with the *ton*. However, when my father chose to befriend him and allowed him to court me, the *ton* quickly changed its opinion, and he is now considered to be a valuable asset to their ranks. You also must not overlook the fact that Christian is now a powerful *ton* member in his own right and you will have his support, as well."

Again Julia made sense, and again Bethany felt compelled to question her words. "While I will grant that your family's and Christian's support might lend me a patina of respectability, there is still the matter of Christian's family. No doubt his parents expect him to make a grand match suitable to his station."

Julia shrugged, visibly unconcerned. "Let Christian handle his family."

"But—" Bethany began.

"But you must address your concerns with Christian," Julia gently interjected, reaching over to take Bethany's hand in hers. "It seems to me that none of this is anything that cannot be settled by simply talking to him. So talk to him, Bethany. I promise that you will see things so much differently if you do."

For a long moment Bethany fell silent, considering everything that Julia had said. Then she sighed and murmured, "You are right, Julia, about everything. Unfortunately, your advice has come too late. As I said earlier, Christian despises me, so I can hardly discuss such things with him now."

"And as I said earlier, I might be able to help you mend whatever trouble lies between you if you will tell me what it is." Julia gave the hand she still held a squeeze of encouragement.

Bethany swallowed hard to dislodge the lump that had formed there at the mere thought of confessing her shameful behavior. But confess it she must if she wanted to heal the breach between her and Christian. Hanging her head as she spoke, her words coming out slow and strangled, she recounted the awful incident under the kissing bough. When she had been silent for several moments and Julia had not responded, Bethany stole a glance at her face.

It was frozen in an expression of disbelief. Not that it was any surprise that she should look so when her tale had indeed been shocking.

"You—you drove him off with your passion?" Julia finally inquired in a choked voice.

Miserably, Bethany nodded.

There was another long pause, during which Julia's face slowly turned the color of a boiled beet. Then she burst into laughter. "Oh, Bethany! You truly are an innocent!" she sputtered between fits of hilarity.

Bethany gaped at her in bewilderment. "However can you say that I am an innocent when I behaved in such a—a—an *un*innocent manner! I told you how shocked and disgusted Christian was by it," she exclaimed.

"Oh, Bethany—love. I do not doubt that you are correct in that Christian was shocked by your passion," Julia gasped out, still possessed by her uncontrolled mirth. "He was shocked to discover his good fortune."

"What!" It was Bethany's turn to be shocked.

Julia, who still shook with laughter, was now clutching her sides. "Silly girl! Do you not know that the greatest prize a man can hope to win is a wife with a passionate nature?" When Bethany merely stared at her, too stunned to respond, Julia nodded and added, "It is true. Gideon says it is so, and mentioned once or twice that Christian is in full accord on that point. It seems that on their long rides in India they often discussed the sort of wives they hoped to have someday, and a passionate nature topped both their lists of attributes their perfect wife would possess."

Chapter 9

"Yes, yes," Brice Fielding wheezed, gasping for breath as he struggled to recover from his most recent fit of hilarity. "I do agree that that was one of his droller wagers. However, my favorite is the one he made with Lord Mifflin."

"Which was?" prompted Christian, the *he* to whom Fielding referred. Though he almost hated to ask about the bet, knowing that he would most probably cringe at its nature, he was determined to learn as much as he could about his forgotten life, no matter how distasteful parts of it might prove to be.

Fielding's red face darkened to a mottled purple. "You—you—b-bet him—" he began, emitting a series of snorting sniggers between the words in an effort to fight back his mirth. Losing his battle before he could finish, he collapsed against his urn-shaped chair back and helplessly surrendered to yet another fit of his distinctive braying laughter.

"That comical, was it?" Christian inquired in a wry voice, shooting a party of nearby diners an apologetic look.

He and his companions presently supped in White's dining room, and as happened every time his circle gathered there, the other men spent the entire time regaling Christian with the details of his seemingly endless bets, most of which were chronicled in the enormous betting book that lay open on a table in the club's foyer.

Lord Illingsworth shrugged one black superfine-clad shoulder in response to his question, politely swallowing his mouthful of pickled kidney beans before saying, "Apparently, Fielding thinks so. Personally, I always considered that particular wager to be more clever than comical."

"Clever, yes." Lord Chafford nodded, a move that sent his spectacles sliding down his long, thin nose. Shoving them back up to his bridge again to peer earnestly at Christian through the thick lenses, he added, "I, too, would most definitely categorize the Mifflin wager as more clever than comical."

Now glancing at Lord Avondale, who was holding his glass at an angle so he could contemplate the color of his wine against the stark background of the snowy tablecloth, Christian said, "Would you care to opine as well, Avondale? Or can I count on you to simply tell me about the wager so I can draw my own conclusion?"

Avondale shifted the glass he was studying to the right to better capture the light from the crystal chandelier overhead. His eyes narrowing at whatever the change in lighting revealed, he replied, "You bet Mifflin ten thousand pounds that his newly acquired governess was not as chaste as he claimed her to be, and that she would have to be sacked within two months of the wager date for having a bun in her oven."

"Oh, but it was not so much the wager as your timing in presenting it that made it so very comical," Fielding pointed out, still gasping from his laughter. "You stood by quietly for a good half hour while Mifflin went on and on to everyone at the club about how the woman was a paragon of virtue and a saintly example for his daughters before interrupting him midboast to propose the wager. You must all agree that the expression on that stiff-rumped coxcomb's face was comical to the extreme." Apparently, he was reliving the moment in his mind, because a loud, snorting snigger exploded from his nose. "Why, he looked ready to expire on the spot at the mere suggestion that someone beneath his roof might be sullied by sin. You most certainly had a chuckle over it, Chaffy, and a hearty one at that." He more brayed than uttered that last in his merriment.

Chafford, whose thin lips all but disappeared as they stretched into a grin over his enormous teeth, repeated the alleged act by chuckling now as he told Christian, "Mifflin is a smug, sanctimonious bastard who fancies himself and his morals to be above every other man in England, including the Archbishop of Canterbury. His greatest sources of pride are his equally starched family and his servants, all of whom he claims have sterling references from households known to be of good moral character."

"Needless to say, he and you were—ahem! Well, let us just say that you two bore distinctly different philosophies on how life should be lived," interjected Illingsworth, swirling a chunk of spiced beef in the accompanying wine sauce. "That he had no tolerance whatsoever for your views was a fact he never missed an opportunity to point out."

"Yes, and it hardly improved matters the way you would shrug off his criticism with a cocky grin. Thus, your wager simply served to add fat to the already raging fire of his righteous indignation." This was from Avondale, who now sampled the contents of his glass.

"I get the distinct impression from Fielding's glee over the affair that I won the wager," Christian commented.

Fielding brayed. "Indeed you did, my friend! Then

again, how could you have lost? You were on rather familiar terms with the governess in question, having kept her as your mistress while you were at Oxford."

"Are you telling me that I cheated?" Christian exclaimed. Not that he would be surprised to learn that he had, not after all he had heard about his scandal-ridden past.

"It was a lark, nothing more," Illingsworth answered with an indifferent shrug. "You confessed to having tricked the man afterward and refused to collect your winnings from him, so you can hardly be accused of cheating."

Again Chafford, Fielding, and Illingsworth left it to Avondale to fill him in on the particulars. Doing so between taking bites of his lamb haricot, Avondale explained, "By your own account, the woman came to you to beg for help after her keeper tossed her out for becoming pregnant. It seems that the poor fellow could not be certain if the child was his since he had caught her with a tradesman two months earlier, and had found evidence that she had had other dalliances, as well."

He chuckled and shook his head, though whether in disdain for the man's obvious inability to satisfy his mistress or in amusement at the woman's wantonness, Christian could not say. "At any rate," Avondale continued, "Mifflin had been boring us all into a coma with his constant complaining about the lack of virtuous governesses in London, so you thought it would be a grand joke to style your old dolly-mop as a pious country vicar's daughter and fob her off on him. You even went so far as to forge a glowing letter of recommendation from a mythical bishop. In exchange for the woman's cooperation, you promised to provide for her until after her child was born. Needless to say, Mifflin was humiliated by your trick and has yet to forgive you. Indeed, he made no secret of his delight when you were thought to have been killed."

In a gusty sigh, Christian released the breath he had been holding during Avondale's tale, relieved to hear that he had not been responsible for the chit's condition. As it was, he could not help cringing at the knowledge that he had once been so callous as to use a woman's downfall to fuel a prank. His loathing for the man he had once been deepening yet another degree, Christian lifted his wineglass, which a waiter had just refilled for the third time, and took a quaff. Ah, well. At least he'd had the decency not to turn the poor woman out into the street to starve after she had served her purpose. Or so he hoped.

His conscience nagging him to find out if he had indeed honored his end of the bargain, Christian glanced around the table and asked the question point-blank.

Swallowing the bite of roasted guinea fowl he chewed, Chafford replied, "For all that you were a rakehell, you always honored your promises, especially those you made to the ladies."

"And the woman? What has happened to her since?" Christian quizzed, genuinely concerned.

"She died in childbirth and took her bastard with her," Avondale supplied.

Chafford nodded. "I must say that we were all devilishly surprised when you insisted on paying for rather a better burial than the pair merited. Indeed, you even went so far as to lie about the woman's marital status so that she and her brat could be buried in hallowed ground." Chafford's offhand remark was accompanied by the sound of silver scrapping against china as he flipped the bird over with his knife and fork and began to pick at the meat on the underside.

Christian nodded, gratified to hear that he'd been responsible for at least one honorable act during his days as Northwick the Notorious, as he had been dubbed in his youth. Hoping to end the other men's discomfiting reminiscences on that note, he turned his attention to boning his untouched baked sole, casually changing the subject by saying, "Speaking of females, I wish to thank you all for giving Lady Mina a turn on the dance floor at the Duchess of Hunsderry's soiree Tuesday night. As I mentioned, Lady Julia Harwood counts Lady Mina as a bosom-bow, and since I look upon the Harwoods as an extension of my family, I naturally feel a duty toward their friends. Besides," he paused to make a show of deftly separating the delicate white sole fillets from their spiny skeleton before finishing with a grin, "I happen to enjoy Lady Mina's company."

"Ah, yes. Lady Julia," Illingsworth mused, sitting back in his chair to rub his flat but undoubtedly full belly, considering the amount of beef he had just consumed. "I remember when she made her come-out, quite elegant and a beauty to boot. I must confess to being taken with her, as were all the bucks in the *ton*. We were all beyond stunned that she chose to wed a commoner when she could have had her pick of England's titled bachelors."

Christian opened his mouth to defend Gideon, bristling, as he always did whenever anyone dared to insinuate that Gideon was in any way inferior because of his common birth, but Avondale cut him off before he could speak, saying, "Judging from the accounts I have heard about the fellow, Mr. Harwood seems a man of parts, so I would say that the girl did quite well for herself." Now smiling at Christian, he added with a nod, "And you are quite welcome, Northwick. Lady Mina seems quite pleasant, so it was really no great burden to dance with her."

Fielding, who took enormous pleasure from the dinner table and was now scraping the last of his creamed hare from his plate, commented, "I cannot say that she uttered more than two words to me during our entire dance."

"And I say hurrah to that," Illingsworth inserted. "There is nothing more tiresome than a chit who natters on about nonsense, which is all that seems to fill girls' heads these days. What little Lady Mina did say revealed a modicum of intelligence, so I, for one, intend to dance with her at every opportunity."

"Mmm, I quite agree with Illingsworth about Lady Mina's conversation. Unlike most girls, she does not speak simply for the sake of chattering but because she actually has something of relevance to say. That she possesses such a highly commendable quality makes her lack of looks all the more of a pity." This was from Chafford, who signaled a passing waiter to indicate his need for more wine.

Avondale shrugged. "I daresay that her looks would not be so very bad if she did not have spots."

"Her spots will go away with time," Christian said, his growing fondness for the girl prompting him to champion her.

"Of course you are correct, Northwick. Point granted," Avondale conceded with a low laugh.

As always happened when Avondale uttered the words, "Point granted," which was frequently, something buried deep in Christian's memory stirred. And as he always did in such instances, Christian stared hard at Avondale, hoping that the sight of him would coax forth whatever memory had provoked the response. But it was to no avail. Whatever his mind had tried to recall was lost and the only thought to come forward was the well-worn question as to how a man as intelligent and evolved as Avondale had come to be friends with the likes of him and the other men. For unlike them, Avondale was free from the notoriety that stained their reputations and was widely admired for his sterling character.

As Christian continued to gaze at Avondale, the other man frowned. "What, Northwick?" he inquired.

Christian shrugged one shoulder. "Nothing really. Just an odd feeling that sometimes comes over me when I am in your company, especially when you say point granted."

"Indeed?" Avondale murmured, visibly intrigued. "And what sort of feeling, pray tell?"

"One of familiarity, like I am at the edge of a memory that is about to reveal itself, but never quite does." Christian shrugged again. "However, I seem to draw closer to doing so each time I experience the sensation, so I am optimistic that I will one day soon remember whatever it is my mind is trying to reveal to me." He nodded once, decisively. "By all indications, it appears that my first real memory of my past shall be about you, Avondale. What say you to that?"

Before Avondale could respond, Fielding who had apparently missed the change in topic during his single-minded bout of plate scraping, abruptly chimed in. "Lady Mina's spots will go away in time, true. Unfortunately that same time will most probably do nothing to improve her figure, which I must confess to finding rather too lumpish for my taste." He paused to lick a dollop of cream sauce from his fork before finishing, "Nonetheless, I believe that I shall follow Illingsworth's example in the matter. Dancing with Lady Mina does indeed provide a man with a moment to catch his breath, so I, too, will seek her out for a dance at every gathering."

"As will I," Christian declared, thinking how pleased both Julia and Bethany would be to hear of their friend's modest success. And they would undoubtedly hear about it since they were now in London, a marvelous piece of news he had learned from the message he'd received from Julia that very afternoon. Though he knew he should wait a decent interval before calling, so as to allow the women time to settle in, he nonetheless intended to go around first thing in the morning and lay his heart at Bethany's feet. If there was one thing he had learned for certain while in London, it was that he could not bear to live without her.

Fielding emitted a derogatory noise and waged an attack on his side dish of artichoke pie. "Considering the Duchess of Hunsderry's talent for constantly filling your sight with her daughter, I doubt you shall have the chance to see, much less dance with, Lady Mina."

"Lady Helene. Mmm. Now there is a delectable eyeful. She can fill my sight any day of the week." Chafford flashed one of his lipless grins to reveal something green stuck between his two blocklike front teeth. "I must say that I quite envy you, Northwick. Not only have you won the Harridan of Hunsderry's approval, but also, it would seem, Famous Helene's heart. That Helene actually seems taken with a mere mortal man and her mother has judged him good enough to wed her famed offspring is something none of us ever thought to see."

"Ah, but does Northwick judge the Famed One as good enough to wed him? I wonder," Avondale mused, eyeing Christian with a sardonic air. "Hmmm. It is a question that is certain to provoke some rather lively wagering once the season begins."

Fielding nodded. "No doubt the odds will be in favor of the match. After all, no man in his right mind would pass up the opportunity to have the Famed One warm his bed."

"Then I am afraid that there are destined to be many lost wagers, and that I shall most probably be declared quite mad, because I have every intention of passing it up," Christian declared.

All jaws dropped at his announcement. After a stunned beat, Illingsworth demanded to know, "How can you possibly reject such an opportunity out of hand? Lady Helene Dunville is an angel!"

"An angel, yes," Chafford cooed, his dewy-eyed expression making him look every inch the love-struck dolt. "She has the face and voice of an angel. . . ."

"And the sweet nature to match," Illingsworth added with a rapturous sigh.

Fielding groaned. "Not to mention the most heavenly tits in England. God! What I would not give for a handful of those."

Christian shrugged, secretly unimpressed by the girl. Despite the fact that she rather resembled Bethany with her dark curls and sapphire blue eyes, in his mind Helene Dunville's admittedly spectacular looks seemed rather ordinary when compared to those of the woman he loved. Nonetheless, he did not wish his lack of interest in the Famed One to be interpreted as an insult to the other men's taste in women, so he diplomatically conceded, "I admit that Famous Helene is indeed very lovely, and were my sights not set on another lady I would most certainly give the chance to wed her serious consideration."

The instant the speech had left his mouth and he saw the glance that passed between the other men, he regretted his words. Bloody hell! He could tell from their look that they fully intended to probe him, and mercilessly, for the identity of his ladylove. And that was a confidence he simply could not share until he had spoken to Bethany.

"Well, then? Do empty the bag, Northwick," prodded Fielding, wasting neither time nor finesse in his prying.

"Yes, do tell us who the lady is whose beauty so eclipses that of the Famed One," Chafford chimed in.

Illingsworth nodded. "I must confess to being rather intrigued myself."

"So, Northwick?" Avondale demanded.

Christian glanced from face to face, all of which wore identical expressions of curiosity, their eyes boring into him from beneath eyebrows arched in query. Slowly he shook his head. "Until I can persuade her to accept my suit, I am not at liberty to say."

All four faces registered shock at that piece of intelligence. "*Persuade* her to accept your suit? Good God! Are you saying that the chit is reluctant?" gasped Fielding. "Why, she must be daft not to jump at the chance to wed the heir to the Duchy of Amberley."

Christian could not help laughing, as much at Fielding's indignant response as at the other men's flabbergasted expressions. "Fortunately—or unfortunately, depending upon how you choose to view the matter—this particular lady's head and heart cannot be turned by riches or a grand title."

"Daft. Unquestionably daft," Fielding muttered, while Chafford inquired at the same time, "What else is there to recommend a man if not riches and titles?" As he spoke, he shoved his sliding spectacles back up on his nose to peer at Christian in astonishment.

"Northwick does have his looks," Avondale observed. "With that face, I would guess that he would do well enough with the ladies without a fortune or title."

"Which makes the mystery lady's reluctance all the more confounding," Illingsworth inserted. "She must indeed be daft not to want to wed a catch like Northwick."

Christian held up his hands to halt their mad-dash speculation, shaking his head as he laughingly replied, "I did not say that she does not wish to wed me. I have every reason to believe that she does."

"Then where is the rub?" asked Avondale. "If you love the chit and are confident that she returns your feelings, why the hesitance in revealing her name?"

Thinking quickly, Christian replied, "She is a widow and is not yet out of mourning, which makes it highly improper to even mention her name in the same sentence as romance."

To his relief, the other men seemed to see the validity of his reasoning, because they all nodded.

"I must say that that does make your situation rather sticky," Illingsworth murmured.

"Rather, yes," Christian agreed, praying that that would be the end of the matter.

He should have known better, especially where Fielding was concerned. Now systematically shoveling a second side dish, this one consisting of pickled French beans, Fielding said between bites, "We all understand that it is a matter of honor that you cannot reveal the lady's identity. Truly we do. However, that does not mean that we shan't continue to try and make you spill it, or that we will not guess at her identity."

Chafford nodded. "Now let me think, who could she be?"

"Well, there are several luscious widows in the *ton*—Lady Ashworth, for one," said Illingsworth.

"Yes, but she put off mourning months ago, so she cannot possibly be the one," Avondale pointed out.

"Then how about Lady Seton? I must say that she looks quite fetching in black," Chafford said, once again pushing his ever sliding spectacles back up his nose.

"Perhaps," Illingsworth agreed. "Or perhaps it is the beauteous Lady Farr? Old Farr crocked up his toes—when? Four or five months ago, was it, which means that she is still in mourning."

All eyes were again on Christian, who merely shrugged.

Avondale chuckled. "So that is the way it is going to be, eh, Northwick?" When Christian merely smiled, he added, "Ah, well. I daresay that we will find out quickly enough once you take up residence with us at the Bachelor Barracks. And make no mistake about it, we fully intend to succeed in convincing you to lodge with us for the season."

"Perhaps you will at that," Christian replied. Though he genuinely enjoyed his parents' company and that of Lucy and Godwin, both of whom resided in London and frequently dropped by for a visit, living in his family's home had done little to awaken his memory, and he could not help wondering if maybe a season of reliving his past in the infamous Bachelor Barracks might just be the thing to do so.

Fielding opened his mouth, no doubt to further pursue the matter, but Chafford cut him off before he could speak, expelling, "Good God! Is that Lord Denleigh?"

"Denleigh?" Illingsworth echoed in a stunned voice, a frown creasing his forehead as he looked in the direction in which Chafford gazed. The rest of the men at the table followed suit, as did many of their fellow diners, Christian noticed.

Compelled to look as well, he saw that they were staring at a trio of men who had just entered the dining room. All were tall, though not inordinately so, all were handsome, with varying shades of brown hair, and all were dressed to the nines. As he watched, several club members rose and moved forward to greet them.

"Damn me if you are not correct, Chafford," Fielding muttered, turning back to his companions to address them. "How very odd that he should make an appearance now. Am I correct in thinking that he has not been seen in society since the duel?"

"You are," confirmed Illingsworth.

As always, it was left up to Avondale to explain matters to Christian. "The Earl of Denleigh is the gentleman aided by crutches." He nodded toward the men.

Christian stole another quick peek. He had not noticed at first glance that one of them had crutches. Now that he looked for them, he saw why. They had been painted black to match the man's suit, thus making them less noticeable to the casual observer.

"Tragic, that, losing a leg in a duel," Avondale continued, shaking his head. "Especially when you consider that he was once thought to be the most dashing buck in the *ton* and every chit dreamed of being his bride. But, of course, losing his leg like he did changed all that. Perhaps if he had lost it in battle or while performing a heroic feat, but—" he broke off with a sigh and another head shake.

"I am not certain that Northwick would have known about Denleigh's leg, even with his memory intact," Chafford said. "As I recall, he was shipped off to India the week before the surgeons took it off."

"I would have thought that someone would have written him about something like that," Illingsworth commented. "It is only right that he should know."

Christian frowned, trying to make sense of the conversation. "Were Denleigh and I friends then?"

Avondale laughed a dry, harsh rasp. "Hardly. You were at the other end of the pistol that shattered his knee. You were dueling over an actress you both wanted for your mistress. As I seem to recall, it was you who issued the challenge."

"You did," Fielding confirmed. "And I should know. I served as your second."

Christian felt like someone had just slugged him in the belly. "Good God," he muttered, sickened by what he had done.

Avondale nodded at his response. "Yes, it was an exceedingly ugly affair. Denleigh retired to the country when he had recovered enough to travel, which, given the severity of his wound, was some months later. It was rumored at the time that he did not wish to live maimed as he was and that he had attempted to take his own life." He shrugged. "At any rate, the duel was what finally prompted your father to ship you off to India. As wild as you had become, he could not help fearing that you would kill yourself or someone else in your recklessness."

"Good God," Christian repeated. His voice was little more than a croak from the horror strangling him. "How Denleigh must hate me." He certainly hated himself at the moment.

Avondale emitted another of his rasping laughs. "Let us just say that I would not turn my back on him if I were you."

Chapter 10

"The poor, poor man. He can hardly set foot outside his door without the Duchess of Hunsderry being there, thrusting Famous Helene in his path," Lady Caroline confided to Bethany and Julia, her brown eyes twinkling in amusement. "And her parties! Mama says that she has never known her grace to throw so many parties outside the season, and most certainly not such lavish ones. She has had—what—four entertainments since Lord Northwick returned to London?" She glanced at Amy and Mina for confirmation.

"Four, yes. There was a musicale, a Venetian breakfast, a card party, and a rout." This was from Mina, who looked rather odd this morning, having tried to disguise her latest crop of spots with a sickly pink paste; a paste that she had reported carried a claim to not only render the spots invisible to observers but also to clear them away posthaste. That the cosmetic succeeded only in making her complexion woes all the more obvious was a fact that no one in her circle had the heart to point out.

Amy grimaced at the mention of the parties. "Bloody awful affairs, all four of them."

"Amy, please. You know better than to use vulgarities like *bloody* while in company," Caroline chided.

Amy, whose mother had died during her birth, leaving her in the care of an overly indulgent father who had allowed her to run wild, shrugged one pink-frilled shoulder, visibly unrepentant. "Well, they were bloody awful. Without a doubt the most agonizingly tedious affairs I have ever had the misfortune to attend. And all thrown, I might add, for the obvious purpose of showing off Famous Helene's dubious talents and charm to Lord Northwick."

Always one to find good in just about everything, Mina softly remarked, "I must confess to rather enjoying the Italian soprano her grace engaged for the musicale."

"Oh, I suppose she was well enough until her grace insisted that Helene join her in a duet," Amy retorted. Her expression now calling to mind a person suffering an excruciating megrim, she more groaned than said, "I thought my eardrums would split from the screeching the Famed One fobbed off as singing during the duet. Exactly where her grace got the idea that Helene has the vocal range to sing such a strenuous piece, I shall never know."

"It was awful," Caroline agreed, her pretty face mirroring Amy's pained expression. "However, my vote for the worst display of the Famed One goes to the amateur theatrical she staged at the Venetian breakfast her mother held the first week Northwick was in town. How the Duchess of Hunsderry could possibly have believed the drivel Helene penned to be worthy of such a sumptuous production is beyond belief."

Amy snorted. "Even more beyond belief was the way her grace boasted afterward about the Famed One's performance. Why, I have seen logs with more animation than Helene managed to muster in her role as a tragically wronged shepherdess." Now parroting the Duchess of Hunsderry's superior tone, her pert nose rising in the air in comic imitation of the condescending manner in which her grace looked down her high-bridged beak at the rest of the world, Amy mimicked, "Such a singularly talented girl, my darling Helene. I became quite misty-eyed during her masterful death scene. Do you not agree that her performance was inspired, Lord Northwick?"

Getting into the spirit of Amy's game, Caroline also struck a pose, this one almost flirtatious in her simpering smile and the way she fluttered her fingers in beckoning. Mimicking the sotto voce the duchess adopted when speaking to Helene's more worthy marriage prospects, she cooed, "My dearest Lord Northwick, do come and tell our darling Helene how very marvelous she was in her role. The precious angel is so modest that she simply refuses to believe everyone's praise of her talent."

Amy snorted again. "The only people to compliment Helene on her talent were either moonstruck dolts who are too blinded by her beauty to see what a rotten actress she is, or those people who were fortunate enough to have slept through her performance."

"And what did Lord Northwick say about it?" Bethany blurted out before she could stop herself.

Having spent the past half hour listening to the other women recount Helene and her mother's endless ploys to snare Christian's affections, Bethany could not help but wonder if they were perhaps succeeding in their purpose. To be sure, if what Julia said about Christian's fondness for passionate women was true and he had thus not been disgusted by her heated response to his kiss, then the only reason she could think of to explain why he had not written to her since his departure from Critchley was that he'd had a change of heart. And she suddenly had a sickening feeling that that change might very well have been prompted by Famous Helene's wiles. Yes. Now that she thought about it, it all made terrible and perfect sense. For how could a man like Christian not prefer a woman like the Famed One, who not only matched him in station and breeding, but also in beauty?

Amy shrugged at her question. "What else could the poor man do but agree with her grace?"

Caroline nodded. "As a gentleman he had no choice but to tender a flattering response. However, I was watching him during the performance and I can assure you that he looked less than enthralled by the sight of Helene's wooden posturing on the stage. Why, I distinctly recall seeing him stifle a yawn twice during her most dramatic scene."

"And I can swear to the fact that he pressed his hands to his ears several times during her duet at the musicale," Amy interposed. "He also begged a prior engagement in order to escape her grace's card party after partnering Helene for only two games of whist—hardly the action of an infatuated man, in my mind."

"Amy and Caro are correct, Bethany," Mina chimed in, gracing Bethany with such a sweet smile that for a moment her plain, plump face looked almost beautiful. "Lord Northwick does not seem at all taken with Helene. Then again, how could he possibly find her attractive when he is acquainted with you?"

"Of course you are right, Mina," Julia declared. She reached over from where she sat next to Bethany on the comfortably padded drawing room settee to give Bethany's arm a fond squeeze. "Lord Northwick is no fool. He recognizes true goodness, such as our Bethany possesses, when he sees it and is thus unlikely to fall victim to Helene's counterfeit charms."

"Besides, Helene's looks cannot hold a candle to yours, Bethany," Mina inserted. "Even Helene knows it is true, though she would no doubt rather be strung up by her thumbs than admit that there is anyone in the world more beautiful than she. I daresay that that is why she and her mother were so impossibly rude to you when we all spent the night at Critchley Manor last summer. They were resentful of your looks and knew that you would present serious competition for Helene in the marriage mart should you decide to seek a new husband this season."

Though Bethany appreciated Mina's loyal little speech, she knew that her friend was merely being kind in comparing her looks so favorably to Helene's legendary loveliness. Thus she smiled her gratitude and demurred, "You are a dear to say such things, Mina, but I have seen myself in the mirror and know that I am no threat whatsoever to Helene. Why, I look like a drab little country mouse next to her refined beauty and elegance."

"Then you are in need of spectacles if you cannot see that you are a hundred times more beautiful than Helene could ever be," Amy said. "Judging from the way Lord Northwick watched you on Christmas Day, I would say that your stunning looks are not lost on him."

"Amy's observation is correct," Caroline concurred. "He truly did appear to be taken with you. Every time I glanced his way, he was gazing at you and could not seem to tear his eyes away."

Despite Julia's conviction that there was yet hope for Bethany and Christian, Bethany still could not bring herself to believe that it was so. Compelled by those feelings of uncertainty to protest the notion now, she softly replied, "Lord Northwick and I are just friends. Nothing more."

"And you will stay just that if you do not do something to encourage the interest we all saw in his eyes every time he looked at you," Caroline countered with a sniff.

"I am sure you are mistaken about the nature of his interest, Caro," Bethany again protested. "Lord Northwick has never said or done anything to lead me to believe that he harbors feelings for me beyond friendship."

"That is because he is a gentleman and understood that he could not honorably offer you his heart until he knew for certain that it was free to give. But of course you are already aware of that fact. We discussed it at length," Julia reminded her.

Bethany sighed. Despite the other women's good intentions in encouraging her feelings for Christian, she desperately wished that they would leave the subject alone. Such talk was uncomfortable, dangerous even, in that it coaxed the seed of hope Julia had planted during their discussion about Christian a week earlier to take root in her heart. And if she allowed it to root it would most certainly grow and flourish, and only a fool would nurture a hope that she feared was doomed to be killed by disappointment.

But, of course, she wished in vain.

Now leaning forward on the settee she occupied, which was positioned opposite the matching one upon which Julia and Bethany sat, Caroline said, "What Julia says makes perfect sense, Bethany. My guess is that he will come up to scratch now that he is certain of his identity." She paused to glance first at Mina, who sat primly beside her on the settee, and then to where Amy more sprawled than sat on a tapestry-upholstered armchair near Bethany. "On our journey home from Critchley Manor, did we not discuss how Lord Northwick is obviously taken with our dear Bethany and air our suspicion that he would propose to her at first chance?"

Mina and Amy nodded, with Mina saying, "We did. And judging from his indifference toward the ladies he has met in the *ton* thus far, I would say that his affection for her has not waned."

Amy giggled, the sharp, agitated titter that always signaled an outrageous remark. "It seems that his indifference toward females is not just limited to ladies. Papa said that Lord Northwick has refused to take a mistress and that he also declined Mrs. Dobeck's fanciest piece when his circle took him to her establishment to treat him to a little sport."

Always the innocent, Mina frowned and murmured, "Mrs. Dobeck's? I do not believe I know her establishment."

"Which is as it should be," Caroline retorted, frowning at Amy, who had dissolved into a fit of giggles at Mina's remark. "Mrs. Dobeck is the proprietress of the most exclusive, ur, accommodation house in London."

Mina's miracle-paste-splotched brow creased. "Accommodation house?" she echoed, visibly nonplussed.

"A fancy house, dear," Julia contributed with a meaningful lift of her eyebrows. When Mina merely stared at her blankly, she sighed and tried again. "A school for Venus? A bawdy house?"

Mina shook her head, to which Julia and Caroline exchanged a helpless look.

Amy snorted. Pulling herself up to sit straight in her chair, she exclaimed in an exasperated voice, "Oh, for heaven's sake! They mean a brothel, Mina. A place where men go to be pleasured by whores. And according to my father and his cronies, Mrs. Dobeck's establishment is an excellent place indeed for such a purpose."

Julia and Caroline groaned in unison, "Amy!" while Mina squeaked and flushed a mottled crimson.

Equally taken aback by her companion's unseemly knowledge, Bethany gasped, "Surely your father does not discuss such things in your presence, Amy?"

"Of course not," Amy retorted, her leaf green eyes dancing with mischief. "I heard my father and his circle discussing Lord Northwick after a dinner party last week, when they thought that I had been safely banished to the drawing room with the rest of the ladies. I have a passion for listening at keyholes, you see." By her tone, it was clear that she saw nothing in the world wrong with spying on her father and his friends.

Though Bethany knew that she should feel disapproval at Amy's unfettered talk, like Julia and Caroline clearly did, or shock, as was the case with poor Mina, she could not help being relieved, and yes, even a bit pleased to hear that Christian had not reverted to the rakish behavior he'd reportedly indulged in before his memory loss.

Apparently, Amy interpreted Bethany's lack of objection to her naughty revelation as a sign that she was to continue, because she leaned nearer and confided in a loud whisper, "According to the gentlemen's gossip, the whores were terribly disappointed by Northwick's refusal to lie with any of them and did all sorts of lewd things in an attempt to entice him to their beds. Not that I can blame them." Another ear-piercing giggle. "Can you imagine how fetching he must look without his clothes on?"

That provoked another shocked squeak from Mina and a chorus of outraged, "Amy!" from Julia and Caroline.

Unfortunately for Bethany, she could imagine Christian without his clothes, and the mere thought of him spread out naked on the bed before her, aroused and ready for pleasure, made something deep in her belly quicken and sent a rush of liquid warmth surging into the secret place between her legs.

As if reading Bethany's mind, Amy nodded and continued, "I would wager that Northwick needs no tailoring tricks to make his shoulders look so very broad, or stays to trim his waist. As for the way he fills the more interesting regions of his breeches—"

"Lord Northwick," interrupted the majordomo's deep voice.

All four women started guiltily at the announcement, their heads snapping around to gape at Simon Rowles, Gideon's roguish-looking majordomo, who now stood just inside the cozy family drawing room door with Lord Northwick by his side.

Amy slapped her hand over her mouth but not before a shrieking giggle escaped it, while Mina turned a deeper shade of red, if such a thing were possible. Always in command of every situation, Julia immediately rose and moved forward to greet her new guest, leaving Caroline to glare in warning at Amy. As for Bethany, she could only stare at Christian, starved for the sight of him.

Today he sported an immaculately tailored coat in a rich shade of red, worn open, as was the fashion, to display a magnificent blue silk waistcoat that had been painstakingly embroidered to recall an exotic oriental garden. In tasteful deference to the ornateness of his waistcoat his breeches were white, as were his stockings, though unlike his breeches, which looked almost stark in their plainness, his stockings boasted a fancy knitted pattern and frivolous gold garters with tassels that bounced jauntily against his muscular calves as he moved forward to take Julia's outstretched hands in his.

Sparing his feet enough of a glance to note his highly polished black pumps, Bethany lifted her gaze to take in the precision with which his frills were pleated and the intricate arrangement of his starched neck cloth. As for his hair—his wonderful, glorious hair—while it was still as long as she remembered it, it had been tamed into an orderly and, yes, fashionable tousle of deep, glossy waves and fat curls.

In short, he was groomed to perfection, looking every inch the wealthy nobleman he was. Gone was the Christian English she knew so well, with his wild mane and simple tastes, replaced by the magnificent Marquess of Northwick, a man almost terrifying in his elegance.

Feeling suddenly awkward, flustered, overwhelmed, and even a bit intimidated by his resplendence, Bethany nervously shifted her gaze to her lap, the sight of which made her desperately wish that she were wearing something nicer than the serviceable gray day dress she had donned upon rising. Then again, she had not expected Christian to call so soon after their arrival in London, instead expecting to spend the day going through the linens with the housekeeper, Mrs. Courter.

Ah, well. She heaved a heavy inward sigh and laced her fingers together to keep them from fussing over what now seemed to be her impossibly rumbled skirts. There was no help for her appearance now. No doubt she had Julia to thank for her present predicament.

"Lord Northwick! What a delight!" Julia was exclaiming, her pleased tone lending veracity to what would normally be a rote greeting. "I must say that you are looking quite well."

"As are you, Lady Julia. Indeed, you grow more radiant each time I see you. Carrying Gideon's child obviously agrees with you." That his voice sounded exactly as she remembered provided Bethany with a small measure of relief, but not nearly enough to settle the nervous fluttering in her stomach.

Julia emitted a sound halfway between a snort and a laugh. "I am as big as a house and we both know it, but I do thank you for the compliment. You are most gallant."

"I am hardly worthy of being called gallant, at least at this moment," he smoothly countered. "After all, I am guilty of blatantly violating the *ton*'s sacred rule that a gentleman must wait at least three days before calling upon a newly arrived lady. However, in my own defense I must plead to having missed you all too terribly to stay away a moment longer, and beg your forgiveness for my lapse in propriety."

"There can never be an improper time for a person to call on his family, and you should know by now that you shall always be considered a part of the Harwood clan," Julia graciously returned. "As for your defense plea, I daresay that we have missed you every bit as much as you have missed us. Indeed, the children have felt your absence so keenly that they have attempted to fill the void by making a game of guessing at all the wonderful things you might be doing in London." She expelled a short laugh. "As you can imagine, some of Bliss's suggestions do not bear repeating."

Christian chuckled. Like his voice, his chuckle was exactly as Bethany remembered—low and warm, and edged with what to her was a tantalizing huskiness. "And where are the brats? I would very much like to see them."

"Bliss is still at Critchley with Gideon. She refused to abandon him in order to travel with us, so she will accompany him when he joins us in town at the end of next month. No doubt she views my absence as a chance to dote over him," Julia replied with another laugh. "As for my siblings, they are presently residing with our parents. Mother expressed a wish at Christmas to have them home for a visit before the start of the season. I do hope that you will call on them there. They would be beyond thrilled to see you."

"Then I will do so. Perhaps I can even persuade your parents to allow me to take them to Gunter's for a sweet." Bethany ventured a peek at Christian as he uttered that last, and saw Julia leading him to where her group sat. Stopping near Amy's chair, Julia said, "But of course you are acquainted with Ladies Amy, Caroline, and Mina?"

As he proceeded to banter with the three women, easily countering Caroline and Amy's witty repartee in like coin, Bethany was again struck by the change in him. The Christian she knew—her Christian—had never possessed the glib tongue this man did. He most certainly had never displayed such ease and confidence around mere acquaintances, which she knew the other women to be. *Hmmm.* It seemed that Christian English had become the Marquess of Northwick in more than just looks.

"What is this, Bethany? No greeting for an old friend?" Christian quipped, at last turning his attention to her.

Quickly looking back down at her lap, unable to meet his gaze for fear that she would not recognize the man she saw in his eyes, she murmured, "Welcome, Lord Northwick." How she managed to shove the mechanical response through the tautness of her throat, she would never know.

There was a long pause then, a tense, uncomfortable one during which it was obvious that everyone expected her to continue. When she merely sat staring at her hands, at a loss as to what to say to such a grand nobleman, Caroline cleared her throat and broke the silence, saying, "Julia promised earlier to show me all the wonderful things she and Bethany have been stitching for the baby. Since I must soon take my leave, I do hope that you will allow me to steal her away for a moment to show me now, Lord Northwick."

"All this talk of sewing reminds me that I am to meet Papa at the drapers this afternoon to help select fabric for our chambermaids' new gowns. So I, too, must depart soon," Amy chimed in. "And like Caro, I, too, must insist on viewing the baby things before I go. After the way Julia has bragged about Bethany's masterful needlework, I simply cannot wait until the next time I call to see them."

"Mina?" Caroline intoned suggestively.

Mina glanced up with a frown, slow, as usual, to comprehend her friends' conspiracy. "Yes, Caro?"

"Did you not say that you wished to see all the lovely baby things, too?" She widened her eyes and raised her eyebrows, nodding almost imperceptibly in an attempt to prod Mina into understanding.

Mina's frown deepened. "Things?" she echoed in a dumbfounded voice. Then her cheeks flamed and she stammered, "Oh, of course. Y-yes. The baby things, yes. Do let us go upstairs this instant and see them."

Julia smiled at Christian. "With your permission, Lord Northwick? I am sure Bethany will provide you with very pleasant company in my absence."

"I am sure she will," Christian agreed, his voice strangely thick.

"Bethany?" Julia said, deferring to her.

Though the last thing in the world Bethany wanted was to be left alone with Christian, she could not think of a reason to insist that the other women stay. So she smiled as best she could and uttered the first inane response to pop into her head. "Perhaps his lordship would like to sample a slice of Cook's excellent iced spice cake in your absence." Iced cake? She almost groaned aloud. How could she have made such a silly suggestion, knowing as she did that Christian disliked icing on anything, deeming it far too sweet for his taste?

"Well, then, shall we?" Julia inquired, nodding to Caro, Amy, and Mina. The three women promptly rose and hastened from the room.

Rather than taking Caro and Mina's abandoned seat across from Bethany or the chair Amy had vacated, as would have been proper, Christian sat next to Bethany on the settee, near enough to gather her hands in his. Lacing his fingers through hers in the intimate manner she had always loved, he murmured, "You do not seem particularly happy to see me, Bethany. Have I done something to vex you?"

"No, no, of course not. It is just that—that—" she stammered weakly, her mind scrambling to find a plausible explanation to excuse her reserve. Instead she found Julia's advice.

Talk to him. Address your concerns to Christian. You will see things so much differently if you do, Julia had said.

Talk to him? Her racing mind abruptly skidded to a halt. *Hmmm.* She had seen the wisdom of Julia's words when she had uttered them, but now that the time had come to actually take her advice, could she? Did she dare to do so? Should she even try? After a brief deliberation, Bethany decided that she could, should, and would. Julia was right: If she was ever going to settle matters with Christian, she must tell him of her concerns—talk to him about her fears. True, doing so was going to be difficult, especially now, when her thoughts seemed to tangle and her tongue tied into knots every time she attempted to speak to him. Oh, if only he weren't so very grand!

"It is just what, Bethany?" Christian quietly quizzed.

Sternly reminding herself that the dazzling aristocrat by her side was just Christian and that he could not have possibly changed so very much beneath his glittering facade in such a short time, Bethany cleared her throat and started again. Her voice stronger now in her determination, she uttered the truth. "It is just that you look so very grand. I must confess to being quite awed by your presence."

She felt rather than saw him draw back and heard his quick intake of breath. "Awed by me?" he said on his exhale. He could not have sounded more stunned or incredulous. "I cannot imagine why. I am still Christian English, the very same man you found such easy company at Critchley."

"The man I knew had a mane of wild curls and a fondness for dusty riding boots. He was a man of simple tastes and a retiring nature. But you, well, just look at you!" She gestured at his ostentatious apparel. "Your new splendor is quite intimidating."

There was a long silence during which Bethany did not dare to steal a glance at him, certain that she had offended him. Then he erupted into laughter, his bubbling guffaws so spontaneous and full of genuine amusement that she could not help staring at him in astonishment. "Oh, Bethany, my love. What a cabbage-head I am!" he sputtered between gusts of mirth. "I had my valet feather me like a peacock out of respect for you and my purpose here today. I had hoped to please you, not frighten you."

"Oh," she murmured for a lack of anything better to say, suddenly feeling rather like a cabbage-head herself.

His hilarity now spent, Christian clasped her hands yet tighter, urging her in a rough whisper, "Look at me, Bethany. Look past my ridiculous attire and fussed-over hair, and you will see that I truly am the same man I was at Critchley."

Disarmed by the fervor of his plea, Bethany did as he asked. The instant their gazes met she felt her tension seep away. These were the eyes she remembered, so warm and gentle and alight with thoughtful intelligence; deep, dark eyes, the sight of which never failed to make her ache to take him in her arms to assuage the haunting pain she saw shadowing their depths. They were Christian's eyes. Her Christian. As she gazed at him, his firm lips slowly curved into the endearing smile she adored, crinkling the corners of those arresting eyes.

Overwhelmed by sudden tenderness, she smiled back. "Of course you are the same man—what a ninny I am! I should have expected a change in your appearance. After all, you are a nobleman now and a member of the *ton*. It is your duty to look the role."

"To the devil with duty," he retorted with a short laugh. "If you want me to wear dusty riding boots and go about town with my hair flying willy-nilly, then I shall do so."

"Oh, but that would never do. Just imagine the scandal you would cause," Bethany exclaimed, only half in jest. "Besides, now that I have grown accustomed to your new appearance, I find that I rather like it." It was no lie. He did look dashing.

Christian gave a good-natured shrug. "Fine. Then I will stay as I am. Since pleasing you is the only thing that truly matters to me, I shall gladly do or be whatever you want. Your wish is my command."

"What I wish is for you to please yourself," she countered, though she could not help being thrilled by his words.

"But I am pleasing myself. Pleasing you pleases me." He seemed about to continue in the same vein, then sighed and shook his head. "Forgive me for speaking as I am about to do without a proper preamble of pretty prose and swainish trumpery, but I have already wasted far too much time in declaring myself and I simply cannot wait a moment longer to do so."

Bethany's breath stilled in her chest. Declare himself? Did that mean—could it be—was he about to—

Before she could fully formulate her thought, he slipped from the settee to kneel before her, ardently declaring, "I love you, Bethany. I have from the moment I met you. And since that time I have wanted nothing more than to make you mine. Now that I am certain that I am free to wed and can offer you the sort of life you deserve, I am begging you to marry me. Be my marchioness. If you will make me the happiest man in England by consenting to be my wife, I promise to do everything in my power to make you the happiest woman."

"Christian," Bethany began, only to stop in the next instant, too torn between the warring demands of her heart and mind to continue. This was everything she had ever wanted, ever dreamed of. And yet—yet—

Talk to him, Julia's voice again rang through her mind.

Bethany swallowed hard, her throat taut and aching with emotion. There were so many reasons why she should say no. To be sure, despite Julia's conviction that a marriage between her and Christian was possible, she still could not imagine how.

Talk to him.

Yes, yes. She must talk to him. She must tell him of her reservations and list all the reasons they could not possibly wed. If he still wished to marry her then and could convince her that doing so was indeed right, well, then and only then could she consider his proposal.

"Say yes, Bethany," Christian begged, clasping her hands to his frilled chest. "Say that you love me, too."

"Of course I love you, Christian. How could any woman not love you? You are so kind and handsome and dear," she replied, adhering to her resolve to speak the truth. "And I would love nothing more than to marry you. But I cannot in good conscience say yes when there are so many very real and troubling reasons why a match between us would be wrong."

"The only real reason a match would be wrong is if we were not in love. And we have already established that we love each other," he returned, grinning in a way that never failed to set her heart aflutter.

Bethany sighed. If he parried all of her arguments with such charming agility, this truth business was going to be harder than she'd first imagined, perhaps even impossible. Especially if he continued gazing at her like he was doing now, with his lips curved into that devastating grin and his eyes smoldering with the promise of a passion she desperately longed to accept. It was all she could do not to groan aloud in her frustration. When he looked at her like that, it took every last ounce of her self-control not to toss aside her better judgment and fall into his arms.

Somehow resisting the delicious impulse, though heaven only knew where she found the strength to do so, Bethany forced herself to retort, "You know as well as I that there is a great deal more to marriage than just love, especially for an aristocrat like you."

He shrugged one shoulder, clearly not about to be deterred from his purpose. "If two people love each other, the rest will take care of itself. Surely you cannot dispute the fact that there is nothing more important for the success of a marriage than love?"

"I agree that love is very important, but—" She broke off as he treated her to another of his fascinating grins, the sight of which completely robbed her of her wits. Blast! She would never be able to speak her piece if she continued to allow him the unfair advantage of his potent appeal. Determined to remedy the situation posthaste, she pulled her hands from his and patted the cushion beside her, saying, "Please do get up and sit beside me, Christian. We need to discuss this in a rational manner and we cannot possibly do so with you kneeling before me." The truth of the matter was that it would be far easier to avoid looking at him and thus save herself from falling under his spell if he sat beside her.

Christian grinned that entrancing grin again—heaven help her poor heart! And then, to her eternal gratitude, obediently followed her directive. Now seated beside her with her hands again in his and his thumb caressing her palm in a way that she found every bit as distracting as his grins had been, he murmured, "Whatever you wish, my love. However, I think it only fair to warn you that I am determined to marry you and that I shall stop at nothing to make you mine. In short, I intend to convince you that you cannot live without me."

As if that would take any great effort! Smiling weakly, her heart aching all the more in its uncertainty, she replied, "You may consider me duly warned."

He nodded. "Good. Then you may proceed with your lecture."

Bethany nodded back. His bedeviling thumb now sketched teasing little circles on her palm, eliciting titillating sensations that made it next to impossible for her to think. Fighting to hang on to her wits, she said, "I daresay that you already know why a marriage between us is impossible."

"I can certainly guess at the reasons. Would you like me to list them and tell you why none of them matters?" Without giving her a chance to respond, he began. "My first guess is that you are using what you view as your sordid past as the grounds for your greatest objection. That you think you are soiled goods and thus unfit to be any man's wife, much less that of a future duke. Correct?" He looked at her for confirmation.

Miserably, she nodded.

He nodded back. "All I can say to that is rubbish! There is no woman in England more fit to be my bride. You are kind, gentle, compassionate, intelligent, generous, and witty, and that is only a partial list of your admirable traits. And do let us not forget that you are also the most beautiful and desirable woman I have ever met. In short, you are everything I could ever wish for in a wife."

Bethany shook her head, not about to allow him to skirt the issue with flattery, no matter how tempting it was to do so. "Even if I were everything you say, and I know for a fact that I am not, it would hardly make up for my past. You know as well as I that a woman's virtue—"

"To the devil with your past!" he forcefully cut in. "It does not matter, any of it. All I care about is the future."

"My past might not matter to you now, but can you honestly say that it will remain inconsequential once you regain your memory?" she countered, desperate to make him see her side of the argument. "By all reports, you were once an aristocrat through and through, with all the aspirations and expectations that come with the station. In view of that fact, is it not possible that you will again be that man when your memory returns, that you will again have the dreams and desires of the aristocrat you once were?"

"Bethany," he began.

But she cut him off, ruthlessly pressing her point. "Think about it, Christian! If such a thing happens, you are certain to resent being tied to a woman who is not only far below you in station, but is also of dubious reputation. And then you will hate me, and most probably yourself for your foolishness in wedding me, and that hatred will ruin both our lives. I simply cannot—"

"*If* I regain my memory, not *when*, Bethany," he corrected her, raising his hands to halt the flood of her argument. "And I can most certainly promise you that I shall never again be the shallow, spoiled man I once was, no matter what I remember."

"But how? How can you possibly promise such a thing?" she exclaimed in heartsick disbelief.

"Because the man I once was is dead. He died in India, leaving behind a man profoundly changed by hardship and suffering. Being enslaved made me realize what is truly precious in life; that freedom, kindness, compassion, hope, and love are the greatest treasures a man can ever have. You are all those things to me, Bethany. You are my treasure. And I am willing to vow on all I hold sacred that I will always cherish you as such."

His speech was so impassioned, so filled with genuine emotion, that Bethany could not doubt that he truly believed what he said. And yet, still—"My station and reputation might not matter to you, but they will undoubtedly matter a great deal to the rest of the world," she blurted out. "Your family—"

"My family has no bearing on the matter, nor does the rest of the world," he said in a voice that brooked no argument on the point. "If they do not approve of our marriage, then to hell with them. I have been through far too much to allow someone else's disapproval to rob me of a chance at a lifetime of happiness. And I would say that you have earned the same privilege. What happened to you is not so very different from my ordeal in India. We both did what we had to do to survive. We were both forced by our circumstances to accept a lot in life not of our choosing."

"But you were enslaved, you truly had no other choice," Bethany cried, unable to countenance what he was saying.

"I was enslaved by pirates and you by poverty, both very real and degrading forms of slavery."

"But I still had a choice!"

"And where exactly was your choice, Bethany?" he gently inquired. "Had you not removed Bliss from the rookery in which your poverty forced you to live, she would likely be in prison for theft by now, or perhaps dead. Even Bliss admits as much. The brat is many things, some of them admittedly quite exasperating, but she is no fool. She knew the fate of the members in the pickpocket ring she had joined and understood that there would be no happy ending for her in her life of crime. Yet she continued, and nothing you could have said or done, short of removing her from that environment, would have made her stop. And do you know why?"

Bethany mutely shook her head.

"It is because she felt an obligation to help you scrape together a living, and picking pockets was the only way she knew how to do that. She has discussed the matter with me on several occasions. She also confided that she had intended to continue down that sorry path until either Gideon returned from India and rescued you, or your situation, by some miracle, improved. And you know how stubborn our dear Bliss is when she takes it into her head to do something. So you see? You truly did not have a choice, not if you wished to save your sister. I might also add that what you did took great courage. Indeed, I can only hope that I would have the strength to make such a selfless sacrifice were I to ever find myself in a situation that required me to do so."

Bethany shook her head, though in truth she was beginning to crumble beneath his persuasive arguments. Her weak voice reflecting her waning resistance, she said, "Nonetheless, I still would not make you a suitable wife."

He made an exasperated noise. "If it is a matter of our difference in stations, then please let me assure you that the disparity is not so very great that it cannot be overcome. As I recall, the Harwood line springs from the ancient union of a knight and a baron's daughter, which I consider to be a very respectable origin indeed. And then there are your parents. I believe that your mother was once a governess and your father a curate?"

Bethany nodded, her heart swelling with pride as she remembered her parents. In her mind they had been the very best sort of people; stellar examples for anyone to follow.

Christian nodded in return. "Both governesses and curates are required to have breeding and learning, which makes them respectable, as well."

Again, Bethany could not dispute what he said.

"As for you, my love," he continued, "it is clear from your ladylike manners and cultured ways that you have enjoyed the benefit of your parents' tutelage. Indeed, I would venture to guess that you are far better educated than most of the chits in the *ton*. Let us also not forgot that in the eyes of the world you are the widow of a wealthy sea captain. Again, not a lowly position by any measure."

"But most certainly not what anyone would call the perfect match for a future duke," Bethany pointed out.

"Perhaps not, but it also would not be so very unsuitable that it would do more than raise a few eyebrows. I do not doubt that once everyone saw you they would know exactly why I married you and agree that I had done very well for myself."

"But if I were to go into society with you, it is very possible that we would meet the father of my baby. And if he decided to expose me—" Bethany finished the sentence with a head shake, panic welling up inside her at the mere thought.

Christian looped his arm around her and pulled her against him, his hand urging her head to rest against his shoulder so he could stroke her hair. Bethany melted against him, instantly soothed by his gentle caress. "Then I will tell the world that he is a liar, as will Julia and Gideon and all our friends," Christian murmured, pausing at her temple to coil one of the curls resting there around his finger. "With such powerful allies you are certain to be viewed as an innocent victim of slander, and the man voicing it will most probably be cast from the *ton* for his ungallant behavior. However, I doubt he will dare to say a word against you. To admit to taking advantage of a decent woman's misfortune as he did and then tossing her into the street to starve when she conceived his child would serve only to expose him for the bastard he is. So see, you needn't worry on that score."

"Yes." She more sighed than said the word in her contentment at being in his arms. She did see his point. How could she not when he and Julia, both people she respected and admired, had said the very same thing in regard to the matter?

"Well, then?" he inquired.

She lifted her now heavy head from his shoulder to frown at him in query. "Well, what?"

"Will you marry me, goose?"

Bethany returned his expectant gaze for several beats, then sighed. There was one last reason why she should not wed him, one that she had hoped not to have to utter, the one that could very well change his mind about her. Closing her eyes so that she would not have to see his face as she stated it, she said in a hoarse whisper, "There were complications when my baby was born, Christian, and the doctors Gideon hired all agreed that I would never be able to have another child. As a duke you will naturally need an heir."

There was a long pause, during which Bethany's heart seemed to shatter into a million pieces. Then Christian said, "I would be lying if I said that I am not disappointed, for I truly would have loved to have a daughter just like you to spoil. But like everything else, it does not matter. Simply having you by my side shall be enough."

"But I could not bear knowing that a man as wonderful as you would never be able to pass down a part of himself for future generations to adore," Bethany exclaimed, genuinely stricken by the notion.

"And I cannot live without you by my side." Christian dipped his head and dropped a brief kiss on her mouth, lingering a scant inch from her lips as he whispered, "I love you, Bethany. Say that you will at least consider my suit."

Emotionally drained and breathless from his nearness, Bethany surrendered to her heart. "I will consider your suit, Christian."

Chapter 11

Fielding paused in devouring his third helping of baked apple pudding to gape at Christian as if he had just sprouted a particularly astonishing second head. "Your mystery lady wishes to found a charity school?" he ejected on a rising note of bewilderment.

Christian smiled faintly at his friend's stupefied expression. Fielding, he had learned, harbored the misguided notion that women served only one purpose in life, and that purpose was to serve men. That a female might actually have a mind of her own and wish to use it for something other than pondering ways to please men was an utterly foreign concept to him. Nodding to approve the bottle of port the White's wine steward was presenting for his inspection, Christian replied, "It shall rather resemble one, yes. However, unlike most charity schools, it will be open to females of all ages and stations, not just the young girls society has judged worthy of help. And it will teach more than just the domestic skills required for them to gain employment."

That last served to again halt Fielding's systematic food shoveling, this time with his pudding-laden spoon poised halfway to his biscuit speckled lips. His forehead alternately scrunching and smoothing in the manner that always signaled an overtaxation of his brain, he ejected, "But what the devil more could a female possibly need to know?"

"Anything and everything," Christian returned, wondering, not for the first time, if Fielding had always been such a numbskull in matters pertaining to the fairer sex. "Like men, women, too, benefit from knowledge, and that knowledge allows them to enjoy a much fuller and more satisfying life than they would otherwise have."

"Anything and everything?" the numbskull echoed, clearly missing the point of Christian's speech. "Ridiculous!" He more snorted than uttered the word. "Everyone knows that it is as useless to teach a gutter blowse as it is to train a rabid dog. Neither has the wits to learn, and both are inclined to bite you for trying."

Though Fielding's bigoted comment chafed at his sense of justice, Christian let it pass without protest, aware that to challenge it would be a waste of breath. Like all the aristocratic men in his acquaintance, Fielding believed that he was in every way superior to the rest of humankind and no amount of argument was likely to change his opinion. Hoping to God that he had never been so small-minded, though he suspected from the sudden and sickening twist in his gut that he most probably had, he pointed out in as even a voice as he could manage, "I did not say that my lady plans to teach her students everything. Such a thing would indeed be impossible, not to mention impractical, given the purpose of her school." He shook his head once, firmly. "I was merely expressing my belief that a woman's sex in no way precludes her need for education."

"Perhaps. However, you did say that your lady intends to teach more than just domestic skills," Illingsworth interjected. "No doubt I speak for the entire table when I confess a curiosity to know what else she deems important for such females to know." Having dined only on dry toast and poached turbot, a Spartan regimen he had adopted upon his tailor's horrifying discovery that his waistline had expanded a quarter inch, he had spent the bulk of the discourse eyeing Fielding's pudding in much the same manner most men eyed a woman they coveted.

Though Christian's opinion of Illingsworth's fanatical vanity generally hovered somewhere between amusement and incredulity, he had been starved as punishment enough times during his enslavement that he could not help pitying the man's hunger, even if it was self-inflicted. Therefore, his voice, which had taken on a brusque edge during his exasperating exchange with Fielding, gentled as he answered, "The teachings to which I refer are the kind that require neither books nor the skill to read for one to learn them. They are what you might call, ur—" Christian paused to search for the term that best described the philosophy of the plan Bethany had explained to him, finally settling on, "life lessons."

"Life lessons?" Chafford repeated. He looked up from the enameled snuffbox he was toying with to shoot Christian a wry look. "The only life lessons I can think of that such a female would need to know are the ones my father had me tutored in on my fourteenth birthday, and I wager that those particular ones shan't be included in your lady's curriculum." The lessons to which he referred were the ones taught to him by the whore his father had engaged to initiate him into the joys of manhood. Since he was rather fond of recounting the tale whenever he was in his cups, a state he managed to be in at least three nights a week, his circle had been privy to every colorful detail of the episode more times than they could count.

Fielding brayed his appreciation of Chafford's bon mot, while Illingsworth favored it with a snort. Avondale, who had been quietly sampling the port Christian had provided for the group's latest round, now and again nodding at the other men's comments, smiled faintly and shook his head.

Tamping down his impatience with Chafford's buffoonery, something he found he was often forced to do while in the man's company, Christian followed Avondale's example, shaking his head with a taut smile as he countered, "They most assuredly will not, Chaffy." Another head shake. "The sort of life lessons my lady proposes to teach are far different from the ones to which you refer and much more fundamental to the success of the women's futures."

"And what, pray tell, can bring a woman more success than knowing how to romp between the sheets?" Chafford archly inquired.

"Knowing that she need not romp to be a success," Christian retorted, his tone again growing brusque.

"How the devil does your mystery lady propose to teach them that?" This listlessly drawled query was from Illingsworth, whose longing gaze had yet to waver from Fielding's rapidly disappearing pudding.

Christian nodded at the question, viewing it as the perfect opportunity to nudge the conversation down a more edifying path than the one Chafford currently had it traveling on. Seizing the moment for all it was worth, he replied, "By showing them that there is a world beyond the harsh one from which most of the women will have come; a civilized world where comfort and contentment can be earned through education and industry. It is my lady's belief that her students will be far more eager to learn a trade once they see the rewards to be reaped from diligence. Thus, instead of expecting them to dwell in the crude lodgings most charitable institutions provide for their charges, she will furnish hers with the comfortable sort of quarters in which they will live when they go into service. Quarters that, I might add, will doubtlessly be far more luxurious than most will have ever experienced before. Furthermore, she intends to ensure the continuation of their agreeable new lives by aiding them in finding posts in London's finest homes and shops."

Illingsworth had completely abandoned his worship of Fielding's dessert during Christian's dialogue to fix Christian with an incredulous stare. "Yah gads, man!" he boomed, unmindful of the attention his outburst was drawing. "Your mystery lady will have every grubber and scab in London looking to leech off her charity once word of her cozy establishment is put about the streets."

Chafford, who had indulged in a pinch of fashionable Spanish snuff at the beginning of Christian's speech, sneezed twice, sending his ever wayward spectacles slithering down his nose. Pushing them back up again with a sniffle, he exclaimed, "You have stolen the words from my mouth, Illingsworth." Transferring his watery-eyed attention to Christian, he lectured between sniffles, "If what you say is true, Northwick, it is clear that your mystery lady has not considered the nature of the class she wishes to help. After all, everyone knows that the poor are, for the most part, a shiftless lot who have brought their poverty upon themselves through their sloth. In view of that commonly acknowledged fact, it strikes me as rather naive of your lady to believe that her females will trouble themselves with learning a trade once they have wormed their way into a snug place at her school."

Illingsworth nodded. "Now it is you who are stealing my words, Chaffy, for I was about to say that our mystery lady will no doubt find her students very quick in making themselves comfortable and exceedingly slow in learning their lessons."

"And why the devil should they bother to learn when the same degree of comfort they would earn in service will be free for the taking at the school?" This gem of reasoning was contributed by Fielding, presented with his mouth full of pudding.

Christian waited until Chafford had finished blowing his snuff-irritated nose to respond, not wishing to have to shout over the explosive noise he was making. "Ah, but you all misunderstand her plan. The places at her school will not be free for the taking. Her students must earn them by performing their lessons for the good of the entire household." When the other men merely stared at him like he had lobsters crawling from his ears, he illustrated his point by saying, "The students who are learning to be cooks will be charged with providing the household meals, while those wishing to become seamstresses will be required to stitch the clothing that each woman will receive when she begins her new life at the end of her instruction. The future maids will, of course, tend to chores such as cleaning and ironing, with the delegation of their tasks being determined by the sort of maid each is training to become. And the would-be nursery maids will care for the young children some of the women shall undoubtedly have with them. In short, the lessons will be taught through the women working at whatever post each hopes to one day acquire, and each woman's work will benefit both herself and the others. If a woman is unwilling to do her part, she will be turned out."

"Which will make your mystery lady's establishment akin to a workhouse." Fielding again. This time his words were accompanied by the sound of silver grating against china as he noisily scraped the remains of his dessert from his plate. Now lifting his sweet-crusted spoon to his mouth to polish off the last sticky morsels, he added between licks, "Very clever thinking for a female. The mere suggestion of work is bound to prompt the vast majority of the great unwashed to cut a wide swathe around the place."

"My lady's school can hardly be compared to a workhouse, in that the women will be the sole beneficiaries of their labors. Moreover, those labors will serve to win them a bright new future, something that cannot be said for a workhouse," Christian pointed out, taking exception to Fielding's analogy. Workhouses were places of misery and hopelessness, while Bethany's establishment would be the exact opposite.

"You are correct, Northwick, just as you are correct in believing that your mystery lady's plan has merit," Avondale said, finally deigning to join the discussion. "A female who is willing to work and learn in the manner your lady proposes will most certainly be in earnest about improving her lot, and shall thus make a stellar servant. I, for one, will be happy to offer any posts I might have open in my household to her students."

"As will I," Chafford chimed in with another snuff-induced sniffle.

"I daresay that we shall all be glad to help in any way we can," Illingsworth concluded. "However, in order for us to do so, we will need to know where and to whom to send our offerings, which will, of course, necessitate that you reveal your mystery lady's identity to us." Christian didn't miss the sly look he shot Fielding and Chafford as he uttered that last, or the way they smirked in response.

Ever since Christian had declared his intention to court Bethany, whom he continued to refrain from naming out of respect for her wish for privacy, Chafford, Fielding, and Illingsworth's preferred pastime during their circle's frequent and lengthy White's dinners had shifted from regaling him with details of his past to quizzing him about his lady love and guessing at her identity. That they had yet to do so could only be attributed to their ignorance of the fact that Gideon Harwood had a beautiful and supposedly widowed sister who had recently come to town.

Determined to foster their ignorance for as long as possible, Christian shrugged and picked up his glass of port, making a show of examining its color as he replied, "Considering the difficulty my lady is experiencing in finding an appropriate place for her school, there is a good chance that we will be wed by the time her first students are ready to be placed. Therefore, you may direct your offerings to the Marchioness of Northwick at whatever address she selects for our London residence."

"That is assuming she accepts you," Chafford reminded him with one of his toothy, lipless grins. The fact that Christian, who currently reigned as London's most desirable bachelor, should have such trouble persuading a woman to marry him amused their circle to no end.

"Right you are, Chaffy. Our mystery lady isn't exactly jumping at the chance to be Northwick's bride," Illingsworth chimed in, joining his friend in his good-natured twitting. He shook his head, emitting a noise that was halfway between a cluck and a chuckle. "I must confess that I never thought to see the day that a female would be reluctant to grant Northwick anything, much less her favor."

Christian had to stifle his urge to grin at that last. Though he wasn't about to share the fact with his present company, Bethany had made it more than clear that she favored him. Indeed, judging from the passion in the kisses he had stolen from her in the two weeks since he'd declared himself, each one more heated than the last, it was obvious that she desired him every bit as much as he did her.

Fielding made a dismissive hand motion in response to Illingsworth's comment. "I, for one, have no doubt whatsoever that she will accept him in the end. Indeed, I have even placed a sizable wager in the betting book to that effect. It is my guess that our widow is dangling him along in order to make him promise her a particularly large allowance after they are wed, or some such foolishness." He shrugged. "Women play those sorts of silly games, you know."

Christian swallowed the port he had been sampling, gratified to find it every bit as excellent as he had somehow known it would be. With its velvety richness lingering pleasurably on his tongue, he retorted, "I can assure you that her reluctance has nothing to do with games and everything to do with my past reputation." It was true. . . . in a manner of speaking.

Chafford visibly stiffened at his response, his fair skin flushing and his spectacles again slipping down his nose as he more roared than uttered, "Reputations be damned! Where the devil has your lady been keeping herself that she expects you to be a saint? You are a man, after all, and everyone knows that men will be men and a part of being a man is sowing wild oats. Bloody hell! It is a man's right to do so." He pounded the table several times for emphasis. "And by gum, any female who takes him to task for doing what comes naturally is a scold and is thus to be avoided at all costs!" Several men at nearby tables nodded and murmured, "Hear, hear!" in response to his impassioned diatribe.

Having witnessed a number of similar impromptu speeches from Chafford and aware that they signaled his descent into drunkenness, Christian remained unperturbed in the face of his friend's agitation, calmly savoring his port as he countered, "I did not mean to imply that my lady is a scold or that her reluctance is in any way intended to be a rebuke for my past sins." He shook his head. "She is merely exercising her *woman's* right to take her time in considering all that having me for a husband will entail and to determine whether or not the good outweighs the bad, which in my opinion is a very sensible thing to do. Perhaps if more women paused to examine the character of the men proposing to them before accepting their offers, there would be more happily wed couples in the *ton.*"

Avondale laughed a low, hoarse laugh crackling with sardonic glee. "Very good, Northwick. Point granted."

Point granted. A vague memory struggled through the shadowy mists of Christian's mind at the sound of the words, only to retreat, like it always did, before he could grasp it. This time, however, he seemed to hear an echo of the laugh Avondale had just emitted and glimpsed a flash of gleaming steel.

Apparently his bemusement showed on his face, because Avondale grinned and said, "Another lurking memory, Northwick?"

Christian nodded and explained what he had just experienced.

"No doubt you were remembering one of your drunken fencing matches with Avondale," Illingsworth interjected. "You used to have a friendly dispute over who was the superior swordsman and would sometimes attempt to settle the matter when you were in your cups."

Fielding made another dismissive motion, this one rather impatient. "I am sure you are correct, Illingsworth, but enough about that. I want to discuss Northwick's mystery lady."

"Ah, yes, Northwick's mystery lady," Avondale murmured. Pausing to sip from his glass, he went on to say, "From what you have told us this evening, it would appear that your lady is preoccupied with her school, almost single-mindedly so. You say she is having difficulty in finding a place for it?"

Christian nodded. "One that meets her specifications, yes."

Avondale nodded back. "Well, then, there you have it. What we have been viewing as reluctance might not be reluctance at all. It could be that she is simply too absorbed with her problem to appreciate your wooing. Now if you were to find a place for her . . ." He completed his sentence with a meaningful lift of his eyebrows.

"If you find her a place, her mind will be free for more important matters, like your courtship," Chafford inserted. He chortled, another thing he was prone to do when in his cups. "No doubt she will be so grateful that she will fall into your arms, sighing her acceptance of your proposal. After all, nothing makes a woman forget a man's sins quicker than when he treats her to a gallant act."

Fielding, who was guzzling his port with the same gastronomical glee he had shown for his pudding, nodded and added, "Finding her a place will also make you appear to have an interest in her project, which can only help to further your cause with her."

"I am interested in it, very much so, and I intend to do everything in my power to help her make it a success," Christian rushed to clarify.

Avondale chuckled. "All the better, Northwick. I have always believed that a man and woman should share at least one interest outside the mundane concerns of home and hearth if they are to maintain an agreeable marriage."

"Well, then, it seems to me that there is only one thing to be done about this matter, and that is for us to help Northwick find his lady a place for her school." This was from Illingsworth, whose gaze longingly followed the plump tart a passing footman carried on his tray.

Chafford nodded. "My thought exactly, Illingsworth. Now let us think."

The men fell into a companionable silence then, with Christian, Avondale, and Illingsworth enjoying their port while Chafford helped himself to another pinch of snuff and Fielding signaled for a footman to bring him yet another helping of baked apple pudding.

At length Chafford snapped his fingers. "Now, why the devil did I not think of this before? How about the hospital Lady Newland purchased when her youngest son decided to become a doctor? Since the cub has abandoned that ambition in favor of being a wastrel, I should guess that her ladyship would be more than happy to sell the property. With your eye for architecture, Northwick, you could renovate the building to meet with whatever particulars your lady has set forth."

"Where is it located?" Christian inquired, his interest genuinely piqued.

"Fi-i-inchley—*ah-ahchoo*!" Chafford more gasped than uttered his response as he was assaulted by a belated response to his most recent foray into his snuffbox.

"Finchley?" Christian frowned and shook his head. "I am afraid that I either do not remember Finchley or am unfamiliar with it. Where exactly is it?"

Chafford shot him a contrite look over the handkerchief he now pressed to his nose. "Sorry. It seems so like old times having you about that I often forget your memory problem."

Christian made a dismissive hand motion. "It is hardly necessary to apologize for being at ease in my company. I am quite glad you are. Now, about Finchley?"

"It is north of the city, about an hour's drive in fine weather," Avondale supplied.

"An hour?" Christian shook his head regretfully. "No, I am afraid that that will never do. It was a good thought, Chaffy, and I thank you for presenting it, but Finchley is too far away given my lady's desire to oversee her project on a daily basis. It is also too removed from the women she wishes to aid."

"Perhaps if you tell us your lady's requirements, we will be better able to accommodate her needs," the ever sensible Avondale suggested. Having finished his port, he was signaling to a nearby footman to refresh his glass.

As the servant rushed to do his bidding, Christian replied, "The building must be large enough to comfortably house at least two dozen students, and should, naturally, be structurally sound. She would also prefer that it have a number of rooms that can serve as bedchambers. Since she wishes to duplicate the conditions in which her students can look forward to living when they are in service, she intends to board them two to a room rather than all together in a large ward, as is the usual arrangement in charity institutions. Of course, walls can be erected to divide large spaces if necessary, so that particular requirement should be simple enough to fulfill. Aside from that," he shrugged, "her only other specification is that the building be located in or near a rookery."

That last brought his company up short, as he had suspected it would do, freezing them amid their various actions to gape at him as if he had taken a total leave of his senses.

"A rookery?" Chafford finally chocked out, being the first to recover his wits. "Good God, man. The rookeries are hardly a place for anyone to be, much less a gently reared female."

"My thought exactly, Chaffy," Illingsworth said, to

which Fielding and Avondale soberly nodded their agreement.

Christian quickly explained Bethany's reasoning to his companions, who admitted to seeing its logic but nonetheless remained critical. Not exactly thrilled with that part of her plan himself, he finished by confessing, "I must say that I, too, find the notion of my lady spending so much time in such a place troubling to the extreme, which is why I would like to propose that we find a location that borders a rookery rather than actually being in one. That way she will not be required to travel through or even enter the foul area to do her good work, and yet it will still be accessible to the women in need of her help." His words as he said that last was accompanied by the tolling of the long case clock in the hall.

"Seven o'clock already? My, my, how time flies when one is engaged in stimulating conversation," Fielding murmured, studying his latest serving of dessert, which a footman had just set before him. "I do believe that the stroke of seven is your usual cue to depart for Angelo's on Wednesdays, Northwick, though why you choose to abandon our dinners every week in favor of practicing your fencing with Winnie, I shall never understand."

"What I have an even harder time understanding is why Winnie chooses to squire Miss Ridgeway to those deathly dull Wednesday afternoon lectures she favors rather than joining us here for a pleasant supper before your weekly game of parry and thrust," Chafford interjected with a sniff. "Then again, I fail to see what he finds so very captivating about Miss Ridgeway. She has no figure to speak of, her face is decidedly unremarkable, and she lacks anything that could possibly pass for wit or charm."

Illingsworth nodded. "I, too, am having a devil of a time understanding where the attraction lies. Perhaps if Winnie were under the hatches and in need of her rich dowry . . . but no." He sighed and shook his head. "As the Marquess of Northwick, he was far wealthier than the Ridgeway family could ever hope to be. And we all know that his income has not been so drastically reduced by his brother's return that he must wed a fortune to maintain his elegant way of life."

Avondale emitted another of his evocative laughs. "I daresay it is instances such as this that led the ancient philosophers to declare love one of life's greatest mysteries. And if such superior minds could not make sense of the phenomenon, then it is highly unlikely that we shall be able to do so, either. In view of that fact, the only sensible thing to do is to accept that Winnie loves Miss Ridgeway and acknowledge that we most probably will never understand why."

"You think he actually *loves* that tedious baggage?" This was from Fielding, who couldn't have looked or sounded more aghast.

Avondale nodded. "I do. Which leaves the question of whether Miss Ridgeway cares enough for our Winnie to accept him without the grand title she anticipated gaining when she first worked her wiles to hook him."

"When one considers that she would only receive titled suitors last season, I would guess not," Chafford said. He shook his head, clucking like a harried hen. "Poor, poor Winnie. He shall no doubt find whatever dubious privileges he enjoys as Miss Ridgeway's favored companion rudely revoked once the season begins and the chit has had the opportunity to snare a title to replace him."

Christian drained the last of his port in preparation to depart, all too aware that what Chafford said was true. From what he had heard about Miss Ridgeway, which was plenty given the lack of new gossip to buzz about in London, it was clear that she'd indeed been out to trap a title when she had entered the marriage mart last season. To be sure, according to the accounts floating about the *ton,* she had been relentless in her quest to win Godwin's heart and had employed every feminine trick known to womankind to bait her tender trap. But now, well, now that Godwin had been demoted back to second son, her once warm demeanor toward him had cooled to frigid indifference, and Christian had seen for himself the ill grace with which she now suffered his attentions. As for Godwin . . .

Christian pushed his chair from the table and rose to his feet, heaving an inward sigh at his brother's plight. When Avondale said that Godwin loved Miss Ridgeway, he had vastly underestimated the fervor of Godwin's feeling. Godwin didn't merely love Miss Ridgeway; he worshiped and adored her. So much so that he doggedly continued to woo her, despite the fact that the scheming little witch had made it more than clear that she no longer favored him or his suit. Caring for his brother as he did, he naturally found Godwin's desperate attempts at courtship painful to watch, especially knowing as he did that those attempts were doomed to failure and that Godwin would suffer a heartbreak from which he would not soon recover.

He also could not help feeling somewhat responsible for his brother's predicament. After all, if he had not turned up alive, Godwin would still be Lord Northwick and Miss Ridgeway would still be eager to wed him. Not, of course, that she deserved Godwin; she most assuredly did not. And, yes, in the end Godwin was bound to be better off for having escaped her greedy clutches. . . .

He only hoped he would be able to convince Godwin of that fact when his romance finally ended, and that doing so would bring him a small measure of comfort.

And if he failed on both counts?

Then he would pray that his brother's hurt didn't sour into bitter resentment over what his return had cost him.

Chapter 12

Having somehow managed to bid his circle a cordial farewell during his ruminations, Christian now stood in the foyer, where he retrieved his greatcoat from White's ever attentive majordomo. After donning the garment, which was lined with marten skins and fashioned to fall almost to his ankles so as to better shield him from the bitter English winter, Christian strode to the door, pausing just inside to put on his leather gloves and tall beaver hat. Bracing himself for the shock of the cold outside, he stepped from White's toasty foyer into the frigid night beyond.

Though he had often been cold in India, and wretchedly so, this was a cold unlike any he could ever recall suffering before. It was a damp, hostile cold that was almost paralyzing in its intensity; the kind of cold that numbed one's flesh and turned his blood to ice, seeping so deeply into a person's bones that there were times when Christian could have sworn that his marrow was freezing. And no matter how many or how weighty the garments he donned in an effort to ward it off, that damn cold never failed to cut straight through them and chill him to the core the instant he ventured outdoors.

Looking around him as he descended the four front steps, Christian noted, not for the first time, that the rest of London's population seemed unaffected by the frigid weather. Indeed, judging from the crush of people thronging the walkways, many of whom stood conversing in gay, laughing groups while others leisurely perused the goods displayed in the brightly lit shop windows, one would have thought that it was late May and that tonight was a warm spring night. Then again, St. James Street was always like this, or so it seemed.

A mecca of masculine delights, where White's, Brook's, and Boodle's stood in genteel testament to the elegance of the men who frequented them, Christian had found that St. James Street teemed with excitement no matter what time of day or night he chose to visit it, lending it a carnival air that never failed to remind him of an Indian bazaar. Indeed, like the bazaars, St. James Street attracted a colorful mix of the city's denizens, both high and low, with every imaginable race and culture represented. Thus aristocrats out for an evening of clubbing rubbed elbows with bustling on-duty servants and sauntering off-duty laborers, while street hawkers crying their wares jostled past beggars whining for alms, and pickpockets preyed upon anyone foolish enough to become caught up in the wonder of it all.

Now threading his way through the seething crush, weaving around a trio of wildly gesticulating Russian sightseers here and dodging a pair of tussling refuse men there, Christian could not have been more at ease. It all seemed so familiar, so very comfortable and right. It had felt that way from the instant Godwin had first brought him to this street to buy hats at Lock's and from Harry and David Rotely Harris's exclusive establishment scented waters, which his brother had insisted he must have if he were ever to be counted as a pink of the pinks. . . . a term he seemed to recall denoted an epitome of fashionable manhood. Christian smiled at the memory of that day as he paused to press several coins into a blind girl's rag-wrapped hand. It had been the day his brother had taken him on what had turned out to be the first of their many expeditions to refurbish his "rustic wardrobe," as his mother had delicately taken to referring to his Liverpool-tailored garments.

Though Christian had dreaded that initial excursion, aware that his appearance in public would put him at the mercy of the *ton*'s wagging tongues, Godwin had thoughtfully arranged to visit the most fashionable shops at what Christian had soon discovered to be an unfashionably early hour, thus ensuring that they avoided the hordes of aristocratic shoppers he had since learned crowded those places on any given afternoon. Oh, true, they hadn't managed to avoid the *ton* completely. However, in the rare instances that they had encountered *ton* members, Godwin had engaged them so thoroughly with tidbits of gossip and in answering queries about themselves that they hadn't had the chance to bring the conversation around to Christian before Godwin begged a prior engagement and whisked Christian off.

In the end Godwin, who had been a virtual stranger to him when they had first set out, had proved to be such jolly company that Christian had enjoyed the day immensely. Better yet, those hours together had forged the foundation for what the brothers had since built into a steadfast friendship. So steadfast, in fact, that a day had yet to pass since their first outing that they did not meet for at least an hour to share their latest news. Though Godwin presently kept quarters in an elegant house on Bruton Street, he had promised to take up residence at their circle's new Bachelor Barrack near Berkeley Square the instant Christian did so, which was something Christian hoped to do soon. . . . and the sooner the better.

Christian sighed. To say that his parents were overprotective of him would be to vastly understate his situation at home. The truth of the matter was that they were smothering him with their fussing and fawning, forcing so much attention on him that he was ready to run mad, if only to gain the comparable peace he was bound to find at a madhouse. And he was not exaggerating the matter in the least.

To be sure, he could not so much as set foot outside the house without his father grilling him on the specifics of where he had been, whom he had seen, and what he had done. . . . that is, when he actually managed to slip out without one or the other of his parents in tow to serve as his nursemaid. And then there was his mother's endless clucking over his health. Why, one would have thought that he was an invalid from the number of physicians she insisted examine him during any given week, despite both his and the doctors' repeated reassurances that he was in prime twig. Oh, and he must not forget her medicinal concoctions. . . . as if such a thing would be humanly possible.

His stomach churned at the mere thought of those nasty brews. Not a morning passed that his mother didn't try to pour some foul-tasting tonic down his throat, with evenings reserved for the plying of the sickeningly sweet caudles she insisted on brewing herself in the stillroom. Adding insult to her assault on his stomach and tongue was the way she constantly monitored his every bodily function, quizzing him morning, noon, and night on everything from what he ate to the number of times he visited the water closet. It was simply much too much!

Christian heaved another sigh in his frustration, this one laced with regret. Having grown to genuinely love his parents, he might have been willing to suffer their intrusions into his life a while longer had they been satisfied to limit those intrusions to matters pertaining to his well-being and his daily doings. Unfortunately, his mother had decided that Famous Helene would make him the perfect bride, and she had taken to tossing the girl in his path at every turn. Talk about being driven mad!

When his mother wasn't chattering about the chit, going on and on for what seemed like hours about Helene's incomparable beauty and boundless talents, she was manipulating him into accompanying her to this affair or that where the Famed One and her harridan of a mother were certain to be in attendance. And as if that in itself weren't quite enough to ruin his day, the two mothers always contrived to leave him alone with Helene, someplace private, of course, clearly convinced that he would fall victim to her charms were he given ample opportunity to sample them.

Christian could not help grimacing at the thought of Helene's so-called charms. While the chit was indeed every bit as fetching to look at as the myriad poems, songs, and toasts circulating town proclaimed her to be, she was also annoying, demanding, conceited, and boring to the point of being painful to endure. Worse yet, she clearly fancied herself in love with him and never missed an opportunity to try to lure him into kissing her.

In short, it was a difficult situation that grew stickier with every passing day. And the only way he could see to extract himself from it was to steer clear of his mother's matchmaking machinations, a feat he was beginning to realize could only be accomplished by moving from his parents' home. But accomplish it he must, and not just for his own sake. As a gentleman, it was his duty to consider the well-being of everyone involved, whether or not they wanted his consideration, or would even appreciate it. Take Helene, for example.

Though he doubted if the chit would view his defection as an act of gallantry, the truth of the matter was that it would be far kinder, and, yes, more gallant, to let her down now, while she could escape with her pride intact, rather than allow her to continue to humiliate herself by fishing for a proposal that would never come. The same held true for their mothers. It was only right that he dash their hopes while they could still be gracefully withdrawn. Which brought him around to Bethany. While it was true that she wasn't precisely involved in this, she was nonetheless in danger of being hurt, and badly, if he allowed the matchmaking madness to continue unchecked, especially if his and Helene's mothers were to grow impatient with their lack of success and take desperate measures in an attempt to force a match.

His dark mood turned positively grim as he contemplated the most likely nature of those measures. In view of the two women's zealous, not to mention unscrupulous, determination to see their children wed, he would not put it past them to try to trick him into compromising Helene. . . . no doubt with Helene's full knowledge and cooperation. Furthermore, they would probably contrive for him to do it in full view of the *ton* so as to further ensure his entrapment. Though Christian was confident that he would be able to extract himself from any trap the women chose to set, Bethany could not help but to be hurt by the gossip the episode was certain to prompt, and her trust in him was bound to be shaken.

Not about to allow his darling Bethany to suffer in such a manner, Christian further steeled his resolve to do what he must to protect her and their love. If he must take a few desperate measures of his own to do so, namely the one that called for him to leave his parents' home, then so be it. He would leave. The only question to remain was how? What reason could he give for leaving that would allow him to do so without bruising his parents' feelings or, worst yet, causing irreparable damage to their newly forged relationship?

Christian considered his dilemma, nodding once when he hit upon a possible solution. Fielding had once suggested that reliving his past in the Bachelor Barrack might help him to regain his memory. Perhaps if he were to offer that same suggestion to his parents . . .

The more he considered the idea, the better he liked it. It made perfect sense, really, given the fact that the flashes of memory and stirrings of familiarity he had experienced during his initial fortnight at his parents' house had since completely ceased. And since his parents were aware of his current memory stalemate . . .

He nodded again, his lips curling into a satisfied smile. Yes, that was it. Perfect. If he convinced them that the change in surroundings might serve to jog his memory, why, they were certain to give their blessing to the move. As to how he should present his case . . .

Now testing possible speeches in his mind, Christian made his way the rest of the distance up St. James, automatically turning right onto Piccadilly Street. In the weeks since his return to London, he and Godwin had met without fail at Angelo's School of Arms on Old Bond Street every Wednesday evening at eight and most Saturday afternoons at four to engage in a friendly fencing match or two, something his family had informed him they had done since they were boys. Because it felt so very right, not to mention that it provided yet another opportunity for him to perhaps remember, Christian had gladly revived the tradition when his brother had suggested that they do so.

Another tradition his brother had told him about that he had chosen to resurrect, as well, was his practice of briskly walking the short distance from White's to Angelo's on Wednesday nights, something that

Christian had quickly discovered served to stretch and prime his muscles for the rigors of his upcoming exercise. Like he was inclined to do when required to go somewhere he had reportedly frequented before his memory loss, he had refrained from asking directions to Angelo's that first Wednesday night, instead allowing his senses to be his guide. They had ended up guiding him along what Godwin had later confirmed was the exact route he had taken in the past. Though Christian could not honestly claim to have recognized any of the buildings or landmarks along the way, he had experienced an exhilarating sense of familiarity at every sight and sound and turn, with his feet instinctively skirting the uneven places in the pavement and his body unconsciously bracing against the constant buffeting from the crowd.

He was rehearsing for the third time now what he had decided was his best speech, automatically working his way to the curb in preparation to cross the busy Piccadilly Street carriageway when—

Wham!—Someone violently smashed into him, sending him flying forward to—

Splat!—Pitch headlong into the hard cobblestone road, where he—

Thump!—Thump!—Somersaulted across the uneven grade with a force that—

Oww!—Seemed to shatter his ribs and—

Oomph!—Completely robbed him of his breath.

So acutely aware was Christian of the uncontrollable tumbling of his body that he felt as though he were trapped in a slow-moving dream, with each surrealistically protracted flip and roll seeming to be a separate action from the last. When he finally slammed to a stop in the middle of the road, he could only stare in helpless horror at the oncoming traffic, too stunned by the impact of his spill to do more. Leading the charge toward him was a coach speeding at such a reckless pace that it took only a single glance for him to know that the driver would never be able to stop in time to avoid running him down.

As Christian struggled to move, wincing at the pain that knifed through him with every fruitless attempt, pictures of Bethany began to flash through his mind. He froze, gripped by a wrenching sense of loss at the brutal reminder that he might never see her again.

No! his mind screamed. No, he could not die now, not yet. There was so much more he needed to say to Bethany, so much left for them to do. He had not survived the hell of slavery to die like this. Damn it! He would not die, not when he finally had something to live for. He would not surrender to death before he'd had a lifetime of loving Bethany, and even then he did not intend to go without a fight. Strengthened by the power of his love, Christian again willed his body to move. This time he succeeded in flinging himself toward the walkway.

Now he was rolling, his shock-numbed body barely registering pain as the cobblestones stabbed and scraped his flesh with every rotation.

Now he slammed into the curb, striking his head hard as he fell back into the gutter, where he lay sprawled in a broken heap, dazed from the blow to his head. Through the resulting ringing in his ears he could hear the grating scrape of wheels against cobblestones and the high-pitched screams of horses, which sounded as if they were bolting out of control.

As Christian resumed his battle to move, he felt the welcome sensation of hands grasping his arms and legs. In the next instant those hands hauled him from the gutter, narrowly rescuing him from being crushed by the wheels of the coach as they grazed the curb against which he had lain only a split second earlier, after which the vehicle veered wildly toward the center of the road and careened off in the direction of Albemarle Street at breakneck speed.

"Gor! Is 'e kilt then, do ye think?" inquired one of his rescuers in a loud, fearful whisper. Clad in a rough coat with a shabby round hat set at a drunken angle on his grizzled head, the man squatted near Christian's left elbow, nervously rocking back and forth on his heels in a way that moved him in and out of the shadows cast by the dozen or so curious people who had gathered around Christian's prone figure.

Shabby Hat's equally coarse-looking companion, who crouched near Christian's shoulder, emitted a derisive snort. "Naw. O'course 'e ain't kilt, Charly. A dead man don't breathe all 'ard like that if 'e's been kilt."

"Sir? Can you hear me, sir? Are you badly hurt?" This was from another of Christian's saviors, a young man kneeling near his knees. Unlike Shabby Hat and his friend, this man was clearly a person of some consequence; a fact evidenced by his smart evening attire and educated voice.

The shock from his near brush with death now waning, Christian gingerly tested his limbs to ascertain their soundness. Though he felt battered and bruised within an inch of his life, nothing seemed to be broken, at least not at this juncture, so he carefully raised himself up to rest on his elbows. After clearing his throat twice in an effort to find his voice, he was able to croak, "No. I do not think my injuries are of a serious nature. However—"

"What is happening here? Why are these people gathered so near my stoop?" an aristocratic voice from outside the wall of hovering humanity demanded to know.

"There has been an accident, my lord. A gentleman was run down in front of the house. I saw the entire incident from the stoop while I was waiting for your coach to be brought around." This voice, of course, belonged to a servant, a footman, judging from the conversation.

There was a short pause, and then the aristocrat responded in a lowered voice, "The man is a gentleman, you say?"

"Yes, my lord. Perhaps even a nobleman. And I must say that he is most fortunate to be alive." By his self-satisfied tone it was apparent that the servant was pleased to be the bearer of such exciting news. His voice rising with each word in his enthusiasm at the telling, he more crowed than said, "Why, with the way he fell against the curb it will be a miracle if—"

"What will be a miracle is if I do not sack you for leaving an injured gentleman lying on the walkway while you jabber on like a rattlepate," the aristocrat snapped.

"M-m-y lord?" the servant stuttered, obviously taken aback by his master's displeasure.

His master made an impatient noise. "For God's sake, Seever, bring the poor fellow into the house this instant and summon the surgeon. I cannot imagine what you could be thinking to allow a gentleman to lie on the walkway like a drunken beggar."

Thoroughly cowed by his employer's castigation, the servant hurried to do as he was instructed. "Move along, now. Move along. My master and I will tend to the gentleman. There is nothing more for you to see or do, so get along," he called out as he pushed his way through the crowd. With the show now clearly at an end, the spectators parted to let him through. As the group began to dissipate, with some spectators drifting off in whispering parties while others hurried off alone, the wine-and-gold-liveried footman kneeled beside Christian, anxiously inquiring, "Are you able to walk, sir, or should I have a litter brought out to carry you?"

Christian again tested his limbs, this time sitting all the way up as he did so. Again finding them sore but sound, he replied, "I believe I am capable of walking, thank you, if you will be so kind as to assist me in rising."

Babbling something about the housekeeper's gentle touch and excellent brandy, the fair-haired footman slipped his hand beneath Christian's arm to provide the requested aid, patiently half lifting and half bracing him as he slowly rose. Christian had just gained his feet, albeit unsteadily, when he heard a hissing intake of breath and the aristocratic voice expel, "Good heavens! It is Northwick."

Christian glanced up quickly to find himself face-to-face with Lord Denleigh, whose shocked expression he was certain mirrored his own. Unlike Denleigh, however, whose shock no doubt stemmed from the fact that he had just offered aid to his arch nemesis, Christian's came more from the jolt of familiarity he felt at the sight of the other man's face. This was the first time he had viewed it closer than from across the room, and then only for brief instances. The impact of it at this distance was nothing short of startling, though why, Christian could not say.

Perhaps it was the astonishing hue of those eyes. They were not merely blue; they were a pure, impossibly brilliant shade of cerulean without the slightest hint of gray or green to muddy them. Add the stunning contrast of those thick, sooty lashes and the dark, slanting brows that echoed their exotic shape, and those eyes truly were a feature a person would be hard-pressed to forget. Then again, his entire face was distinctive, with its blade-sharp cheekbones, aggressively square jaw, and high-bridged nose. Of course, it could be—

And then it struck him. The most startling thing about that admittedly extraordinary face wasn't its features; it was its unexpected expression. There was no hate in those jewel-like eyes, no telltale tautness in that firm jaw, or even the slightest bitterness twisting those precisely sculpted lips. Lord Denleigh looked almost . . . uncertain.

Feeling uncertain himself, knowing that he must say something to the man he had so recklessly maimed, yet unable to imagine what, Christian steadily returned Lord Denleigh's gaze, praying for the right words to come. It was Denleigh who spoke first. After searching Christian's face for a long moment, he smiled faintly and said in a quiet voice, "I suppose we both knew that this moment would eventually arrive, Northwick. It is odd, but I never expected—"

"Good God, Christian! What happened? You look like you were run down by a refuse wagon," Godwin's alarmed voice abruptly interrupted.

His gaze still locked with Denleigh's, Christian absently replied, "It was a coach, not a refuse wagon."

"The devil you say! Really?" Godwin ejected.

"Really." Far more interested in hearing what Denleigh had to say than in recounting the accident to his brother, Christian tipped his head and raised his eyebrows, signaling for Lord Denleigh to continue.

Denleigh returned his quizzical gaze for several beats, then shrugged one shoulder and looked away.

Before Christian could further pursue the matter, Godwin latched on to his arm and pulled him away from the footman who still braced him on his other side. Spinning him around to face him, thus forcing Christian's gaze away from Denleigh, he exclaimed in a babbling rush, "Jesus, Christian! You could have been killed! Oh, bloody, *bloody* hell! Just look at you!" He made a jerky hand motion that encompassed Christian's entire length. "You are bleeding in several places, and God only knows what sort of injuries are hidden beneath your clothes." Now wedging his shoulder under Christian's arm and with his arm wrapped around Christian's waist to aid him in walking, he finished in an urgent voice, "We must flag down a hackney and get you to a doctor posthaste."

"I am fine, Winnie. My injuries do not amount to more than a few cuts and bruises," Christian protested, glancing back to where Denleigh stood. He was gone. In his place stood the footman who had helped him rise. Disappointed, for he truly did wish to know what Lord Denleigh had been about to say, he sighed and returned his attention to Godwin, who was now going on about a knot that was apparently forming on his forehead.

As he resigned himself to his brother's fussing, wincing as Godwin prodded the knot in question, Christian was suddenly struck by the irregularity of his brother's being there. After all, the lectures he attended usually ran until seven, at which time he was required to drive Miss Ridgeway home and pay his respects to her parents. That generally left him a scant quarter of an hour to make his way to Angelo's and prepare himself for their eight o'clock match. That he should be here now, and on foot no less, was very irregular indeed.

When Christian vocalized his thoughts, Godwin shrugged and replied, "The lecture ended early and Miss Ridgeway's parents were out, so I was not detained by them. And since there was nothing of note happening at Angelo's, I decided to walk out to meet you and accompany you part of the way there. I must say that it was propitious that I should decide to do so. Judging from your appearance, I am not so sure that you would have made it home alone."

"I was hardly alone. Lord Denleigh and his servant, Seever"—Christian paused to nod at the footman, who smiled at the acknowledgement and nodded back—"were graciously aiding me when you arrived. Do not tell me that you did not notice them?"

Godwin recoiled a step, visibly taken aback. "That was Lord Denleigh?" He more gasped than said the words.

Christian opened his mouth to reply, but the ever eager Seever beat him to it. "Yes, sir. That was indeed

Lord Denleigh, my employer. And he has asked me to convey his offer of his coach to take you home." He gestured to the street, where a smart wine-and-gold landau emblazoned with what Christian assumed was the Denleigh family crest seemed to have magically materialized at the curb. So noisy was Piccadilly from the constant traffic that he hadn't heard it pull up.

Not quite certain what to make of the offer, yet not about to decline it, aware that to do so might be regarded as a rejection of what could possibly be a bid for a truce, Christian smiled and replied, "You may tell his lordship that we accept and thank him for his kindness on our behalf."

"We do?" Godwin blurted out, staring at him like he had lost his mind.

"We do," Christian returned firmly.

Godwin continued to gape at him for several more beats, then emitted a short, snorting laugh. "Considering the circumstances and the person making the offer, do you really think that wise, brother?"

Christian frowned. "What are you getting at, Winnie?"

Shooting Seever a wary glance, Godwin tilted his head closer to Christian's and replied in a hushed voice, "If you ask me, it is rather too convenient that you should almost be killed where his lordship could watch from the comfort of his window."

"Are you saying you believe that Denleigh arranged my accident?" Christian hissed back, unable to believe what he was hearing. Unless Denleigh was blessed with a superb talent for acting, he had hardly looked or behaved like a man bent on murder.

Godwin shrugged. "Well, he does have reason to wish you dead, you know."

"As does half of London, at least according to what Chaffy, Illingsworth, and Fielding have told me,"

Christian retorted. He shook his head once, firmly. "No, Winnie. It was an accident—one of a coincidental nature, true, but an accident nonetheless. I was pushed into the street by the bustle of the crowd, something, I might add, that happens every day. Indeed, one cannot open a newspaper without seeing an account of someone being inadvertently shoved into the street and run down."

There was a long pause, then Godwin sighed. "I suppose you could be right, Christian. I most certainly hope that you are."

"I am," Christian retorted with confidence.

Of course he was right.

Chapter 13

"Wherever are you taking me?" Bethany asked for the tenth time in as many minutes, this time edging forward on her seat in an attempt to steal a peek through the gape in the drawn coach curtains.

Christian chuckled and pulled her back against the plush upholstery, his arm curling around her to snuggle her close to his side. "Oh, no, love. No fair peeking," he lightly chided. "I said it is a surprise, and I intend to keep it that way."

"You could at least give me a hint," she retorted with a merry laugh, happily nestling into what was now his familiar embrace, her head automatically finding the place on his shoulder that seemed to have been created to pillow it.

She felt rather than saw him shake his head. "What?" he quipped. "And risk spoiling my surprise? Never!"

"But—"

"But," he interjected in a firm voice, "you will see where we are going when we get there, which will be very soon, I might add, and that is that."

Bethany tipped her head back to look up at him, her heart giddily missing a beat, like it always did when she gazed at his handsome face. The sight of the livid purple-and-yellow bruise marring his forehead made it skip again, this time in terror at how close she had come to losing him five days earlier. He could have died that night in the road—he *had* almost been killed—he had—

Refusing to spoil the playful moment with grim thoughts of the accident, she made a saucy face and bantered, "So very mysterious, my darling."

"So very curious, my sweet," he tenderly bantered back, taking advantage of her upturned face to kiss her.

Bethany sighed her pleasure at the feel of his skilled mouth moving against hers. If ever a man knew how to kiss, it was Christian. His lips—oh! Those wonderful, beautiful lips! The way they claimed and possessed hers, so commanding in their firmness yet worshipful in their gentleness—pure bliss! And when he explored her mouth with his tongue like he was doing now, teasing every ticklish plain and valley, caressing every sensitive nook and cranny—sheer heaven! Then there was how he lightly kneaded her shoulders and neck—

A soft moan escaped her as her bones seemed to melt beneath his magical touch and she sagged against him, her every thought and inhibition dissolving in the liquid heat of their passion.

To her disappointment, the kiss was a brief one and he pulled away before she'd had her fill. . . . if such a thing were even possible. To be sure, how could anyone tire of such marvelous kisses, especially knowing, as she did, that they were a mere promise of the rapture yet to come? And, oh! How she longed to experience that rapture! For all that she adored his kisses, they never failed to leave her body taut and aching with need and her flesh crying out for more. But, of course, Christian was too much of a gentleman to do more than kiss her outside the bonds of marriage, and since she still could not bring herself to agree to wed him . . .

Heaving another sigh, this one in frustration at herself, Bethany laid her head back on his shoulder and tried to content herself with sitting chastely in his embrace. But it was no use. It was impossible for her to be near him like this and not want him to love her. Why, the very scent of him, a heady mélange of spicy soap underscored by the natural musk of his manliness, seduced her almost as much as his kisses did. And then there was the way his body pressed against hers. How could she feel it, so strong and hard and contoured to perfection, and not envision it naked and crushed against her in a carnal embrace?

By now she was fighting to keep her breathing even and to bridle her overwhelming urge to squirm in her wanton urgency. All she had to do was say yes to Christian. Yes, and he would be hers for the taking. Yes, and everything she desired most in life would be hers. *Yes.* Such a small word for the enormous consequences it carried, especially in this instance.

The mere thought of those consequences seemed to turn her blood to ice, effectively freezing her desire. Seized by a sudden chill, she shivered and burrowed deeper into the folds of Christian's greatcoat, desperately seeking the comforting heat of his body through the heavy fabric of their garments.

His arm automatically tightened around her. "Are you cold, sweet?" he murmured against her hair, ending the question with a kiss on the top of her head.

"How could I possibly be cold when I am in your arms?" she returned truthfully, to which he hugged her yet closer and kissed her head again.

Loving him so much that she was certain she would burst from the greatness of the emotion, Bethany turned her head and kissed the side of his neck. For all that Julia and Christian's arguments and reassurances had eased the qualms she'd voiced to them, there remained one last fear she hadn't had the courage to address, a weighty one that only she had the power to put to rest. . . . but only if she could find the strength to do so, which at the moment felt as likely as traveling to the moon. Truth be told, she didn't even know how to begin going about doing so. Perhaps if she could share her fear with Christian or Julia they might be able to advise her . . .

But no. How could she tell Christian that she would not marry him because she feared the humiliation of being vilified by society when they learned the truth about her past? How could she explain to Julia that the support of their family and friends was not enough to make her venture public scorn; that she was so weak and shallow that she could not bear the thought of being cut by strangers on the street and suffering their jeering whispers as she passed? How in the world was she to confess her selfish cowardice to those she loved when she could barely stand to admit it to herself?

As always happened when she did force herself to admit to it, Bethany was shamed to the core of her being. Christian deserved better from her. He deserved from her the same kind of grace and courage he'd displayed in all the difficult things he had been forced to do since his return from India. He deserved to have her stand proudly by his side and show the world that her love for him was strong enough to withstand whatever hardship it chose to heap on her. He deserved someone who would take a chance on their love and sacrifice anything to keep it. In short, he deserved someone much stronger and better than she.

As if sensing her troubled thoughts and wishing to offer her comfort, Christian hugged her again and dropped yet another kiss on the top of her head. Rather than ease her inner turmoil, his loving gesture served to make it worse.

Despite all he had been through, all he had suffered,

painful and degrading experiences that would have either crushed or embittered a lesser man, Christian had somehow managed to remain everything that was good and admirable. He was kind and compassionate, not to mention generous, honorable, and just. And then there was his unfailing thoughtfulness. Why, everything he did was done thoughtfully and with a conscientious consideration for how it might affect others and their feelings. Take this outing, for example.

In deference to her wish to escape society's notice, he had hired a plain black coach, manned by a driver and footmen garbed in nondescript clothing so as to avoid the attention and speculation the crest-emblazoned Moncreiffe vehicles and liveried servants were certain to excite. Furthermore, he had arranged their excursion for an hour when most of their aristocratic neighbors would still be abed. Best of all, he had refused to take no for an answer when he had proposed it.

Then again, how could she have possibly refused him anything? He had been so charming in his exuberance when he had tendered the invitation the day before, his eyes bright and eager and sparkling with boyish excitement. And then there was the grin lurking at the corners of his lips. That endearing little smile had made her suspect that the secret he harbored was a particularly delicious one and had promptly piqued her curiosity to learn what it was. Indeed, so great was her curiosity that she had been able to voice only a single and decidedly weak protest to his suggestion that she venture forth from her Grosvenor Square sanctuary before surrendering to his infectious excitement.

"Julia mentioned that Gideon will be detained in the country for another week or so," Christian commented, breaking their companionable silence. "She said something about the cloth guild having difficulty with their looms?"

Bethany smiled at the mention of her brother and his dedication to his tenants; a fealty she knew to be returned tenfold by his admiring tenants. "I cannot say for certain what the problem is. All I know is that a number of the looms have proved to be unsuited for weaving the delicate new muslins the guild is now producing."

"Well, knowing Gideon's knack for resolving mechanical problems and the weavers' talent for overcoming the more aesthetic obstacles, I daresay that they will have whatever is plaguing them worked out posthaste and that the resulting cloth will be well worth the initial trouble of weaving it. As I recall, their last batch of muslin fetched a tidy sum in London, and it was of a coarser quality than what they are now making." Having aided Gideon in establishing the village cloth guild, Christian was naturally privy to the business details of the endeavor.

"It is their best cloth yet," Bethany declared, her voice ringing with pride in the guild members, all of whom she counted as her friends. "Gideon sent Julia and I several samples to solicit our opinion on the new print patterns and colors, and we both agreed that the guild has quite outdone itself this time. To be sure, every lady in London will be clamoring for a length of it when they see the gowns Julia intends to have made up from it as gifts for her mother and her circle."

"What makes Julia think that garbing those particular women in the cloth will spark a demand for it?" Christian inquired. "It seems to me that it would be displayed to a far greater advantage on someone young and lovely, like you and Julia." He paused to dip down and kiss her forehead. "Then again, your radiance always outshines whatever you wear, so perhaps she is wise not to waste the cloth on you."

Bethany smiled faintly at his compliment. "Julia says that if one wishes to create a rage for something, that something must first be shown to be desirable to the innermost circle of society, since everyone else follows their lead. And according to Julia there is no one of better *ton* or more imitated in fashion right now than her mother and her circle."

"Quite the little slyboots, our Julia," Christian quipped. The affection in his voice was unmistakable. "I must say that Gideon is a very lucky man indeed to have a wife who takes such an interest in his affairs."

"Which is as it should be," Bethany countered. "After all, Julia is Gideon's wife and the mistress of his manor. Besides, the guild members adore her and look forward to her visits to their workrooms."

"Just as our tenants will adore you and look forward to your visits after we are wed," he tossed back. The possibility that she might say no to his proposal seemed to have never crossed his mind. At that moment the coach lurched to a shuddering stop, and there was the sound of footmen's feet pounding against the pavement as they jumped from their perches to hurry about their duties. Lifting a corner of the curtain to peer outside, Christian said, "Excellent. We have arrived. I told you we weren't going far."

Eager to see where they were, Bethany moved forward to look out as well, only to again be drawn back against the seat.

"Not yet, love," Christian murmured.

"But why?" Bethany almost whined the words in her exasperation.

Christian chuckled and kissed the tip of her nose. "Because I wish for you to enjoy the full impact of my surprise, and in order for you to do so you must first step from the coach."

"Well, then?" She lifted her eyebrows and cast the coach door a meaningful look.

He chuckled again. "Patience, love. Your surprise

is not going anywhere." Shaking his head in amusement at her agitated eagerness, he rapped the ceiling three times, something that elicited an unintelligible shout from their driver. He then retrieved a sheaf of rolled-up papers from beneath their seat.

"What is that? Part of my surprise?" Bethany inquired in the same fretful tone as a child anxious for a long-overdue treat.

"Patience," Christian again chided.

Fortunately for Bethany, who felt ready to burst at any moment from her growing impatience, only a small measure of forbearance was required, because several seconds later a footman opened the door.

Again she moved forward and once more Christian stopped her. "Sorry, love. I am afraid that I must insist on exiting the coach first." She opened her mouth to ask why, but he answered her before she could issue the words, having obviously anticipated her question. "Because I wish to see your face when you first glimpse your surprise," he explained. "Here." He handed her her bonnet, which he had pulled from her head and tossed on the opposite seat when he had kissed her upon entering the coach. Eyeing the dainty creation with a jaundiced look, he added, "I doubt if this wisp of fuss and furbelows will provide much protection against the cold outside, but I suppose it is better than nothing, so tie it on tight. Perhaps if you pull your hood up over it you will at least save your ears from freezing solid." With that he picked up his tall beaver hat, which he was required to don outside due to the truncated height of the coach doorway, and exited.

Bethany smiled at Christian's typical male opinion of women's hats, though she did have to admit that her mourning bonnet, with its black ribbons and wreath of black satin flowers, did provide rather flimsy protection against the icy winter weather. Tying the somber confection securely into place, as directed, she lifted the drapey hood of her black velvet cloak and arranged it around her face. Like the cloak itself, the hood was richly lined and trimmed in sable. When she had retrieved her matching muff from where it had somehow become wedged beneath the opposite seat and had tucked her gloved hands inside it, she waited for either Christian or the footman to claim her.

She waited. And waited. And waited. Now sighing, now fidgeting with the wrist strap of her muff, and now tapping her foot in an antsy tattoo. Just when she was certain she would scream if she was forced to wait a second longer, Christian appeared at the door.

"Ready to see your surprise, love?" he inquired. His eyes again danced with boyish glee and that endearing grin had reclaimed his lips.

Instantly forgiving him for making her wait—how could she not when he looked so very charming?—Bethany slipped to the edge of the seat nearest the door and prepared to exit. With one hand lifting her skirts while Christian braced her opposite elbow to aid her in her descent, she ducked her head and stepped from the coach.

Though there was no snow in sight, the dampness from the foggy night before had glazed the pavement with a treacherous sheen of glossy gray ice, upon which the smooth soles of her half boots slipped the instant they touched the ground. Back and forth she teetered, desperately fighting to regain her footing. Then her feet slid out from beneath her and she began to pitch backward.

For what seemed like an eternity Bethany flailed in the air, her heart racing with fear and her mind cringing in dread of what was certain to be a painful, not to mention humiliating, spill. Then Christian's strong arm whipped around her and yanked her body hard against his, the violence of his motion sending her voluminous hood tumbling over her eyes, blinding her to her surroundings. To her everlasting relief, his solid form served to instantly brace her faltering one.

When at last she was steady and her feet were firmly planted on the walkway, Christian lifted the hood from her eyes, inquiring with a ceremonious arm flourish, "Well, what do you think?"

Bethany looked in the direction to which he motioned. They stood before a gate; a dilapidated wooden one that was splintered by age and weathered an ugly mottled gray, with broad double doors that were warped and sagged brokenly from their rusty iron hinges. Judging from the height and width of the gate, through which a sizeable coach could easily pass, and the rutted pebble drive leading from the equally poorly paved street, she guessed that a carriage yard of sorts lay beyond. Glancing first to her right and then her left, trying to determine where she was, she noted that the gate was anchored to twin buildings. Mirror twins, to be exact. Bethany frowned at the sight of them, wondering why anyone would wish to erect one, much less two, buildings of such unattractive design.

Awkwardly proportioned and constructed from what had to be the drabbest dun-colored brick on earth, each building boasted a long-abandoned shop at street level featuring a wide rectangular front window from which the glass panes were either missing or cracked in their battered sashes. Above the shops rose three unadorned stories, their floors marked by two real and one blind window, with the third story crowned by a trio of attic gables beyond which jutted several smoke-blackened chimneys. Like the deteriorating window sashes, the shop doors had once been painted a cheerful green but were now peeling to reveal chipped and faded undercoats in variegated shades of red, blue, and yellow.

As Bethany continued to glance around her, she could not help noticing that the walkway was cracked and broken away in places and littered with rotting refuse, the origin of which she did not dare contemplate. The sight of that refuse instantly awakened her senses to the squalor around her, rousing an awareness of its stomach-turning smell with a force that sent a sickening flood of bile rushing to her throat. She swallowed hard, frantically fighting her rising nausea. That smell . . . dear God! Deliver her from that awful, wretched smell!

Certain that she would vomit if she did not escape it, Bethany closed her eyes and turned her face away, pressing her hand to her nose in an attempt to block out its foul assault. It was a stench she knew too well; one she had desperately hoped to never again smell.

It was the reek of despair, the obscene perfume of poverty, hopelessness, and misery.

Wondering why Christian would bring her to such a place, knowing as he most certainly must that it would dredge up memories she would rather forget, Bethany looked up at him in wounded query.

His expectant smile flattened at the sight of her face and the dancing lights faded from his eyes. "You do not like your surprise." It was a statement, not a question, and he sounded as crushed as she felt.

Not quite sure what to say about his so-called surprise or even what it was supposed to be, she shook her head, gesturing helplessly as she replied, "I am afraid I do not understand it."

For a moment he simply returned her gaze, visibly nonplussed, then his grin slowly reappeared. "Ah, I see. Well, then, with your permission, I shall explain it to you." At her nod he motioned to the nearby footmen, one of whom sprang forward with a key to unlock the gate and throw the heavy bolt, though why anyone would bother to lock and bolt a gate that was clearly ready to tumble down, Bethany could not imagine. When the footmen had wrestled the heavy doors open, Christian ushered her inside. She had been correct in that the gates concealed a carriage yard, a large, rubbish-strewn one she now saw, surrounded by what she immediately identified as an old coaching inn.

Indicating their surroundings with a sweep of his arm, Christian crowed, "Feast your eyes on your new school, milady."

Chapter 14

"M-m-my school?" Bethany echoed in a stunned voice, gaping at him in astonishment.

"If it suits you, love, yes," he replied, wrapping his arm around her waist to hug her against his side. "I believe it meets your requirements in both its size and location."

"Where exactly are we?" she murmured. Suddenly the smell of the place didn't seem so very bad.

"St. Giles. We are close enough to the Church Lane rookery that your prospective students will have easy access to the school, but far enough away that you will not be subjected to the dangers there." Nodding to their surroundings, he asked, "So what do you think? Do you approve?"

Bethany tore her gaze away from his smiling face to glance around her, examining her surrounding with new eyes; ones that saw not only what existed there now but also the possibilities of what it could be. Her mind racing with those possibilities, she moved from the shelter of Christian's arm to slowly walk to the center of the courtyard, where she stood taking in every detail, thrilled by the potential before her.

Standing foursquare around the unkempt courtyard, three sides of the admittedly inelegant brick building featured a double tier of bedchamber galleries set above what she guessed to be the public and service rooms on the east and west sides, with the north gallery spanning the top of a second gate that was reminiscent of the one through which she had just passed. From her vantage point she could see that each bedchamber boasted a heavily sashed window and a stout wooden door, above which was mounted a plaque announcing what she guessed to be each room's designated name. All and all it looked to be a most promising structure to house her school.

Oh, true. It was in a greater state of disrepair than she would have liked. The clumsy timber balustrades surrounding each tier sagged and were broken in places, and many of the bedchamber doors had been pried from their hinges, no doubt by vagrants seeking a dry place to sleep on a wet winter night. And of course the entire building would require extensive cleaning, painting, and, no doubt, many renovations. Nonetheless, the basic structure appeared sound. Indeed, only a few tiles were missing from what she could see of the roof, and the partially enclosed staircase to her left leading up to the bedchambers appeared in good repair. After noting that most of the windowpanes seemed to be miraculously intact, as did all the street-level doors, Bethany wandered through the second gateway to discover another, larger courtyard, this one walled by stables with a third gate that opened into a back street.

As she skirted the long water trough in the center, picturing the courtyard as a neat garden where her students could stroll and study on fine days, and where those aspiring to be cooks in great houses could learn about kitchen gardens, Christian came up behind her and wrapped his arms around her midsection to draw her back against him. Dipping his head to kiss her cheek, he murmured, "So? What is the verdict?"

Utterly taken with what she now considered to be the most marvelous building in the world, Bethany shook her head over and over again, her mind racing with plans and her heart with excitement. "Oh, Christian!" she exclaimed breathlessly, turning in his arms to hug him. "It is wonderful—perfect! However did you come to find it?"

"It belongs to the Earl of Markland. Perhaps you remember him from your Christmas gathering at Critchley?" he replied, punctuating his words with kisses dropped lightly onto her now available lips.

Bethany did not have to think long or hard to remember Lord Markland. How could one forget such a comical old man with his silly child bride and prune-faced daughter, especially when it was he who had restored Christian to his rightful place in life? "Of course I remember him. Had his lordship not recognized you, you would most probably still be at Critchley living a simple, quiet life as Christian English."

He grinned and kissed her yet again. "And I would undoubtedly be happy as a king doing so, since you would be nearby."

She smiled back rather wistfully. "As would I." A soft sigh escaped her at the thought of what she viewed in retrospect as their halcyon days. "I must confess that I sometimes miss those days—not that I am not glad that things have turned out so splendidly for you," she hastened to amend, not wanting him to think that she wasn't pleased by his good fortune. "I could not be happier that you have found your identity and that your rediscovered life is one of such privilege. Why, if anyone deserves to have everything good in life, it is you. To be sure, I can think of no one more suited to be of the nobility—"

He cut her off then, pressing his gloved index finger against her lips to halt what she suddenly realized was her babbling deluge. "I would have been perfectly happy with any life that would allow me to make you my wife, love, and you will marry me, you know." With every word he uttered his face drew nearer to hers.

"Ummm," she intoned, mesmerized by the simmering heat in his eyes. It was compelling, magnetic, irresistibly drawing her to him.

"Ummm? Is that a yes?" he inquired softly. His lips were so close to hers now that they brushed against them as he spoke, teasing and tantalizing them with a promise of passion.

Wanting nothing more than for him to honor that promise, she huskily whispered, "It is just an *ummm*. Make of it what you wish."

He pulled away a fraction to grin down at her, a wickedly seductive grin that sent a delicious tingle of sensual anticipation racing up her spine. "In that instance, I shall take it as a sign that you need further persuasion." With that declaration, he covered her mouth with his and proceeded to persuade her.

Bethany twined her arms around his neck, eagerly urging him on. He had no sooner parted her lips with his tongue to deepen their kiss when they were interrupted by the sound of someone discreetly clearing his throat. Embarrassed to be caught in flagrante delicto, Bethany tried to pull away, but Christian refused to release her, allowing her to move only to his side where he held her with his arm wrapped possessively around her waist. Eyeing the red-faced footman before them with an air of unapologetic nonchalance, Christian quizzed, "Was there something you wished, Guy?"

"A thousand pardons, my lord, but you did say that I was to fetch you the instant Ralph had the buildings unlocked," the flustered servant replied, looking everywhere but at them, clearly wishing to be anywhere else in the world at the moment.

"Indeed I did. Thank you, Guy. We shall be there posthaste." Looking down at Bethany, who was certain her face was as red as poor Guy's, Christian inquired with a smile, "Would you like a tour of your school, love?"

Her school. Oh, how she loved the sound of that! Her pleasure now supplanting her embarrassment, she smiled back. It appeared that her dreams were about to come true—well, at least one of them. Resolutely pulling her thoughts away from her desire for Christian and back to the business at hand, she said, "I would adore one." Now searching for a safe topic of conversation to keep her thoughts on the school while he escorted her, she settled on the first appropriate subject to come to mind, saying, "So this building belongs to Lord Markland?"

"Yes." Guiding her around a particularly nasty-looking pile of refuse, he explained, "According to Brice Fielding, Lord Markland's third son—I am sure you remember me talking about Fielding?" He glanced at her for confirmation.

She gave it with a nod. Christian had told her all about his circle, including many amusing anecdotes. To be sure, she almost felt like she knew Fielding, Chafford, Illingsworth, and Avondale from his vivid descriptions of them.

Nodding back, he started again. "According to Fielding, his great-great-great-grandfather—I believe it was three greats." He seemed to consider a moment and then shrugged one shoulder. "How ever many greats it was, the fellow is said to have purchased the inn as bait to lure a woman he fancied into his bed."

"Indeed?" Bethany prompted, her curiosity piqued.

"Indeed," Christian returned.

When he did not continue, she blurted out, "And

did the ploy work?" Oh, she knew it was indelicate to ask such a question, but she simply had to know.

He laughed, his dark eyes dancing with deviltry as he met her gaze. "It did. You see, the woman in question was the widow of the man who owned this inn at the time, and she very much wanted to stay here and continue on as innkeeper in his stead. Unfortunately, the couple was childless, so the law dictated that the property must go to her husband's wastrel nephew or uncle or some such male relation, whom she was certain would not only toss her out of the inn she considered her home, but would also run the business to ruin. Thus, when his lordship approached her with an offer to keep her, she proposed a bargain in return: her services as his mistress in exchange for the inn."

"She sounds to have had a good head for business," Bethany commented, though again she knew that it was unseemly to vocalize such a thing. Nonetheless, she could not help admiring the woman's shrewdness. Had she been clever enough to demand such a settlement from the man who had kept her, she never would have ended up in the dire straits she had found herself in when he'd discarded her.

Christian nodded at her observation. "A very good head indeed, though not as good as his lordship's. He purchased the inn, as she requested, but stipulated in the papers that the property would revert back to his estate upon the woman's death. By all accounts, she did not read the papers before signing them, and thus went through life believing that she owned the inn, which in turn prompted her to work hard and make it a great success."

Bethany sniffed her disapproval of the man's deception. "What a vile trick. I daresay her children would have been left in a very bad way, had she borne any."

"She had several by the man she wed after his lordship tired of her, but their state did not change after her death, thanks to the Fielding family's charity."

"How can you say that their state did not change?" Bethany exclaimed, appalled by his reasoning. "To my way of thinking, living off charity is a very big change indeed from being a property owner with a thriving enterprise."

"What I meant by charity was that the Fieldings allowed the woman's family to continue on as if they owned the inn and to keep all the profits from their endeavors. They would most probably still be doing so had the succeeding generations not chosen to pursue other professions. In truth, it was for the best that they elected to do so, for the inn had fallen out of favor by the time the last of the innkeepers died. After that the Fieldings saw no reason to keep the inn open. So you see, the family's state did not really change so very much."

"Yes, I do see," Bethany said, and she did, though doing so did little to change her view of the man's deception. Nonetheless, she refused to allow her and Christian's difference of opinion on the matter to spoil the day, so she changed the subject by saying, "You still have not told me how you came to discover this building. Or did you suddenly remember it?"

Christian shrugged. "When I mentioned to my circle that a lady who wished to remain anonymous was searching for property to house a charitable institution, Fielding remembered the inn and asked his father if we might have it. Since the property is entailed it cannot be sold, but Lord Markland is willing to give us a ninety-nine year lease for the price of a mere pound."

"A pound a year?" Bethany exclaimed, unable to believe her ears.

"A pound for the entire ninety-nine years," Christian clarified.

Bethany came to an abrupt stop to gape at him in disbelief, certain that he had misspoken. "A pound for the entire ninety-nine years?" she repeated, incredulous. "Are you sure?"

He nodded. "Quite sure."

"But why? Why so little? The inn is in rather poor condition, true, but still—" She broke off, shaking her head, finishing the sentence with a helpless hand gesture.

"Because he wishes to do his part in aiding the poor," Christian replied. They were now in the main courtyard, and as they resumed walking it appeared that he was leading her toward the open door at the front of the building to their right. "I also suppose that it does not hurt that he is fond of me."

At that moment, the footman stationed at the front gate spied them and rushed forward bearing what Bethany immediately recognized as the mysterious roll of papers Christian had produced from beneath the seat upon exiting the coach. Taking them from the servant with a nod of thanks, Christian removed the black ribbon binding them, adding, "I came here yesterday afternoon and made a few sketches showing the improvements I think will be necessary to make the buildings suitable for your purpose. Of course, if you have other ideas I will naturally be happy to sketch them, as well, so you can present them to whatever contractor you choose to hire." He met her gaze then, his expression suddenly rueful. "It seems odd that of all the things I could have remembered about my past life that I should best remember my schooling in architecture."

"Perhaps it is because it was what you loved best about that life," Bethany replied with a gentle smile.

He returned her smile with a faint one of his own. "Perhaps. However, I can assure you that the same cannot be said for this life." She did not have to ask him what he meant; she could see the answer in his tender gaze, hear it in the warm caress of his voice. What he loved best was her. But, of course, she already knew that. "I must admit that I am glad I remember as much as I do," he continued, looking away to unroll the papers, "because it allows me to be a part of your project."

"You wish to be a part of it?" she asked, thrilled by the notion of working side by side with the man she adored.

"If you want me, yes. Nothing would please me more than to be a part of something so very important to you."

"If I want you? Oh, Christian! Of course I want you. Why, I doubt if I can do it without you," she exclaimed, wanting nothing more at that moment than to throw her arms around him and kiss him. However, she had made quite enough of a spectacle of herself in front of the servants for one day, so she firmly bridled the impulse and instead directed her attention to the beautifully sketched architectural plans he held in his hands.

"Shall we proceed, then?" he inquired with one of his infectious grins. Smiling back in spontaneous response, she nodded. He tipped the plans toward her to allow her a better view of them and began to explain the exterior renovations he felt were necessary to bring the building before them up to date, now and again referring her to his plans, which illustrated each idea in detail. When she had approved his suggestions and had made a few of her own, which he duly scribbled on his plans, they moved inside. To her delight, the interior appeared to have aged far more gracefully than the exterior.

From room to room they wandered, pausing to poke at this and discuss that, with Christian explaining his ideas for each room and then noting her remarks and instructions. The more they planned and explored, the more excited Bethany became. It appeared that the number and arrangement of the rooms would suit her purpose to perfection.

There was a narrow hall on the ground floor flanked by what a tarnished plaque declared to be the coaching office, a space that Bethany promptly decided would make a fine office in which to interview prospective students, with a well-proportioned parlor on the opposite side that could serve as a reception area. Four rooms that gave no clue as to their original purpose lined the remaining length of the hall, which terminated in a rather ornately carved wooden staircase leading up to what Christian informed her had once been the ladies' drawing room and the private sitting rooms, all of which they both agreed would make splendid classrooms. After examining the attics above, which they found in acceptable condition, they made their way to the opposite wing.

There Bethany found a cavernous cellar, an enormous dining hall, a cozy coffee room, a taproom with tall wooden settles, and kitchens that seemed to go on forever. On the floor above were four private dining rooms, which, too, would make excellent schoolrooms. When they had inspected every nook and cranny there, they turned their attention to the double tier of bedchambers. Unlike the rooms in the front portions of the structure, these were filthy and in dire need of repair. Nonetheless, Bethany was equally delighted with them, for once they were set to right they would provide more than enough chambers to house her students in the comfortable fashion she desired. After returning to the back courtyard for a quick tour of the laundry, Christian led her through the front gate and around to one of the vacant shops. The door now stood open, almost as if in expectation of customers.

When Bethany glanced at Christian in query, wondering what it meant, he said, "Lord Markland owns the shops, as well, and said we could have them as part of the bargain if we wish. I thought you might turn the one over there," he gestured to the opposite shop, "into a dressmaking establishment, where those students desiring employment as seamstresses can work to gain shop experience after they have completed their schooling. Of course, the sort of women who will patronize the shop shan't be able to afford the lavish garments your students will undoubtedly dream of creating, but they will be paying customers, which will enable you to pay the students for their services. And what better way to teach them about the rewards of industry than to grant them wages? As for this shop," he nodded to the one before them, "might I suggest a bakeshop? It was what was here previously, so it has the required ovens."

"A bakeshop and a dressmaking establishment—what a marvelous idea!" Bethany exclaimed, instantly taken with the idea. "Not only will the shops serve to benefit our students, but they will also provide the less fortunate women in the area with affordable clothing and baked goods."

"My thought exactly," Christian countered with another of his heart-stopping grins. "The floors above each shop are divided into several apartments that could serve as lodgings for your instructors, if you wish. Would you care to see them?"

Bethany grinned back, her elation bounding to new heights. "Of course I do. I want to see everything."

"Then you shall." With that declaration he produced plans for the shops and apartments, as well.

An hour later they had finished touring what would someday be the school's bake- and dressmaking shops and their apartments, the sight of which filled Bethany with so many ideas that her tongue kept tripping over her words in her rush to share them. Now in the back-room of the future dressmaking shop, where Christian leaned over a scarred oak table making the final adjustments to his plans, he murmured, "I take it that I shall be safe in informing his lordship that we accept his offer?"

"Yes, oh yes!" Bethany cried. Never in her life had she been so happy or felt such hope and excitement for the future. Never had she loved Christian more. He was the guardian of her heart, the champion of her dreams, and with him by her side the word *impossible* held no meaning. For when they were together, his strength and courage became hers; his indomitable spirit infused her, inspiring her to rise to undreamed-of heights. Being with him made her better than she had ever imagined she could be. With him life was full of endless possibilities. And without him in her life—

Unwilling to even contemplate such an empty life, Bethany watched as Christian added the finishing touches to the final set of plans. She simply could not be without him—she could not bear to do so!

But did she have the courage to do what she must to ensure that he stayed with her forever? Did she dare to say yes to his proposal?

Take the risk! Say yes! Dare to choose love! her heart urged her. *What does it matter if the world shuns you? You will have Christian to love you, and is that not what truly matters? Do it! Gamble on love!*

As always happened when her heart cried out, her fear rose up to silence it, sallying forth with its army of hopelessness, pain, and doubt. But this time those grim forces lost the struggle, this time the cries were so strong, so impassioned, that her heart easily triumphed.

She could do it. Oh, yes! She would do it!

Strengthened by her heart's victory to do what she must to enforce her newfound resolution, she said, "Do you remember what you were trying to persuade me to do in the courtyard earlier, Christian?" Her voice was thick and throaty from the power of her emotions.

His pencil jerked to a halt at her question and he slowly straightened up. "I do." His dark eyes were narrowed and guarded as his gaze met hers.

"I am persuaded," she softly proclaimed.

"Are you." By his tone, the words were not so much a question as an expression of wariness.

Unperturbed by his response, knowing that his uncertainty stemmed not from a wavering in his love for her, but from his need to protect his heart, Bethany slowly approached him, nodding over and over again as she replied, "The answer is yes, Christian. Yes, I will marry you." Now standing toe to toe, she twined her arms around his neck to guide his lips to hers.

Rather than meet her halfway, as she expected, he pulled away a fraction to scrutinize her face. His eyes soberly searching hers, he whispered, "Are you quite certain? You are not promising to wed me out of a sense of obligation for finding you this building, are you?"

She emitted a short laugh. "Silly man, of course not! I am promising out of an obligation to my heart. I love you, Christian, and I want nothing more than to spend the rest of my life showing you how much." This time she did not have to guide his lips; this time he swooped down and caught her mouth beneath his.

His lips were hot and demanding as they seized hers, his tongue hard and aggressive, possessing her mouth so thoroughly that she sagged against him, weak and dizzy with breathless pleasure. Never before had he kissed her with such abandon, never with such rampant desire. The way his mouth plundered hers, his teeth now and again scraping her lips in his eagerness—it was almost as if he wished to devour her.

Flares of white-hot fire raced through Bethany's blood as she met his passion with her own and she instinctively dropped her arms from around his neck to grasp his buttocks, shamelessly urging him on. He groaned into her mouth and convulsively thrust his groin against her. The feel of him, so long and hard and thick in his arousal, further inflamed her and she thrust back, moaning aloud as liquid heat rushed to the secret place between her legs. He jerked in savage response, his lusty moan echoing hers. Again she thrust against him. Again he thrust back. Overcome by her desire, mindless of everything but her burning need for him, she tightened her grip on his flexing buttocks before he could pull away again and pinned his pelvis firmly against her, trapping it. Over and over again she rubbed her belly against his erection, her body quickening at the feel of its powerful thrust.

Oh, how she wanted him! She wanted to touch his rigid sex, to feel the pulsating heat of him in her hand as she wantonly fondled him, to tease and entice and stimulate him until he cried out in erotic torment. Most of all, she wanted to feel him buried deep inside her, to be filled by the fire and fierceness of his responding desire. Maddened by her now desperate need to touch him, Bethany slipped one hand into his coat and down into his breeches to grasp him.

Christian arched back in violent response, a rough growl breaking from his throat as he rammed his arousal hard against her palm. For a brief second he stayed that way, shuddering and jerking as she groped his impressive length, now and again groaning when she brushed a particularly sensitive place. Then his hand moved to hers to grip it through the fabric of his breeches and he began to guide her movements. Up and down he guided her, her hand pausing when his did, her fingers tightening around him whenever he exerted pressure. Only the sound of their harsh breathing, punctuated by an occasional moan from Christian, pierced the silence around them.

Thrilling to her rush of feminine power, Bethany closed her eyes to concentrate on their movements, the fire in her own sex burning higher and hotter with every stroke of her hand. When at last she could bear the heat no longer, she dragged his free hand between her legs and pressed it against her through the fabric of her gown, mutely begging him to relieve her. He groaned, a deep, agonized sound, and hauled her up onto the edge of the table, forcing her legs apart with his hip while pulling up her skirts with his free hand. In the next instant she felt his hand on her bare thigh.

His touch light and advancing in short, feathering strokes, he inched his way upward, caressing her inner thigh in a slow, meandering motion that made Bethany squirm and gasp in her mounting urgency. He was almost there. . . . almost to the place she so desperately wanted him to touch. He was . . .

To her sensual frustration he traced around it, continuing up and over the curve of her stomach in a deliciously tickling caress. Bethany whimpered her disappointment into his mouth, which had recaptured hers, her pelvis undulating and jerking in an attempt to propel him lower. Instantly he complied, his fingers brushing downward to first rake and then draw tight circles in the curls on her woman's mound. Bethany squirmed and sobbed in fevered response, her legs straining farther apart to expose her hardened core, urging him to stroke her there. When he merely continued to toy with her curls, she dragged her lips from his, hoarsely begging, "Please, Christian. Oh, please." She lifted her hips and thrust her mound meaningfully against his hand to illustrate her plea.

"Only if you tell me again that you will marry me, love," he demanded. His breath was labored now and tearing from his chest in ragged gusts.

"I will marry you," she more gasped than said as she felt his fingers edging closer to her most needful place.

"Say that you will marry me soon," he whispered. He was seductively outlining her womanhood now, skillfully skirting the aching bud of her desire.

Certain that she would die if he did not touch her there, she moaned, "I will marry you anytime, anyplace you wish."

His dipped his face close to hers again, positioning his lips over hers, poised to reclaim them. "You promise?"

"I promise," she fervently vowed. The instant the words left her mouth he touched her, his lips coming down forcefully on hers to swallow her cry of shattering pleasure.

His fingers were spreading and stroking her now, teasing and tantalizing her slick woman's flesh. Held in thrall to her passion, Bethany sat frozen beneath his ministrations, her urgency mounting with every skillful caress.

"God, Bethany, how I want you," Christian groaned. His index finger was now inside her, pumping in and out while his thumb continued to flick her bud.

Wanting the hardness that still surged against her palm to replace his plundering finger, Bethany whispered, "Then take me, Christian." Not waiting for his response, afraid that his sense of honor would rear its sterling head and force him to deny her appeal, she recaptured his mouth in a sweeping kiss and began to unbutton his falls. A moment later his sex sprang forth, hot and swollen and ready to take her. Not about to give him a chance to voice gentlemanly protests, she rose up and impaled herself on him.

He shuddered and jerked at his initial penetration; a low, strangled cry tore from his throat. Clasping him hard between her thighs, she arched up and thrust downward onto his piercing shaft, driving him deeper inside her. For several beats he remained motionless, his eyes squeezed closed and his breath ripping from his chest in harsh, guttural moans. Then he plunged yet deeper, filling her completely.

As Christian began to move with her, easily catching her rhythm, Bethany wrapped her legs around his hips and her arms around his neck, clinging to him as he thrust again and again, her pleasure heightened by the roughness of his untamed passion. Utterly immersed in each other, their bodies melding to become one, they climaxed together, sobbing their rapture in unison as they shared their ecstasy. Their passion now spent, they slumped in each other's embrace, with Bethany's cheek pillowed against Christian's chest and his head resting atop hers.

When at last their euphoria had passed and they were able to rouse themselves from its blissful languor, Christian murmured, "You are obligated to wed me now, you know. So be warned: If you change your mind and try to cry off, I shall whisk you off to Gretna Green and force you to utter the marriage vows."

"Is that a threat, my lord?" Bethany teased.

"No, my lady, it is a promise," he lightly returned, kissing her head.

Bethany smiled faintly at his tender repartee. "Never fear—I shan't change my mind. You are as good as leg-shackled."

"They are shackles I cannot wait to don," Christian countered. Pulling back to grin down at her, he added, "I daresay we should make ourselves presentable, lest one of the footmen comes looking for us."

Though Bethany would have loved nothing more than for him to take her again, this time slowly and with his clothes removed so she could thoroughly explore his body, she knew that this was neither the time nor the place for such intimacy, so she nodded, suffering a momentary pang of bereavement when he pulled from her. The next few minutes passed in companionable silence as they righted their garments and retrieved their hats, which had tumbled from their heads in their passion.

Their appearances now righted, Christian again took Bethany in his arms. "I was not merely bantering when I demanded that you promise to wed me soon. It is a vow I have taken to heart and fully expect you to honor."

"And it is one that I fully intend to keep," she returned, rising up onto her tiptoes to engage him in another ardent kiss.

"Well, well. Now ain't this cozy. Two lovebirds billin' 'n' cooin' in their nest," a coarse voice intruded.

Bethany and Christian swung around to stare in the direction from which it had come to see a man, holding a pistol standing in the doorway. He was a large man with massive shoulders and a bull-like chest, clad in the rough, nondescript sort of clothing one often saw on laborers. Though Bethany doubted if either she or Christian would have recognized his face, he had taken pains to conceal it by tying a strip of black cloth over his lower face, while the wide brim of his shabby round hat had been pulled low on his forehead to obscure the upper portion. Only his mouth was visible, exposed by a crudely cut hole in the cloth.

"What do you want?" Christian growled, his arms tightening protectively around her.

"Yer purses and jewels, to start," the man replied. He had begun to advance toward them, the barrel of his pistol clearly pointed at Christian's head. "Then I'll have a bit o' wot you was gettin' when I came in. Ain't nivver had the pleasure 'o nubbin' such a fancy piece."

Christian's arms tightened around Bethany a fraction more. "You may have our purses and jewels, but if you so much as touch a hair on the lady's head you will be a dead man," he calmly replied, though Bethany could tell from the tension radiating from his body that he was anything but calm.

The thief emitted a sound that was halfway between a snicker and a snort. "Ye don't say?" he sneered. Halting mere inches from where they stood, his pistol primed and ready to fire at Christian should he try to make good on his threat, he continued, "Well I'm the one holdin' the barker, me boy, so I don't think so. What I think is that ye'll be the dead man if ye try 'n' stop me." Now turning his attention to Bethany, he cooed, "Never ye fear, me dear. I know how to diddle a lady good, so ye'll be enjoyin' yer ride."

"I am warning you—" Christian hissed. Bethany could feel every muscle in his body tighten and coil.

The thief ignored him. "Yer slit 'ell feel so fine when I'm done that ye ain't nivver again gonna be satisfied by a pokin' from a gent's lazy lob." As he spoke he slowly and deliberately lifted his hand to Bethany's face. She could not help noticing that the skin on his hand was weathered and cracked, like leather left out in the elements for too long, and that his ragged nails were almost black with filth. Smirking in a way that made her shrink back against Christian, repulsed as much by the sight of his rotten teeth as by the stench from their decay, she shuddered and closed her eyes, bile rising in her throat as he brushed his thumb over her lower lip.

He had no sooner touched her than she heard Christian snarl—a fierce, feral sound. And in the next instant she was soaring through the air, flung violently sideways by Christian, away from the pistol and the thief. Her eyes flying open in her surprise, she saw Christian lunge at the man, toppling them both to the ground. Then her head slammed against the wall and the world dissolved into nothingness. But not before she heard the pistol's chilling report.

Chapter 15

"I cannot believe that you are actually considering marrying that—that—creature!" the appalled Duchess of Amberley exclaimed, her voice quivering in outrage.

"That *creature's* name is Bethany Matland, and she is a respectable widow, and the sister of the man who rescued me. And I am not *considering* marrying her, I am *going* to do so," Christian coolly informed his mother. "I have proposed, she has accepted, and I intend to meet her at the altar on the soonest date to which she will agree."

His mother halted abruptly in her agitated pacing, something she had been doing since the beginning of their interview a quarter of an hour earlier, to stand directly before the settee upon which Christian sat, her arms akimbo and her hands braced on her trim hips. Fixing him with what he sensed he had once found a most intimidating glower, she expelled, "Surely you jest!" You would have thought by her face that he'd just announced that he was secretly wed to a Covent Garden doxy and had just gotten the next Amberley heir off her.

More annoyed than daunted by her show of bombastic disapproval, he tossed back, "I can assure you that I have never been more serious in my life."

She threw up her arms in what Christian considered a rather excessive show of exasperation and resumed her pacing, her green-and-cream striped muslin skirts snapping furiously around her legs with every turbulent step she took. Her voice sharp and her speech precise in her ire, she ranted, "I cannot even begin to imagine what you could have been thinking to become entangled with such a person, much less why you should feel obligated to wed her in the face of this hullabaloo. After all, she is a commoner, and scandals such as this one are of little consequence to the common crowd. To be sure, they regularly engage in the vulgar sort of display in which you and that woman indulged three days ago, so they shall most certainly let the incident pass without comment or detriment to her reputation."

"I hardly see how carrying a woman in need of aid from a coach into her home can be counted as a vulgar display, especially when the woman in question was unconscious from a blow to her head," Christian retorted, his normally slow-burning temper rising a degree with every passing second. "Indeed, the only thing I can see that is even remotely vulgar about the episode is the fact that no one in this household has bothered to ask after the lady's health."

His mother deflected his barbed comment with a snort. "I suppose it should come as no surprise that you should be unable to see the error of your ways, given your memory loss. And I daresay that I must shoulder a measure of the blame for this debacle since I did not think to reacquaint you with the niceties of society before allowing you to go about in the *ton* alone."

"And what, pray tell, would you have counseled me to do in such a situation?" Christian interjected, genuinely curious to hear what the *ton* considered proper etiquette in dealing with a savage attack.

"Had I been counseling you, you never would have strayed anywhere near that abominable part of town, so none of this would have happened."

"Indeed?" Christian murmured, not bothering to inform her that he had not strayed into the area, but had gone there deliberately.

She jerked her head to the affirmative, a gesture as imperious as it was curt. "Indeed. You would not have dared to do so, not after I pointed out the myriad dangers to be found in that wretched place and made you understand that to go there is to take your life into your hands. As you discovered for yourself, I would have been justified in my warning. Why, just look what happened to you." She paused before him long enough to fling a hand in his direction. "You were set upon by thieves and shot!"

It was Christian's turn to snort. "Thief, not thieves—there was only one," he corrected her, "and I was hardly shot. The bullet merely grazed my arm. Even the dozen or so physicians you insisted upon having examine me agreed that it was nothing but a flesh wound, and a slight one at that." He had to bite his tongue to keep himself from informing her what it was really like to be shot, having suffered a grave bullet wound during the battle in which Gideon had rescued him.

She snorted back. "The point is that you would not have been wounded at all had you known to stay where you belong."

Christian shrugged. "Point granted," he conceded, Avondale's favored retort springing readily to his lips. "Nonetheless, you still have not explained how I could have better managed the situation, since it did happen, or even why my display afterward should be considered vulgar."

His mother's furious pace slowed to a measured tread, and he suddenly sensed that he was in for a lecture. The instant she began to speak, crisply and with the authoritative air of a university don, he knew his intuition was correct. "It was vulgar because you are an aristocrat, and as an aristocrat it is your duty to behave with the dignity befitting your station, especially when in public. Thus your error was in carrying the woman yourself. Not only is such an act considered to be a menial chore and thus best left to the servants, but in handling her with such familiarity you fostered a highly improper impression of intimacy between the two of you."

Christian stifled his grin at that last, wondering what his mother would say if she knew just how accurate the impression they had given truly was. Not particularly eager to find out, he replied, "In short, you are saying that an aristocrat must take care to check his chivalrous impulses." The irony in his tone was unmistakable.

"If they involve handling a female beyond taking her hand or arm in a socially sanctioned manner, yes. Of course, a man is naturally allowed to make an exception if the woman in question is a close family member. Under dire circumstances he may also aid his intended or a distant female relative, such as a cousin."

"If what you say is true, then I can in no way be accused of wrongdoing," Christian said. "I had asked Mrs. Matland to marry me earlier in the day and she accepted, so she was my intended when I was spied carrying her. And even you must admit that the circumstances under which I did so can most certainly be counted as dire."

"Of course she accepted you," his mother retorted, pointedly refusing to acknowledge the validity of his reasoning. "You are the heir to an exceedingly old and respected title, not to mention a fortune of legendary proportions. It is my guess that she has been scheming to trap you from the very start of your liaison."

"Actually, it is I who have been scheming to trap her," Christian countered, the heat from his rising anger creeping into his voice. "It so happens that Mrs. Matland shares your reservations about the suitability of marriage between commoners and aristocrats, and she turned me down the first time I proposed."

"Games!" his mother scoffed with a disdainful sniff. "Were you still in possession of your wits you would have easily seen that she was merely playing her cards to better her advantage."

Christian shook his head once, emphatically, his temper now on the verge of snapping. "No, Mother. You are wrong. I do not need my memory to determine that her concerns about our stations were, and still are, quite genuine. Just as I do not need it to know that her love for me is true."

His mother heaved a gusty sigh and again threw up her hands, her eyes rolling toward heaven, as if imploring the powers that be for help.

Christian ignored her dramatics, continuing, "Furthermore, I love her in return. I have from the very moment I met her. She is everything a man, aristocrat or commoner, could ever hope for in a wife, and if you were to make her acquaintance I am confident you would agree that she will be a credit to our name." His voice rose with every word he uttered, ringing with passion and conviction.

His speech was greeted with a dry chuckle and the sound of a single pair of hands applauding him. "Bravo, my boy. Stated like the Xander of old. Perhaps more of Northwick the Notorious remains than we know, eh?" This wryly framed observation was stated by his father, who had been sitting silently in the chair to Christian's right during the entire interview, in a pose that Christian somehow knew was deceptive in its ease.

Flinching at his father's words, praying that they were not true, Christian stonily inquired, "What makes you think so?"

"You were always quite passionate about your liaisons with the fairer sex in the past," his father replied, now rising. "And this is not the first time you have announced your intention to wed one of your women. This is what, Margaretta? His fifth, or is it his sixth, marriage announcement?"

He glanced at his wife in query, who promptly supplied, "I am quite certain it is his sixth."

Accepting her verdict with a nod, he continued, "Fortunately, you always came to your senses before you did anything regrettable, and in most instances made your ladybird of the moment your mistress instead of your bride—something, I might add, for which you were always exceedingly grateful a month later when you tired of her."

Struggling to master his temper, which he knew would erupt if he attempted to respond at that moment, sensing—or was it remembering?—that his sire viewed nothing with quite as much contempt as a loss of control, Christian mutely marked his father's progress as he strolled to the graceful étagère where his impressive collection of snuffboxes was displayed. Watching as he carefully selected a box and helped himself to a pinch of the fine snuff inside, Christian finally managed to contain his anger enough to utter, "I do hope that you are not suggesting that I make Mrs. Matland my mistress?" Though he succeeded in keeping his voice even, his tone simmered with quiet fury.

"I do not see why not," his mother answered before his father could do so, lowering herself into his abandoned chair with a regal sweep of her skirts. "No doubt she will pout when you amend your offer from marriage to carte blanche, but she will come around quickly enough once you make it clear that that is all she shall ever get from you, especially if you dangle a pretty bauble before her eyes."

Christian's hands balled into fists at her cavalier suggestion. Clenching them so hard that his nails gouged into his palms in his struggle to maintain his control, he spat through gritted teeth, "If you were a man, I would call you out for that."

"No doubt you would," his father interposed with a discreet, snuff-fostered sniff. "Dueling, another Northwick the Notorious trait, though again one of his less-than-admirable ones." Closing the enameled box in his hand with a decisive snap of its lid, he returned it to its designated place and then moved to the nearby fireplace to position himself against the white marble surround. Leaning against it in a casual manner that Christian again sensed was illusory, he said, "See here, my boy. I know things have been exceedingly difficult for you of late, what with trying to adjust to a life you have forgotten and that no longer seems to fit with the man you have become. And in view of that fact I can understand your desire to marry this Mrs. Matland. She was the first female to befriend you upon your return to England and the one you know best, so it is only natural that you should wish to cling to the familiar."

"I intend to marry her because I love her, and for no other reason," Christian retorted with a calm he was far from feeling. "I cannot understand why you both find that fact so very hard to comprehend."

"Oh, we comprehend it well enough, and I am sure that I speak for your mother, too, when I say that I truly wish we could accept this woman as your bride. But we cannot. As the Amberley heir, you have a duty to wed a female of noble blood, one whose title and fortune are equal to your own; a woman who will genuinely understand the honor being bestowed upon her and will possess the breeding to carry the Moncreiffe name with the required grace and dignity."

"Ah, but what about my duty to myself? What about my right to happiness and to live a fulfilling life?" Christian quietly demanded.

His mother made a dismissive hand motion. "You shall have no difficulty whatsoever finding all that and more with one of the girls in the *ton*. Once the season begins—"

"No, Mother," Christian cut in. "What I share with Mrs. Matland is no ordinary love—it is the rare and priceless melding of heart and soul that most people spend their lives seeking but never find. She is my treasure, my light . . . my greatest joy. She is everything to me." Now rising to drive home the strength of his determination, he met his father eye to eye as he finished. "I shall wed my sweet Bethany, and only her, and nothing either of you can say or do will dissuade me from doing so."

His father pushed away from the fireplace to square off with his defiant son. "Indeed? Well, I wonder if your 'sweet Bethany's' heart and soul would continue to meld with yours and if her love would remain so very extraordinary were she to suddenly learn that she shall never be the Duchess of Amberley or enjoy the fortune that goes with the title?"

Christian nodded once, not about to be cowed by his father's veiled threat. "I do not doubt for a moment that it would."

"Indeed? Hmmm. I wonder," his father murmured, his eyebrows lifting in unmistakable challenge.

For several tense moments Christian refrained from responding, his gaze dueling with his father's, their dark eyes snapping with anger as they clashed. Then he accepted the challenge, parrying, "Shall we find out?"

"The choice is yours," his father countered.

"Do not be a fool, Christian," his mother chided. "We shall find you someone new, someone you will love even more."

Christian ignored her. Boring his gaze yet deeper into his father's so as to ensure that there would be no mistaking the resolution behind his words, he softly declared, "I chose love."

"Christian, no!" his mother wailed.

He tore his gaze from his father's then to spare her a cool glance and polite nod. "Now, if you will excuse me, I must see to arranging new quarters. I shall send someone for my belongings."

"Damn it, Xander!" his father boomed.

But before he could continue on with what was no doubt about to be a tirade on duty, Christian cut him off, saying, "The name is Christian English, your grace." Turning on his heels to make his exit, he added, "I believe I saw Godwin come in as I was entering the drawing room. I shall send him in so you can give him the good news."

A silence followed Christian as he made his way across the coldly elegant blue-and-silver drawing room. Pausing at the door, he said without looking back, "Godwin is a good man. I have no doubt whatsoever that he will make a fine Duke of Amberley." With that he stepped from the room, closing the door softly behind him.

He had just stepped into the foyer and was glancing around for the majordomo so he could collect his coat and hat when an amused voice he instantly recognized as his brother's drawled, "So? Did he give you a rough time of it?"

Christian glanced in the direction from which the voice had come to see Godwin and Lucy sitting on the stairs, the latter now elbowing the former in the ribs, hissing at him to hush.

Another picture instantly flashed through his mind,

one of a budding Lucy and child Godwin waiting for him on the steps as they did now, anxious to hear about his latest punishment and ready to soothe the sting if he had been switched. Despite his inner turbulence, he could not help smiling at what could only be a memory.

"Well?" Godwin persisted, which earned him another jab from Lucy.

"He will tell us what happened if he wishes for us to know," Lucy chided. She rose as she spoke and descended the stairs with much the same grace of movement that Christian had noticed their mother possessed. Stopping before him to cup his chin in her palm, she searched his face with eyes full of tender concern, murmuring, "Are you quite all right, Christian? Is there anything I can do to help?"

"I daresay I will survive," he replied, touched by her show of support. Over her shoulder he saw Godwin bound down the stairs to join them. Nodding at his brother, he added, "However, I will be requiring new quarters posthaste. I do hope the invitation to take up residence at the Bachelor Barrack still stands?"

His brother's genial grin disappeared, as if slapped from his face, replaced by an expression of complete and utter shock. "Of course it is, but—good God, man! Do not tell me that they tossed you out?"

Christian shrugged with a nonchalance he did not feel, hoping to ease the distress from Lucy's face. "It is I who decided that new quarters are in order." When she continued to look stricken he chucked her under her chin, a gesture that seemed so familiar that it felt natural, and teased, "Never fear, Goosey Lucy. I shall still be at your beck and call to squire you about town on those occasions when your husband is loath to move from his chair before the hearth."

"Oh, Christian. It *was* awful," she softly exclaimed,

unappeased by his attempt at levity. "I can always see it in your face when you have had a row with Father. Your eyes look so sad."

"As I said, I will survive," Christian replied with another shrug. "By the bye, Godwin. Father wishes to see you in the silver drawing room."

Godwin groaned. "I do hope he isn't going to take me to task again for marring the paint on his new gig. I did not scrape against the stone gatepost in front of Miss Ridgeway's house on purpose."

Christian shook his head, suddenly feeling very sorry for his brother. "Worse. He is going to reinstate you as the Amberley heir."

There had been so many callers to the Harwood town house in the wake of the scandal that by the end of the first week, Bethany and Julia had agreed that they should hang a shingle outside their door that marked the place as Bedlam for the madness of the *ton*'s rush to see the woman for whom the future Duke of Amberley had tossed away his title. Now early evening on the sixth day since the scandal had erupted, Bethany sank into her favorite chair near the fireplace in the cozy family drawing room, grateful that the seemingly interminable hours for calling had at last ended, relieved to be free from the staring eyes and slyly prying tongues of the elegant crowd that all afternoon had paraded in an endless stream through the more formal Italian drawing room.

Heaving a weary sigh, Bethany kicked off her dark blue Spanish leather shoes and put her stockinged feet up on the footstool she had placed before the chair upon her arrival at the town house, toasting her cold toes before the cheerfully crackling fire as she contemplated all that had happened during the past few days. She had feared that society's discovery of her and Christian's love would throw their lives into a coil, and now that the discovery had been made, those fears were being borne out in ways she had not even begun to imagine.

To be sure, while she had expected the majority of the *ton* to look down their noses at her in scorn for her commonness and to converse in thinly veiled insults interspersed with barbs dressed up as wit, all uttered to condemn her for daring to love above her station and insinuating that she had seduced her way into a title, she had been unprepared for the leering innuendoes she had suffered from several of the so-called gentlemen, the wildly speculative stories complete with caricatures of her and Christian that graced every newspaper, and most startling of all, the martyred posturings exhibited by a number of the unmarried young women and their outraged mothers. The worst by far of that last category had been Famous Helene and her horrible mother, who had paid Bethany a visit two days after the incident at the school, turning up on her doorstep a good two hours before what society had deemed to be the accepted time for calls. Bethany's head began to throb at the mere thought of the episode.

Unlike the other thwarted matchmaking mothers who had called, the Duchess of Hunsderry wasted no time on false niceties or even tendering a proper greeting before launching into a tirade accusing Bethany of stealing Christian from Helene by using methods that no decent woman should know, much less employ. Helene, playing the tragic martyr to perfection, had more stumbled than walked into the drawing room, where she had collapsed upon the chaise longue to assume a studied pose of abject sorrow, sobbing and clasping at her breast as she keened over her broken heart.

Stunned into speechless by the pair's singular performance, Bethany could only stare at them with what she had hoped was a modicum of dignity, at a loss as to how to respond to their rude display. Julia, however, had suffered from no such loss. When she had come upon the scene a few minutes later, she had promptly jumped to Bethany's defense, crossing words with her grace and chiding Helene for her peevish pouting with a ferocity that had sent the pair packing, but not before her grace had gotten in a parting shot. "I wonder if you realize that you are leading his lordship down the road to ruin, Mrs. Matland?" she had said.

Though Julia had scoffed at the notion of Bethany's love ruining Christian, as had Caroline, Amy, and Mina when they had called a short while later to offer their support in the wake of the scandal, Bethany could not help wondering if perhaps her grace had been correct, especially when the news of Christian's rift with his parents over his intention to wed her had begun to circulate around town.

Oh, true. Christian claimed that he would rather spend his life as her husband than as the Duke of Amberley, and she had no doubt whatsoever that he sincerely meant what he said. And then there were the reassurances she had received from Christian's charming sister Lucy and his genial brother, Godwin, who had requested a private interview with her the day before yesterday in order to make her acquaintance. Had they not seemed genuinely confident in their claims that their parents would come around in time on the matter of their marriage and restore Christian to his rightful place as heir? And yet—yet—how could she not feel a measure of guilt over what their love had cost Christian, especially when she had been so very selfish? And she truly had been selfish.

Indeed, for all the time she had spent fretting over the impact the revelation of their love might have on her life, she had spared little thought as to how it could affect Christian or the sacrifices he might have to make. She most certainly had never paused to consider that he might be forced to choose between her and his parents. That she could have been so very stingy with her concern for the man she loved shamed her to the bottom of her soul.

Heartsick with remorse, Bethany hugged herself tight and did what she should have been doing all along: she contemplated Christian's feelings, thoughtfully and with unstinting deference. Though he had neither said nor done anything that would lead her to believe that he had any regrets or was pained by the choices and sacrifices he had been forced to make, she knew that he must ache inside over the fracturing of his relationship with his parents. Why, just thinking about how she would feel if she were in his place made her want to weep.

Wishing that Christian were near so she could offer him solace, Bethany closed her eyes and rested her head against the tall chair back. The butter-soft leather gave beneath her weight, molding to her head's contours to cradle and support it. But unlike most evenings, Bethany took no pleasure in its comfort now, too stricken by the thought of Christian's suffering to do so.

Her poor, poor darling. The truth of the matter was that all this had been much worse for him than her, yet true to his selfless nature, he thought only of her and how she was faring. And as if that weren't quite enough of a burden for one man to bear, he also insisted on blaming himself for what happened at the inn, and not a day had passed since that he had not apologized profusely for what he viewed as his reckless injury to her person, though in truth he had most probably saved both their lives in flinging her aside. That the thief had escaped justice served only to deepen his anguish over the incident.

Bethany was deep in thought, trying to devise ways in which to relieve him of his unwarranted guilt, when there was a soft scratching at the door. Instantly recognizing its distinct pattern as belonging to Simon Rowles, the majordomo, she called out, "You may enter."

Rowles, who usually wore a politely sardonic expression, which was in keeping with his droll wit and wry tongue, looked uncharacteristically dour as he entered the room. Coming to a halt several feet from where she sat, he announced, "You have a caller, madame. A gentleman, and a most insistent one, I must add." By both his tone and face it was clear that he did not quite approve of her visitor.

Bethany glanced at the small marquetry clock on the nearby table, the dial of which was nearly obscured by the embroidery hoop holding the half-finished cradle sheet she had left heaped there the night before. It was a quarter after six, long past the acceptable hour for visits from all but family and the closest of friends. Frowning at the irregularity, she inquired, "Did he, by chance, state his business, Rowles?"

"He did not. However, he did offer this." He held up a crisp calling card. Closing the short distance between them as he spoke, he added, "The gentleman said he was certain that you would wish to receive him once you saw it, and refused to leave until I had presented it to you." With a flourish, he did exactly that.

Bethany angled the card into the light to view it, the blood draining from her face the instant she saw the elegantly engraved name.

He was here.

Now.

For all that she had resigned herself to the fact that she was bound to attract his notice in the wake of the scandal, she had hardly expected him to come calling.

Wanting nothing more than to run upstairs and hide, to flee from the man who held the power to further complicate and perhaps even destroy her and Christian's lives, Bethany forced herself to meet the majordomo's sharp-eyed gaze and utter, "I will receive him." To her relief, her voice came out strong and steady.

Rowles inclined his fashionably-coiffed dark head. "Very good, madame. I will show him into the Italian drawing room."

Bethany began to nod her agreement, but then changed her mind and shook her head. "No. I believe I would rather see him here." Better that the uncomfortable interview take place in the room where she felt the most comfortable. Besides, what they had to say to each other was of a personal nature and much more suited to the close confines here, where they could speak in muted tones, rather than in the Italian drawing room, where the spacious arrangement of the furniture groupings necessitated that a person must practically shout to be heard.

Apparently, her turmoil showed on her face, because Rowles frowned and inquired, "Shall I request that Lady Julia join you?"

Again Bethany shook her head, not wishing to disturb Julia from her much needed rest. Large with child and nearing her time, Julia tired easily these days and usually went upstairs to rest during the interval between the end of calling hours and supper. Moreover, her presence would serve only to prevent Bethany and her caller from saying the things that needed to be said.

For a long moment Rowles merely contemplated her, his brow furrowed and his dark eyes narrowed, as if in indecision—indeed, by his expression she almost expected him to insist that Julia be present for the interview. Then he inclined his head and murmured,

"As you wish, madame." With that he turned on his heels and departed.

Though Bethany hated herself for doing so, she could not stop herself from rushing to the tall console mirror to inspect her appearance. As she scrutinized every detail, her image bathed in the flattering golden candlelight that spilled from the gilded mirror's twin triple-branched sconces, she was suddenly grateful to Julia and her insistence that she don the most elegant gowns from her new London wardrobe to receive her onslaught of callers. Since Julia had also insisted that the gowns be made up in more sophisticated designs than Bethany usually favored, and in colors that while far from gay were nonetheless departures from the usual drab shades worn in second mourning, Bethany was dressed in a manner that could only be described as *dernier cri,* the very latest in fashion.

Lingering there only long enough to ensure that everything was in order, she straightened her modish dark blue silk half-robe, making certain that its delicate gold lace trim lay flat, then turned her attention to smoothing the blue-and-yellow-sprigged muslin round gown she wore beneath it. Noting with approval that the artless coiffure of waves and cascading ringlets that Julia's maid had so painstakingly arranged for her still looked perfect, she turned from the mirror to survey the room. After a moment of deliberation, she chose to return to her favorite chair, deciding it best to present a picture of relaxed informality.

As she heard the sound of footsteps approaching the door, she snatched up her embroidery and bent over it in a pose that she hoped conveyed a sense of unflappable tranquility, not wishing her caller to suspect how unnerved she was by his visit. A moment later there was the sound of Rowles's distinctive scratch, to which she somehow managed to bid him to enter, followed by the creak of the door opening and footsteps entering.

"Viscount Kirkland," Rowles announced.

Bethany's racing heart seemed to thud to an abrupt halt at hearing his name uttered aloud. Commanding herself to breathe, fighting to hold on to the last frayed threads of her unraveling composure, she slowly looked up to acknowledge him.

Him, the man who had so tenderly introduced her to the pleasures of love and had vowed to keep her safe; the same man who had so cruelly abandoned her to the harshness of London's pitiless streets. Harry Clay, Viscount Kirkland, the man who had made her a whore, the father of her dead bastard child.

Wanting to weep at the bitter memories stirring within her at the sight of him, she forced herself to smile and cordially utter, "Viscount Kirkland, how very kind of you to call."

"Not nearly as kind as you are to receive me at this hour, Mrs. Matland," he smoothly countered.

Bethany blinked at the sound of his voice, wondering if it had always been marred by that nasal whine. Pushing the question from her mind in the next moment, wishing to get on with the unpleasantness she suspected lay ahead, she nodded at the majordomo, saying, "You may leave us, Rowles. Lord Kirkland and I are—"

"Good friends," his lordship cut in with a broad smile.

Bethany could not help raising her eyebrows at his choice of words. She had been about to say that they were old acquaintances. Not wishing to argue the point in front of the majordomo, she said, "Yes. We were once very good friends indeed."

Apparently sensing the tension between her and her visitor, Rowles fixed the viscount with a hard look, his voice holding a wealth of meaning as he replied, "As you wish, madame. Should you require my assistance, you have only to call out. I shall remain close at hand."

As the majordomo made his exit, rather more slowly than was usual, Bethany indicated the chair beside her, the one usually occupied by Julia when they shared the fire in the evenings, saying, "Please sit, my lord. I do hope that you will not mind if I continue to work. My sister-in-law is nearing her lying in, and I wish to have this sheet finished for her baby's cradle before it is born." Though there was a certain truth to her statement, her real reason for wishing to stitch on her embroidery was so that she would have something to occupy her hands and someplace to look other than at him.

She felt rather than saw him lean over to study her handiwork. Though his head was far too close to hers for her comfort, Bethany restrained her urge to jerk away, not about to allow her discomfiture to show. At length, he murmured, "How lovely. Then again, you always were quite skilled with the needle. I still have the exquisite waistcoat you embroidered for me for my birthday." His voice sounded odd, husky with emotion.

Bethany looked up sharply at his tone to see him watching her, smiling in much the same manner as he had done when she was his mistress and he'd wished to make love. Resisting her impulse to grimace, she glanced at the door to make certain that Rowles had exited, determined to get to the heart of the interview as quickly as possible. Seeing the servant gone, she returned her gaze to her former lover and bluntly countered, "I am sure you did not come here this evening to reminisce the past with me, my lord."

"Harry," he corrected her, moving his head away from hers to assume a relaxed pose in his chair. "After what we once were to each other, I see no need to stand on formality."

Bethany gritted her teeth to keep herself from informing him exactly what he was to her now, not wishing to antagonize him any more than was necessary.

Nonetheless, she could not bring herself to his utter his given name, an act suggestive of intimacy in her mind, so she demurred, saying, "If you do not mind, I would feel more comfortable referring to you as my lord."

"As you wish, my dear." He more cooed than uttered the words, the sound of them making Bethany recoil as if from an unwanted caress. Again pressing his head close to hers, he whispered, "Dear God, Bethany, you are beautiful. Even more so than the last time I saw you, if such a thing is possible."

Unfortunately, Bethany couldn't say the same for him. Looking at him now, she wondered how she could have ever thought him so very handsome. True, she supposed that some women would find him attractive, what with his thick golden hair, which was always coaxed into the latest style, his clear, cornflower blue eyes, and dimpled cheeks. And there were no doubt women who actually preferred his unimposing stature and more slender build to the commanding splendor of Christian's muscular physique. But in her eyes, his looks faded into insignificance when compared to Christian's blatantly masculine beauty.

Now wary and wondering at his game, praying that he hadn't come to try to blackmail her into granting him her favors in exchange for his silence, she blurted out with far more bluntness than she had intended, "What do you want, Lord Kirkland?"

There was a long pause, during which she was beginning to think that he might not answer, then he said, "I came to tell you that I am sorry."

Bethany could not help snorting at that. As if simply saying that he was sorry was enough to dissolve the bitterness she felt toward him. Unable to stop her tongue from responding, she snapped, "If that is all you came for, then you have completed your mission, and I shall bid you farewell."

He sighed, and when she glanced up from stabbing

her needle through the fine linen in stitches she would be required to rip out later, she saw that his face looked suddenly weary and that his shoulders slumped, as if in defeat. "I know I deserve your hatred, Bethany," he muttered.

"Yes, you do," Bethany agreed, setting aside her needlework to prevent herself from doing it any further damage.

"Perhaps it will make you feel better to know that I hate myself for what I did to you."

She shrugged, "Not particularly, since I do not really care how you feel."

He sighed again. "You have to understand that I had no choice but to do what I did."

"One always has a choice," Bethany tartly interjected.

He shook his head, his gaze seeking hers, his eyes pleading for understanding. "Not always, not in this instance. I know I give the appearance of being a wealthy man, but the truth of the matter is that I have nothing but my title to call my own. All my funds come from the generous yearly allowance I was granted as a part of my wife's marriage portion. She is a commoner, you see, an American who very much wanted to marry into the English aristocracy. So her papa purchased her a noble groom, a man destitute and desperately in debt. Me."

"I hardly see what any of that had to do with me," Bethany said with a sniff, as short on compassion as she was on patience for his tale of woe. Let him freeze and starve in a rookery for a few months and see just how much sympathy he had for the person who put him there.

"It had everything to do with you once my wife found out about our relationship. She is an exceedingly jealous woman, Bethany, a colonial who does not understand the ways of the aristocracy or that a man needs to find pleasure outside of marriage." He began to lean near her again, his eyes still clinging to hers. "Please believe me when I say that I did not wish to end things the way I did and that there was nothing I would have loved more than to have held our child in my arms. Whether or not you choose to believe me, the truth of the matter is that I loved you. I loved our unborn child, too. But there truly was nothing I could do for either of you. I was at the end of my yearly stipend when you gave me your news, and my father-in-law refused to replenish my coffers until I ridded myself of you. Apparently, my wife had been venting to him her unhappiness over my relationship with you, and since he doted on her . . ." He finished the sentence with a shrug. "So you see, I had no real choice."

"Oh, I see well enough," she retorted waspishly. "You sacrificed our child for monetary profit. Do you know that the doctors said that our daughter—" She saw a shadow of pain cross his face at her revelation that the child have been a girl. "Yes, my lord. You had a beautiful daughter, one who the doctors said most probably died due to the privation I suffered after you tossed Bliss and I into the streets. By the bye, I noticed that you did not ask after my sister, and as I recall, you two were fast friends."

"I know that Bliss is well, just as I knew when I came here that our child had died and that you have been living in Lancashire on your brother's estate, one called Critchley Manor, I believe."

That revelation brought Bethany up short. "And how, pray tell, did you learn all that?" she exclaimed, stiffening.

"I have made it my business to learn about you," he replied. "After I received my allowance, I searched for you. I wanted you to have the funds for a decent place to live, and I intended to pay for our child's keep, even though I knew I must keep the fact a secret and I could never again take you as my mistress. But I could not find you. You seemed to have disappeared off the face of the earth. And then Gideon Harwood arrived in town and I instantly remembered all you had told me about your brother in India and knew who he was. From then on I had him followed, and eventually found you. Since your brother is a wealthy man who clearly loves you, I saw no reason to disturb you in your new life."

"Then why come now?" Bethany softly inquired, hating the note of pleading that had crept into her voice.

"Because I heard you were to marry Northwick." Bethany opened her mouth to respond, though what she intended to say, she did not know, but he cut her off before she could speak, saying, "I came only because I want you to be happy. I do not know if Northwick is aware of your true past, and I shall not ask you to tell me. All I wish is for you to know that neither he nor anyone else will ever hear the truth from me. As far as I am concerned, you are indeed Mrs. Matland, a respectable widow. And you needn't worry that my wife or her father will empty the bag, either. They never knew your name or particularly cared to learn it. So you should be safe from scandal in all quarters."

"Why?" Bethany asked, unable to believe her ears. "Why are you doing this for me?"

"Because I owe you at least that much."

Indeed he did. Nonetheless, Bethany was disarmed by his gesture, so much so that she actually managed to smile at him as she said with heartfelt gratitude, "Thank you."

He nodded. "You are welcome." After several awkward moments during which neither of them quite knew what else to say, he murmured, "Well, then. That is that, I suppose."

"That is that," she quietly agreed.

"Then allow me to extend my best wishes for your upcoming nuptials." He rose as he uttered the felicitation, clearly preparing to take his leave.

Bethany, too, rose. Though it would be a very long time before she could truly forgive him, she felt like she was now well on the road to doing so. Impulsively presenting her hand, she said, "Good-bye, Harry,"

He took her proffered hand in his, smiling rather sadly in response to her use of his given name. "Of all the things I shall regret at the end of my life, what I will regret most is that I was never able to make you mine. I shall go to my grave envying Northwick for having the good fortune to do so."

Chapter 16

"Lord Northwick, ur, I mean—umm—" the footman stationed at White's front door sputtered inarticulately several more times before breaking off completely, visibly nonplussed over how to address Christian in the wake of the scandal.

Christian halted in the center of the club's foyer, turning to smile his sympathy for the man's chagrin. "It is quite all right, Hollingsworth. There seems to be much confusion over what to call me of late. Personally, I prefer Mr. English, but I suppose you must refer to me as Lord Christian, since it is my correct title as the deposed Amberley heir."

Hollingsworth nodded and discreetly cleared his throat behind his white-gloved hand. "*A-hem!* Lord Christian, yes, very good. Thank you, my lord." He nodded again, returning Christian's smile. Now advancing toward where Christian stood, he said, "There was a letter delivered for you a quarter of an hour ago, my lord. The man who brought it cautioned me that it is of the utmost importance and specified that I was to place it directly into your hands myself the instant you entered the club." He produced a rather dog-eared letter from his pocket and did exactly that.

Christian raised his eyebrows at the servant's message, mystified by its cryptic nature. After rewarding the man with several coins, he broke the plain wafer sealing the missive and unfolded the single sheet of paper. Glancing first at the signature, which identified it as being sent by Chafford, he read the short, hastily scrawled note, shaking his head at the contents.

"Not bad news, I hope?" the footman solicitously inquired.

"No, nothing like that." For all the drama of its delivery, Chafford had penned the note merely to inform him that he, Illingsworth, Avondale, Fielding, and Godwin, who were to meet Christian at the club at seven, had been detained at Tattersall's due to a complication in Illingsworth's purchase of horses for his new sporting gig. Since Chafford had also indicated that they would arrive at White's no later than half past the hour and had asked him to wait, Christian added, "When Lord Chafford arrives, please inform him that I am in the reading room."

After securing the servant's promise to do so, Christian divested himself of his coat and hat, and then made his way to the club's comfortable reading room, looking forward to passing the next half hour reading the latest newspapers and enjoying a solitary glass of port. Though he had been invited to join his fellow Bachelor Barrack dwellers on their daylong itinerary of excursions, which had included visits to several shops, calling upon the women his circle had decided they fancied that week, and a sale of fine horses at Tattersall's, Christian had declined in favor of accompanying Bethany to what in a few months' time would be her new school to consult with the contractor they had hired to make the required renovations.

Unlike the first time they had visited the old inn, Christian had since taken measures to ensure Bethany's safety by hiring four recently retired soldiers to stand as armed guards over the place, giving them strict instructions that Bethany was never to enter a room alone or be allowed to stray out of earshot for the entire time she was there. And he intended to continue their employment, perhaps even adding to their number, once the school was in operation. Anything to keep his darling Bethany safe.

Engaging the soldiers had been Avondale's suggestion, one that had been made the night after the scandal had broken while Christian and his circle had lounged about the Bachelor Barrack's library, drinking fine port and conversing, something that had become somewhat of a nightly ritual for them on those evenings when they were all at home. Their conversation that particular night had been more of an interrogation than a discourse, with his friends attempting to first tease and then pry details about Bethany from him, the whole while lending him their support in their typically circuitous male fashion.

Christian smiled at the thought of life at the Bachelor Barrack. Though his circle was long past the age for engaging in the reckless pranks for which they were famous in their youth, they still enjoyed jolly times when in each other's company and shared an easy sense of camaraderie that had made Christian feel instantly at home in his new accommodations. Moreover, living there afforded him the opportunity to become better acquainted with his brother.

Unlike the other denizens of the Bachelor Barrack, who often stayed abed until noon, Godwin, like Christian, preferred to rise early, and seldom a morning passed that they did not breakfast together. Being alone in the stillness of those gray postdawn hours allowed them to further strengthen the bond of intimacy they had forged through their brotherhood, and Christian now felt like there was nothing he could not share with Godwin. And share he did, telling his brother all about his hopes, dreams, and plans for his life, and for his future with Bethany. He had also shared his pain and disappointment over his rift with their parents, to which Godwin, in his typically droll fashion, had recounted the numerous times in which their parents had disowned Christian for his wickedness in the past, pointing out that since they had always come around back then they were bound to do so in this instance, as well.

There was something in Godwin's face as he spoke, or perhaps it was in his voice, that gave Christian the disquieting sense that his brother's wry humor was but a facade to conceal his bitterness at being used as a pawn to keep Christian in line. When Christian, wishing to learn the truth, had asked his brother the question point-blank, Godwin had remained silent for a very long time before finally replying, "It is difficult not to feel a measure of resentment at being knocked back down to second son after enjoying the privileges and pleasures afforded the Amberley heir." The words had no sooner left his mouth than he rushed to say that he would rather have Christian for his brother than all the titles in the world, adding that while he enjoyed the privileges of being the heir, he found the responsibilities unbearably tedious. Though Godwin had seemed to genuinely mean what he said, Christian could not help being troubled by his confession.

"Northwick!" someone hailed.

Instinctively responding to the name, Christian glanced in the direction from which the voice had come to see Viscount Dent, one of London's most notorious bloods, and his young protégé in debauchery, Marcus Rhodes, the newly anointed Earl of Landseer, standing outside the subscription room. Lord Dent was signaling for him to come over.

Casting a wishful glance toward the reading room at the end of the hall, longing for its peace, Christian willed his reluctant feet to carrying him over to the men, praying that they weren't in one of their chattier moods. "Gentlemen," he murmured, nodding his greeting.

Lord Landseer, a portly, spotty-faced youth fresh from Oxford, exclaimed, "I daresay your ears were burning, Northwick. We were just talking about you."

"Indeed," Christian politely intoned, not bothering to correct the young man on the change in his title for what would have been the ninth time.

Lord Dent, a dissolute-looking rake whom Christian would have guessed from his stained teeth and the pouches beneath his eyes to be middle-aged but knew to be much younger, chuckled and took a swig from the glass in his hand, saying, "We happened to spy you with your widow through Gunter's window yesterday. She is an exceedingly fine article, no doubt about it. We were just saying that it might actually be worth sacrificing one's title to marry a female like that. We applaud your fine taste."

As if to illustrate his friend's words, Lord Landseer began to lightly applaud, stopping again in the next moment when Lord Dent shot him a withering look.

Christian inclined his head in acknowledgement to their compliments. "Thank you, gentlemen. I am pleased that you approve of my choice. Now, if you will excuse me?" He nodded toward the end of the hall, as if to indicate that he had a prior engagement.

"Of course, of course," Lord Landseer bluffly exclaimed, thumping him jovially on the back. "No doubt you have many toasts to drink to your beautiful future bride."

"Yes," Christian replied. And it was most probably the truth. It seemed that just about every member at White's had either seen or called upon Bethany in the wake of the scandal and now wanted to drink a toast to her beauty. Not that he had any objections to their doing so.

Ever since he'd come to London he had dreamed about escorting her around town, proudly and openly, wishing to show her off to the entire world and to publicly proclaim their love. Though Bethany still shied away from accompanying him to the many gatherings they had both been invited to of late, knowing as he did that the invitations had been tendered more out of a wish to provide the *ton* with the sport of watching them together rather than from any real desire for their company, she had allowed him to escort her to Gunter's for a sweet when they had completed their business at the school the day before. As he had walked through the shop door with Bethany on his arm—Bethany the picture of serene beauty and refinement in her midnight blue ermine-edged pelisse and matching round fur cap, he had known the true meaning of the word pride. How could he not feel pride at having by his side the woman he considered God's most miraculous creation; a woman who was not only breathtakingly lovely to look at, but also possessed a heart and soul to match? How could he not glory in knowing that such a woman loved him in return and had consented to be his wife?

Bubbling with effervescent joy, like he always did when he contemplated his good fortune in being loved by Bethany, Christian entered the quiet reading room with its clusters of comfortably deep leather armchairs, solitary reading desks, and tables around which the gentlemen sometimes gathered to discuss the news in the papers they were reading. Tonight the room was free of patrons save for a trio of ancient peers in old-fashioned white powdered wigs, one who snored loudly in an armchair with his mouth wide open, displaying a dislodged set of false teeth, while his nearby companions whispered and guffawed.

Nodding politely to the two awake men, who grinned broadly in return, he strolled near the door to the long table, upon which was neatly arranged a selection of reading materials. Finally settling on the latest edition of *The Globe,* he glanced around for a place to sit, doing a double take when he spied a fourth club member sitting at a table in the far corner. He was sitting so still, clearly deeply involved in whatever he was reading, that Christian had overlooked him during his first casual glance around the room. Now that he had noticed the man, his eyes narrowed at the sight of him.

It was Lord Denleigh, whom he had not seen since the night he had almost been run over, and for once he was alone.

After a brief moment of deliberation, Christian began to move toward him. For all the peace he had found in loving Bethany, a part of him would never rest until he had made amends with Lord Denleigh. Whether or not Denleigh would allow him to do so, or if such a thing was even possible given the situation, well, that was yet to be seen. But judging from the man's conduct the night of the accident, he guessed that his bitterness did not run beyond reason.

Now stopping near where his old nemesis sat, Christian quietly said, "Denleigh?"

Lord Denleigh slowly glanced up, his pure cerulean eyes registering surprise when he saw who had uttered his name. An odd smile touching the corners of his lips, he murmured, "Northwick, or should I call you Moncreiffe? It is hard to keep up with the gossip these days, it flies so fast and furious."

That the man was speaking in a civil voice struck Christian as a good sign. Smiling in response to his comment, he replied, "I must confess that it is getting rather hard for me to keep up on it all myself, so much so that I am sometimes at a loss as to how to refer to myself. Since, however, I do not recall hearing that I am back in my parents' good graces, I believe that Moncreiffe is correct."

Denleigh's enigmatic smile broadened a hint at Christian's attempt at humor. "Ah, well. I daresay they will forgive you soon enough. They never could deny you for long, no matter how outrageous your actions."

Christian made a face at Denleigh's reference to his less-than-admirable past self. "So I have heard, though from what I have been told, I would have been better served had they shipped me off to India sooner."

"As would I," Denleigh countered with a short laugh.

Christian smiled tautly at his quip, taken aback by his tone. The bon mot had been uttered dryly and with genuine humor, wholly free from the taint of bitterness one would expect, given the situation. Tipping his head to gaze down at the other man's starkly handsome face, which was the picture of urbane poise, Christian said, "I wish to thank you for lending me your coach on the night of the accident. It was most gracious of you."

Denleigh made a dismissive hand motion. "I received your note the following day, which was thanks enough. Of course, my coachman has never been quite the same since. After the sizeable gratuity you insisted he accept for driving you home, he has taken to spending an inordinate amount of time loitering near the front of the house. I could almost swear that he is hoping that another gentleman will come to grief so he can drive him home, as well, and perhaps earn another handful of gold."

Yet another jest? Perplexed, Christian frowned, blurting out without thinking, "Were you always so witty?"

Denleigh shrugged. "There were some who considered me to be so, though, as you have probably guessed by now, you did not rank among them."

Christian shook his head, suddenly wanting nothing

more than to know what had made him view with such loathing the man whom he presently found rather pleasant company. Somehow sensing that Denleigh would appreciate candor, he asked, "What made us hate each other so very much that we would attempt to kill each other? Surely it was not simply a matter of coveting the same bit of muslin?"

That odd smile again touched Denleigh's precisely sculpted lips. "Ah. That will take time to explain." Raising his arm to summon the nearby footman, he inquired, "Are you still a port man, Moncreiffe?" At Christian's nod, he turned his attention to the footman, saying, "Do be a good fellow and fetch a bottle of your finest port." When the servant had bustled off to do as he was bid, Denleigh glanced back at Christian, who stood frowning down at him, again at a loss as to how to interpret the other man's actions. His eyebrows lifting in a meaningful quirk, Denleigh said, "Why don't you be a good fellow, as well, and sit down. My neck is getting devilishly stiff from looking up at you, and as you might imagine, it is rather inconvenient for me to stand."

"Yes, I can indeed imagine," Christian murmured, awash with shame at the reminder of what his recklessness had cost the other man. Doing as requested, he took the chair to Denleigh's right, squarely meeting his gaze as he did what he had come over to do. "Whether or not you choose to accept my apology, and I shall not blame you a whit if you do not, I want you to know that I am truly sorry and deeply ashamed by what I did to you. And I would like a chance to make amends, though how one can possibly amend for such an atrocity, I do not know."

Denleigh returned his gaze for several tense beats, a thousand emotions flitting through his startlingly blue eyes. Then he made a soft sound halfway between a sigh and a laugh, and quietly uttered, "Tell me about India, Moncreiffe. Was your ordeal truly as grueling as everyone seems to believe?"

"No. It was far worse," he softly retorted. Aware that he was speaking to someone who knew what it meant to truly suffer, he added, "I was not only beaten and starved and forced to live in ungodly conditions, like everyone says, I was subjected to unspeakable humiliation and violated in ways that haunt me still." Aside from Gideon, to whom he had confided everything, this was the first he had admitted to that last. And though Lord Denleigh had every reason to hate him and to wish him ill, Christian felt a strange sort of kinship with him and somehow knew that he could trust him with whatever confidences he chose to share on the matter.

At that moment, the footman returned with the port and two glasses. When he had poured them each a measure and retreated to his station in the opposite corner, Denleigh lifted his glass, saying, "Here is to our partnership in misery."

With a nod, Christian touched his glass to Denleigh's, thinking how aptly the man had read his thoughts and put them into words. Partners in misery indeed.

For several moments thereafter they drank in companionable silence, strangely at ease in each other's presence. At length Denleigh said, "It would appear that we have both paid a very dear price for our hatred. I have paid with my leg and you—" He tipped his glass in Christian's direction to indicate that he was to state his own price.

"My soul," Christian supplied in a hoarse whisper. "I paid with my soul."

"Ah. But it would appear that you have gained a new one, a far better one, from all that I have heard and observed, while I," he thumped his leg, producing a dull thud, "while I have gained a new leg of steel and iron." He heaved an exaggerated sigh. "Ah, well. At least I suffered no pain when my horse stepped on my foot last week. Of course, my boot was ruined, which was a terrible pity."

Christian choked on the port he had just sipped, unable to believe that the man could joke about such a thing. If he were conversing with the bastard who had robbed him of his leg, the last thing he would be inclined to do was jest about his maimed state.

Denleigh grinned at his response. "I rather like that story myself."

Christian shook his head, incredulous. "How can you jest so about such a terrible tragedy?" he exclaimed.

Denleigh's smile faded, and for the first time since they had begun their conversation he looked wholly serious. "Because I must." He uttered the words softly and without the slightest inflection.

Christian shook his head again, frowning. "I am afraid that I do not understand."

"No, I daresay that you do not." Denleigh paused to take another drink, to fortify himself, Christian suspected, and then continued. "No doubt you have heard that I tried to take my life after I lost my leg." Christian opened his mouth, compelled to apologize again, but Denleigh cut him off with a wave of his hand. "Oh, I am not reiterating the point to further shame you or to beg for pity. I am stating a simple fact. I could not bear to live with the humiliation of being maimed in such a manner. I felt like less of a man for the loss of my leg, and if you were able to remember what I was like in those days you would know how deeply such a feeling would affect me. I shall never forget the pain in the wake of my amputation, not the pain from the operation, though God knows it was horrendous. Worse was the pain of knowing that I would never again be the envy of the men in the *ton,* and that the women who had once gazed at me with such desire in their eyes would now view me with scornful pity. How I hated you then. Not a day passed that I did not wish for you to suffer as I did."

"If it is any consolation, I can promise you that you got your wish," Christian interjected in a soft voice.

Denleigh shrugged. "I decided long ago that it did not matter, that I could not let it matter. You asked me why we hated each other so? I can tell you in two words: pride and arrogance. In all honesty, I cannot claim that we actually knew each other. We were like two young lions fighting for possession of a pride: we both wished to be the dominant male in the *ton*. We were locked in a constant battle, each struggling to prove himself the strongest and the best, determined to win at any price. And in the end—"

"We both lost," Christian finished for him.

"Perhaps it is because we deserved to lose," Denleigh countered, again meeting Christian's gaze. "Perhaps losing will end up being the making of us both."

"Do you really believe that?" Christian asked.

"When the choice is between believing and having your soul eaten up by hate and self-loathing, yes." He paused to drink deeply from his glass, then explained, "You see, over time I came to understand that I was as much to blame for what happened that night as you were. I was as guilty of tweaking your pride at every turn as you were of tweaking mine. I was every bit as arrogant and overbearing as you, and as much as it pains me to admit the truth, the actress we dueled over was rightfully yours. She made no secret of the fact that she preferred you, and in my overweening conceit I could not accept that any woman would prefer you to me."

"But I was told that it was I who called you out," Christian said, his mind spinning with what Denleigh was telling him, trying to reconcile it with what he had heard about the incident from his circle.

Denleigh looked away then, but not before Christian saw a shadow pass through his eyes. "I gave you every reason to do so. I told the female in question that you were fond of sordid sexual acts—all lies, of course—and painted you as a man with perverse appetites. After that, she refused to have anything to do with you. In your own way, I think you rather loved her."

"Why are telling me all this?" Christian asked, staring at Denleigh's strong profile.

Denleigh turned his head, his gaze reconnecting with Christian's. "Again, because I must. Let us call it an unburdening of my soul. Neither of us are the men we were in our youth," he made a wry face at his own words, "though, of course, neither of us are exactly what one would call in our dotage, either, yet I feel like I have aged at least a hundred years since the night of the duel. And in my newfound maturity," another wry face, "I have decided that though I can never again be considered for the title of the strongest or most desirable man in the *ton,* I shall find it very satisfying indeed if someone someday says that I am one of the best men. I daresay such a title will stand in better stead for me when I am their age." He nodded at the ancient peers, all of whom now snored in a discordant chorus.

Christian smiled at the sight of the comical trio. "From our conversation this evening, I would say that you are well on your way to earning that title," he returned, genuinely meaning what he said. "I can only hope that I shall someday be worthy of such a title myself."

"Perhaps that is what we should drink to, then," Denleigh said, refilling his glass and Christian's, which Christian was astonished to see he had drained during their conversation. Raising his glass once again, Denleigh said, "Here is to being worthy of the title 'good men.' "

As Christian began to drink to the toast, he heard Chafford's distinctive voice exclaim, "There he is!" He turned to see Chafford, Illingsworth, Fielding, Avondale, and his brother trooping toward him. When they saw who his companion was they stopped short, their faces set in identical expressions of thunderstruck disbelief.

Christian and Lord Denleigh exchanged an amused look, with Denleigh calling out, "I was just about to propose a toast to Moncreiffe's beautiful bride-to-be. Perhaps you gentlemen would care to join us?"

Always the first to recover his wits in all situations, Avondale blurted out, "Well, I'll be damned!"

Chapter 17

"You are going to bite the tip off the index finge of your glove if you continue to gnaw it like that,' Gideon commented.

Bethany, who sat opposite her brother in his elegan town coach, silently fretting over Christian's failure t appear that morning for their daily appointment t view the school's latest renovations, jerked from he mouth the finger she had been unaware she was chew ing, frowning when she saw the damage to her glove Judging from the teeth marks marring the fine kidski and the fact that the stitching at the end of the inde finger was beginning to come undone, it was obviou that she had been nibbling it for quite some time now Dropping her hand to her lap with a frustrated sigh she said, "I cannot stop worrying about Christian. I is utterly out of character for him not to show up fo one of our appointments like this. In the past, he ha always sent a note around if he is going to be mor than a few minutes late."

"Well, notes have been known to be accidentall misdirected. It is also not unheard of for the servan assigned to carry said note to be detained or distracte along the way," Gideon replied with his usual unru fled logic. "I am sure that such is the case in this instance, and that it will all turn out to be nothing more than a comedy of errors. No doubt we will all have a hearty laugh over the incident in the end."

"No doubt," Bethany murmured, her concern unalleviated.

"I am only glad that I was here to accompany you to the school myself," Gideon continued. "I must say that I am exceedingly impressed with what you have accomplished thus far. You should be very proud of yourself. I most certainly am."

Bethany managed a faint smile in response to his praise. "I could not have done nearly so well without Christian's help. The contractor says that he has never seen such well-conceived and expertly drawn plans as the ones Christian presented to him. Did you have any idea that Christian is such a marvelous architect?"

"I rather suspected that he had a talent in that direction from the sketches he made for the carpenters when we converted the old village mill into the guild cloth factory." He shook his head, chuckling. "More unexpected yet was his expertise with tools. Even Christian was surprised to find that he could not only identify every tool in the carpenters' workboxes, but he also knew how to wield them with impressive skill."

Bethany's smile broadened a fraction at the thought of Christian and what she was discovering day by day to be his astonishing range of knowledge. "Christian is a remarkable man full of hidden talents, and I look forward to spending my life discovering each and every one of the them," she said.

Gideon leaned over then to take both her hands in his. Giving them an affectionate squeeze, he murmured, "Have I told you yet how happy I am for you and Christian?"

"Not since you have been in London, no. Then again, you arrived late last night, so I suppose I shall have to forgive you your lapse," she teased, squeezing his hands in return. "You did, however, make your approval for the match more than clear in your last letter."

"How could I not approve of such a match when it shall be the union of two people whom I hold so very dear to my heart?" As Gideon spoke, his eyes began to dance with an impish light and his lips curved into the grin that Bethany had recognized since childhood as being a precursor to deviltry. "Do not tell Julia that I told you this, for I do not wish to encourage her in her meddling, but I secretly approved of her matchmaking between you two and hoped it would be a success. If ever two people belong together, it is you and Christian."

"Do you really think so?" Bethany asked, her doubts about the marriage renewed by Christian's rift with his parents.

Gideon nodded. "I have from the very instant I saw you two together. It was clear that you are very alike in all the ways that are important, and that you complement each other in your differences. Furthermore, you are exceedingly good for each other. I watched you both grow and blossom in each other's company while at Critchley, and am certain that you will continue to do so if you spend the rest of your lives together."

"Perhaps. Nonetheless, I cannot help feeling like our love has been somehow tainted by Christian's falling-out with his parents. I hate that he was forced to choose between us."

"It was his parents who forced him, not you, so it is their love that bears the taint. Had they loved and nurtured him properly, they could be certain that the values they had instilled are now standing him in good stead and they would trust his judgment in selecting a bride. That they cannot or will not trust him suggests that they do not bear for him the unconditional love that family members must have for each other if they are to maintain their ties. Christian had a choice and he chose you, Bethany. He chose you because he knows that the love you bear for him is pure and unsullied by unreasonable conditions and selfish expectations, unlike the love of his parents. To allow his parents' selfishness to poison what you have together will be a betrayal of the trust he has put in your love for him."

Of course he was right. Why should she allow the Duke and Duchess of Amberley's selfish prejudices to ruin something so very wonderful and right for her and Christian, especially when Christian refused to do so? Her heavy heart lightening and lifting, she asked with a smile, "Have you always been so very wise, big brother? Or has your wisdom come with your advanced age?"

Gideon laughed. "As much as I would like to plead the former, I must credit that particular piece of wisdom to loving Julia. She has taught me much about trust and the importance of unconditional love." Giving the hands he still held another squeeze, he added, "As for your other concern regarding Christian, if he is not at the house nor sent a message by the time we arrive home, I will go to his quarters and see what has detained him. I promise."

"Thank you, Gideon. I would appreciate that," Bethany replied, allowing herself to relax for the first time that morning.

But Christian wasn't at the house, nor had he sent a message. Now rather concerned himself, Gideon, in the company of Jagtar, his manservant, who always accompanied him on his business about town, promptly departed for Christian's quarters.

Now in the family drawing room with Julia and Bliss, the former stitching an elaborate blue silk bonnet for her baby while the latter worked on a tiny red wool greatcoat for Kesin, who napped in his flannel-lined basket on the floor near where Bliss sat, Bethany was finding it impossible to concentrate on the cradle sheet she was trying to embroider, anxious for news of Christian. Gideon and Jagtar had been gone for well over an hour, more than enough time for them to have visited Christian's quarters and returned, thus she tensed with anticipation every time she heard the clatter of an approaching coach, only to slump in disappointment every time it passed by.

Finally giving up on her needlework, she set it aside and rose from her favorite chair to wander to the window, which overlooked the street. Parting the filmy subcurtain to allow her an unobstructed view, she rested her forehead against the cold window glass, staring at the scene outside. As was usual for this time of day, callers could be seen arriving and departing from the town houses on the fashionable square, while servants and laborers with business there hurried on their way, taking care not to brush shoulders with their betters. Every now and again a caller would come to their door, only to be turned away with the news that the household wasn't receiving that day.

As Bethany watched Ladies Trudgill and Townsend, two of the *ton*'s most malicious gossips, disappear up the front steps and then reappear to depart a few moments later, she could not have been more grateful to Julia for instructing Rowles that no one, save for Christian, was to be allowed to call this afternoon.

Oh! If only he would call! Bethany thought, idly sketching a looping line in the fog her warm breath had haloed on the cold glass. She had become so accustomed to seeing him every morning that she felt oddly incomplete having missed doing so today.

"Looking for them shan't make them come any sooner, Bethany, dear," Julia said in a gentle voice.

Sighing, Bethany dropped the curtain back into place. "I know," she replied, turning away from the window. "I just do not know what to do with myself while I wait. I am much too restless and distraught to sew."

"I am sure there is no need whatsoever to worry," Julia said. "My guess is that Gideon has found Christian by now and that they have forgotten the time in their pleasure of seeing each other again. You know how they are when they are together. They talk and talk and quite forget the rest of the world."

"Of course you are right," Bethany murmured, remembering all the times she and Julia had been worried to distraction waiting for them to return from the village for supper, only to have them appear an hour or so late, confessing to having been caught up in a particularly stimulating conversation.

For the first time since Gideon had left for Christian's quarters, Bethany smiled, picturing the sheepish looks on their faces at those times. Of course, she and Julia had always forgiven them. How could they not? Loving the men as they did they naturally valued Gideon and Christian's friendship, almost as much as Gideon and Christian did, thus they would never have done or said anything that might in any way discourage the closeness the men felt.

"Oh, bloody, *bloody* hell! Friggin' sleeve!" Bliss cried, stamping her foot in frustration.

"Bliss!" Julia and Bethany chorused in unison, while Kesin popped his woolly head up out of the basket, hissing in protest to being awakened.

Bliss reached down to soothe the disgruntled little beast, shooting Julia and Bethany a mutinous look as she gently massaged Kesin's shoulders. "Well, the sleeve *is* being a friggin' nuisance," she retorted unrepentantly, her gaze shifting to the hearth in a narrowed, sidelong glance, as if considering tossing her recalcitrant tailoring project into the fire. "I measured exactly like you taught me to do, Julia, and followed your instructions on cutting it out, Bethany, and the damn thing still won't fit into the friggin' armhole."

Grateful for something to distract her mind, Bethany went to where Bliss more sprawled than sat on the settee facing the window, kneeling down next to her to try to determine the problem. Seeing it instantly, she said, "You measured and cut perfectly, dear. The trouble is in your stitching. Do you see how the seam does not quite match up on the side?" Taking the little garment from her sister's hands, she showed her the mistake, then demonstrated how to remedy it. She was so engrossed in her instruction that she did not immediately respond to the sound of a coach rattling to a stop in front of their door. It wasn't until she heard Gideon shouting instructions outside that her mind snapped back to her worry over Christian and she jumped up. Running to the drawing room door, she flung it open wide and raced the short distance down the hallway to the foyer.

"Gideon!" she called out at the sight of her brother standing near the front door, where he appeared to be meting out a series of terse orders to the majordomo and several footmen. When Gideon heard her voice he turned, stretching out his arms to catch her as she skidded on the marble floor in her attempt to stop before him. Her words tumbling out in a blather-filled rush, she exclaimed, "Where is Christian? Is he with you? Did you—"

"Bethany," he cut in, his hands tightening on her arms.

There was something in his voice, a terrible, guttural tautness that rendered her silent and made her jerk her head back to look up at his face. The instant she saw it, a tingle of fear crept up her spine. His steel gray eyes were bleak and darkened with worry, and his mouth was set in a harsh line. The only word to describe his expression was *grim*. "C-C-Christian?" she stammered in a broken whisper, somehow forcing the utterance through the alarm constricting her throat.

"He is in the coach," Gideon replied. His gaze was boring into hers now, commanding her attention, forcing her to see what he was clearly having difficulty putting into words.

Bethany promptly glanced away, terrified by what she saw in his eyes. Refusing to believe that anything could be so very wrong, she frowned and shook her head, more babbling than saying, "I must go to Christian. I must see him—talk to him." But when she tried to pull her arms from Gideon's grasp to do so, his hands tightened around them, holding her immobile.

"Let me go, Gideon. I need to see him—I shall see him!" she cried, now struggling in earnest, desperate to go to the man she loved.

Gideon gave her a shake, a hard one. "Stop fighting me and listen, Bethany. Christian appears to have been poisoned, and he is in a very bad way. He might even be dying. If you want to help him, you will stay out of the way and let Jagtar and I do what we can for him."

The panic that had been welling up inside Bethany exploded at his news and she began to back away from him, shaking her head over and over again. "No. No! It cannot be, he cannot be so very bad off as that," she choked out, as if simply voicing the denial would make it true. As she uttered the words, Gideon pulled her away from the door to allow Rowles and four footmen bearing a litter to hurry outside.

"He is," Gideon retorted flatly, trying to steer her from the foyer.

She jerked away from him, still shaking her head. "Then we must summon a surgeon posthaste," she exclaimed, wildly flailing her arms in her agitation. "I hear that Doctor Gilbertson in Finsbury Square is the best to be had. Julia says that all the *ton* consult him on their ailments, so I shall—"

"He has already been seen by the man, who told us that there is nothing he can do for him," Gideon cut in.

"Then we shall get another surgeon, and if he cannot help Christian then we shall get another, and another, until we find one who can," she cried, not about to let Christian go without a fight.

"Gideon? Bethany? What has happened?" Julia inquired in a worried voice, coming, with Bliss close on her heels, to where they stood.

From outside came the sound of Jagtar's distinctively accented voice as he supervised Christian's removal from the coach and placement onto the litter, followed by the slam of the coach door. Frowning, Gideon glanced over his shoulder at the front door, which the servants had left ajar. Clearly not wishing the women and young Bliss to witness Christian being carried inside, he began to tow Bethany down the hall toward the family drawing room, herding Julia and Bliss in their wake.

"You did not answer my question, Gideon. What has happened?" Julia demanded to know.

"Christian has been poisoned," Gideon replied.

"Bloody friggin' hell!" Bliss exclaimed, coming to an abrupt stop.

Julia, too, halted in her steps. "What! But who—how—" she stammered, either not noticing Bliss's cursing in her shock or not caring enough at that moment to reprimand her.

"What the hell does it matter who did it or how? We should be helpin' him, not standin' around natterin'!" Bliss cried, trying to rush past Gideon. He caught her and pinned her against his side, still restraining Bethany with his other arm.

"Bliss is right. We must go to him and help him. I daresay you have already summoned a surgeon?" Julia said. For all that she was doing her best to maintain her composure, her voice quivered and her beautiful amber eyes glistened with tears.

"He is being helped as much as possible. Now if you will all hush and come into the drawing room, I will explain everything," Gideon said, half-carrying and half-dragging the wildly squirming Bliss and now weeping Bethany in that direction, while Julia followed behind, fretfully listing all the things they should be doing as they went.

Once they were in the drawing room and Gideon had deposited Bethany and Bliss on the settee, instructing Julia to sit beside them, he began to pace back and forth in front of them, saying, "As I have already explained to Bethany, Christian is in a very bad way. According to the surgeon who was at the house when we arrived, he appears to be dying." He held up his hand to silence their responding wails of despair, adding, "However, Jagtar believes that with proper treatment and care he might pull through."

"What the hell does Jagtar know about anything?" Bliss muttered with a sniffle.

Gideon fished his handkerchief from his pocket and handed it to her. "Plenty. And I will thank you to watch your tongue, young lady."

"Well?" Julia prompted, while Bliss blew her nose with unladylike vigor.

Gideon nodded. "Unfortunately, or perhaps it shall prove to our good fortune in this instance, poison is a rather popular mode of doing away with one's rivals and enemies in the Indian courts."

"So?" Bliss challenged impatiently.

"So Jagtar's cousin had, and I daresay probably still possesses, a rather tidy business concocting poisons in the court where I first met Jagtar. Since his patrons sometimes had a change of heart after utilizing his wares and decided that they did not wish their victims dead after all, he also supplied remedies. Of course, unlike the poisons, there was no guarantee that the remedy would work. At any rate, Jagtar learned a great deal from observing his cousin at work."

"Then Jagtar knows the remedy for Christian's poison?" Bethany exclaimed in a rush of hope.

"Jagtar knows many remedies for many poisons. However, since he cannot be certain what poison we are dealing with or even if it is one of which he has knowledge, he must treat Christian according to his symptoms. Since we also do not know how, where, or why Christian was poisoned, we have brought him here to ensure that if someone has indeed poisoned him on purpose that they shan't have the opportunity to do so again. In his current condition, another dose of poison would kill him for certain."

"You think someone tried to kill him?" Julia exclaimed, visibly aghast. "But why? Why in the world would anyone wish to do such a thing to Christian? No one has had anything but wonderful things to say about him since his return to London."

Gideon shrugged. "I do not know."

"Did his friends at the Bachelor Barrack have any idea as to how this could have happened?" Bethany asked, horrified by the thought that someone might be trying to kill the man she loved.

"They were not there to question. According to the servants, the other occupants of the house left for a shooting party in the country this morning. Since Christian had elected to remain in town to help you with the school, no one thought anything about it when he failed to appear for their early breakfast. His valet did mention that Christian was quite ill shortly before dawn, but that both he and Christian had assumed it to be from the drinking his circle had done the night before. When Christian finally became quiet, the man assumed that he was sleeping. Not wishing to disturb him, he did not check on him until early this afternoon. When he finally did so, he found the sheets soiled with vomit and bloody urine, and Christian in convulsions. Of course, he summoned a surgeon."

Always in command, Julia rose, briskly declaring, "I am glad you brought him here, where we can properly see to his care. Naturally, I shall assist in his nursing."

"As will I," Bethany said, rising as well. She wanted to be with Christian; she *needed* to be near him. Though she knew she was silly for thinking such a thought, she believed that she could somehow shield him from death if he was in her arms.

Gideon shook his head. "There will be plenty you can do for him later. If he survives, he is bound to have a long convalescence and require a great deal of care. Right now, however, it would be for the best if you stayed away from the sickroom. What we shall have to do to Christian is neither pleasant nor dignified, and he would not wish for any of you to see him in such a condition."

"But I have to do something," Bethany whispered brokenly. "I shall go mad if I do not do something to help him."

"Then pray," Gideon said, gathering her into his arms.

Chapter 18

All afternoon and into the evening Bethany stood vigil outside Christian's bedchamber, sometimes pacing restlessly before the door, her steps short and rapid and her turns so abrupt that she often made herself dizzy, and other times sitting motionlessly in the hard, straight-backed side chair she had dragged from down the hall and stationed across from Christian's room. Every second felt like a year, every hour an eternity, as she awaited news of the man who was everything to her. Now and again the door would open and a footman would exit carrying soiled linen or a bucket filled with matter Bethany would rather not identify, but aside from the men sparing her a nod and a sympathetic smile, no one bothered to acknowledge her presence or tell her of Christian's condition.

When Julia had come searching for her just before supper and found her sitting there, she had had the footmen replace the chair with a well-padded settee from one of the unoccupied bedchambers to allow Bethany to wait in a modicum of comfort. She had then sat beside Bethany for a very long while, silently holding her hand in a mute offering of comfort and strength, aware that there were no words to ease her fear.

Now sitting alone, weariness and discomfort from her pregnancy having driven Julia to seek her bed, Bethany hugged herself, tears streaming down her cheeks at the anguished screams coming from behind Christian's door. Oh! The sounds that had been emanating from that room all day. Bethany sobbed aloud and hugged herself tighter, wondering if she would ever forget those heart-wrenching sounds—those terrible cries of torment, the painful retching, and, worst of all, those agonized, whimpering pleas from Christian begging Gideon and Jagtar to stop whatever it was they were doing to him at that moment.

Of course, she had been warned that the sounds would be awful. When Gideon, upon leaving the chamber to fetch something for Jagtar, had spied her in the hall, he had demanded that she wait downstairs, warning her of the horrors she would hear and perhaps even see if she remained there. Yet how could she not stay? As dreadful as the sounds were, they meant that Christian was at least alive. And though she was not allowed by his side, where she so desperately wanted to be, she was close at hand, near enough that she could rush to him at a second's notice, should he need her.

To Bethany's everlasting relief, Christian's latest bout of screaming was short-lived, followed by a lull during which she heard Gideon and Jagtar conversing, or perhaps they were speaking to Christian, soothing and reassuring him. She prayed it was the latter, hating the thought of Christian lying in pain with no one thinking to offer him comfort.

The instant that last thought entered her mind, she promptly dismissed it. But of course she was a goose to even imagine such a thing. If Gideon was anything, he was compassionate, and she knew from experience that he was always quick to offer comfort to those in need. He most certainly would not allow someone he cared for as much as he did Christian to suffer without giving him what solace he could.

Wishing that she were allowed to comfort him, too, wanting nothing more at that moment than to cradle him in her arms and croon soft, soothing nonsense to him, Bethany lay down on the settee, snuggling deep into the cushions with her feet tucked beneath her skirts in an attempt to evade the night chill that now crept down the corridor. An hour passed during which there were no more sounds from Christian's room, then two, the time marked by the deep-throated chiming of the long case clock in the foyer. Exhausted from her worry, Bethany drifted into a fitful slumber.

She was awakened sometime later, at an hour she determined to be deep in the night, judging from the stillness of the house around her, roused by someone sharply and insistently poking her shoulder. Her neck stiff and aching from sleeping with it at an odd angle, she gingerly lifted her head to see who it was, gritting her teeth at the pain knifing through her neck and down her shoulder as she did so.

It was Bliss. Clad in a white frilled nightgown and ivory woolen wrapper, with her long hair severely scraped from her pale, tearstained face into a braid that dangled down her back, she looked like a wraith standing in the dim light of the sputtering candles.

"Bliss? Sweetheart?" Bethany murmured, instantly wide awake at the sight of her sister's tears. Bliss almost never cried, and then only at the most dire tragedies. Like when their mother had died and they had been forced to bury her in one of the awful, trenchlike pauper graves, where her body had lain among a multitude of other corpses, all in various states of decay and left uncovered by earth until the grave was at last determined to be full, which had occurred several days later. Knowing that the mother she adored had been laid to rest in such a horrifying fashion had haunted

Bliss then, plaguing her with nightmares from which she would awaken screaming and weeping, and Bethany knew that it haunted her still. It most certainly still haunted her.

Aware that should he die like this Christian's ghost would take its place besides their mother's in haunting Bliss, and praying that he would live, not just for her sake but also for Bliss's, Bethany held her arms out to her weeping sister, murmuring, "Come, love."

Bliss flew into her embrace. Her lips trembling so badly that she had difficulty forming the words, she brokenly whispered, "I am so afraid, Bethany. What if Christian dies? I shall not be able to bear it if he dies." She was weeping in earnest now, her sobs ripping from her chest in deep, rending gusts.

"There, there now, sweet. Hush. Christian will be all right, just you wait and see," Bethany crooned, holding her sister close, gladly offering her the comfort she was unable to give to Christian. "He is a strong man. If anyone can survive this, it is he."

Bliss lifted her wet face from where it was pressed against Bethany's shoulder to stare up at her face, her eyes woefully begging for hope. "Do you really"—*sniffle!*—"think so?"

"I do," Bethany replied with a firm nod. "You heard Gideon. Jagtar believes that Christian has a very good chance of survival, and he would know. Besides, Christian has all of us to take care of him. How can he not live with people who love him as much as we do to nurse him back to health?" Oh! If only she felt as confident as she sounded.

Bliss stared at her solemnly for several moments, her damp gray eyes, which were so like Gideon's in both their color and luminous intelligence, keenly searching her face. At length she sniffled and nodded so imperceptibly that Bethany would not have seen her do so had she not been watching closely. "I truly do love him, you know, very much," Bliss whispered. "Do you think he knows that?"

Bethany tightened her arms around her in a fierce hug, forcing herself to eject a light laugh. "Of course he does, goose. How could he not know with the way you constantly cosset and spoil him? I also happen to know that he loves you in return."

A faint smile touched Bliss's lips. "Yes, he does. He loves us all. It is what makes him so very dear to us. He loves each and every one of us individually for who we are, not just because we are Gideon's family and he feels an obligation to do so. He has made me understand that he loves me for myself, enough that he shall never willingly abandon me." She nodded. "He promised me, and I believe him."

"As well you should, dear. You are very wise for one so young," Bethany countered, stunned, as she often was of late, by the maturity of Bliss's introspection. She was also touched that her sister trusted Christian so completely. After all that had happened in Bliss's short life, all the tragedy and betrayal she had suffered, she did not trust often or with ease. That she harbored such a perfect trust in Christian spoke volumes about how close he was to her heart.

"Can I stay with you here, just for a while?" Bliss murmured, snuggling against Bethany.

Bethany shook her head, not wanting Bliss to hear the sounds of Christian's agony, should they begin again. "I do not think—"

"Please?" Bliss softly implored, her arms twining around Bethany, practically clinging to her. "I wish to be near him, too."

How could she deny Bliss's request when she so well understood her need to be near Christian? Though it went against her better judgment to do so, she relented. "All right, then. But just for a short while." Lying again, she drew Bliss down to cradle her in her arms, pressing her front against her sister's back, holding her tight. Before long Bliss was asleep. Cuddling beside her, lulled by the soothing rhythm of her even breathing and comforted by the warmth of her small body, Bethany, too, drifted into slumber.

She dreamed that she was back at Critchley Manor with Christian. Once again, they were under the kissing bough, but this time they were alone, and this time they did not stop at a mere kiss.

It was still dark when Bethany woke from her delicious dream, darker, in fact, than when she had fallen asleep. The candles, which had burned low in their gilt wall brackets when she had drifted off, had since expired, leaving only the glow from the tapers in the girandole that someone had recently placed on the mirrored console at the end of the hall.

Wrapped in the lingering, somnolent pleasure of her dream, Bethany simply lay there for a long while, her body too relaxed to move and her mind too lethargic to think. Then her awareness of where she was and why abruptly intruded, and she bolted into a sitting position, gripped by panic.

Christian! Dear God! How was Christian? Was he better? Or worse? Was he even still alive?

Glancing wildly around her, it suddenly struck her that Bliss was no longer there, and she noticed that someone had tucked a warm wool blanket around her. That someone was no doubt a servant who had seen Bliss there and carried her to her bed, returning with the blanket to cover Bethany. Wondering what she had missed while she slept and feeling like she had somehow abandoned Christian by not staying awake to fret over him, Bethany tossed aside the blanket, her attention riveted to Christian's bedchamber door.

A thin ribbon of golden light spilled from beneath it, an auspicious sign, in her estimation, for it signaled that there was life within. Besides, if something had happened to Christian while she slept, someone would have awakened her. Wouldn't they?

Not if that someone was Gideon, she reminded herself. If Christian had died while she slept, it would be just like her brother to insist that she be allowed to continue to sleep, knowing that her grief over Christian's death would rob her of rest for a very long time thereafter.

Now rising, her heart twisting painfully in her chest at the thought of never again seeing Christian's beautiful smile or feeling his loving caress, Bethany crept to the door. After a brief moment of deliberation, she bit her lip and turned the knob. Despite the fact that Gideon did not wish her to see Christian so ill, and his certainty that Christian would not wish her to do so, either, she simply had to see him. . . . to touch him and feel his pulse beating beneath her hand . . . to know that he was still alive and that there was still hope. Bracing herself for what she might face in the room, be it Gideon's reprimands or Christian's lifeless body, she eased open the door. After a pause during which she sucked in a sustaining breath, she stepped over the threshold.

The room was warm, wonderfully so in contrast to the cold corridor where she had passed most of the night. Not wishing the heat to escape she quietly closed the door. She then forced herself to look at the scene before her. Remembering the terrible sounds of earlier, she expected to behold the usual sickroom disarray, to see the floor littered with soiled linen, overflowing slop buckets, and perhaps a hastily discarded chamber pot, with the surface of every table cluttered with medical paraphernalia and vials of curative potions.

What she saw instead was a clean, cozy chamber, with only the slop bucket by the bed and the inordinately high stack of clean towels by the pitcher and basin on the nearby table betraying the fact that its occupant was gravely ill. Well, that and the stench of vomit, sweat, and bodily waste, but even that wasn't nearly as pervasive or foul as she would have expected. Spying Gideon at the opposite side of the bed, sprawled, fast asleep, in an easy chair, Bethany slowly approached Christian.

He lay in a blue silk-draped tester bed with a gracefully carved mahogany headboard and cornice, his long, still form shrouded in shadows cast by its canopy and side curtains. As she drew nearer she saw that he was naked, his modesty saved only by a sheet that had been folded neatly over his loins. Now at his side, her hand flew to her mouth, pressing against it hard to stifle her cry of distress at the sight of him.

His skin looked waxen and bloodless, deathly in its translucent pallor, its ghostliness serving to cast the dark circles ringing his sunken eyes into stark relief, making them look like the angry bruises from grievous wounds. His beautiful lips, which were usually so full and soft, were painfully cracked and dry; their lush, rosy hue was blanched to a sickly ashen gray. As for his hair . . .

Her hands trembling with the power of her emotions, Bethany reached down and gently stroked one of the sweat-drenched curls spilling across his pillow. His poor hair, his wonderful, magnificent hair, it was impossibly matted and tangled. Sitting on the bed beside him, she resolved that when he was well enough for her to do so she would gently comb every snarl from those curls. Indeed, she looked forward to doing it for him. As she tenderly smoothed several damp strands away from his face, frowning at the cold clamminess of his skin, he cried out sharply and jerked over onto his side, tears spilling down his cheeks as he convulsively gripped his belly, his legs flexing up to his chest as if in response to terrible pain.

"Oh, Christian! My poor love," she whispered, frantically stroking his hair and back, desperate to ease his agony.

"Jagtar says that some poisons generate a burning in the stomach, bowels, and bladder, which causes the victim to suffer terrible pain in his belly and groin," she heard Gideon say. She glanced up to see him approaching the bed from the opposite side. In his fatigue, he looked almost as bad as Christian did. Now sitting on the edge of the bed, gazing down at Christian, his face drawn and his features taut with worry, he continued, "Judging from Christian's pain and the blood in his waste, Jagtar is almost certain that such a poison was used on him."

"If Jagtar knows what sort of poison was used, surely he can do something to help him," Bethany exclaimed, noting for the first time that Jagtar was absent from the room.

"He has done a great deal for him already," Gideon replied, his bleak gaze still on his friend, grimacing in sympathy when Christian sobbed and expelled a strangled whimper. "He spent the afternoon and most of the evening purging as much poison as possible from Christian's body, and he administered the antidotes for the poisons that match with his symptoms. Unfortunately, we did not get to him in time to prevent the poison from beginning its deadly work, so aside from giving him what comfort we can, there is nothing we can do but pray that he has the strength to survive."

Bethany opened her mouth to further question her brother about Christian's condition, to beg him for hope, but before she could form the words Christian again convulsed, a hoarse scream tearing from his throat as he rolled his pain-racked body into a tight ball and clutched his belly yet harder. Both Gideon and Bethany reached out to comfort him at the same time, with Bethany stroking his cheek and crooning encouragement, while Gideon massaged his friend's tense shoulder, making soothing noises deep in his throat.

When Christian cried out yet again, sobbing and muttering what sounded like a garbled plea, Gideon gritted his teeth and ground out a string of foul curses. Running his hands through his hair in his frustration—hair that was so badly tousled that it was apparent his fingers had been worrying it all night—he snarled, "Damn it to hell! I hate feeling so bloody helpless. If only there were something I could do to ease his pain."

"I am sure you are helping just by being here," Bethany reassured him, though even to her own ears her words sounded pitifully hollow.

Gideon snorted. "He is out of his mind with pain. He does not even know I am here. All he knows is that he hurts and he desperately wants the pain to go away."

Desperately wanting it to go away, too, Bethany anxiously quizzed, "Did Jagtar say when the pain would pass?" She prayed it would be soon.

"He says that the worst of the pain will pass in two or three days, if it does not kill him first, and that he is likely to continue to suffer a more mild discomfort for at least a fortnight thereafter."

Their conversation lulled then, with Gideon moving to the hearth, where a large iron pot had been set over the fire, while Bethany continued to stroke and soothe Christian. After several moments his pain seemed to pass and he began to relax, his deep, labored breathing easing into a softer, more natural pattern. Giving his cheek a final stroke, she reached down to straighten the sheet that had slipped from his hips in the violence of his last movement. As she pulled it up over his muscular buttocks, she caught a glimpse of his famous birthmark. It was indeed bright red and shaped like a perfect starburst. She also saw something else, something that made the tears she had been so valiantly fighting spill over in her eyes and course down her cheeks.

"Oh, Christian! My poor, poor, darling! I did not know they had hurt you so terribly," she whispered brokenly, her heart shattering at the evidence of the brutality he had endured while in slavery. She had been so caught up in trying to soothe him that she hadn't noticed the disfiguring scars crisscrossing his back and shoulders. Now gazing at his body with new awareness, she saw that his torso was marred, as well, though, blessedly, to a far lesser degree, and that his wrists and ankles still bore the marks from the manacles he had once been forced to wear.

Gideon, who had fished what appeared to be a steaming poultice from the pot and now waited for it to cool to a tolerable temperature, shot her a troubled look. "What is it, Bethany?"

"His scars. Oh, Gideon. How awful! How he must have suffered! How could anyone have hurt him like this?" she cried, shaking her head over and over again in her horror.

Gideon drew back slightly, frowning, visibly nonplussed. "You have never seen them before?"

"Of course not. Why would I—" Then the implication of his question struck her and she gasped, utterly taken aback. "You thought that I had been intimate with him?" Not that she had not given him reason to presume such a thing, not after what she had done and been. Nonetheless, he was her brother and she was stunned that he would even imagine, much less suggest, such a thing about her.

Gideon shrugged. "The thought had crossed my mind. After all, I have seen the way you two look at each other. It is clear that you are hungry for more than just a few chaste kisses."

"Gideon," she began to protest, her face burning with embarrassment at his observation.

"Oh, do not act so missish," he cut in. "You are a grown woman who has had relations with a man and borne a child. Surely we can speak frankly to each other about these matters?"

"I—I—I s-s-suppose so," she stammered, suddenly feeling like a complete ninny. After all Gideon had been through with her, how he had helped her through the difficulties of her pregnancy and comforted her in the wake of her baby's death, there was no reason why she should feel embarrassment at their present conversation. Heaven only knew they had discussed much more intimate matters in regard to her pregnancy.

Firmly reminding herself of that fact, she said in as even a voice as she could muster, "You are right, Gideon. We should be able to speak with frankness. So to answer your question: This is the first time I have seen Christian naked." It was the honest truth. While they had engaged in sexual relations, she had never once seen what lay beneath his clothes. Now that she did, she saw that he was as wonderfully made as she had imagined, his body a miracle of symmetry with its long, lean lines and hard, sculpted muscle.

Now approaching the bed with a steaming poultice in hand, Gideon shook his head, replying, "Nonetheless, I am surprised you do not know about the scars. Surely he has told you about his ordeal in India?" By now he had stopped beside the bed. Nodding down at Christian, he added, "Roll him onto his back and pull his hands and legs away from his belly so I can lay this over it. The heat might help ease his pain. He is so weak that he shan't put up much resistance to being moved."

Bethany did as Gideon requested, gently turning Christian over onto his back and straightening his limbs. Gideon had been correct in that he was too weak to fight, though he did moan and sob in protest. Lacing her fingers through Christian's to secure his hands, which he kept trying to return to his belly, she watched as Gideon carefully arranged the poultice over the painful area, gasping loudly when he pulled back the sheet while doing so to expose a hideous scar on his groin.

Gideon glanced up quickly at her response, a grim smile twisting his lips. "I am afraid that I must lay partial claim to the wicked appearance of that particular scar. It is the result of Jagtar and me digging a bullet from his belly after we found him on the battlefield. We had a great deal of difficulty finding it, which necessitated that we widen the wound to search for it. I am still amazed that nothing vital was damaged when he was shot. Gunshot wounds to the gut are fatal more often than not." The poultice now arranged to his satisfaction, Gideon straightened up, his gaze still on Christian.

Christian, who had stiffened at the feel of the poultice, slowly relaxed beneath its soothing effect. Gideon nodded his satisfaction. "Good," he murmured, more to himself than to Bethany.

Realizing from listening to Gideon's story how little she knew about Christian's life in India, and feeling a sudden, wrenching need to learn about it now, she laid Christian's now limp hands at his sides, admitting, "Truth be known, I know little about his ordeal in India. He has never volunteered the information, and I have never asked. I did not wish to pry, you see. I was afraid that in doing so I would stir up painful memories for him."

"Christian never told you about India because he did not wish you to view him with pity. However, I am certain that if you ask him about it when he is well again that he will gladly tell you whatever you wish to know."

"I was rather hoping that you would tell me now," Bethany countered, half expecting him to deny her request. When people asked Gideon about Christian's time in India, he always shrugged and told them that it was Christian's story to tell, not his.

To her surprise, he met her gaze steadily and inquired, "What do you wish to know?"

She made a helpless hand gesture. "Anything. Everything. Perhaps you will tell me about his scars first."

"The worst of the lash marks on his back and the burns on his chest," he pointed to several ugly, puckered, disk-shaped scars on Christian's chest, "are the result of the first night he spent with his first owner, a depraved Arab bastard by the name of Ghassan bin Hanif. He purchased Christian for his beauty and spirit, wishing to make him his *garzóne,* which is what a male concubine is called in Algiers. He was first sold in a marketplace there."

Bethany shook her head, holding her hands up to halt him, not understanding. "Are you saying that he was purchased to—ur—" Now, how did she put this delicately? She settled on, "service the women in the man's household?" It was all she could do to keep the shock she felt at the notion from her voice.

"No. He purchased him for himself, to use for his bestial pleasures."

"What! No!" Bethany gasped, sickened by the thought of Christian being used in such an unspeakable manner.

Gideon shook his head, his expression grim. "I am afraid it is true. When Christian fought his advances, the bastard beat and tortured him into submission, though by Christian's own admission, the pain from his torture was far easier to bear than the humiliation of his violation."

"My poor love. I had no idea," Bethany crooned to

Christian, her heart feeling as if it were shattering at what he had suffered. "How long did that awful man own him?"

"Three days. You see, it was highly irregular that a slave should be taken directly to his new master's house like Christian was that day. Slaves are generally taken to the dey's palace after the slave auction—"

"The dey?" Bethany interrupted, wanting to fully understand Christian's story.

"The ruling official," Gideon supplied with a nod. "At any rate, it is customary for the slaves to be taken to his palace directly following the auction, where he then examines them and decides if he wishes any of them for himself. If he does, the new owner is obligated to sell the slave to him. In Christian's instance, the dey fell ill the day of the auction and the slaves were not taken to the palace until three days later."

"And he bought Christian?" Bethany interjected eagerly, wanting nothing more than to hear that Christian had been removed from Ghassan bin Hanif's vile clutches.

Gideon laughed—a harsh, grating sound. "Yes, after he killed one of his guards."

"What!"

"When the dey declined to buy him, Christian became so desperate to escape bin Hanif that he attacked one the dey's guards and slayed him with his own sword, hoping that the other guards would kill him in retribution. He would rather have died than endure further violation. The dey, however, was impressed by his skill with a sword and insisted on buying him then. Like the Indian princes who engaged me to train their troops in the European style of fighting, the dey knew the value of an Englishman skilled in weaponry."

"So Christian was a soldier in the dey's army?"

"No. He trained his troops, like I did, except without the rewards. A year or so later, he was sent as a gift to a cousin or some such relative. That is often a slave's lot, being passed from one court to another as a gift, especially a valuable slave like Christian."

Bethany considered all she had been told for a moment, then said, "I have read that slaves are sometimes able to work their way out of slavery in that part of the world. Do you suppose that Christian would have been able to do so if you had not rescued him?"

Gideon shrugged. "Perhaps, though not from the tyrant he was being forced to serve when I rescued him. As soon as the Muslim bastard received Christian as a gift, he had his body shaved and forcibly circumcised him to turn him into a Mussulman. He then drove a silver earring with a knob through his right earlobe to mark him as a slave among the Muhammadans. When Christian had recovered from being circumcised he was sent to the tyrant's *chaylah* battalions, which is where slaves condemned to perpetual slavery and captives of war are kept."

"What is a Mussulman and a Muhammadan, and what is involved in being circumcised?" Bethany asked with a frown, wanting to completely understand Christian's history.

"*Muhammadan* is a name for a Muslim, an adherent of Islam. The term *Mussulman* also refers to a Muslim, but in this instance it was being used to signify a man who had been converted to Islamism, in Christian's case, unwillingly so. Circumcision is an operation that is performed during the conversion to Islamism in which the foreskin of a man's penis is cut away." When Bethany gasped, pressing her hand to her mouth in her horror at what had been done to Christian, Gideon grimaced and retorted, "My thought exactly. For all that circumcision is a common practice in some parts of the world and most men emerge from the operation no worse for it, I am glad that I have never had to endure it."

"But Christian did, poor darling," Bethany murmured, lifting Christian's limp hand to kiss it.

Gideon nodded, grimacing again. "In case you are wondering, he healed quite nicely, so he should have no trouble engaging in marital relations."

Bethany nodded back numbly, though, of course, she already knew that Christian was perfectly fine in that regard. More than fine, actually. He was magnificent.

"There is, naturally, much more to his story than I have told, but I will leave the rest for him to tell," Gideon said, now removing the poultice from Christian's belly, which had grown cold during their discussion.

Christian made a soft noise, in protest, Bethany thought by the sound of it, and his chiseled belly muscles visibly tensed. So she laid her hand where the poultice had been, lightly stroking the area. He made another low sound, then sighed and relaxed again beneath her touch.

"You shall live to tell me the rest of your tale. I promise," Bethany whispered, leaning close to his ear. "Damn it! I will not let you die, Christian English, not now. After all you have endured, I refuse to let you die before you have had a lifetime of happiness to make up for your years of suffering."

Chapter 19

The first thing Christian saw when he opened his eyes was Bethany. She sat by his bed in a comfortable armchair, frowning at the embroidery in her hands, turning her hoop this way and that, as if trying to decide whether to keep her stitches or pick them out. Feeling strangely fatigued, far too exhausted to speak or move, he contented himself with simply lying there watching her.

Dressed in a serviceable woolen day gown in a jewel-rich shade of red, a hue that he could not help noticing made her ivory skin glow, with her long, dark curls pulled back in a wide embroidered ribbon and a green Kashmir shawl tied around her shoulders, she was the very picture of domestic tranquility. She was also the most beautiful sight he had ever beheld. Then again, she always looked impossibly beautiful, so beautiful, in fact, that she never failed to take his breath away every time he saw her. And yet as he gazed at her now, he somehow knew that even if he lived to a hundred he would never find her quite so lovely as he did at that moment, though why he should think such a thing, he did not know. As he watched her finally nod her approval of her handiwork and again pick up her needle, he was struck by the queerest sensation that he had not seen her for a very long while, though, of course, it had only been . . .

When? When had he last seen her?

Christian frowned, trying to recall, but his brain was slow to respond. He would have shaken his head in an attempt to rattle his wits back into place, but, strangely, it seemed much too heavy to lift, much less shake.

Why? Damn it! Why was he so bloody weak?

Then it struck him; the irregularity of his lying in bed while Bethany sat beside him, his unnatural weakness, and the dull, burning pain in his belly, of which he was only now becoming aware, wretchedly so. Then there was his stiffness—dear God! His entire body felt stiff and sore, and there wasn't an inch of him that had not begun to ache.

Suddenly horribly nauseated and certain that he was about to vomit, he opened his mouth to call out to Bethany, to ask for her help, but only a garbled croak issued from his raw throat. But it was enough, for Bethany glanced at him in response, dropping her embroidery when she saw him awake.

Rushing to the bed and falling to her knees beside it, she exclaimed, "Christian, oh, Christian, my love! Thank heavens!" Her hands were on his face now, stroking his cheek and smoothing back his hair. "I must tell the footman outside to alert the household that you have awakened. Everyone will be so relieved! You have had us all so very worried."

Somehow mustering the strength to grasp her arm, to halt her from rushing off before she helped him, he croaked, "Sick."

"Yes, I know, darling. You have been very sick, and you no doubt still feel quite ill," she crooned, laying her cool hand against cheek.

At that moment a burning pain knifed through his

abdomen and stabbed deep into his groin, doubling him over and increasing his nausea tenfold. Grasping his belly in agony, he began to choke and gag on the bile rising in his throat. For several awful seconds he was certain he would vomit on his pillow, then he felt his head being lifted and saw a chamber pot positioned beneath his chin. Sobbing helplessly as he vomited, as much from the torture of his bile scalding his raw throat as from the new wave of pain ravaging his belly, this pain more intense than the last, he miserably closed his eyes, willing himself back into blessed unconsciousness.

But his body refused to cooperate, instead treating him to another bout of nausea. When he had vomited up the contents of his stomach, which, luckily, were scant, Bethany held a glass of water to his lips, tipping it enough that the cool liquid flowed over his tongue. "Rinse your mouth and throat, love, and then spit the water back into the glass. You will feel more comfortable once you have washed away the awful taste of bile."

Christian obediently did as commanded and found that he indeed felt better. Well, at least his throat was better and the nausea had subsided. His belly, on the other hand, hurt like hell, and he was suddenly plagued by a desperate need to relieve himself.

"Gideon, do come see!" Bethany suddenly cried out, merrily waving to a point beyond Christian's view. "Christian is awake and he looks ever so much better."

A moment later Gideon's face appeared in his field of vision. He looked awful, like he had neither slept nor shaved for at least a week, nonetheless he was grinning broadly. "Good of you to rejoin the world of the living, Christian, my boy," he quipped, lightly clapping Christian's shoulder.

Christian gritted his teeth in his urgency to relieve

himself. "Need—the chamber pot—now," he managed to croak.

Bethany smiled at him, then at Gideon, as joyously as if he had just delivered the most wonderful news in the world. Pressing a tender kiss to his forehead, she rose, saying, "I shall leave Gideon to help you attend to that particular need."

As she closed the door behind her, Gideon did exactly that. As with vomiting, relieving himself proved to be an excruciating ordeal because of the misery in his belly and groin. Eyeing him sympathetically as he emitted a particularly pained groan, Gideon murmured, "I take it that it hurts like the devil?"

"That is putting it mildly," Christian rasped, his voice improving with practice.

Gideon squeezed his shoulder. "Jagtar says that the pain down there should pass completely in a fortnight."

"And that is supposed to make me feel better?" Christian grumbled, indicating that Gideon could take the pot. God, he didn't think he could bear such pain for another day, much less a fortnight.

Gideon took the pot, nodding his approval at its contents. "No blood. Excellent."

Blood? Christian recoiled in horror at his words. If he had been bleeding from there . . . "What the devil is wrong with me?" he hoarsely bit out, gripped by sudden panic.

"You were poisoned," Gideon replied, covering the pot and setting it aside.

"What!" Christian's voice returned in full force with that exclamation.

Gideon nodded. Now sitting at the side of his bed, he explained what had happened to Christian during the four days he had been unconscious, his descriptions of Jagtar's treatments making Christian eternally grateful that he had been insensate during their administration. Gideon finished by saying, "If someone indeed tried to murder you, which Jagtar and I think is likely, given the nature of your poisoning, then there is a good chance that they will make another attempt on your life. If we are to ensure their failure, we must try to determine who the culprit might be and then set a trap to flush him out. But, of course, all that can wait until you are better. Right now you must focus all your energy on getting well. I shall have Jagtar concoct a draft to help with your pain now that you are awake to take it."

Jagtar's potions, combined with the poultices he and Gideon laid over Christian's belly and groin when the pain was at its worst, served to allow Christian enough comfort that he was able to sleep a great deal during the following week. And during that time, he never once awoke to find Bethany gone from his side. He had only to open his eyes for her to rush to him and take him in her arms, greeting him with her radiant smile and ready kisses. Indeed, she did almost everything for him.

It was she who fed and nourished him, gently and tenderly coaxing him to take the broth or caudle she insisted he swallow every time he awoke. It was she who was near to comfort and soothe him when pain tore him from his slumbers. She sang to him when he was restless, read to him when he grew bored, and no matter what he required or when, she seemed to have already anticipated his need and readily provided for it.

Only his most private needs, such as bathing, assisting him with the chamber pot, and changing his bedclothes were tended to by someone else, usually by Gideon or Jagtar, and occasionally by Gideon's valet, a peacock of a man named Darby. Though Christian would have preferred to have been bathed and clothed by Bethany, despite the fact that he was in no condition to take masculine pleasure from the intimacy of her touch, Julia had primly declared it to be highly inappropriate for Bethany to tend him when he was naked since they were not yet wed.

By the middle of the second week, Christian's pain had waned enough that he was able to sit up for much longer periods of time. It was during those times that he, Gideon, and Jagtar began to try to piece together the puzzle of Christian's poisoning. Though Christian found it hard to believe that anyone in his circle, or even Lord Denleigh, would wish to kill him, the preponderance of suspicion naturally fell on them since he had been in their company the night before he had fallen victim to poisoning.

The second week passed into the third, and as Jagtar had predicted, Christian's pain finally abated. Though he was still frustratingly weak and slept far more than was usual for him, he was well enough to begin receiving visitors. The first to be allowed to call were Bliss and Julia's sisters, who couldn't be kept away any longer, so anxious were they to assure themselves that the man they adored was truly on the mend.

How Christian enjoyed their visits! Bliss proved to be every bit as attentive a nurse as Bethany, spending her visits fussing over him, straightening his covers, and smoothing his pillow, every now and again touching his face to make certain that he was not fevered. Maria and Jemima, having been informed by Bliss that Christian's throat and belly were paining him, Bliss having gleaned the information from eavesdropping on Julia and Gideon, had arrived bearing an ice from Gunter's in hopes that it would soothe his throat. They had then taken turns spooning it into his mouth, delighting him the whole while with their girlish chatter. Having declared his throat much improved by their treat, they had brought him an ice every day since, along with drawings they had made and bouquets of flowers they had picked from their parents' conservatory, all intended to add cheer to his chamber.

When Christian was finally strong enough to leave his bed, to walk short distances with Bethany and Bliss's aid, and to sit for an hour or so by the bedchamber fire, it was decided that the time had arrived to begin their hunt for the would-be killer. Enlisting Julia's aid in setting about the news that Christian was now well enough to receive sickbed visits, and attributing his illness to a severe case of gripe rather than poisoning so as not to alert their prey to their suspicion, they baited their trap.

In the days that followed, during the appointed hours for calling, one could not walk down the corridor where Christian's bedchamber was located without seeing clusters of his acquaintances from White's loitering there, awaiting their turn to visit. Though his parents were off visiting somewhere in the country and had yet to respond to the letter Julia had sent them, Lucy called daily, as did Justina, who was in town to prepare for the season, and both of them clucked over Christian like a pair of hens with one chick between them, something that Christian enjoyed immensely. What he did not enjoy so very much were his daily visits from Godwin. That his brother might wish him dead cut him to the very core of his being, and every time he called Christian prayed that he would not do or say anything to prove himself to be the one they sought, that he would not be the one they caught in their trap.

Fielding, Chafford, Illingsworth, and Avondale, too, called almost daily, always in each other's company and always bearing snatches of amusing gossip or droll tales that never failed to make Christian smile. Even Denleigh came. Unlike most of Christian's male callers, who filled their allotted time with manly banter and forced conversation, visibly ill at ease in the sickroom, Lord Denleigh brought him a book titled *The History of Tom Jones: A Foundling,* by Henry Fielding, a bawdy work of fiction in which Denleigh laughingly claimed that the hero's misadventures rather reminded him of Christian's youthful exploits. They had then passed the remainder of their time sardonically commiserating on the indignities of being bed bound, a state that Denleigh understood all too well.

Though Christian enjoyed the company of his friends and family, the constant parade of visitors never failed to leave him fatigued by the time the hours for calling had ended. So much so that he usually fell into an exhausted slumber soon after the last visitor had departed, awakening only when Bethany came to his room with his supper.

It was the evening of the sixth day since he had begun receiving, a particularly tiring day for the inordinate number of visitors he'd received, and as had become their routine of late Bethany had come to him after the last caller had departed to straighten his chamber and bedding and to wash his face and hands before settling him down to sleep. Completing her fussing with a kiss, she extinguished all but a single candle, and then left him to his rest.

He was asleep almost as soon as she closed the door. When he awoke again it was to the feel of someone carefully pulling back the covers Bethany had so tenderly tucked beneath his chin earlier. That that someone was not Bethany was immediately apparent, for Bethany never pulled back his blankets or did anything to his person without first awakening him, not wishing to startle him. Neither did Jagtar or Gideon.

Instantly on the defensive, an instinct that had been honed during his perilous years in slavery, Christian abruptly flung himself to the opposite side of the bed, rolling into a low crouch, aggressively prepared to attack, if necessary.

There was a low, rumbling chuckle followed by the sound of soft applause. "Bravo, Northwick. I see that you developed an instinct for survival during your time in India." It was Lord Avondale. That his visit was unacknowledged and unsanctioned by any member of the household was evidenced by the fact that he still wore his outdoor clothes.

"I have developed a great deal more than mere instinct," Christian countered, his muscles flexing with tension.

Avondale ejected a short, snorting laugh. "Yes, I daresay you have, to have survived what would have killed most men."

"What do you want, Avondale?" Christian asked with a low growl in his voice. "Surely you did not sneak into my bedchamber to exchange cryptic banter?"

Avondale shrugged one shoulder. "I shall give you a clue: you have not been suffering from the gripe."

By now Christian's arms had begun to tremble with fatigue from his weakness, and he shifted his weight to his haunches in an attempt to preserve what little strength was left in them. "Indeed?" Christian inquired, playing along with Avondale's assumption of his ignorance, hoping that Gideon would come into the room to check on him before Avondale attempted whatever nefarious act he had obviously come to accomplish. In his current depleted state, Christian knew he hadn't a chance to survive if it meant pitting his strength against Avondale's.

"You were poisoned," Avondale coolly informed him. "I should know—I poisoned you myself."

"You poisoned me?" Christian repeated, feigning horrified shock.

"Mmm, yes. With a rather inventive concoction of castor beans and just a pinch of ground cantharides, the effects of which were calculated to mimic a very severe case of gripe before it killed you." Avondale sighed, his face genuinely regretful in the dim candlelight. "I am sorry about the pain I caused you. I truly hated to inflict such a miserable death on you, but you gave me no choice. You are an exasperatingly hard man to kill, Northwick."

"But why? Why do you wish to kill me?" Christian inquired, sickened that a man he had once considered a good friend could so coldly talk about murdering him.

"Because you are on the verge of remembering and might someday remember what I was, what I did in India, and ruin me."

Christian recoiled at his words. "You were in India?" he expelled, caught off guard.

"I was, at the same time you were. However, nobody in England but you knows that. I explained my absence from England by setting about the I rumor that I had been forced to spend many years in Scotland putting my estates in order, though truth be known, there was no money left to do any such thing. My lie enabled me to avoid questions about my activities in India."

"And what were your activities that you should be desperate enough to kill to cover them up?" He was no longer simply trying to buy time; he genuinely wanted to know the truth.

Avondale shrugged. "I was a spy for the Barbary pirates, the very ones who captured you, in fact."

"What!" Christian exclaimed, rolling back on his heels in his shock.

Avondale nodded. "It was all quite simple, really. I assumed a false identity and took a position as a lowly clerk for the East India Company, which allowed me to learn which ships were to sail when, what cargo they carried, what route they intended to take, and how many guns were on deck. It was information for which I was handsomely paid, especially when the pirates took a particularly valuable cargo or captured a group of promising slaves."

Christian felt like someone had just gut-punched him. "Good God, Avondale. Are you saying that you knowingly committed me to a life of slavery?"

"As with poisoning you, I really had no choice in the matter. You see, you discovered me there and soon after discovered my little secret." He snorted and shook his head. "For all that you were a rake, you were an honorable one, and when I invited you to join me in my fruitful endeavor, you turned me down, calling what I was doing treason." He leaned forward slightly, his glittering gaze boring into Christian's. In a low voice that held a wealth of meaning, he said, "They hang men for treason, you know."

"And I threatened to report you," Christian murmured. It was a statement, not a question.

"Unless I returned to England with you and reformed my wicked ways, yes. At the time, you were preparing to return home. Since, as always seems to be the case in my dealings with you, you gave me no real choice in the matter, I boarded the ship with you and pretended to do your bidding. I had, of course, alerted my pirate friends about our sailing, and they attacked the ship."

Christian's hands balled into fists, remembering all the pain and horror he had endured during his slavery. Gritting his teeth in his fury, he spat, "You bastard! I was simply trying to be your friend, and you betrayed me in a manner I would not wish upon my worst enemy."

He shrugged. "Point granted."

Point granted. The instant the words left Avondale's lips, a scene flashed through Christian's mind. He was on the deck of a ravaged ship surrounded by what he recognized from their dress and long beards as Algerians. Avondale stood before him, and though he could not hear his words, he somehow knew what he was saying, knew that he was condemning him to a life of slavery. When Christian lunged at him in fury, calling him a traitorous bastard, Avondale smiled grimly and clearly enunciated, "Point granted."

"Point granted," Christian murmured. "That was the last thing you said to me that day."

"Well, I might have said more, but you attacked me, giving me no choice but to strike you across the head with the flat of my sword. Since your return to London, I have sometimes wondered if perhaps it was that act that robbed you of your memory." He seemed to consider the thought for a moment, then shrugged dismissively. "I suppose it hardly matters at this point."

"Was it worth it?" Christian growled. "Was the wealth you gained from your treason and betrayal worth the price of your soul?" Before Christian's mind could register what was happening, Avondale abruptly lunged across the bed and tackled him, pinning him hard against the mattress. Easily immobilizing him in his weakness, Avondale pressed his face close to Christian's ear, hissing, "Oh, yes. I would have done anything then to gain the wealth and power and glory that are now mine, and should have been mine from the beginning, had my foolish father and grandfather not squandered our family fortune. And I am now willing to do whatever I must to preserve all I have gained."

Struggling weakly to free himself, Christian flung back his head to see that his opponent held a tiny, wickedly sharp-looking dagger poised over his neck. "A single prick and there will be no saving you, Northwick. Your death with this poison will come swiftly and quietly, and everyone will assume that you had a relapse and died in your sleep. As one of your oldest friends, I will naturally be quite overwrought by your death and shall weep in a most unmanly fashion at your funeral."

His gaze riveted to the deadly dagger, Christian snarled. "I suppose that you learned all about poisoning from your pirate friends?"

"Mmm, yes. And a very handy skill it has turned out to be, since all my other attempts on your life have failed."

"Other attempts?" Christian echoed, his eyes narrowing.

Avondale lightly ran the point of the knife down the side of Christian's neck, taunting him. "There was the man I engaged to push you into the street in front of the coach I hired to run you down. And the thief at the inn. He was supposed to kill you both. As I said, Northwick, you are proving to be vexingly hard to kill. I still find it impossible to believe that you survived my first draft of poison. However, I can assure you that you shan't survive this one." He lifted the knife to cut Christian's neck.

But Christian had had enough time to gather his strength and he was able to knee Avondale, hard, in the groin. Avondale, however, seemed to have anticipated his move, because he shifted to the right and Christian's knee connected instead with his hip. Christian had no sooner lunged against Avondale, attempting to shove him off, when he heard Bethany scream. In the next instant a rain of broken crockery and food spilled over him and Avondale as she slammed the supper tray in her hands over Avondale's head.

Avondale roared and reared up, rounding on Bethany to brutally backhand her across the face. Bethany spun around and then fell, her head hitting the floor with a sickening thud. Strengthened by his rage at seeing the woman he loved hurt, Christian grabbed the arm holding the poisoned knife, wrenching and twisting it until it fell from Avondale's hand. Oblivious to the abuse his body was taking from the other man's kicking legs and thrusting knees, he viciously slammed his fist over and over again into Avondale's face, not stopping until someone grabbed his arms and pulled him away. Avondale fell back upon the mattress, unconscious.

The someone who had pulled him off Avondale was Simon Rowles. Promptly jerking himself free from the majordomo's grip, Christian rolled off the bed, crawling toward where Bethany sat on the floor, rubbing her head. "Bethany, dear God!" he exclaimed, stricken by the sight of blood on her lower lip.

She shook her head and flexed her jaw, checking to make sure both were sound. Finding them so, she murmured, "I am all right, love. Did I get him?"

She looked so bloodthirsty when she asked that question that Christian could not help laughing. Pulling her into his arms to gently kiss her split lower lip, he murmured, "Oh yes, love. You most assuredly got him."

She nodded. "Good. I wanted to kill him for what he did to you."

"You heard?" Christian asked, now carefully inspecting her face for damage.

"Just the end, but it was enough. I—"

It was then that they both became aware of Rowles standing over them, loudly clearing his throat. When they looked up at him, he jerked his head toward the door and announced, "Your parents, my lord. The Duke and Duchess of Amberley."

"Christian?" Bethany called out, softly knocking at Christian's bedchamber door. At his command to enter, she pushed open the door and stepped inside. Expecting him to be resting after the excitement of the night before, she automatically glanced at the bed, and was surprised to see it freshly made up and unoccupied.

When she looked up again, she saw him walking toward her from where he had been standing at the window, gazing outside. Her heart seemed to jump into her throat at the sight of him. He looked wonderful, better than she had seen him look since before his poisoning. It was clear from his wet hair, which he was dabbing with a linen towel, the rosiness of his freshly shaved cheeks, and the fact that he was garbed only in a blue velvet dressing gown that he was fresh from his bath, his first real one since his illness. Smiling at how much healthier he looked in his groomed state, she said, "I must say that you are looking very well this morning."

He draped the damp towel over one shoulder to free his hands so he could hold out his arms to her to invite her into his embrace. When she had flown into it, he cupped her chin in his hand to raise her face to study it, frowning down at her as he replied, "I wish I could say the same for you. I do not like the way your cheek is swelling, and I could kill Avondale for splitting open your lip like that."

Bethany snuggled against his solid chest, considering the damage to her face a price well worth paying to have Christian alive and safe in her arms. "From what I heard from the watchmen who hauled Avondale off, you came very close to doing exactly that."

Christian kissed the top of her head. "After striking you he deserved much, much worse, and had Rowles not stopped me he would have gotten it."

Bethany laughed and tipped her head back to gaze up into his wonderful face. "That is exactly what your mother said, that Avondale deserved much worse than you gave him. From the way she was glaring at him while Gideon and Jagtar were tying him up, I half expected her to give it to him herself."

He grinned. "There is apparently nothing quite like nearly being murdered to put me back in my mother's good graces. My father's, too. It seems that I am again the Marquess of Northwick."

Bethany hugged him tight, genuinely thrilled for him. "Such wonderful news, Christian. It is what I have been praying would happen."

"You wanted to be a marchioness that badly, did you?" he teased.

She playfully slapped him for his impudence. "Of course not, wicked man. I simply wished the rift between you and your parents to be mended. I know your estrangement from them must have hurt you after being separated from them for so very long."

"It did. Nonetheless, it was necessary. I had to teach them that they cannot rule my life in matters that pertain to my happiness; that happiness is my first priority and that I shall not allow anything to stand in the way of my taking it when and wherever I might find it. Most importantly, they had to come to terms with the fact that I am going to marry you."

"And have they?" She tipped back her head to again gaze into his face, this time in searching query.

He laughed and dipped down to kiss her, taking care not to hurt her damaged lip. "Indeed they have. In fact, had you not been whisked away by Julia to have your face examined by a surgeon, I am quite certain that they would have told you so themselves. My mother was exceedingly impressed with how you jumped into the fray to defend me and said that the fact that you would risk life and limb to dash to my rescue proves to her that you indeed love me for myself and not for my title."

"And your father," she inquired breathlessly, her heart swelling with joy.

He kissed the tip of her nose. "My father thinks that you are the bravest and most beautiful girl in the world. He said that your spirit rather reminds him of my mother's in her youth, and I can assure you that you could have received no higher compliment from him."

"And what about you, my lord," Bethany murmured, rising up onto her tiptoes to steal a kiss from his beautiful lips. "Do you still wish to wed me?"

He kissed her back, lingering over her mouth, his lips lightly caressing hers. "At the first opportunity, love."

"Mmmm. I was rather hoping you would say that." She paused to run her tongue over the opening between his lips, slowly and sensuously teasing the pink silky lining of his lower one. "You see," she explained between licks, "I hear that a couple as much in love as we are can get a special license that will allow us to wed any time and place we might wish to do so without having to wait for the banns to be published."

His tongue darted out to briefly twine with hers. "I also hear that such licenses are only good for three months from the date of issue, which means that we should probably use the special license I got for us soon."

Bethany froze in nibbling his lip, then pulled back to meet his sparkling gaze. "You have a license?" she asked, smiling. "Whatever possessed you to get one?"

"Let us just say that I was optimistic about my abilities to persuade you to marry me." He shrugged one shoulder. "Or perhaps it might be better termed as lovelorn wishful thinking."

"Whatever we choose to call it, if you have a license we must most certainly use it."

"Just name the time and place, and I shall be there," Christian declared, sealing his vow with a kiss.

"Today, or tomorrow, or—" She broke off to hug him with all her strength. "Oh, Christian, my dearest, darling love. I shall wed you the instant you are able to meet me at the altar. I want to begin our life together as soon as possible. After almost losing you, I have come to realize that I do not wish to spend another moment without you." With that, she rose up onto her tiptoes and covered his mouth with hers.

Groaning aloud, Christian tightened his arms around her, hauling her hard against him, his sex instantly springing to life at the feel of her luscious body pressing against his. Her lips were so soft and warm, so supple and responsive. The feel of them clinging to his, her mouth open beneath his and her tongue teasing his, inviting him to deepen their kiss, filled him with a mad and almost undeniable desire to drag her over to the bed and spend upon her the passion she was kindling within him.

"I love you, Christian, and I want you," she whispered, her lips now leaving his to blaze a sizzling trail of kisses over his chin and down his throat. "Let me show you how much."

He grinned down at her. "What do you have in mind?"

Slanting him a saucy smile, she led him to the bed.

"You know that I am still weak from my illness and that I shall not be able to resist you should you decide to have your way with me," he teased.

She gave him a playful shove, pushing him back onto the bed where he lay sprawled, his legs splayed apart and his arms outstretched in a pose of unconditional surrender. "That is what I am counting on," she retorted with a low, husky laugh. Leaving him only long enough to lock the door, she kneeled between his legs and untied the belt securing his dressing gown. That done, she drew the fabric apart, exposing him. Gazing down at him with an expression of awe, she softly exclaimed, "Just look at you, Christian. You are so beautiful." She shook her head, her gaze wandering over his bare torso. "I always knew you would be beautiful."

He reached up to pull her down on top of him, to kiss her, but she firmly pinned his arms to the mattress, shaking her head. "Oh, no. You are to lie there and let me ravish you." Her hands were back on his dressing gown now, tugging it over his shoulders, working to divest him of it. Christian raised first one shoulder and arm to help her do so, then the other. When he lay completely naked before her, she began to caress him.

Her touch was light and her motion feathering as she traced and skimmed the contours of his body. Now she stroked his chest, her fingers drawing tight, tickling spirals around his nipples; now she gently pinched and flicked the tender centers, making them harden and crest beneath her touch. Christian moaned, arching in heated response.

When the aggressive thrust of his sex rammed her thigh, grinding and rubbing against it in needful demand, she grasped his hips and pushed him away, pinning him firmly against the mattress until he had regained enough control to hold his hips there himself. Wagging her finger at his impatient sex like a mother scolding a willful child, she softly chided, "Patience," imitating the tone he had used the day he had first taken her to view the school and she had been so anxious to claim her surprise. Now wagging her finger beneath Christian's nose to reinforce her reprimand, she added, "Do not forget that good things come to those who wait." Shooting him a look that was no doubt supposed to be stern but was instead adorably naughty, she returned to her previous ministrations, her hands now advancing down his torso.

For the fierceness of his desire, it was all Christian could do to remain still as she explored the tight grid of his belly. Then she brushed lower, raking through the inky thatch of curls from which his pulsing sex jutted. The resulting sensation made his groin tighten in savage response.

"Bethany," he groaned, his pelvis again flexing and thrusting in his uncontrollable urgency. God! He would burst if she did not relieve him soon.

To Christian's erotic disconcertion, she slipped down to lie on her belly between his legs, cupping and toying with his manly sac as she soberly contemplated his penis. At length she sighed and said, "While you were ill, Gideon told me about what happened in India, what they did to you." She gestured to his sex. "How they cut you."

He grimaced at her reference to his circumcision. "That is hardly the sort of thing a man wishes to discuss while in the throes of passion."

She tipped her head to meet his gaze, her face suddenly serious. "I know. I just wanted to make certain that you are truly all right now."

He could not help smiling at her innocent worry. "Do I not look all right?"

She bit her lip and resumed studying him, this time closely. At length she nodded. "Yes, except for the scar." She lightly touched the area, making him jump from the explosion of resulting sensation. She jumped, too, grasping his flailing hips, awkwardly patting them. "I am sorry—sorry, Christian. Oh, dear. I thought—Gideon said that you were fully healed. I did not realize that you would still be tender."

"I am sensitive there, Bethany, not tender. There is a great deal of difference between the two," Christian gritted out in his lustful agony. "And I love the way it feels when you touch my male member."

She grinned, shooting him an impish look over the member in question. "Indeed?" she murmured. "Do you mean like this?" She lightly ran her finger down the underside of it, pausing to caress its sensitive cleft, something that again made him jump.

"Yes," he growled. "I like that very much."

"And this?" she quizzed. Her hand was now wrapped around him, firmly pumping.

His pelvis began to thrash and thrust, roughly catching her rhythm. All too quickly he felt himself nearing his climax. Now dangerously close to losing himself and wishing for her to find her pleasure with him, he closed his eyes and groaned, "Bethany, no, I—I—"

But she interrupted him before he could finish voicing his protest, saying, "Perhaps you will like this even better." Then he felt her sheathe herself on him. She was so hot and wet, so obviously aroused and as desirous of him as he was of her, that Christian had to fight hard to keep from instantly spilling his seed. Grasping her hips to control her, hoping that in doing so he could control his urgency, he forcefully slowed her motions. Into her center he plunged and then pulled out, driving back in again in the next instant, the whole while guiding her, dictating their rhythm and thrust. Now moving as one, he took them over the edge, driving them home.

Lying there in the aftermath of their climax, too weak and limp with pleasure to do more than rest in each other's arms, Christian murmured with a frown, "You still have your clothing on. I would have liked to have removed it and had my way with you in return before taking you."

Bethany smiled lazily, lifting her head from where it rested in the hollow of his shoulder to kiss his jaw. "You shall have plenty of time to do so in the future. We have a whole lifetime to enjoy each other's bodies."

Growling playfully, Christian rolled over with her clasped in his arms. Now on top, he slowly and thoroughly made love to her, setting a high standard of pleasure for the future that he silently vowed to keep.

EPILOGUE

Christian wrapped his arms around Bethany's waist, pulling her soft backside against his muscular front. Angling his head around the beribboned brim of her bonnet to kiss her cheek, he murmured, "Is it everything you dreamed it would be, love?"

Standing in the courtyard of her newly renovated school, gazing raptly around her, barely able to believe that the neatly painted and landscaped building surrounding them was the sad, neglected inn Christian had first shown her four months ago, Bethany softly exclaimed, "It far exceeds my dreams. Oh, Christian! It is simply too wonderful for words!"

"As are you," he whispered. "Have I told you yet today how thrilled I am to have you for my wife, Lady Northwick?"

She giggled and turned in his arms to embrace him. "You told me when you made love to me this morning, and again over breakfast, and then again when you chased off my poor maid and insisted on fastening my gown yourself. You also mentioned something along those lines on the ride over here, and you told me just now. That makes—hmmm, let me see—five times so far today."

Christian leaned down to press a kiss to her mouth, lingering over her lips. "Then let us make it six. I am thrilled to have you for my wife and consider myself the luckiest man on earth."

There was a loud snort behind them. "Don't you two ever stop kissin'?"

Christian and Bethany laughed. Bliss, of course.

"Hush, Bliss," Julia chided, casting the smiling couple an apologetic look. "They have only been married a short while. It is what newlywed couples do—they kiss."

Bliss snorted again. "You and Gideon ain't newlywed and you're always kissing."

"*Are not,* not *ain't,*" Julia corrected her. "And we kiss all the time because we love each other. When you find a husband you love as much as Bethany and I love ours, you will be wishing to kiss him all the time, too."

Bliss wrinkled her nose, the distaste on her face expressing her opinion of that notion far more eloquently than words.

Firmly clasping the girl's shoulder, Julia led her off, saying, "Maria and Jemima are inside stuffing Kesin with cake from the refreshment table. We must stop them before they make him ill."

Bethany watched Julia's newly trim figure disappear around the corner—Julia having given birth to her and Gideon's son a month earlier—then glanced around to survey the milling crowd around them.

Ever since the *ton* had heard about Bethany's charitable project, Christian having proudly boasted about it at every gathering, everyone in society wished to be a part of it. Not that they were actually interested in Bethany's concept for the school or the day-to-day workings of it. Their motive for attending the reception today, which Christian's mother had insisted they must have to celebrate the opening, was derived strictly from their desire to be a part of the Marquess of Northwick and his beautiful bride's circle, the Northwicks now considered to be one of the finest couples in London. Bethany, however, did not care where their motive lay, not when everyone present had promised to fill their posts with her future students.

"Mina seems to be getting on rather well with Lord Denleigh," Bethany observed, nodding toward where the couple sat on a bench in what had been the former inn's stable yard but was now Bethany's desired school garden.

Christian smiled at the man who was quickly becoming one of his closest friends. "He could certainly do much worse than Mina," he said, grimacing at the sight of Famous Helene and her harridan of a mother approaching the couple. As usual, the Duchess of Hunsderry was thrusting her daughter into the path of the season's most eligible bachelor, who, to Christian's amused delight and surprise, had turned out to be Lord Denleigh. Then again, he could not think of a man more worthy of the *ton*'s admiration.

"Oh, dear," Bethany exclaimed. "What in the world is Bliss doing?"

Christian glanced in the direction in which she was staring to see Bliss scampering up the tree near the entrance with much the same agility as the monkeys he had often seen climbing trees in India. Speaking of primates, he shifted his gaze higher to see Kesin, dressed in a green coat and frilled shirt, swinging from a branch just of her reach, clearly taunting her. Standing below were Maria and Jemima, cheering Bliss on.

"I do not know what I am going to do with that child," Bethany exclaimed with an exasperated sigh. "She seems to grow wilder everyday, despite Julia's and my best efforts to tame her."

"Why tame her? I think she is perfect exactly as she

is," Christian replied honestly. "If I had a daughter, I would not mind in the least if she were just like Bliss."

Bethany smiled faintly at his words. He had just given her the perfect opportunity to share her wonderful news. Coyly averting her face, she said, "I will be sure to remind you of that sentiment if the child I am carrying is a girl and turns out to be a hoyden like Bliss."

She felt Christian grow very still beside her. "What did you say?" He grasped her arms and spun her around to face him.

"I said that I would remind you of what you just said about Bliss if the child I am carrying turns out to be as wild as she is," she replied, watching the play of emotion flit across his face. There was shock, followed by incredulity, and finally a look of thunderstruck hope.

"Are you telling me that you are going to have my baby?" He more squeaked than uttered the words.

"A woman carrying a child almost always eventually has a baby, and since the baby in my belly was most definitely planted there by you, the answer is yes. I am going to have your baby."

"A-are you certain?" he stammered, clearly wanting to believe what she was telling him but afraid to do so in his desperate desire for it to be true. "I mean, you were told that you would never be able to bear another child."

She laughed. "Oh, yes. I am quite sure. The doctor has confirmed it and I am showing all the signs. The closest we can guess, you will be a papa in about seven months."

Christian again froze, then the most magnificent expression of joy spread across his face and he let out a loud whoop, earning smiles from several passersby. "We are going to have a baby," he told them, looking ready to burst in his happiness.

Turning back to her, he swept her into his arms. After thoroughly kissing her, he said, "Come. We must tell our families the wonderful news."

Smiling at his excitement, Bethany allowed him to lead her away. When he had lay dying she had promised him a lifetime of happiness to make up for his years of suffering. What a wonderful start she had made in doing so!

SIGNET

SCANDAL

A man of new-found wealth enters society—and an arranged marriage—by striking a gentleman's bargain with an aristocrat with something to hide. But his charade of a marriage catches him off guard when it explodes into a passion strong enough to blow every lie and misconception apart.

0-451-20767-X

Available wherever books are sold or to order, please call 1-800-788-6262

S908